SPHINX

by

David Lindsay

Published by Bookship, 2019, 2023.
First published by John Long, 1923.

ISBN 978-1-9996269-1-4

Cover and title design © Murray Ewing 2019.

Sphinx

BOOKSHIP

Contents

I

ARRIVAL

The local train, with its three coaches, pulled up at Newleigh Station at half-past four, and Nicholas Cabot alighted. It was a Friday afternoon in early June. The day was gloriously fine, without a cloud in the sky, but with a crisp breeze tempering the otherwise overpowering sun. He sniffed the air, which was particularly fresh and sweet to London nostrils, and it was more by force of habit than any feeling of unpleasantness that, in gazing around him at the same time, his mouth took on a half-contemptuous expression. There was little to see, for the platform was nearly deserted; no one else appeared to have got down. He was a pale, lean, shortish, inconspicuous young fellow, in the middle twenties, with rather delicate upper features, but with strong-looking eyes, a determined jaw, and the full, thrust-out lips belonging to an audacious mind, as distinguished from an audacious temperament. He wore grey flannels, with a new white straw hat, of the straight type affected by the city dweller. As he was in the act of making his way to the rear van to see after his trunk, which a porter was already tumbling roughly on to the platform, another man, dressed in a soiled white chauffeur's coat and uniform cap, came up to him and saluted.

"For Mereway, sir?"

"Mr. Sturt's house—yes."

"Car waiting, sir. That all your luggage?"

"That trunk and this bag. Has a packing-case arrived for me, do you know?"

"Haven't seen aught of it, sir."

The porter lending a hand, the trunk was installed in the somewhat dirty and battered four-seater which stood waiting in the station yard. Nicholas gave up his ticket and followed them out. He thought it strange that none of the family should be here to meet him, but was relieved that he should not be called upon to talk platitudes with unknown people on his way up to the house. He guessed that, Sturt himself being an ex-actor, they were rather on the Bohemian side. The conjecture was supported by the appearance of the car and its driver. The latter had great hands, like horn, a bowed back, and was getting on in years; he evidently combined the care of the garden with his other occupation.

When all was ready for a start, the car moved out of the yard into the village street. Newleigh proved to be quiet, ugly and undistinguished. With the exceptions of the railway tavern and half a dozen shops, it consisted, as far as he could see, entirely of labourers' cottages. Few people were about. They were soon past the houses, but the road for the first half-mile had no features of interest. When, however, it commenced to ascend, it grew leafier and more picturesque. The rays of the burning sun were intercepted by the over-hanging branches, while the cool, green woodland on either side of the road became increasingly exquisite.

The journey was a quite short one, the modern, fashionable residential settlement being less than two miles from the station, and very soon the first of the nice houses began to appear. Some enterprising builder had conceived the notion of dividing the whole estate into lots of three, five or ten acres, for the purpose of erecting high-class residences in the bungalow style for that numerous class of leisured people who delight in sunshine, nature, pseudo-solitude, and new art. Each house so far erected— there might be twenty or thirty of them—stood in its own grounds, and was red-tiled, many-gabled, and of fantastic shape. Each was separated from its immediate neighbours by strips of scattered pines—the melancholy residue of the original forest, which had held a population of birds. The woods began just beyond the last houses. There was a little forest lake not far off. Most of the houses possessed bizarre names, and each had its tennis court and rose pergola.

Mereway, when they came to it, turned out to be just as grotesquely pretty as the rest, though rather larger than some. It had the same queer, unmeaning gables, chimneys and window-bays, sticking out at all sorts of angles; and the same cobbled pathways, pergolas, arbours, trellis-work and rustic garden furniture. A tennis net was up on one lawn; another was set for croquet. Gay flower-beds showed everywhere, while Nicholas caught a glimpse at the back of the house of kitchen gardens and a fowl-run. The whole establishment had a holiday air. The house, from its appearance, might have been put up yesterday, yet, actually, it had been standing for more than twenty years.

The car turned up the miniature drive to the front door, which was next to the conservatory entrance, and he got out. A smart maid was standing in readiness just inside the porch.

"Where's this trunk to go?" demanded the driver.

"Stand it in the hall a minute, George. I'll show the gentleman to the drawing-room, then I'll come back to you."

"Is your mistress at home?" asked Nicholas, as he followed her through the hall.

"The ladies are out visiting, sir, but I will go and fetch the master."

"In that case, perhaps I had better go straight to my room."

"Afterwards, sir, if you wish, but I was told to show you into the drawing room."

As she spoke she opened the door of the room in question, stood aside to allow him to pass in, and immediately returned on her steps. Nicholas seated himself on a chair near the open window, overlooking the lawn, with its background of dark trees. The sunlight streamed in, and the caressing breezes were delightful. The apartment was elegantly appointed. The carpet was soft and rich, the chairs luxurious, expensive Japanese coloured prints were on the walls, while a Bechstein baby-grand stood obliquely across one of the corners. It was open, and a torn paper-covered volume of Chaminade was on the rest. A half-worked daffodil-yellow jumper, with its companion skein of silk, was lying on a chair-seat.

The maid came back, bearing in tea on a three-tiered table, which she set in the bay. The sun, shining full on the red china, made it a blaze of splendour.

"The master wishes you to begin tea, sir. He will be here directly."

Nicholas nodded with assumed carelessness, but thought that he had come to a queer place. Pouring himself out a cup of tea, he took it, with a cake, to his seat by the window. A minute later a man, who could only be his host, entered the room, stifling a yawn. It was a tall, thin, rather jauntily-dressed individual, true to a professional type, scarcely handsome, but quite distinguished-looking, with the long, reposeful face and incurved lip of the old-time tragedian. His cheeks were somewhat blue. He extended three fingers negligently, before dropping on to the sofa.

"Charmed to make your acquaintance, sir!" He spoke in a sort of sepulchral boom, drawling most of his long vowels. . . . "Would you be so good as to give me tea?"

Nicholas stared, but obeyed.

"They have just aroused me from sleep," proceeded Sturt, depositing the cup on the carpet beside him, and yawning again. "A drowsy country! . . . I see you have weird cakes there—are they eatable?" He examined the proffered plate at some length, his guest standing before him the while, and ultimately selected one. For a few moments he munched it meditatively, with drooping eyes.

"I am informed that you have but this minute arrived!"

"Ten minutes ago."

"And you have had a pleasant journey down?"

"Yes, thanks."

The young man's curt responses caused Sturt to regard him more attentively.

"That is good. . . . The ladies are out, I find. It is unfortunate, but doubtless could not be avoided. Here we all go our own ways very much. You will drop into the fashion of the house, and you will not find it unpleasing. After tea they will show you your room. . . . You have been with my brother-in-law, Spireman, a number of years, I hear?"

"Yes."

"His secretary, or something, I believe?"

"No, his ledger clerk."

The host raised his eyebrows the merest shade.

"That must have been deuced monotonous! However, he is a pleasant enough fellow, and I dare say you got on excellently well together. One has not the same prejudice against the trade of estate agent as against certain others. If it is not quite a profession, it is almost an art, for after all, a fine mansion is a distinct advance upon a consignment of coal, or bricks, or coffee. You have probably met good people in the course of your employment?"

"No, that wasn't my department."

Again the eyebrows went up.

"It is your uncle, or your grandfather, who has just died, I think?"

"It was an uncle."

"And you are his sole heir?"

"Yes."

"Spireman mentioned an amount to me, but I have forgotten it. I have an impression that it was a very large sum of money!"

"I have come into, roughly, fifty-five thousand pounds. At least, that is what Dangerfield, the lawyer, tells me. It may be a little less, or a little more."

"A splendid fortune for a young man, my dear fellow, and I congratulate you, heart and soul! 'Pon my honour! I have not handled so handsome a sum in the whole course of my life, and now never shall. In my best days, in the nineties, I made my five thousand, and my ten thousand, a year, but a professional has so many calls—believe me! my existence was, even then, one long struggle with shopkeepers. The accumulation of riches was a thing altogether outside my province."

"Mr. Spireman told me you had to leave the stage on account of a motor accident."

"A common or garden hansom, my dear boy! The wretched apparatus shot me through the glass front on to my spine, and my career was wrecked at one swift blow! Who knows? I might by now have been a baronet."

"It was certainly bad luck."

"It was devilish malice on the part of fortune, my dear fellow! . . . And that is why I now economise in the depths of Hampshire. For, since we are to be fellow-residents for a time, why should not we be frank with each other? The times are bad, expenses soar, and my income is stationary. Rates and taxes are fierce, and domestics no longer consent to give their labour for a song. A wife and three grown daughters are charming luxuries, but, go where one will about the house, drapers' catalogues meet the eye! . . . I open myself to you in order that we may not start our mutual relations on a basis of false shame. The ten guineas a week you have agreed to pay for your board and residence will be deuced useful to me. That, of course, is not to say you will not get your money's worth."

"No, I understand all that."

"Permit me to enumerate once more, that there may be no ground of discontent left in your mind. For the sum you are willing to pay you may live at any good hotel, with luxuries possibly superior to those we shall offer you. *But* . . . in an hotel you will not meet solid, family people, established in their own homes. You will enjoy no privacy. You will be a solitary stranger, among strangers. You will have no delightful home life, with the daily and hourly society of attractive girls—for my daughters *are* attractive, and why should not I say so? And you will scarcely find an hotel where you will be able to step out of the back door, as it were, into the very heart of the pine woods. So . . ."

"Yes, I understand all that," repeated Nicholas, with a trace of impatience. "The real reason I accepted Mr. Spireman's invitation to come down here was to get a quiet place where I could work undisturbed. I expect he told you?"

Sturt, without rising, produced a gold case from his breast-pocket and held it forward.

"You smoke?"

"Thanks!"

After getting up from his seat to cross the floor for the cigarette, the guest did not sit down again, but went over to the window, where he stood looking out at the sunlit garden.

"You have a grand situation here!" he remarked.

"Charming, my dear boy! And it is the sort of place that does not exhibit all its beauties during the first half-hour. You will grow much attached to it. . . . But we were discussing your work, I fancy! My good brother-in-law informs me that it is in the chemical line—that, vulgarly speaking, it has to do with *stinks*. So long as you do not send us sky-high, or render the house uninhabitable, there can, of course, be no objection to that."

"I shan't meddle with explosives, and there won't be any unpleasant smells."

His back was turned, and Sturt's half-closed eyes shot him a single queer glance, then seemed to retire within themselves. "I am reassured. But are you a proficient or a student?"

"I'm experimenting."

"Quite so! . . . Pardon my inquisition, but there is a certain hiatus between . . . well, between, let us say, your estate agency experience and this other predilection of yours. Have you interested yourself in chemistry for a great while?"

"Ever since I was a boy."

"That is very remarkable, for, with so marked a preference, one would think that you would have chosen a more congenial career!"

"I wanted to retain any originality I might possess," explained Nicholas curtly.

"And you believed that a professional training would destroy this original cast of mind?"

"I was sure of it. By the time you have learnt all the rules, your brain is too dull for anything else."

Sturt yawned, and said nothing for a minute. Then, stretching his shoulders, he remarked:

"Do you know, my dear fellow? I fancy that opinion is responsible for sending more youngsters to the devil than almost any other. I have seen so much unsupported originality in my time that I am even inclined to doubt whether it be not due to a certain softness of temper. . . . However, undoubtedly there are exceptions, and, in any case, we will not fall to blows on this our first meeting!"

"I think I hear someone coming," said Nicholas, pitching his half-smoked cigarette out of the window.

Unaccustomed as he was to meeting women, his face assumed a deep flush as the door suddenly opened, upon the very heel of his remark, and his hostess walked into the room. He attempted a slight and awkward bow, but this did not prevent his eyeing her rather keenly, as the person upon whose temperament would depend the degree of his comfort in that house during the weeks, and possibly months, to come.

Mrs. Sturt looked considerably younger than her husband. Nicholas had already placed him in the neighbourhood of sixty, whereas she, but for the illuminating fact of the three adult daughters, might well have passed for thirty-seven or eight. The modern outdoor fashions permitted her to wear garments which would equally have suited an unmarried girl, and she carried herself with an elastic alertness that told of athletics comparatively recently abandoned. In person she was a tall, big-framed, stately, foreign-looking woman, more fair than dark, possessing high cheek-bones, full lips, a good colour, a face very handsome, but expressing character and purpose, imaginative eyebrows, and eyes full of vivacity and humour. When she spoke her voice was breezy, pleasant and sympathetic. It required no great judgment to guess at once that she was the ruling spirit of the household.

She ignored the bow and his embarrassment, and held out her hand, as to a familiar acquaintance.

"Forgive me for escaping so disgracefully! I have had to call on a very dear friend, who returned home only yesterday. I say 'home,' though, as a matter of fact, she spends most of her time in London and Manchester, and such places. Lore Jensen—the well-known composer. Have you met her?"

"No. I've heard music of hers."

"I wonder what? But it's all perfectly sweet. A woman's music, I always think, has a delicacy of sentiment one never meets with in a man's. It is like a very subtle perfume. . . ." She paused and laughed. "It's so exciting to know that there is a whole undis-covered mine of art lying sealed up in our sex! . . . She's working at the moment on a delightful little fancy, to be called 'Pamela in the Rose Garden.' You must be introduced. She will come round here one evening, when she will play. She plays divinely."

"Is she Swedish or British?"

"English-born, but she takes her mother's name, for some reason known only to herself. Her mother—it would be before your time—was a beautiful and talented singer, Swedish or Norwegian, I don't know which. . . ." Again she broke off and laughed. "It's too bad to carry on a general conversation with you when you are straight off a tiring train journey! Have they shown you your room yet?"

"Not yet."

She turned to her husband. "The girls are not back, Leslie, I suppose?"

"I conclude not."

"They are playing tennis with friends, Mr. Cabot. They live for tennis—at least, we may say that of Audrey, my youngest. You will make their acquaintance at dinner. . . . If you will come with me, I will take you upstairs—that is, if you have finished your tea? I expect you have, as you were standing up when I came in—"

Nicholas having signified his readiness, she preceded him to the door and up the stairs. She showed him an airy little bedroom on the first floor, having a large window—at present wide open—which had for prospect the flower garden at the side of the house and the distant woods in the west. Everything was beautifully sweet and clean. His trunk and bag were already installed there.

"Will this do?" asked his hostess smilingly.

"Capitally, thanks!" He hesitated. . . . "Was there not to be another room?"

"Next door!" She indicated a second apartment, communicat-ing with the first, and immediately led the way there. It was of identical size and situation, but had been furnished as a sitting-room. Nicholas gazed around him reflectively.

"May I knock a few nails in, I wonder?"

"Why not? I imagine you are a fairly reasonable being, and won't do more damage to my walls than you can help."

"Of course I won't. . . . Has a wooden box arrived for me yet?"

She questioned him about its dispatch, and he told her.

"Then it should be here in the morning. Nothing of pressing consequence inside it, I hope?"

"Only my chemicals and apparatus."

"You don't propose to blow us all up, by the way?"

"No, there's nothing of that sort. You can rely on my not being a nuisance to anybody."

"Is it experimental work you are doing?"

"Yes."

"I took a course when I was a girl at school, but everything has sadly progressed since then, I fear!"

"There are limits even to the speed of science!" returned Nicholas. Such a compliment from him was unexpected, and Mrs. Sturt, overlooking the somewhat mumbling delivery, smiled pleasantly.

"You make me feel quite contemporary!"

"Aren't you?"

"Well, for one thing, I have three daughters."

"I know. I thought you were one of them when you first came into the room."

His hostess laughed and coloured slightly.

"I didn't know you were like this!"

"You're offended at my speaking the truth?"

"Perhaps I'm not offended, but my daughters might be. In their eyes I have entered upon the stage of mere usefulness, I'm afraid!"

"How old are they?"

"Katherine, my eldest, is twenty-three, Evelyn is twenty-one, and Audrey is nineteen. . . . You must have thought them very much older, and so your compliment turns out to be exactly the reverse!"

"I didn't intend a compliment, and I had formed no idea of their ages. But, if it is an admissible question, which is the one that is either engaged or on the point of being?"

Mrs. Sturt looked up sharply. "Whoever told you that?"

"Your brother, Mr. Spireman."

"I can't imagine how he came to speak of it at all, and it's quite untrue. Not one of the girls is engaged, or in any way approaching it. You must surely have misunderstood him." . . . She recovered her jocular, friendly manner. "But why this strange interest? Your reputation has preceded you, of being a misogynist!"

"That's not true, either."

"Really, my brother James must be trying to throw us all into confusion! So you don't hate and despise us?"

"I could never understand why avoiding women should be considered equivalent to hating them."

"But why do you avoid us even?"

"I simply happen to have other interests."

"Your work?"

"Yes, my work."

"And you fear you will be carried too far away from it! . . . Do you know, in one sense that is rather admirable! But have you never, never been attracted by anyone?"

"Not seriously. I don't pretend that I'm proof against natural forces. That's another reason for keeping away."

They were standing talking by the open window. Mrs. Sturt now lightly perched herself on the edge of a low table set before it. Evidently she meant to take this opportunity of understanding her guest.

"How old are you?"

"Twenty-five."

"No sisters, or female cousins?"

"No; I'm alone in the world."

"Poor boy! . . . But hasn't it ever struck you that you are just the sort of man that ought to get married?"

"I'm only just out of one cage, so it isn't likely I shall make a bee-line for another!"

"Oh, well, these things happen very suddenly!" She made a feint of rising, but still remained where she was. . . . "Who *were* your people, by the way? I don't think it's a very rude question, and I might as well know."

"My father, when he died, was first violinist in a theatre orchestra, and after his death my mother opened a milliner's shop in North London. The uncle whose estate I have just come into was her brother, but they were on bad terms, on account of her marriage with my father. I haven't any brothers or sisters."

"You served in the war, of course?"

"Yes," replied Nicholas shortly.

Mrs. Sturt asked no more questions, but, getting up, laid a friendly hand on his shoulder in passing.

"As long as you are with us I want you to regard this house as your own home. We are quite simple people, and if you stand on ceremony with us I shall be greatly offended! Do what you like, go where you like, and smoke where you like! . . . I must go now. If you want anything, press the bell and the maid will come up. We dine at half-past seven. In summer we don't dress, for one or other of the girls is usually playing tennis up to the last available moment."

When she had disappeared he returned to the bedroom, where he made himself clean and put out the contents of his trunk. A clock chimed half-past six as he was in the act of descending the stairs again.

In the drawing-room, to which he made his way, the elder Sturts were reading in separate corners, but the daughters had not yet returned home. After asking and receiving the permission of his hostess, Nicholas proceeded to light the pipe which he had been filling on the way down. Immediately feeling that he had committed a blunder, he began to cast about in his mind for an excuse to retreat into the garden.

"How does everybody pass the day in this establishment?" he inquired with a self-conscious smile.

"In different ways."

"Who superintends the work of the house?"

"I endeavour to, assisted by a more or less incompetent staff, consisting of two maids, a cook, and a gardener-chauffeur."

"Your daughters help, of course?"

"Oh, they are good girls! Audrey, in particular, is my chief of staff. Katherine resembles her father; she is inclined to be intellectual. She reads the minor poets and has a dramatic gift which is very much wasted down here. She has a literary pen, too, if only she could gain her first footing. Evelyn is musical."

"She plays the piano?"

"And very well! . . . I see you keep looking at the garden. Would you like to see it?"

"Very much."

They passed out through the conservatory, leaving Sturt still ensconced behind his newspaper on the sofa.

The afternoon was as delightful as possible, but Mrs. Sturt at once perceived that the interest of her guest was not in her rose-beds and perennials. He kept looking at the distant trees. She tactfully steered him to a rustic seat, facing the lawn, upon which they sat down side by side.

"You are not a flower lover?"

"I prefer nature."

"Do you play tennis?"

"I have played."

"You don't care for it?"

"I think it is much ado about nothing."

"Still, I hope you won't refuse the girls a game occasionally. I want you to be nice to them. They have so built on your coming!"

"I'm afraid niceness isn't one of my virtues."

"But why shouldn't it be?"

Nicholas sucked at his pipe discontentedly.

"Hitherto I haven't met the right people to make it worth while."

"You are far too young to be a Diogenes! Won't you let me undertake your education!"

"I must see a sample lesson first."

"The very first lesson of all is that young girls are sensitive, and that the difficulty is not to *hurt* them, but to *avoid* hurting them. Try that for to-day."

"Are you afraid of my being rude to your daughters?"

"Of course not. Only vulgar people are rude, and you are not vulgar. But a blunt manner has the same effect."

"Is my manner blunt?"

"Perhaps *blunt* is a misnomer. *Abrupt*."

"I appear to have made a bad impression!"

"Don't misunderstand me, my dear boy! You haven't made a bad impression. Very far from it, and you and I are going to be the best of friends. I am thinking of the girls. . . . You say that hitherto you haven't met the right people to make it worth your while to be nice. Well, now we shall see whether your words mean something or nothing."

"I hope I shall be decently polite to them, but if you're referring to the tennis, I rather came down here to *work*."

"Not all the time, surely?"

"Yes, all the time."

"You are indeed an enthusiast!" said Mrs. Sturt, and her tone was noticeably stiffer. She paused a moment before proceeding. "But perhaps you may need an assistant? They would be delighted to be permitted to participate."

"Thanks! We'll see later on."

"And in the meantime you won't snub them too unmercifully?"

Nicholas first pulled out and glanced at his watch, and then got up, but all in a mechanical way.

"Why should I? The chances are they'll snub *me*, from my experience of girls. . . . Hadn't we better be getting back?"

"You go. I'll follow in a minute."

As he walked away, she absently pulled a flower-head and began twisting it round and round in her fingers, while the smile dropped from her face, and two vertical creases made their appearance between her eyebrows. Nicholas, during his short passage to the house, was scarcely less thoughtful. The first flush of triumph had faded, and some of the disadvantages attached to his newly-acquired fortune were already becoming apparent to him. He had a shrewd suspicion that, in installing himself as a paying guest in a household where there were unmarried daughters, he had acted as an impulsive fool.

II

A FAMILY PARTY

The first thing Nicholas saw upon entering the hall was the back of a straight, slim, not very tall, fair-haired girl in tennis garments, who was reading a letter which evidently she had found waiting for her on her return. She turned her head a little to see who had come in, and then he caught a glimpse of a pale, delicately-pretty face, wearing an expression of scorn which seemed as though it might be habitual. When she realised who it was, she turned quite round.

"Oh! . . ." The smile which accompanied the ejaculation was shrinking and reluctant, rather than cordial. He bowed awkwardly.

"You probably know who I am!"

"You must be Mr. Cabot. I'm Evelyn Sturt."

"Your mother has been speaking of you."

"Oh, yes?"

"Don't let me hinder you!" He indicated the letter in her hand.

She responded with a cold, momentary glance.

"It's of no importance, thanks! . . . Well, I have to go upstairs to dress. We shall see one another at dinner, of course. My sisters have just gone up."

He saw nothing more of her, and nothing at all of the other daughters, until the time for the evening meal. When he looked into the dining-room it was still broad daylight, and the three girls were clustered round the open window, talking and laughing among themselves in low voices. They formed a highly picturesque group in their tinted frocks. The scent of the pines came through the window, and the long table was resplendent with dazzling napery, glass and silver. Sturt had not yet come in, but his wife was near the door, giving instructions to a maid.

She put a hand on his sleeve. "Come and make yourself

known to my daughters!"

The girls stopped talking, glanced round, and assumed a constrained manner.

"Here is Mr. Cabot!" announced Mrs. Sturt, smilingly leading him forward. . . . "This is my eldest, Katherine . . . My second. . . ."

"We've already met," said Evelyn.

"Evie generally does contrive to steal a march on us!" complained the daughter who had not yet been introduced. "You would think her thoughts among the icebergs, wouldn't you, Mr. Cabot?"

"I happened to be in the hall when he was passing through."

Audrey, though younger, was taller than either of her sisters, but it was obvious that her rapid growth had not dulled her spirits. She was like her mother, not only in appearance, but in voice and bearing, and she would be still more like her as the years passed. Her limbs were large, her complexion fresh, her cheek-bones high, her eyes clear and animated. Everything about her, however, was at present loose and youthful.

"My baby, Audrey!" laughed Mrs. Sturt, completing her introductions. . . . "What were you girls in committee about?"

Audrey replied for the others:

"We were discussing a certain neighbour of ours."

"Who is that?"

"Mrs. Hantish. She was at the doctor's, and fastened herself upon Katherine—presumably as being the least sophisticated of us. Katherine has just been telling us about it."

"I'll hear it another time. . . . Mrs. Hantish is a very charming widow, Mr. Cabot, reputed, like all other young widows, to be dangerous. You will have the pleasure of meeting her sooner or later."

"Probably sooner!" said Audrey.

"Why, did she mention anything about coming round?" asked her mother.

"Oh, Celia Hantish isn't *crude*, mother!" Katherine opened her lips for the first time.

Her person, though not exceedingly striking in itself, served as a connecting link between Evelyn and her father. Evelyn was slight, classically fair, and clear-cut in all her features and motions, whereas Sturt was tall, thin, dignified, dark-eyed, languid in manner and drawling in speech. No stranger would have identified her as his daughter. Katherine, however, who possessed the physical characteristics of her father, his stateliness and his romance of nature, who was inclined to drawl her words in the same way, and who fell into the same long and somewhat alarming silences without apparent cause, was at the same time continually shooting out little reminders and echoes of her sister, so that there should be no mistake about the relationship. Her delicate skin flushed easily, like Evelyn's, their voices, in peremptory moments, were identical in timbre, in repose their faces bore the same aspect of half-scornful calm, and she was accustomed to use exactly the same involuntary gestures in expressing impatience, surprise and displeasure, but not gratification and enthusiasm, which she displayed far more ingenuously. She was taller than Evelyn, not quite so tall as Audrey, slender and gracefully proportioned, with beautiful hair, hands and feet, of which she took the utmost care. She was neither blonde nor brunette, but half-way between the two. Women called her handsome, but the men more or less passed her over, a fact which was a constant source of perplexity to her.

"When was the last time she came?" asked Audrey, opening her eyes innocently.

"She has certainly rather neglected us lately," replied her mother, "but I suppose she has had other things to do. Personally, I am always glad to see her. She is not only a very nice woman, but an exceedingly decorative one."

"She believes that art, like charity, should begin at home!" explained the youngest daughter for Nicholas's benefit. "You ought to see her wardrobe!"

"She goes in for dress?"

"She changes her frock every time she feels a new emotion coming on! She has a long purse, and she can afford it. I sometimes feel she is the only contented, truly contented, person on the face of the earth.”

Nicholas laughed. “She’s quite young, then?”

“That’s subtle! . . . She calls herself thirty-two, but I’m not going to endorse another woman’s age.”

“I should have thought that a woman of that description would be out of her element in a place like this.”

“Thanks for the compliment!”

“No, I mean one would think she would want to go where men are.”

“Is it for the corresponding reason that you have come down here, where women are?”

Katherine’s face coloured.

“Mr. Cabot will have plenty of time to find out how clever you are, Audrey!” she said quietly. “I shouldn’t go too far at once if I were you.”

“You see how they squash me, Mr. Cabot!” laughed Audrey. “Don’t I look squashed? . . . Hallo! here’s father.”

Sturt strolled into the room, dressed in a dark lounge suit, and dinner was immediately served. Nicholas found himself placed between his hostess and Katherine. The latter almost at once began to address confidential little remarks to him in an under-tone.

“I’m so glad you are to be here for quite a long while! I don’t know anything more horrid than to make acquaintances only to lose sight of them again directly. . . . The next thing to discover is whether we have any sympathetic tastes. Are you a reader?”

“Oh, yes!”

“What sort of books do you read?”

“Science and philosophy.”

“No belles-lettres?”

“Hardly ever.”

“Do you mind telling me why?”

“I’m a realist.”

“But aren’t poetry and romance real? If you think not, I’m afraid you will despise me, for I have to plead guilty to spoiling good paper on those very things."

"Of course they're highly unreal," replied Nicholas, smiling good-humouredly.

Katherine, nonplussed, did not speak again for five minutes.

"We have claret and Moselle—which will you take?" inquired Sturt as the fish course came on.

"I only drink water, thanks!"

"Principle," asked Audrey, "or regimen?"

Nicholas imitated her laconism. "Habit!"

"Do you never discard habits?"

"When the counter-attractions are stronger."

"Isn't the present a case in point?"

"I've never tasted alcohol, so it offers no temptation."

"But don't you ever feel the crying need of exhilaration? Don't you ever want to feel as though you could fly over mountains, or bring beautiful women to heel?"

"Never."

"Perhaps Mr. Cabot prefers the exhilaration of moral altitude!" suggested Evelyn in her calm, disdainful voice.

Nicholas glanced across the table at her. The cool antagonism of her attitude towards him, which he had felt from the first, seemed to be beginning to take definite shape, and a secret irritation grew up in him. At the same time, he was obliged to admit that the pose suited her beauty. It enabled her features to retain their still delicacy of outline, which was their distinction, for smiles and animation would have reduced them at once to mere prettiness. Yet he declined to believe that she was a girl to adapt her moods to the requirements of her physical appearance.

Mrs. Sturt perceived his embarrassment and tactfully came to the rescue.

"Are you looking unusually pale this evening, Evelyn, or is it my fancy?"

"When am I ever not pale?"

"I expect you have over-exerted yourself at tennis again. You really ought to respect your limitations. . . . The girls met Mrs. Hantish, Leslie."

"Ah, indeed! And what had she to say?"

"She was trying to pump Katherine about Mr. Cabot, father," said Audrey. "Your entry into the community is quite triumphal!" she added, addressing the guest.

"I don't see why."

"Our supply of men is so limited that every new arrival is discussed for days beforehand. What will you do about it? The invitations will flow in, from now onwards, in a steady stream, and I foresee that we shall be the most popular girls in Newleigh for quite a little time to come!"

"If it is to be on my account, I'm sure I feel greatly flattered!"

"But aren't you especially interested in the fascinating Mrs. Hantish, who is so interested in *you*?"

"Do try not to be absurd, Audrey!" said Katherine with a quick, private scowl for her benefit. "She is far too old to be mentioned in connection with Mr. Cabot, even by way of joke. . . . Besides, it isn't nice!"

"If I were a young man I should think it very nice indeed to flutter the heart of a lovely and experienced widow—all the more so if she were a few years older than myself."

"It's ridiculous! They belong to altogether different worlds. I am sorry I said anything to you."

"Mrs. Hantish's world is the big world, which includes all the little worlds. . . ."

The maid at that moment entered the room, and she had to stop abruptly. Katherine seized the opportunity to resume her interrupted exchange of confidences with the guest.

"She's only a child, Mr. Cabot! . . . Now do tell me about yourself! I have such a deep literary interest in new personalities. You have come down here to work, have you not?"

"Yes."

"Chemical work?"

"Yes."

"And is that compatible with an *ideal*?"

"I hope so."

"Do you mind telling me what your ideal is?"

Her voice had gradually diminished in volume until it was inaudible to every ear but his. He looked round, to find the other members of the family regarding their plates. It bore too unpleasantly close a resemblance to a conspiracy, and he reddened a little.

"In the first place," he replied quietly, yet with sufficient distinctness to be heard around the table, "since the talk is of beautiful widows, I may as well tell you that an essential condition of my work is a celibate existence."

"Oh! . . ." Katherine laughed nervously. "That wasn't exactly what I was asking! Please don't suspect me of prying into your personal plans."

After an awkward silence, during which Nicholas wondered whether perhaps he had not gone too far, the conversation again became general, and a quarter of an hour later they rose from table.

Sturt immediately retired to his study, for the purpose of smoking an after-dinner cigar, while Audrey, slipping on a wrap, escaped out of doors somewhere. The elder sisters and their mother accompanied the guest to the drawing-room.

"Won't you play us something, Evelyn?" Mrs. Sturt settled herself on the sofa in anticipation.

"I don't care to."

The maid entered with coffee, and they waited till she was out of the room.

"Please do!" said Nicholas.

"What do you wish?"

"A Chopin nocturne," said Katherine, pushing back the hair from her brow with a white and beautifully-shaped hand.

Evelyn looked out the music without a word, and sat down before the piano. After the nocturne she played a polonaise. Her execution was very correct, but rather dry and hard. Releasing the last note, she wheeled half round on her stool, and waited, not so much for commendation as to learn if anything else were required of her. Nicholas thanked her simply, without praising her performance. Mrs. Sturt, sitting on the sofa, with her head propped by a cushion, had socially detached herself from the others, though her narrowed, contemplative eyes never ceased to note the smallest movement or change of facial expression on the part of any of them. Katherine wished to appear enthusiastic for her own purposes, but also to pave the way to a conversation offering possibilities.

"I *adore* Chopin!" she declared. "He is the twilight musician *par excellence!*"

No one, however, seemed disposed to discuss Chopin.

"Shall I play any more?" inquired Evelyn.

Nicholas rose to set his cup on the table. Instead of resuming his seat, he walked across to the piano.

"Mrs. Sturt was speaking of Miss Lore Jensen's compositions. Have you anything of hers?"

"I think so. Is there any particular piece you want to hear?"

"Which is considered her best?"

"I suppose that is a matter of dispute—though not so much in her case as in the case of some others. Her earliest work is the best. Later, she has written for money."

"Evelyn! . . . You *know* that isn't true!" Katherine's voice had a genuine ring of indignation.

"It's too pitifully true! . . . Katherine chooses to regard herself as Lore's especial friend, and so she champions her. It's very loyal, but, unfortunately, facts speak for themselves."

"To endeavour to reach a wider public is not to write for money. Her earlier works were intellectual, while her later ones address the heart. Since they represent entirely different stages of her development, it is uncritical even to bring them into comparison."

Evelyn curled her lip in silence, and began to rummage in the music cabinet.

"There's this!" she said a minute later. "One of her *very* earliest. It's called 'Sphinx.' Do you know it?"

"No," said Nicholas.

"It's rather difficult, and I haven't played it for ages, so you must overlook mistakes."

She set the music up, and reseated herself at the piano.

It was what used to be called a "tone-poem," a work built round a single central idea. Evelyn evidently found its freshness attractive, for she played it with far greater sympathy and feeling than either of the Chopin pieces. Despite her protestation, she made no obvious blunders. It was quite short, in length a mere trifle, but after the first minute Nicholas grew interested and impressed. The opening was calm, measured and drowsy. One could almost see the burning sand of the desert and feel the enervating sunshine. By degrees the theme became more troubled and passionate, quietly in the beginning, but with a gradually rising storm—not physical, but of emotion—until everything was like an unsteady sea of menace and terror. Towards the end, crashing dissonances appeared, but just when he was expecting the conventional climax to come, all the theme-threads united in a sudden quietening, which almost at once took shape as an indubitable *question*. It could then be seen that all that had gone before had been leading the way to this question, and that what had appeared simple and understandable had been really nothing of the sort, but, on the contrary, something very mysterious and profound. . . . Half a dozen tranquil and beautiful bars brought the little piece to a conclusion. . . .

Evelyn got up and walked across to the window, where she stood, looking out. Nicholas had sat down again to listen. Nobody spoke for a few moments.

"That was really fine!" said Nicholas at last.

"Lore will never tell us what it means," said Katherine. "She pretends she has forgotten what was in her head at the time."

"Doesn't the title explain it?"

"In a general way, of course. We all know that the Sphinx was a monster that used to ask riddles, and that those who were unable to solve them correctly lost their lives. The enigma is, what is the riddle that Lore's Sphinx propounds?"

Evelyn turned round.

"Surely the Egyptian Sphinx was a personification of Nature?" she said, looking not at her sister, but at Nicholas. "The question which she asks, and which no one can answer, is, 'Why are you living in the world?' As none of us can answer it, we all have to die."

Nicholas's face showed his disagreement.

"What do *you* think it is, then?" asked the girl.

"It doesn't seem to me that the earliest Egyptians were likely to have been quite so abstract in their notions. Probably the Sphinx was neither more nor less than the goddess of *dreams*. Only civilised people are metaphysical, but even savages dream."

"The Egyptians weren't savages."

"The Sphinx is prehistoric."

"But we don't die because we can't explain our dreams!"

"I don't mean the ordinary so-called dreams. I mean real dreams."

"I'm afraid I don't follow you."

"The dreams we dream during deep sleep and remember nothing of afterwards. The light dreams on the fringe of consciousness are a different thing altogether."

The ladies regarded him with surprise.

"How do you know that we dream at all in deep sleep?" objected Evelyn.

"Because we sometimes have *visions*, which are identical."

"And have visions fatal consequences?"

"They make us act, and we may misinterpret them. That's what I understand by the riddles of the Sphinx. It was the same with the Greek oracles. Many a man has died through mistaking their meaning."

There was a pause.

"You seem to have studied the subject!" said Evelyn.

"I have."

"Then you do seek relief from chemistry sometimes?"

Nicholas hesitated, then suddenly appeared to retire into his shell.

"Sometimes."

Evelyn gave him a long, strange look, after which, without another word, she returned to the window.

"But you deceived me!" said Katherine. "You scoffed at poetry, and all the time, it seems, you are a poet of the first water!"

"It depends on one's definition of a poet," said Nicholas in an altered tone. He gave an impression of wishing to close down the conversation.

"A poet is one who understands through sympathy."

"That's an impossibility. You can guess at things through sympathy, but you can only understand them through practical work."

"Now you are deliberately trying to mystify me, Mr. Cabot, and it is too bad!"

Mrs. Sturt, from her coign of vantage, observed the shade of disgust on his face, and hastened to bring everything to an end.

"Don't you think you young people might drop formalities among yourselves? You are all members of one household now, and it will become positively absurd if you keep it up. I shall call you Nicholas, and I'm sure the girls won't mind your giving them their own names. They are quite nice ones. . . . And now, before it gets too dark, you may perhaps like to explore the neighbourhood on your own account, Nicholas. I don't want you to think that you are to be tied to petticoats during the whole of your stay with us."

"Thanks! I think I will," said Nicholas.

Katherine turned away in offended silence.

III

THE WOODLAND LAKE

The following morning ushered in the first really hot day of the summer. The wind had dropped entirely, leaving the air close and burning, the earth was parched, many of the garden flowers were already drooping, while the song-birds were singularly quiet; everything in nature, in fact, told of a coming ordeal to be got through. Only the bees and butterflies were as busy as ever. Breakfast was served in the open, under the shade of a veranda. Everyone was dressed in the lightest of summer attire, and the conversation was lazy, languishing and desultory, as befitted such a morning. As soon as the meal had drawn to its leisurely close, the girls and Sturt went about their business, Mrs. Sturt being left behind with her guest, still sitting at table. He lit his pipe.

She brushed the crumbs from her skirt. "It's too hot for tennis, and I suppose you can't work till your materials arrive. Have you made any plans for the day?"

"No. I thought I would just wander about."

"Are you feeling misanthropic, or would you care to be joined? I can't spare Audrey, but either of the others would be delighted to cicerone you."

His first day of freedom in the country had raised Nicholas's spirits.

"Aren't you disengaged yourself?" he asked, laughing.

Mrs. Sturt coloured, and also laughed. "How absurd you are! . . . But, seriously, would you care to have one of the girls accompany you?"

"No, thanks! I have only just enough energy to breathe. A polite conversation would be the last straw."

"Need it be so formally polite? However, I dare say you are right—you will find plenty of other opportunities of making their better acquaintance. . . . Incidentally, I hope you have modified your views since we last spoke together!"

"In what respect?"

"As to the possibility of there being people sufficiently nice to be nice to! Have my daughters converted you?"

"They are certainly very nice girls."

"I may as well tell you that *you* have made an impression, too. I can't repeat what Katherine said after you had left the room last evening, but it was highly flattering!"

"I'm sure I am greatly obliged to her!"

"I *will* tell you—in part, at least. She said she felt as if she had stepped from under a cold shower-bath. Your society evidently had a tonic effect upon her!"

"It might be a compliment or the reverse."

"She said something else, too, which I can *not* repeat, for she would be too angry if it came to her ears! . . . But I won't detain you. Which way have you thought of going?"

"Into the woods."

"Delightful! They have told you of our lake?"

"No."

"It's about three-quarters of a mile from here. You can hardly fail to hit it." She rose from the table, and Nicholas followed her example. "Go out through the gate in the kitchen garden at the back, cross the lane into the woods, and follow the main footpath."

They re-entered the house together, he to fetch his hat and she to enter upon her domestic duties.

"Lunch is at half-past one!" she called after him as he passed out through the front door. By way of acknowledgment he partly raised the limp white panama.

Five minutes later he had left the blazing sunshine for the deep shade of the straight, slender, red-boled pines. Everything was still, except that distant sheep were bleating faintly, and that the tinder-dry leaves rustled under his feet as he sauntered on. A rich blue sky appeared overhead through the tops of the trees. He was content to saturate his soul with the beauty of the morning, without actively thinking, yet by degrees his mind crept towards his work again, and his brow became overcast. Clutching his hat down nearly to his eyes, he slouched forward with bent shoulders, like a very much older man. Occasionally he stopped to kick aside a fallen pine-cone. The ground was a handsome russet carpet.

Presently, without expecting any such thing, he stumbled on the little lake. It was only a few hundred yards across from shore to shore, and the colour of its water was scarcely attractive, possessing a muddy opacity. The environing woods, however, succeeded in giving the sheet a romantic aspect. The trees came right to the banks, which in some parts were little cliffs and in others were practically level with the water. The dark, splendid green of the tree reflections helped to redeem the lack of beauty of the broader sunlit surface. A cart-track crossed the top of a dam which had been constructed at the lower end of the lake, but it was one of those tracks which lead from nowhere to nowhere, and no noise of traffic interrupted the stillness of the day. Only a few natural sounds were audible, and they rather served to intensify the silence of the rest of the world. A bird twittered in a tree, a bee hummed its way along, a water-rat plunged from shore, a tiny fish leapt above the surface of the water. The torrid sun outside caused the cool retreat of the forest to appear all the more voluptuously desirable.

He selected with some care a luxurious perch overlooking the lake, produced, loaded and lit his pipe, and for close upon an hour contemplated the scene before him, without fundamentally changing his attitude.

Voices and the snapping of dry boughs at length startled him out of his dreaming repose. The noise came from a little way off, on the same bank. It sounded as if a party were directing their footsteps obliquely towards him and towards the water, but, though he kept his eyes strained, quite a minute or two elapsed before the interlopers came into view. He just distinguished their forms scrambling through the tangle about fifty yards away. It was a woman and a man, and for a brief instant he believed they were making their way forward to address himself—possibly to inquire their route somewhere. . . . Suddenly he recognised the woman as Evelyn! . . .

She was in company with a slight, tallish, dark young fellow dressed negligently in a sweater-coat and light flannel trousers. She herself was all in white. Her face was nearly as devoid of colour as her frock, but such pallor appeared in perfect harmony with the delicacy of her beauty, and she showed no sign of indisposition. She was dangling a shady hat in her hand.

Evelyn was pioneering the way, while her companion, keeping close behind, held back for her the more troublesome branches. They had already advanced another dozen steps and, although she called out no words of greeting, he never doubted in his mind that she had seen him and was coming forward to speak. He wondered mildly who the man was and what they were doing together in so solitary a place. . . . Then she looked up quickly, their eyes met, and he understood that she was aware of his presence for the first time. Halting abruptly, with a quite perceptible tension of the muscles, she remained standing for a moment as if transfixed. Then, whispering a hurried word in her escort's ear, she dived back out of sight among the trees, retreating on the same path by which they had just come. . . .

The young man threw a single glance of inquiry at Nicholas, gave a twirl to his dark moustache, smiled cynically, and, sacrificing dignity to chivalry, proceeded without more ado to join Evelyn on her somewhat ignominious retirement.

Nicholas shrugged his shoulders and knocked out and refilled his pipe. The situation was clear enough. If Evelyn chose to select the woods for a morning rendezvous, it was no business of his. He supposed that he would have to find an opportunity to reassure her tactfully that he had seen nothing, and there the matter would end. The fellow was rather good-looking, and it was natural that she, so fair, should be attracted by a dark type. Doubtless this was what Spireman had alluded to when he had offered the information that one of his nieces was on the road to becoming engaged.

The mystery was cleared up on his way back to the house later in the morning.

In the wood, just before emerging into the lane, he encountered Evelyn's companion, now alone, lounging not ungracefully against a tree, smoking. At these close quarters he appeared still darker than before. His skin was Oriental for sallowness, the eyes were of the deepest shade of brown—nearly black—while his hair was blue-black, straight and glossy. His face, small-featured and handsome, had the bulging forehead of the mechanician. Although his present attire was for comfort, his meticulously neat person seemed to indicate that he was a smart dresser in general. As Nicholas approached, he straightened himself and addressed him in a high-pitched modern voice.

"Good morning, sir! . . . Pardon me, but could you spare a moment?"

"Certainly."

"You are Mr. Cabot, aren't you? Staying with the Sturts at Mereway?"

"Yes."

"Miss Sturt told me so. You saw us by the pond, of course?"

"Yes. I hope I didn't startle you both?"

The dark young man laughed, showing excellent teeth. "Miss Sturt did run a bit! I told her it was piffle! You're a sportsman, I hope?"

"I hope so."

"Girls will be girls! . . . My name is Maurice Ferreira, in case you'd care to know. I'm the son of the local practitioner here."

"Half a minute! Wasn't it at your house that the girls were playing tennis yesterday?"

"We had some sets. Why?"

"Nothing. I just wanted to connect things in my mind. You want to speak to me about something?"

"I wanted to speak to you about this. . . . Will you have a gasper?" He proffered his cigarette-case, and Nicholas accepted one. . . . "You came down yesterday, didn't you?"

"Yes."

"Intimate with the Sturts?"

"I know Mrs. Sturt's brother, and he gave me the introduction."

"Are you staying here long?"

"Some weeks."

Ferreira threw away his own cigarette end and wiped his fingers vigorously with a handkerchief.

"You see, it's like this, old chap! The house is taboo because the worthy mother won't look at me, consequently we have to meet when and where we can. I thought that you, as a reasonable man, would throw your weight in with us. It's Evelyn I'm worrying about. She'll come in for a howling row if it gets about!"

"Oh, I shan't say a word, of course."

"I knew you wouldn't; but she was a bit uneasy in her mind about it, and as *she* couldn't very well approach you, it was left to me. So that's all right and square, then?"

"Excuse my asking, but if she can visit your house why can't you visit hers?"

"It isn't my house, old chap! Theoretically, she visits my respected parents. It's a question of etiquette, and so forth. No doubt the good lady sends her little brood there under strict injunctions! . . . Anything else?"

"No; it only struck me as a curious arrangement. I suppose you are on holiday?"

"I'm resting. I'm a civil engineer, very much out of a job!"

"Are you likely to get one in these parts?"

"Not in these parts, of course; but one sees the papers and hears this and that. I have the offer of a crib in East Africa, but I'm not keen."

An idea suggested itself to Nicholas, but he was not quite sure of its feasibility, and hesitated to open himself to Ferreira.

"You've struck lucky, I hear!" pursued the latter casually.

"Yes."

"Katherine's a nice girl."

"I don't doubt it in the least; but I came down here to work."

"Work, eh?"

"Yes; I'm doing some chemical research work."

"That's not in my line."

"We might be useful to each other, but I expect you wouldn't look at a small job?"

Ferreira regarded him carefully as he pulled out his cigarette case again.

"It all depends. I might."

"I want a piece of rather complicated clockwork. I suppose it would take about a week or a fortnight. You could work in my room. You haven't been absolutely forbidden the house?"

"I'll chance the reception. I could fix you up some clockwork. But what's your idea of a professional fee? I wouldn't want to work for a ten-pound note!"

"I don't know what it's worth. . . . I'm very anxious to get it done quickly and satisfactorily, so I would be willing to pay you a sentimental price, according to results."

"How much?"

"Oh, I would go to a hundred guineas, perhaps. It isn't worth anything like that, but I want to get it started, and I don't know who to go to. You could begin work on Monday."

"Ten o'clock?"

"Yes, ten o'clock would do."

"I'll come straight up to you. No tools required, of course, till we've had our palaver?"

"I expect you'll need to run up to town for materials."

"Expenses?"

"Naturally."

"Good man!"

They put themselves in motion and strolled out into the lane together. At the Sturts' kitchen garden gate they prepared to separate, Nicholas to go into the house, Ferreira to proceed down the lane to his own home. It was five minutes to one.

"There's one thing," said Ferreira. "How do you propose to wangle your acquaintance with me? I don't want Evelyn brought into it."

"What do you suggest?"

"I guess we've met in town somewhere, haven't we?"

The glitter of his dark eyes and the double row of small, sharp, intensely white teeth, revealed for a second in a wicked smile, gave the man a distinctly foreign appearance, so that Nicholas for the first time entertained doubts concerning his nationality. He began to feel a certain repugnance towards him.

"Why not stick to the fact?" he asked. "We got into conversation in the woods."

"Just as you like, old chap—as long as we tell the same story!"

Nicholas, having unlatched the gate, raised his hand in a silent salute, and they went their respective ways. As he entered the hall from outside, Evelyn appeared from somewhere. She threw him a questioning look, as though desirous of ascertaining his attitude towards her.

"Did Mr. Ferreira speak to you?" she asked.

"Yes; I have just left him."

"Is it all right?"

"Of course it's all right! Other people's affairs are not mine."

"There's nothing wrong in it, but please don't say a word to anyone."

"Very well."

After casting a quick, timid glance around her, Evelyn hesitated for an instant, and then, obviously acting on sudden impulse, turned her back quietly on him and retreated along the passage to the back of the house.

While he was still staring after her a maid entered the hall.

"A large wooden box has arrived for you, sir, and has been taken upstairs into your sitting-room. I have placed a chisel and hammer there, in case you wish to open it yourself."

"Thanks very much!" said Nicholas. "I'll open it after lunch."

IV

EVELYN IS INITIATED

"Have they told you that your box has come?" inquired Mrs. Sturt while still at the table.

Nicholas replied that he had already seen it, and proposed to deal with it after lunch. Evelyn, who had scarcely spoken throughout the meal, looked at him sharply but immediately returned her eyes to her plate.

"I happened to meet a neighbour of yours in the woods," he proceeded steadily, thinking this opportunity of announcing the arrangement entered into as good as any other. "Young Ferreira. We got into conversation together."

His hostess's manner perceptibly stiffened.

"Oh, indeed!"

"I was wondering if you would have any objection to his working in my room for a week or a fortnight? I find he can be very useful to me."

"Did he propose it, or did the idea originate with you?"

"It was my suggestion."

"But I expect he led up to it?"

"How could he have done?" He fell instinctively into a defensive attitude. "He didn't know I should have any use for him. I want a clockwork apparatus put together, and it occurred to me that he was on the spot. . . . However, if you have the slightest reluctance—"

"Oh, no!" replied Mrs. Sturt rather coldly. "I want you to feel that your rooms are perfectly your own, and that you are at home in every sense of the term. I understand that Mr. Ferreira is quite clever in his profession."

An unpleasant silence descended on the party. Evelyn showed signs of restlessness, and, murmuring an apology, left the table before the conclusion of the meal. Nicholas began to repent not having taken advice before arranging for assistance in a house where he himself was no more than a guest.

As he was on the point of going upstairs after lunch Mrs. Sturt intercepted him. With one of her most charming smiles she laid an intimate hand on his arm.

"Forgive me my grudging consent just now! I had a reason, but it was impossible to explain things before the others. May we have a *tête-a-tête* in your room? You're about to open your box, aren't you?"

"I was going to, but I can put it off."

"I mean just the reverse. While you are working I can be talking."

She preceded him up the stairs. In his sitting-room the packing-case presented an unsightly spectacle in the exact middle of the floor, and he hastened to drag it to one side. His hostess sank into an easy chair by the open window, through which the sunshine was streaming.

"Smoke if you want to, Nicholas! . . . I wonder if you could lower that blind about half-way? The sun glares so. And perhaps it might be as well to close the door."

He fulfilled her requests.

"Now you can get on. They brought you up the necessary tools?"

Nicholas replied in the affirmative, and lifted the chisel, with intent to start levering the wooden lid of the case.

"Do take your coat off to it!" said Mrs. Sturt. "You make me hot in sympathy."

The atmosphere of the room, in fact, was fiery and even though he accepted the invitation, the moisture stood upon his face before he had fairly commenced his task. Mrs. Sturt fanned herself with a piece of newspaper she had picked up. After she had watched him for a few moments, she addressed him languidly.

"Understand, my dear boy—no, don't get up, I can talk to you quite well while you are at work!—I haven't the remotest objection to Mr. Ferreira's being with you, but, considering the terms we are on together, it rather astonishes me that he should care to be a party to such an arrangement. What is more, I can't help thinking that he has some ulterior motive, which, naturally, he hasn't confided to you."

"Oh, I can assure you he's doing it for money, as far as that goes. Of course, Mrs. Sturt, if you really don't want him in your house he must keep away, and there's no more to be said."

"Oh, no; I'm not so prejudiced against him as all that!" She paused, then uttered a nervous little laugh. . . . "What I am really worrying about is my daughters. . . . I'm afraid you don't quite understand. Mr. Ferreira is a rather dangerous young man."

At this Nicholas stood up and looked round, chisel in hand.

"What do you mean by 'dangerous'?"

"I mean what is usually meant. Fascinating and unscrupulous. And I haven't the least doubt, *ubiquitous!* Instead of being at work at his profession, as every healthy-minded young man ought to be, and is, he spends the greater part of his time lolling in flannels in the society of girls and women. I have seen something of it myself, and have heard a lot more. The disagreeable part of it is that I suppose one would call him *attractive!* He hasn't a penny to his name and I regard him as a most undesirable person to associate with my girls. Of course, they are at the most romantic and impressionable age."

Nicholas cleared his throat, and thought of Evelyn.

"He didn't allude to them in any connection?" inquired Mrs. Sturt.

He hesitated before framing an answer which should be true, yet discreet.

"He did refer to Katherine in rather flattering terms."

"Katherine? Oh, fiddlesticks! . . ." Her face suddenly became pink and energetic. "That was to put you off the scent. Katherine interests him as little as I do. It's Evelyn! . . ."

Nicholas said nothing. His hostess fanned herself still more vigorously.

"I must talk to someone about it, and that's why I am talking to you, though it isn't exactly a pleasant subject. Mr. Sturt is so unpractical, and Katherine is too young and inexperienced. After all, you are a man of the world, Nicholas. I wish you could help me out. . . . You see, even if he *were* in a position to support her—which he is very far from being—how could I depend upon his remaining faithful to her when all the evidence goes the other way? There's very little doubt that he is corresponding with half a dozen other women at this very moment. . . . And Evelyn is so dreadfully secretive! One doesn't know how far they have carried it already. I have to guess at her feelings. There may be an actual understanding between them."

"Has he formally proposed?"

"*That* I don't know! I'm in the dark about everything. All I do know is that they have been seen together more than once lately. . . . That's why I dread having him here. Of course, as long as he remains in this room it will be all right, but how is one to guarantee that he won't occasionally slip away to other parts of the house? I might try to put Evelyn on her honour not to see him, but I'm perfectly convinced beforehand that she would refuse to fetter herself in any way."

"Then I had better cancel the whole scheme!"

"No, don't do that. He would guess who was responsible for your change of plans, and it would only make him more vindictively eager to thwart me. He will have to come now. But do promise me to keep an eye on his movements! You don't realise how much may depend on it."

"But what can I do? I can't escort him from and to the door every time!"

"I'm sure you don't sympathise with a man like that!"

"Of course not, from what you say. But—"

"What I really fear is that he may attempt to persuade you to aid and abet them. I know you wouldn't do that!"

"Oh, no!"

"If you hear anything serious—even if you merely suspect anything serious—do let me know at once! He may inadvertently drop some hint in the course of casual conversation. . . . I don't ask you to do anything against your code—"

"Would you like me to have it out with him on Monday?"

Mrs. Sturt made a gesture of horror.

"Good gracious, no, my dear boy! Don't dream of doing any such thing! The house would be on fire immediately. No one is supposed to know anything about it—least of all I. I simply want to get them quietly away from each other."

"It was merely a suggestion."

"Not a word to him on the subject! . . . Unless, of course, he introduces it. In that case, I wouldn't discourage him. Just listen quietly to what he has to say, and put in a response here and there, to lead him on. . . . I am sure you will agree that the end justifies the means!"

"I quite see your standpoint," said Nicholas in a reluctant tone.

"You *will* help me?"

"I'll do what I can."

"It is *so* important!". . . She sank back in her chair with a deep, soft sigh. "Well, so now we'll leave the subject! . . ."

He reapplied himself to his task with gloomy vigour, and the noise of cracking boards followed. The last section of the cover was wrenched off and thrown aside.

Mrs. Sturt leaned forward again, forcing a smile.

"I'm not as communicative as this with everyone, so you must regard it as a great proof of confidence!"

"It's very kind of you to say so."

"I mean it. I don't pretend to understand your character in less than twenty-four hours, but I do see that you are honourable and straightforward, and that's why I ventured on this rather risky conversation. . . ." She raised herself slowly to the erect position. "And now may I wait and witness your unpacking? You have excited my curiosity!"

"With pleasure! But there's little to interest you. A few bottles, and so forth."

Several layers of wrapping required to be removed before the interior packages could be reached. The floor quickly became a litter of paper, cardboard, shavings and string, and more than once Nicholas glanced apprehensively at his hostess to see how she

was taking the hard treatment of her carpet. She remained perfectly good-humoured about it, and presently even began to assist
him to unwrap some of the smaller parcels. When he saw that her
fingers were as deft and delicate as his own, the silent protest
already framed in his mouth died away. Instruments and recept-
acles, fragile glass retorts, tubes and phials were stood carefully
upon the table in neat order as they came to light. His face gradually cleared when it became apparent that there were to be no
breakages.

"But this is a veritable laboratory!" exclaimed Mrs. Sturt as
the collection grew. She ceased from her labours and dusted her
hands, one against the other.

"It's fairly complete, I think."

"What are those bigger packets still in the box?"

"This is a furnace, and this contains liquids and chemicals."

"And *that?*" She indicated a circular metal box lying stowed
in a corner of the packing-case in a thick nest of cotton-wool.

"Oh, that's what I'm working on." He did not offer to remove
it.

"Is it a secret?"

"I'm afraid it can't be exposed."

She laughed. "It might be a bomb!"

"Something very much more useful than a bomb, I hope!"

"How terribly circumspect you are! Surely you can't suspect
me of wishing to steal your processes?"

"No; but the difficulty is, I'm still experimenting, and haven't
anything completed to show."

"But what are you trying to accomplish?"

"Oh, I haven't the gift of explaining things in words. . . . I'm
very sorry! . . ."

"Well, whatever it is, I wish you all possible luck and success!
There is nothing I can do for you now?"

"Nothing, thanks."

At the door Mrs. Sturt swung her body gracefully round again.

"I hope you are taking tea with us downstairs at half-past
four?"

He appeared uncertain.

"Do try and be down. The girls think Mrs. Hantish may be calling. She will quite extend your ideas, besides being very easy to get on with."

She went out, closing the door behind her. For a moment or two Nicholas stood perfectly still, in an attitude of listening; then, walking across to the door, he reopened it softly and swiftly. Mrs. Sturt had gone away, and there was no one about in the passage. He closed the door again without sound.

Stepping to the curtain in a corner of the room which concealed a row of hooks for hanging garments on, he jerked it suddenly aside.

"You can come out now!" he said in a quiet, sharp voice. "The coast is clear."

Evelyn came forward into the room.

"So it's *you*!" said Nicholas, completely taken aback. The girl tried to meet his eye, but failed. She turned her head impatiently away with a smile, half scornful, half humorous.

"I suppose you are disgusted? This is the second time to-day you have caught me in a ridiculous situation!"

"But what on earth have you been doing there?"

"At any rate, I wasn't *eavesdropping*, so please don't imagine it! I came up here to speak to you alone. Then I heard you and mother coming in together, and as I naturally didn't want her to find me in this room, I had to hide somewhere. I had just time to scramble behind the curtain."

"I see! . . . Won't you sit down?" He pushed a chair towards her, and she seated herself. Nicholas continued standing.

"Perhaps you don't believe me?" demanded Evelyn, with a shade of defiance.

"Why shouldn't I believe you?"

Her smile had by this time faded. "May I ask how you guessed I was there?"

"I happened to see the toe of a woman's shoe move underneath the curtain. I didn't know it was you, of course."

"I was the last person you would suspect of such conduct!"

"You were."

"Thank you, at all events, for keeping your word to Mr. Ferreira!"

"And to you."

"And to me. . . . As you have behaved so decently about that, I suppose I have no right to allude to the rest of your conversation with mother. . . . I couldn't very well help hearing it, could I? . . . Just tell me one thing, though. Are you really going to act as mother's spy?"

"No, I'm not."

"I wanted to know. . . . I quite see how awkward it is for you, being placed, as it were, between two fires. . . . Then how will you manage?"

"It's no business of mine, and I don't propose to take sides in it."

"That's all I ask. Incidentally, you needn't believe all that mother told you about Mr. Ferreira. She dislikes him, and nothing he can do finds favour in her eyes. He isn't that sort of man at all. . . . Now I'll tell you what I came up to speak about. I want you not to have him here with you."

"Why?"

"Won't you oblige me without a reason?"

"I shall have to give Ferreira a reason for putting him off."

"Yet you offered mother to break the agreement!"

"That was different. It's her house, and she has the right to say who shall and who shall not come into it."

"Very well, if you insist! I don't want him to come here, because it will be said that he is here for another reason altogether. It puts me in a humiliating position at once. You weren't to know, but I wonder at Maurice not seeing it. The mere suggestion of an intrigue of that sort sets my teeth on edge! It is the kind of thing a housemaid would do."

"You needn't see him."

"I *shouldn't* see him, but am I to go round explaining that to everybody, including the staff?"

"I'm very sorry, but I'm afraid it's too late now. He is to get a

hundred guineas for the job, and though there's no written contract, I don't see how I can go back on my offer."

"If I write a note will you convey it to him?"

Nicholas neither said "Yes" nor "No," but started pacing the
room in thought.

"It's a thousand pities you ever came down here at all!" said
the girl, looking after him. "I foresee complications all round. The
attention of everyone in the place is being focused on Mereway,
and I suppose Maurice and I will receive a double share of scrutiny! . . . What made you do it?"

"It was your uncle's suggestion. I thought it would be a con-
venient place for me to work in. I still don't see why my presence
should be so upsetting."

The colour was stealing into Evelyn's cheeks.

"Apart from this other affair, don't you realise what a false
position you are putting us all in by staying in the house, total
stranger as you are?"

"I don't," replied Nicholas doggedly.

"Haven't you any imagination? Can't you understand what
people are saying about us?"

"What are people saying about you?"

"Do you really think your money is a secret from
everybody? . . . Oh, it's ghastly! . . ." Resting her elbows on her
knees, she buried her face in her two hands, and for a single
moment he fancied she was sobbing. When she looked up again,
however, her eyes were quite dry.

"Surely that's very far-fetched!" he remarked. "It isn't even as
if I were down here for a holiday. I shall be shut up in my room
all day long, working."

"So much the worse, for in that case I see no sense in your
coming to us at all. Any place is good enough to work in. . . . Oh,
I do wish you would go home again and leave us all in peace!"

Nicholas stared out of doors for the best part of a minute,
without responding. Now that he was ready to begin operations, it
did not suit him at all to be called upon to pack up again, and
once more begin house-hunting. On the other hand, Evelyn had a

good deal of reason on her side. He could quite understand the mortified feelings of a proud and sensitive girl at having her name coupled by sarcastic neighbours with that of a young man who had recently inherited a fortune. It made matters worse that perhaps she knew her parents' ambitions better than he did! . . . He wondered what arguments he could employ to turn her thoughts, if only temporarily. If they could all get through the first few days, no doubt things would settle down into a routine. . . .

"You must see yourself that you aren't justified in stopping here!" said Evelyn, getting up from her chair slowly.

"My work—"

"Oh, your work! your work! What *is* your work? I suppose the world won't stop going round because you postpone your amateur experimenting for a week or a fortnight, until you can find somewhere else to go! You don't seem to have any sense of proportion."

Nicholas coloured. "Perhaps I'd better show you what I've done so far, then you'll be better able to judge its importance."

She was immediately silenced. He went to the packing-case and lifted out the circular metal box to which Mrs. Sturt had called attention.

Evelyn, who by this time was on her feet, drew closer, in a sort of timid wonder. He laid the box on a corner of the table and removed the lid. A smaller box, lying inside it, was revealed, which he took out. It was of the size and shape of a tooth-powder tin, but was constructed of aluminium. There was a revolving lid to it, having a narrow horizontal slit extending from the centre to the circumference.

"You had better sit down," suggested Nicholas.

She obeyed, with a half-frightened look on her face.

"What is it? What are you going to do?"

"I'm going to release the spring which rotates this lid, so that the slot visits each part of the exposed gelatine inside in turn. The whole process won't last two minutes, but you had better keep your seat to it."

"I don't understand. There is not to be an explosion or a

shock?”

“No; it won’t hurt you. Just remain sitting down, and look on quietly.”

While she waited with considerable apprehension for what was to take place, Nicholas, standing before the table, drew back the little release-spring which liberated the revolving lid. The moment he had done so, he dropped into the nearest chair himself.

Suddenly Evelyn was in the middle of a nightmare!

The room streaming with sunlight, the open window with its blind only half lowered, the glorious green, blue, and golden world outside, the sweltering heat—all, without warning, had given place to a mad, fantastic dream, into which she had not even time to wonder how she had fallen. She was not frightened, but it seemed to her as if her nature had parted from its moorings and that she had somehow become transported into chaos!

The world in which she now was bore much the same resemblance to the ordered world of reality as a cubist painting to an actual scene or group of persons. It was a kaleidoscope of colours and sounds, odours and skin sensations. Everything was accompanied in her by such a variety and rapidity of emotion that she had scarcely the ability to realise her internal feelings at all. She was just one big *nerve*! . . . All was hopelessly mixed together— darkness and brightness, heat and coolness, one landscape and another, triumph, gloom, laughter, exaltation, grief! . . . The things only came in vivid hints and momentary splashes, immediately to be lost again. It was no dream, but the dream of a dream. Supposing reality to be solid and dreaming fluid, this was *gaseous*. The elements of life were in a condition of disintegration. They still existed, but in combinations so impossible that she could not even understand their meaning. . . .

It was as if she were in the dark-bright bowels of the sun, where nothing yet exists, but where everything already begins to fight desperately to realise itself, even down to men and passions! . . . Every emotion was plastered over by others, while all the outward semblances of individual life were inextricably confounded. . . .

She seemed to herself to be passing through a weird and awful tunnel. The end must surely come, but she had no idea of time. . . .

"It's all over!"

Evelyn, sitting back in her chair, in a nearly fainting condition, heard Nicholas's remark, but was unable to respond to it. The sudden cessation of her extraordinary experience had left a strong paint-like impression of it upon her mind, and she could not adapt herself immediately to the outer world. She consequently failed to see the self-satisfied look of triumph and excitement on his face as he proceeded in a leisurely way to restore the aluminium box to its metal case and place the latter on the table. The look, in fact, was succeeded at once by a constrained one of impassiveness. He slipped on his coat and came forward to stand over her.

"I should have been burnt or boiled for this in the Middle Ages, I expect! I hope you're not feeling upset?"

"What was it?" The words came in a whisper.

"Nothing!" replied Nicholas, smiling.

"What do you mean?"

"What I say! It was *nothing*—nothing *real*, that is. . . . How can I explain it to you? Imagine a dozen gramophones all playing different tunes at once. What you have just been through was a *dream*, reproduced by means of physical impressions on a sensitised substance. Only, for want of proper adjustment, the sensitive surface of the film has been exposed several times over, with the result we have just experienced. It's purely scientific and explainable, so you might as well pull yourself together!"

"A *dream!*"

"Why not? It is only an extension of the established fact of thought transference. If a thought can pass from one brain to another without spoken words, why shouldn't it pass to a prepared receptive gelatine? It must travel by mean of material waves."

"But a dream! . . . And it was so *real*!"

"I hit on a way of intensifying the impressions, so that they are practically captured intact. As for its being a dream, a dream is as much brain-activity as ordinary thoughts are."

Evelyn got up. She passed her hand over her eyes, as if dazed or tired.

"May I speak to you about it some other time?"

"Certainly."

"I can't grasp it all at once. It's too gigantic!"

"So now you can see why I'm keen on settling down to work!"

"Please forgive me for bothering you with my petty personal troubles! You must go on staying here—and if Maurice is to be of any assistance to you, you must have him with you. I had no idea that you were doing anything so wonderful, though from your remarks last evening I might have guessed it."

"Of course, you will say nothing to anyone!"

"Of course not."

She went out, and Nicholas wandered to the window, where he stood for a considerable while gazing absently at the garden.

Evelyn, as she retired to her own room, grappled with a dim and confused intuition that her real motive in visiting him must have been to learn this very secret—though, of course, without any suspicion of its nature—and *not* to speak of Maurice or of Nicholas's presence in the house, which had been mere excuses, even if she had honestly believed in them herself. His remarks on the previous evening, when they had been discussing the Sphinx, had corresponded to very strange feelings inside her, which she had not understood at the time, and which she still did not understand. But it seemed to her now as though she had all along been waiting for this discovery of his, and that both she and he were intimately concerned in it, in a personal sense. Now that her first surprise was dying away, she began to assure herself that it had been no surprise at all, but that she had expected something of the sort from the beginning. She wondered with a sort of dread where it was all leading to, and what was to follow. . . .

V

TWO SIRENS

An animated babel of feminine voices fell upon Nicholas's ear as he approached the drawing-room door. He entered rather diffidently, to find tea in full progress. The Sturts were all assembled, and Mrs. Hantish, or someone whom he took to be she, had actually arrived.

She proved to be a tall, graceful, supple, shapely young woman, on the slight side, with a wealth of coal-black hair, a creamy skin and exquisite features—unmistakably a beauty and, what was more, an *interesting* beauty, with clever looks. The daughters of the house appeared quite inconspicuous beside her, despite their superior youth and freshness. She was attractively dressed in a sheath-like frock of some shade of green, and the brown and gold parasol resting against her chair seemed a constituent part of her attire. The upper part of her face was overshadowed and partly hidden by the brim of her large hat.

She sat opposite to her hostess at the tea-table, and, at the moment of Nicholas's entry, Katherine, Audrey and their mother were engaged with her in one of those simultaneous conversations peculiar to women, in which four persons address themselves to the same subject, but divide themselves into parties of two for the sake of intimacy and convenience. Evelyn was sitting apart, gazing out of the window. Sturt, sprawling languidly in his accustomed place on the sofa, sawed the air idly with a lighted cigarette, as though rehearsing a declamation in his head.

Mrs. Sturt, always alert, looked round smilingly towards her house guest, and beckoned him with her finger.

"Come and be introduced! This is Mr. Cabot . . . Mrs. Hantish. . . . You should assimilate excellently, you are such opposites!"

Mrs. Hantish gave him the slightest of bows.

"In what respect?" Her tone was even and friendly, yet she contrived at the same time to erect a barricade of reserve between herself and Nicholas, as though to intimate to him that if his acquaintance was tolerated, it was not particularly desired.

"He regards social life, and all that pertains thereto, as suspect," explained Audrey.

"Indeed?"

"Ask him!"

"As a frivolous person, I won't risk disaster!"

Nicholas was uneducated in this kind of talk. Saying nothing and with a rising colour, he took his cup from his hostess, and hastened to sit down beside Evelyn in the window bay. Mrs. Hantish, apparently dismissing him from her mind, resumed the discussion with Mrs. Sturt and her daughters which his arrival had interrupted.

"What do you think of her?" asked Evelyn rather quickly, in a low voice. "She is *quite* striking, isn't she?"

"Yes, she's beautiful."

"But her looks vary from day to day, so I expect she has a nervous temperament, notwithstanding her easy manner. Would you care to hear about her?"

"Please."

"She is one of those women whom everyone back-bites, but whom everyone secretly admires. Her husband died seven or eight years ago. He was a wealthy Ceylon planter. He was excessively in love with her, they say, while she did not even trouble to conceal her indifference for him. He left her fifteen hundred a year, the capital of which she can't touch, and every penny that doesn't go in housekeeping and travel she spends on her back. She lives here for about three months in the year. The rest of the time she just disappears into space, and is no more heard of, though it is believed she winters abroad. A few years ago she became madly infatuated with a man in the Midlands. No one knows anything about him, or what happened exactly, but he died, and she came back here looking smarter and gayer than ever. The year before last it was the turn of a youth in the Foreign

Office. It went so far that he broke his engagement to a very charming girl. Before many weeks Celia Hantish grew tired of him, and sent him about his business. That's the type of woman she is!"

"But what does she do down here?"

"One supposes she lies fallow! . . . I tell you all this because I think you ought to be put on your guard against her. Don't run away with the idea that she is mercenary. She isn't. She has enough money of her own for all reasonable needs, and all she looks for outside is excitement and occupation. You may not credit it, but she is at this very moment turning you over and over in her mind! It's what she has come for."

Nicholas uttered a protest, but nevertheless shifted his position in order to glance at the visitor. She had her back towards him, and was expressing herself with a friendly ease to the ladies of the house, with speaking little movements of the arms, shoulder and bare neck. There was certainly no appearance of any great anxiety on her part to develop her acquaintance with him, so, if Evelyn's theory were correct, presumably she had not been impressed. The girl glanced with him, the shadow of an ironic smile on her lips.

"If she finds you interesting enough you may be quite sure she will try to lead you on!"

"Then let's hope she won't! But how do you suppose she would set about it?"

"Oh, there's only one way of doing these things! She would do her best to kindle admiration in you, first of all, knowing that the rest would follow. . . . She and Lore Jensen are a pair! That is another siren, but I don't warn you against her, because I don't imagine she would be particularly attractive to a man of your temperament. One fine day there will be a tragedy in this district, and either Lore or Celia will play a leading part in it—possibly both! I've had that intuition for a long time."

"You don't share the others' enthusiasm for Miss Jensen, then?"

"How can I? They don't know, and I do. She laughs at all of us behind our backs. She's unmarried, and still little more than a girl, but she's utterly sophisticated! She writes pretty-pretty music, has a whole host of flabby worshippers in all parts of the country—in short, is fully conscious which side her bread is buttered on, and has gauged public taste to a hair, while all the time and in reality she drinks like a fish, habitually swallows drugs, and in town never contemplates the possibility of bed before three or four in the morning, so I've been told by one who knows. A middle-aged male cynic is not exactly a thing of graciousness, but a girl cynic is a monster! Yet thousands are taken in by her. Mother and Katherine, for instance. The people who *are* in the secret, the initiated few, consisting mainly of men about town and fast women, regard the pose of innocence as a huge joke, and pat her on the back for what they are pleased to term her astuteness. The real joke, if they only knew it, is their patronage of her. She doesn't discriminate between white sheep and black sheep, I can assure you!"

"Then what brings *her* here?"

"Presumably she has her musical output to keep up, and needs the quiet."

"Is she intimate with Mrs. Hantish?"

"As far as I can understand, they know all about each other and have a sneaking regard for each other, without actually being bosom friends. Celia is a better class woman, and things go on inside Lore's house which she wouldn't countenance inside her own."

Nicholas had suspected from the first that Evelyn's rapid and fluent descriptions, so uncalled for and so alien to her character, were intended to prevent his alluding to the incidents of the earlier afternoon. Either she did not care to refer to the subject in the presence of other people, even if they could not overhear the conversation, or else she had been slightly offended by his inflicting such an experience upon her without her previous consent. He thought the latter the more probable hypothesis of the two, and decided to relieve her of his doubtless irksome society without further delay. At the instant of his forming this resolution, by one of those coincidences which seem to belong to the realm of telepathy, Mrs. Sturt addressed him across the room.

"Won't you come and speak to us, Nicholas? Katherine is defending you!"

Evelyn gave him his dismissal with a little grimace. He walked over to the tea-table, capturing the music-stool on his way, and seated himself on it between the two daughters. The fashionable guest smiled, but looked elsewhere.

"Mrs. Hantish suggested that you are shy," explained his hostess. "Katherine, on the contrary, thinks it isn't shyness, but preoccupation."

"A young man *ought* to be shy in the presence of ladies," said Audrey. "It is the essential beginning of better things. It is a becoming confession of ignorance."

"Ignorance of what?" asked Nicholas.

"Of everything that ladies excel in—the graceful and polished side of life. The afternoon tea-table is a sort of finishing school for young men."

"Yet one always feels a man to be put out of place there," remarked Mrs. Hantish indifferently, glancing down at her clothes.

"I like to picture a man *working!*" said Katherine.

Audrey looked sarcastic. "You always did display a marked preference for symbolic art. Men are no more always at work than St. Catherine was always on the wheel! My experience is that they are usually running about after big or little balls."

Her mother smiled tolerantly and immediately turned to the visitor.

"Mr. Cabot is down here to carry on chemical research. He has just been unpacking and arranging his appliances."

"How interesting!" was the cool response.

"Nicholas mustn't imagine he's going to be allowed to hide himself behind his bottles eternally though!" said Audrey. "His education has to be attended to."

"And have you constituted yourself instructress?"

"I don't think he would have me. My manner is not sufficiently impressive. He needs someone more experienced."

Mrs. Hantish for the first time turned directly to the subject of the discussion.

"Are you staying here long?"

"I don't quite know how long."

"I hope you will come and see me occasionally! I should like you to know my cousin, who shares my house with me. She is older and very much more intellectual than I."

"Thank you very much!"

"The girls will bring him over one day," said Mrs. Sturt.

"Soon, I hope!"

Katherine and Audrey glanced at each other involuntarily as the visitor rose to go. Evelyn came forward, while her father got up from the sofa.

"*Must* you go?" asked Mrs. Sturt. "We seem to see nothing at all of you nowadays!"

"I am like Mr. Sturt. The hot weather always makes me misanthropic."

Sturt bowed. "It is a lady's privilege to say unkind things, and her happiness to say them without hurting! Misanthropy is a term which covers a multitude of virtues."

"I don't believe in the virtue of an interesting man who deliberately hides himself in a corner!"

He responded in the same vein, and Mrs. Hantish chose the moment of laughing to effect a graceful and successful escape from the room.

Less than half an hour afterwards, the ladies of the house having dispersed to attend to their respective duties or pleasures, Sturt approached his guest in one of the rooms where the latter was reading the newspaper, pipe in mouth.

"Ah! I see you are engaged!"

"Not at all. Do you want me?"

"No, no! I merely came to suggest that we should take a turn together before dinner. We have seen so deuced little of each other! But there will be other opportunities."

Nicholas threw his paper aside and jumped to his feet.

"I'm agreeable. It will be something to do. But which way shall we go?"

"Have you a preference?"

"No; I don't know the place. I've only seen the woods."

"Then we will not go to the woods. Let us tour the environs a little. You will find it useful to ascertain where our friends are housed. You have met one already and you will meet others."

They captured their hats from the rack in the hall and passed out of doors, descending the drive into the roadway. It was nearly six o'clock. The excessive heat of the middle of the day had subsided, so that it was possible to walk without discomfort, but the natural world had not yet recuperated from the heavy hand of the sun. The flower-beds were parched, the trees looked sickly, while the roads were white with dust which, airless though the evening was, penetrated to their lungs as a fine powder.

"I've met *two*," corrected Nicholas tranquilly.

"To be sure! I had forgotten young Ferreira. Your acquaintance is extending. I think you did not say how you came to speak together!"

"He just stopped me and introduced himself."

"Characteristic, my dear fellow! He is a fantastic youth, and does the weirdest things. . . . Pardon the question, but he did not mention *me*, by any chance?"

"No, I don't think he did."

"I merely asked." He heaved a deep sigh. . . . "This house we are now passing is The Arbour—Mrs. Hantish's place."

"I didn't know it was so close."

"How did you find the dear lady?"

"She seemed very nice."

"One of the most charming of our friends. Nature has richly endowed her, Fortune has followed on the very heels of Nature, and education has accomplished the rest. A finished woman! From her admirable Italian hair down to her *ballerina's* instep she stands out as a true representative of her sex. She gives all her circle much pleasure."

Nicholas continued staring at the house until he could no

longer do so without turning his head. It stood well back from the aesthetic road, with which its glittering new paint, feminine-looking window-curtains and pretty garden, gay with roses, were in perfect harmony. The windows were all flung open to their full extent, but no one appeared. When they had passed it by, he returned reluctantly to his companion.

"Yet you didn't seem to have a great deal to say to her!"

"I have finished with all that sort of thing, dear boy! I am an ancient, and my professional training has taught me how not to overstep my rôle. In conversation one is too apt to forget one's disabilities, but I do not care to make myself ridiculous before a pretty woman. The times are changed!" . . .

"What kind of person is she really?"

Sturt hummed the fragment of a tune with closed mouth while pondering his reply.

"I do not think it is to malign her to place her in the *fatal* category. Her personality is magnetic, she allures, but it seems her victims have not always benefited from the connection. That, at least, is her reputation, my dear fellow. One does not assume that she *intends* harm, yet, if the effect is to be the same, it makes small odds. Young men are much governed by their passions, and a *liaison* built upon physique is always dangerous to a career. I speak generally. *Verbum sat sapienti!*"[1]

Nicholas coloured, without replying. They strolled on in silence past other houses, which occurred at irregular intervals of a few hundred paces on either side of the road. The trim lawns, showy flower-beds, and intervening clumps of pines invested the locality with a stylish, semi-rural air which was very attractive.

"Miss Jensen, on the other hand," proceeded Sturt, in sonorous, measured accents, "possesses a quite different type of character. She has a soul above intrigue, and if on occasion she is somewhat disconcertingly outspoken, that proceeds only from the demands made by the idealism of her nature. I should much like you to know her. I think you would agree well together. We are actually approaching her house—which is what has led me to

1. "A word to the wise…"

name her. How would it be, my dear fellow, if we were to run in, *sans cérémonie*, to pay a flying call? It is just the sort of friendly attention which will delight her. I have no doubt we shall find her in."

"I don't mind; but have you been intending this all along?"

"The thought has but just entered my head. . . . Here we have the house!—Yetholm. No false modesty, I beg! She has heard of you, and she can be nothing but flattered by so spontaneous a tribute."

"The tribute being yours! Has she an instep, too?"

Sturt laughed artificially and appeared rather strangely agitated. He took his companion's arm to detain him at the gate.

"She is no more than a very delightful, talented lady, my dear boy, for whose acquaintance you will afterwards thank me. Let us enter."

"Tell me her age, then I shan't fall into any holes!"

"Thirty—thirty-one or so. It is not her years that signify; it is her intellectual vigour, her breadth of vision! . . . You will see. . . ."

Nicholas tolerantly permitted himself to be conducted up the tiled pathway through the garden to the house door. A page-boy appeared in response to Sturt's thunderous knocking.

"Your mistress is at home, boy?"

An affirmative answer was returned.

"In her work-room, doubtless? Is she alone?"

It appeared there was a visitor.

"No matter. We will go through. You need not announce us."

He motioned airily to Nicholas to follow him along the passage leading out of the hall, and without again turning his head, strode forward until he was outside a door at the end, on the lefthand side. Grasping his companion's arm, to arrest him, he composed his features to a smile, preparatory to calling out:

"May one enter?"

After a silence lasting a few seconds a lazy feminine voice drawled from within: "Who is it?"

"Mr. Sturt and friend!"

Undertones were exchanged inside the room.

"Very well, you may come in," said the same voice.

The visitors entered, to find themselves in a small, rather barely-furnished and untidy room, illuminated by the rays of the late afternoon sun. Women's out-door garments and paraphernalia were mingled everywhere with books, papers, score-sheets and the refuse of composition work. An upright grand piano stood open. On an occasional table were a couple of empty champagne bottles, with three used glasses, while the atmosphere of the room was disagreeable with the stale smell of tobacco smoke. A middle-aged, sallow, French-looking woman, in a low-necked black dress—presumably a companion—was employing herself with fine needle-work on the window-seat.

Lore herself reclined on a sofa. She possessed bobbed chestnut-red hair, over a somewhat puckish face, which might be judged handsome or the reverse, according to one's taste. The features were delicate, giving an impression of extreme sensitiveness, but the eye-ridges were prominent, and one eyebrow slanted up more than the other. Her eyes were grey, with a greenish tinge, and were constantly roaming, as if from an excess of cynical energy. A vivid spot of rouge standing on each cheek-bone contrasted with the pallor of the rest of her face, and seemed to supply the one other bizarre touch which her aspect needed. She was rather short, and full in figure.

In the exact middle of the room, perched on a cushioned easy chair, with his legs tucked crosswise under him, tailor fashion, was Maurice Ferreira. He had a woman's coloured scarf bound round his forehead, to simulate a turban, and was smoking a cigarette from an ivory holder of exaggerated length. His small white teeth disclosed themselves in welcome beneath the curling, thin black moustache, with its pointed ends, as he caught sight of the new arrivals. He flung the book he had been holding right across the room.

Sturt stopped at the door, hat in hand, with a courteous smile, while Nicholas ranged himself beside him.

"Well!" said Lore affably, but without offering to rise. "Since when have you taken to marching into people's private apartments like this?"

"I came to proffer you a gift in the shape of a new acquaintance! But we can retire." He spoke as one who was sure of his ground, and the first glimmerings of a mystery entered Nicholas's mind.

"Sit down, both of you. . . . We have been drinking champagne. Shall I send for another bottle?"

"Not for me, and Mr. Cabot takes nothing in that way, I believe."

This was Nicholas's only introduction.

"What a paragon!"

Sturt turned the subject rather hastily. "Have we interrupted a recital?"

"Maurice was reading to us. What were you reading, Maurice?"

Ferreira removed the scarf from his head and threw it down.

"Balzac's 'Droll Stories,' for my sins! The dreariest rot imaginable!"

The lady turned an eye on Nicholas. "You are staying at Mereway, aren't you?"

"Yes."

"Are you fond of this part of the country?"

"It's my first visit to it."

"He's here to work," explained Ferreira, yawning. "I am to help him. Something in the chemical line."

"That's splendid!"

In the meantime, the companion at the window sewed on as though unconscious of the presence of visitors. Lore wriggled herself into an easier position, and stared up at the ceiling.

"Since you are scientific, I suppose you are not musical?" she asked next. Nicholas, as the only one whose tastes were unknown, took it upon himself to reply.

"I enjoy hearing music."

"But, like everyone else, no doubt your enjoyment is strictly demarcated? You don't pretend to rise to a sympathetic appreciation of all forms of musical art? No outsider does."

"I'm not particular about forms, as long as the material is sincere."

"What does that mean?"

"I mean, as long as it is art, and not money-making." The words were hardly out of his mouth before he realised his *faux pas*, but it was too late to rectify it. Sturt looked uneasy.

"Are you aiming at me?" demanded Lore, not changing her position.

"Of course not. Why should I be aiming at you?"

"You had better not, or I might have something to say back! It's all very well for superior persons to insist on pure art, as opposed to money-making, but, in the meantime, who is to provide the artist's bread and butter? The exalted few who know all about it, or the crowd who know nothing whatever about it, but are quite prepared and willing to put their hands in their pockets if they see what they want in the shop window? . . . You don't for one minute imagine that anyone with brains—or without brains, for that matter!—writes everlastingly round roses, and nightingales, and thatched cottages, and convent-windows, for the sheer love of the thing? Of *course* it's done for money! Of *course* it's pot-boiling! But if I don't boil my own pot, are you going to boil it for me? I suppose you think it's bad art to *have* a pot! An artist ought to be above such trifles as food, and clothes, and house-cover! . . . I expect it never once in your young life struck you how very much more useful it would be to start an endowment fund for struggling musicians than to wander around criticising the poor devils' output? Oh, I've no patience!" And she flung herself round to face the wall.

"I don't see anything wrong with that!" remarked Ferreira tentatively, after a pause.

"I hope you don't think I was in any way reflecting on your work!" said Nicholas. "As a matter of fact, Miss Sturt played me a composition of yours last night which impressed me tremendously. A little sketch called 'Sphinx.' I understand it is one of your very early pieces?"

To his increasing confusion, the speech produced exactly the opposite effect to that intended. Lore, with a sudden twist of her body sat right up on the edge of the sofa, positively glaring at him.

"What you evidently mean, only you daren't say it in so many words, is that my later work belongs to a different class! Why not call me a mercenary wretch right out, and have done with it! It's obvious you are extremely anxious I shouldn't misunderstand what is in your mind. But get *this* right, my dear young man— whoever you are, and whatever you may be—I work as I please, and I propose to go on working as I please, and I haven't the very slightest intention of soliciting your sanction in the matter, and in fact and in short you may go to the devil, for all I care, as an ignoramus! I hate insolence!"

"My dear Lore! . . ." began Sturt, approaching her.

"I don't care—I mean it! I've worked hard all my life, I've put my very best energy and brains into it, and this is what I get! Insults and abuse! It's enough to make me throw up the whole wretched business. . . . And where do I hear it all? In my own private sitting-room, if you please! He walks in here, without a word, as if it were a museum, and I a beetle under a glass case! Are these the new manners?"

"But I don't even know what it's all about!" expostulated Nicholas.

"I suppose if I want privacy I must shut myself up in my bedroom! It's really and truly a most extraordinary state of affairs. Even now he doesn't budge! . . ." She broke into hysterical laughter.

Ferreira signed to Nicholas to bend down over him.

"It's the *fizz*, old chap! Better slip quietly away!"

"Thanks."

Lore called excitedly to the companion, who was smiling tranquilly over her work. "Germaine, ring the bell, please."

The Frenchwoman rose like an automaton.

"Don't trouble!—I'm going," said Nicholas. "Please accept my apologies for intruding, Miss Jensen. Are you coming, or staying, Mr. Sturt?"

Sturt hesitated, as though hoping that peace might even yet be made.

"You needn't look so dumbfounded," said Lore, impatiently turning her back on him, with twitching shoulders. "I'm perfectly in my right senses. I don't want apologies, and I don't want explanations. All I want is to be allowed to sit in my own room, with my own friends. Since you have brought him, you had better take him away again. In any case, I shan't be pleasant company. He has quite succeeded in upsetting me for the evening."

Sturt bowed. Ferreira again drew Nicholas down towards him.

"I'll smooth things over after you've gone. Not a word to Evelyn about finding me here."

Nicholas said nothing, but, after also bowing to the lady of the house, at once moved to the door. Sturt, stately and impassive at last, followed him. Meanwhile Lore, retaining her seat on the sofa, lit a cigarette, and laughed bitterly.

Once outside the gate, in the roadway, the ex-actor showed signs of wishing to address his companion. He was obliged, however, to clear his throat more than once before he was able to overcome his embarrassment.

"Miss Jensen has a temperament, my dear fellow, and that is all about it! You were unfortunate enough to jar a nerve, with the result we see. On another occasion, doubtless, things will run more smoothly, and then you will discover how charming she knows how to be."

"Oh, you don't catch me there again," said Nicholas.

"That is as you wish. I was rather alluding to the probability of your meeting her at Mereway. Miss Jensen is not malicious, and she will not for one minute permit your residence in our house to prohibit any visits she may wish to make us. . . . It would not be a bad thing, dear lad, if we were simply to regard this evening's call as not having taken place! The contre-temps reflects credit on no one. There is nothing to be gained by recording it. I will take an opportunity of requesting Miss Jensen to forget it, and do you do the same. Say not a word to the ladies!"

"Oh, you needn't be afraid of my speaking," replied Nicholas curtly.

Sturt threw him a questioning glance, but was unable to decide whether the words were intended to express reassurance or merely agreement.

VI

MORNING, NOON, AND NIGHT

At half-past ten on Monday morning Nicholas had already been at work for half an hour, when Ferreira was announced by one of the maids.

"Hard at it, eh? What do we do—take our coats off?" The day, in fact, was hot, and Nicholas was in his shirt-sleeves.

"Do! Sit down, won't you? We might as well start right away." He motioned to Ferreira to bring a chair beside his own before the little table at the window.

"I say, this looks ominous!" He threw his coat aside, and seated himself. . . . "Oh, while I think of it—I've made it all square for you with Lore! She wants me to bring you along one afternoon."

"Thanks very much, I don't think I'll risk a second outburst!"

"Oh, she *is* like that. You mustn't mind her funny little ways. You didn't mention to anybody about my being there, I hope?"

"No."

"The first time I catch old Sturt alone I'm going to rag him about butting in on us like that. He seems to imagine he has the run of the place!"

"May I ask what you were doing there yourself? I thought you were so keen in another quarter!"

"I can pay an afternoon call, I hope! Lore is one of my pals."

"That's all right, but why are you so anxious to keep it dark?"

"When you've seen as many girls as I have, old chap, you'll know why! I've tried explaining other women away before now! It takes too long."

"I suppose you know your own business. . . . Well, shall we start?"

"I'm ready and waiting!"

Nicholas turned over his papers, to find one he wanted. He

smoothed it out in front of him, and consulted it. Ferreira lit a cigarette.

"What I need is clockwork to revolve a length of sensitive film. The film is covered, and each part of it in turn passes underneath an open slit. Supposing a single revolution of the whole film lasts four hours, and supposing the slit to be a tenth of an inch across, and the exposure to it one second—what length the total reel?"

"Forty yards," replied Ferreira, without hesitation.

"Exactly. That will have to be deferred to the distant future, I'm afraid! We'll try again. . . . Make the revolution one hour, the slit a twentieth of an inch, and the exposure two seconds. What length reel now?"

"Seven feet, six inches."

"That's much better! . . . Now the next point. The surface of the sensitive film won't be quite set, so it mustn't be coiled. I propose that it shall be an inch wide. How can we manipulate that?"

"Make a travelling band of it, inside a circular box, thirty inches diameter. Any joiner will knock you up a box to specification."

"All right. But now we come to a difficulty. I want the film to sensitise itself, by passing through a tank filled with gelatine brought to a liquid condition by heat."

"So as to avoid exposure?"

"Yes. I suppose the film container itself would have to be the tank? It could be filled, the reel wound through it, then empty it again immediately. To prevent all possible risk of exposure, I expect you would want a double filler at the top, and a double emptier at the bottom. You understand what I mean?"

"That's quite feasible," said Ferreira. "And the only other point is how to connect the clock and the revolving carriage. But that's my job."

"One other thing still! There must be a clock face, with hours and minutes, and a regulator, on the alarm-clock system, so that the motor can be set in advance to start at any given time. . . . I think that's a rough outline of what I want."

Ferreira blew out a cloud of smoke.

"Is it allowable to inquire what the scheme is?"

"I haven't taken out the patent yet," replied Nicholas, diplomatically, believing that the other would appreciate this argument the best of any. His answer had the desired effect, and Ferreira refrained from further questioning on the point.

For half an hour longer the two young men discussed ways and means. Nicholas insisted that the box should be of aluminium, and it was arranged between them that Ferreira should run up to town next day to place the order for its construction with a City firm of his acquaintance. He could take the opportunity of bringing back with him whatever tools and materials were necessary towards putting together the clockwork, so that they might make a clear start on Wednesday morning. Nicholas proposed to confine his own labours to the chemical side. A larger quantity of the sensitive gelatine would be required than he had yet been able to obtain. But before that was put in hand, he contemplated further experiments directed towards improving its quality. He thought that it would be possible to make the film-coating substance still more susceptible to the thought-waves, and he also wished to find a means of causing it to set more rapidly after exposure.

When they had settled the preliminaries to their satisfaction, and nothing else remained to be discussed Ferreira slipped on his coat. Just as he had reached for his hat, a soft knock sounded on the outside panel of the door. Nicholas went to open it.

It was Evelyn.

She was dressed in white, and a sunshade was in her hand, but she was without a hat. Her eyes looked positively dismayed as they fell on Ferreira, and evidently nothing had been further from her thoughts than to find him there.

"I'm very sorry! I didn't know you were here, Maurice." As she spoke, she retreated backwards into the passage.

"I say!—you're surely not running away for me!"

"Alice—the maid—thought you had gone. I only wanted to say something to Mr. Cabot, but another time will do."

The smile faded from Ferreira's face. "Well, anyway, since you've come so far, you might come a bit farther, and sit down!"

Evelyn hesitated, looking extremely annoyed, but finally entered the room, and took the easy chair which Ferreira hastened to push forward. The latter perched himself on the edge of the table. Nicholas continued standing.

"Cabot's been keeping me at it like a Yankee contractor! Don't I look wan?"

"You can't have been here more than half an hour."

"Come, be sympathetic!"

She smiled rather sourly, and turned to Nicholas.

"Have you arranged everything according to your wishes?"

"I think so. Ferreira is to go up to town to-morrow to get the materials, and starts work here the first thing on Wednesday morning."

"So you aren't doing any more to-day?"

"He isn't."

Her obvious coolness to Ferreira led him to wonder what exactly the relations between the two were. If the intimacy were still in its first stages, he could discern no great danger of its developing; but if some sort of understanding existed between them, it was quite possible that she was deliberately concealing her true feelings. He decided that the latter was the more likely of the two cases.

"What about tennis at our place this afternoon?" demanded Ferreira. "Bring the fair sisters along, and stop to tea!"

"It can't be done. We came last Friday."

"Last Friday was last week, and to-day's this week. The fine weather isn't going to last for ever!"

"If you're serious, you had better speak to Katherine about it. She is the eldest."

"I shan't see her. Outside this room is out-of-bounds for me. You ask her!"

"I really can't."

"Come by yourself, then!"

"How can I possibly? You make the most absurd suggestions!"

"Where there's a will, there's a way! Slip over after lunch, and clear off before tea, if you must. Nobody will be any the wiser. Cabot's a sport."

"No, I shall be seen by someone or other."

"Well, hang it all, *let* them see you! If I'm not afraid, why should you be?"

Evelyn began to look reflective, which was a sign of weakening.

"I can't walk out of the house with a racket in my hand."

"I'll lend you a racket."

"But that will be worse and worse, for I can't come to yours *without* one."

"You girls are all the same! You're frightened to put your foot down before you've examined the road for half a mile ahead! . . . If you don't care about coming to the house, come somewhere else?"

"Where?"

"Do you mind if I leave you a minute?" asked Nicholas. "I want to get something downstairs."

"Do, old chap!" said Ferreira heartily. "We'll wait here." Evelyn pretended that she had not heard the question, but a faint pink crept into her face.

Nicholas, to reconcile his conscience, searched the pockets of his rainproof coat, hanging up in the hall, for a letter which he knew was not there. When he returned to the room, five or six minutes later, the others moved guiltily apart. The colour in the girl's cheeks was heightened, while the expression of weary indifference which she had assumed could not altogether conceal the underlying sparkling pleasure. Ferreira twisted an end of his moustache, and simulated a yawn. He picked up his hat again.

"Then I'll see you at ten on Wednesday, Cabot!"

"Right!"

"Good-bye! . . . Au revoir, Evelyn!"

She moved her lips, and Ferreira went out.

"Did you want to speak to me?" asked Nicholas.

"Yes, but I think I'll leave it till later, if you don't mind. . . . I hope you don't imagine . . ." The sentence remained unfinished.

"Oh, no, I could see it was accidental," said Nicholas.

"I am to meet him this afternoon."

"You know there's no need to tell me that."

"I felt you ought to be informed."

"Why?"

"Because you are behaving so decently in the matter, and . . ."

"And what?"

"Since last Saturday I have had the feeling—very presumptuous, no doubt!—that we are *friends*. I want to be friends." She laughed unconvincingly. "Perhaps you are not so keen!"

"On account of what I showed you?"

"Not wholly."

He reddened. "Never mind. I hope we shall be friends, too. . . . You think you are *right* in going with young Ferreira?"

"I do, Nicholas!"

"Then don't let's say another word about it."

At the end of the morning, as lunch was on the point of being served, an unstamped letter was brought to Nicholas in the hall by one of the maids.

"This came for you, sir, from young Mr. Ferreira, about three minutes ago."

He thanked her and tore open the envelope on the spot. The handwriting struck him at once by its distinction. It was thin, sloping, uncommercial, yet perfectly legible—almost a feminine Italian hand, but full of unnecessary flourishes. He passed over that to read the note itself, which was a quite short one.

> *My dear Cabot* (it ran),
>
> *I have just this minute heard from L. J., who wants me round at her place early this afternoon, 'urgently'— whatever that means. I shall have to go, so will you be a good soul and help me over the stile with E.? See her as soon as you get this, and put what you like across, 'except'*

Greatly perplexed as to his proper procedure under the circumstances, Nicholas stopped Evelyn as she was entering the dining-room, and requested a word apart. She took him into another room.

"Ferreira has just sent round to say he's sorry he finds he won't be able to keep his engagement with you this afternoon."

She started as if stung.

"May I see his note? The message wasn't a verbal one, of course?"

"It was a note. I can't show it, because it's confidential."

"About your work as well?"

"Oh, no!"

"Only about me?"

"Yes."

"And confidential? I don't understand."

"Would you mind discussing it with him on Wednesday?"

"Tell me one thing. What is this other engagement?"

"That's exactly the confidential part of it."

"Then I do understand. He's seeing some other woman. . . . Who is it? Lore Jensen?"

"I am not allowed to tell you."

She looked at him and laughed sharply. "Oh, you needn't put on that air of mystery, Nicholas! It isn't the first time it has happened. It's all new to you, of course. . . ."

The lunch gong sounded.

"We'll talk about it later," continued Evelyn. "Perhaps I'll get you to give him a return note from me. I haven't any animus against Lore, but I must confess that I *am* getting rather tired of playing second fiddle! . . . . However, I had better not say too much till I have thought things over."

Nicholas kept his furnace going all the afternoon, and for a part of the evening. He did not descend to tea, but a tray was thoughtfully sent up to him. It was consequently not till after dinner that Evelyn was able to secure her postponed conversation.

He was then pacing the lawn by himself lethargically after the labours of the day, pipe in mouth. Twilight was setting in, and the air was sweeter and crisper than it had been, with the faintest suggestion of early summer frost to come during the night. A bird, either black-bird or nightingale, was trilling in a neighbouring thicket. Evelyn advanced upon him, wearing a coloured woollen coat over her dinner frock, but with head uncovered.

"May I speak to you now?" she asked.

"Certainly."

"Let's come away from the house. It will look so strange if we are constantly seen confabulating."

They accordingly sauntered down the drive, and, under Evelyn's guidance, crossed the road into a romantic descending spinney of tall trees, through which ran the unfrequented footpath to the village and station. Here the dusk immediately became more noticeable.

"I want to talk about Maurice, and I also want to talk about your work," began the girl, halting as soon as they were out of observation from the house. "Which shall we take first?"

"I expect your affair is more urgent."

"After all, I only wish to tell you that I have decided to do *nothing*. It isn't worth making a fuss about. I know he is fascinated by Lore—that's really why I called her a siren the other afternoon. But what then? I am not one of those foolish women who expect to keep a man entirely to themselves. . . . and when I say she *fascinates* him, I don't mean he has any regard for her personally for I have never been able to discover that he has. She isn't even attractive. But he goes there to have a good time. She drinks with him and indulges in free speech with him, and is hail-fellow-well-met generally, and so he is always sure of finding relaxation there, with no possibility of reproaches, covert or expressed. It's her mode of living, and not herself, that fascinates him. . . . So I should be very, very foolish—shouldn't I?—to take offence at being put off in her favour? If he asks you what I said on receiving his message, simply tell him that I was rather annoyed at first, but relented afterwards. Please not a word about my guessing it to be Lore!"

"Very well."

Evelyn sighed deeply, as though relieved at having cast her decision and put the incident behind her.

"I think that's all about that! . . . Now tell me about *your* business. Let's breathe a little fresh air by way of a change."

"What do you want to know?"

"All through the week-end I've been thinking about what you showed me, but I haven't dared to address you on the subject. It seems almost too wonderful to talk about. What I principally want to ask you—only I can't express it—is what you're working up to. Where will this discovery lead you, and what exactly have you got in your head?"

"I want to find out what happens to us when we lose consciousness."

"I must raise objections, even if I don't feel them, for the purpose of getting you to speak. Supposing you do succeed in securing coherent records of dreams, how will that help? A dream can only belong to the physical brain, and in the meantime the soul, if there is one, may be far away."

"No, I don't think so," replied Nicholas.

"Then what do *you* think?"

"I think that as long as the soul is present the body is alive, and when it leaves the body we die at once. Consciousness and unconsciousness, I take it, are merely states of the body, and don't affect the soul. When the soul retires inside the intellectual part of the brain system, and leaves the locomotive and sensitive parts to themselves, to allow them to recover themselves from their exhaustion, what happens is . . . what I want to ascertain. Since it is no longer occupied with the things of the physical world, it is probably occupied with other things—and these other things may be rather illuminating for us! . . . It may throw considerable light on the problem of *death,* for example."

Underneath the tall larches the darkness grew rapidly.

"Well, you have a grand ambition!" said Evelyn after a pause. . . . "How did you come to think of it first of all?"

"I can not only tell you that, but I can almost tell you the exact date. It was in May, 1913, at an exhibition. In one of the side-shows a man and a girl gave a rather crude performance of thought-reading. It was probably faked, but it set me thinking, and I very soon came to the conclusion that there were genuine cases. Then my chemistry came in, and I started wondering and experimenting, and experimenting and wondering, until my brain gradually got crystallised round the idea. My first real hint of the right direction came two years ago, and I have been working steadily at it in my spare time ever since."

"But what gave you the notion of recording *dreams?*"

"I wasn't ready for an associate, so I had to be my own subject, and I believed that dreams, being richer and more emotional than common intellectual thinking, would give me a clearer definition."

"Then what are you engaged on now? What is the next step?"

"Ferreira is making me a clockwork apparatus which should enable me to get the record of a dream lasting a full hour. That's a big advance on that two-minute box I showed you on Saturday, and this time everything ought to appear consecutively and in its right order. It should be completed in under a fortnight. After that, we shall see."

There was another pause.

"I had some more questions I wanted to ask," said Evelyn, "but I have forgotten them. . . . Of course, Maurice knows nothing of all this?"

"No. Not a soul in the world knows except yourself, so I am relying on you not to tell anyone."

"Oh, I couldn't speak of such a thing, even if I wanted to. . . . Before we turn back may I beg a favour of you?"

"Certainly. What is it?"

"Permit me to participate in the first experiment with your

new mechanism."

"The first trial result, you mean? Very well, I shall be delighted. I'll let you know when it is to come off."

They started for the house, and on the way back talked of other things. Upon reaching the garden they separated. Evelyn returned indoors, while Nicholas resumed his pacing up and down the lawn.

VII

THE SONG

The week sped by quietly and swiftly. Ferreira brought his materials with him on Wednesday morning, and as soon as he had sketched out his plans, started to piece the mechanism together, using for that purpose a separate table in an inner corner of the room. The aluminium box had been ordered from the manufacturer, and would be completed and forwarded with the least possible delay.

Nicholas was anxious to be ready for the machine by the time it was constructed, while Ferreira, on his side, appeared by the grim energy with which he worked either to stand in need of his cheque or to be impatient to recover his freedom. Hardly any words were exchanged between them, and neither Evelyn nor Lore, after the first morning, was again referred to. Nicholas had delivered the former's message, which had been received without comment. A change of some sort had come over Ferreira. His manner was reserved and sullen, so that it appeared as if he had something disagreeable weighing on his spirits. Nicholas noticed it, but he was only too pleased not to be called upon to talk while working. Moreover, his depression had the salutary effect of causing Ferreira to concentrate on his job more severely than he would otherwise have done. Their hours that week were from ten to one, and again from two to seven, with no interval for tea, which was regularly sent up, but which they took intermittently, without quitting their work.

Evelyn did not visit the room again. She and her sisters went about their customary routine just as though there were not two young men buried all day and every day in an upper apartment of the house. The fine weather persisted and they were fully occupied with their tennis, housework, social calls, and respective hobbies. Perhaps Katherine's imitation of the nonchalance of the others was not very successful, for it appeared that she had expected more exciting things from Nicholas's arrival, and the disillusionment was too rapid and thorough for her equanimity. Her mother had to caution her privately about her new frigidity to the guest at meals. Evelyn and Audrey, however, seemed not to feel the lack of male society so deeply, and allowed no change to appear in their manner towards him on account of his neglect. His only punishment, as far as they were concerned, was their continued avoidance of him in the evenings after dinner. On the first two occasions after his conversation with Evelyn in the spinney he made his way into the drawing-room, after the meal, anticipating a pleasant hour of relaxation with the girls, only to find no one there to entertain him but his hostess, whose company, no doubt, was very charming, but not exactly what he wanted. After this had happened for the second time, his pride rebelled, and he started the habit of taking solitary walks.

On Saturday evening, however, the young habit was shaken, before being properly established, by the unexpected arrival of a visitor immediately after dinner. The girls, who were on the point of leaving the house together, were heard at the front door effusively welcoming the possessor of a feminine voice, and Nicholas, who had taken refuge for a moment with Mr. and Mrs. Sturt in the drawing-room until they should have disappeared out of doors, fancied that the voice had a familiar ring. It sounded uncommonly like Lore's. She was the last person he wished to meet, and he was about to beat a quick retreat when his hostess prevented him.

"You positively *must* meet Lore! She particularly wants to know you, and has probably come specially."

He exchanged glances with Sturt, but had to remain in the room. Lore came in on Katherine's arm, followed up by the two younger girls. She looked exceedingly affable, smiling, and self-possessed. Her figure, now that she was on her feet, was certainly over-stout for one of her age, but this was to some extent neutralised by the clever, quizzical face, with its youthful crown of chestnut-coloured bobbed hair. Her eyes roamed round the room and took in everybody. She kissed her hostess, bowed to Sturt, then stole a humorous glance at Nicholas, who was unable to subdue the hot flush which he felt creeping to the surface.

Mrs. Sturt effected the introduction with her usual aplomb.

"Lore, this is Mr. Cabot, of whom I spoke to you last week. . . . Nicholas, you are already an admirer of Miss Jensen's music."

Sturt, still standing, assumed a mask of stately unconcern, while Nicholas came forward, looking still redder.

"Very pleased to meet you!" said Lore, smiling. As the young man murmured his response, she half turned to throw Sturt an indescribable look from under her lashes. The latter made a movement of easing his collar and sat down.

"I'm afraid I have picked an absurd time to call," proceeded Lore, "but I have just finished setting one of your poems to music"—addressing Katherine—"and I thought you might like to try it over, hot from the oven!"

Katherine's face lit up with unfeigned delight.

"But how *sweet* of you, Lore! Whatever made you think of it? Which one is it?"

"'Joy'."

"Really? But that's such a wisp of a thing!"

"That's why I fixed on it. I prefer you as a miniaturist." She produced a beribboned manuscript from the music-case in her hand and put it underneath the girl's fingers, to which at the same time she contrived to give an affectionate little squeeze. "There it is. Shall I sing it for you, to give you an idea as to how it ought to go? And after that I'll vanish again. I only came to bring it."

Katherine examined the manuscript with all the rapture of new proprietorship, and her pleasure was reflected on her mother's face, but Audrey contrived to grimace to Nicholas, unperceived by the donor.

"How very, very kind of you!" repeated the favoured girl, turning over the pages tenderly. "How can I thank you for it?"

Lore, in her turn, glanced rather maliciously at Nicholas.

"Perhaps, after all, I'd better not sing it. It may be inflicting an annoyance on other people. Try it over yourself some time when you're alone. It really belongs to you."

"We should all *love* to hear it!" said Mrs. Sturt.

"I know *you* would, dear Mrs. Sturt, but I am afraid of critics!"

"There are none here."

"One can't tell. Mr. Cabot may be a purist in art!"

"And if he is, how will that concern you?" demanded Katherine with considerable warmth. "*Your* music is safe against attack, I should hope!"

"It seems not, my dear. Every second day somebody accuses me of pot-boiling."

"What contemptible people there are in the world! Just because you love beauty and simplicity and broadness and leave the manufacture of clever artificialities to others! And their contention is not even plausible, for nowadays it is so easy to be freakish, and it pays so well."

"May I sing?" asked Lore of Nicholas with a whimsical look.

"As I am not one of your critics, please do!"

While Katherine was in the act of drawing her friend with gentle violence to the piano, the latter turned her head.

"*This* wasn't written for money Mr. Cabot! It is a spontaneous tribute to a very dear acquaintance. . . . Katherine, your little gem has haunted and haunted me until, out of sheer desperation, I have had to lay the ghost in a musical grave. Now it will haunt no one any longer!"

"Because its destiny is accomplished, Lore, dear, and it has inspired a work of living beauty in the shape of your setting! For I can see that is very beautiful indeed!"

Lore smiled tolerantly as one accustomed to hear much adulation, and not to take it too seriously. Seating herself at the piano, she proceeded to pull off her remaining glove, while Katherine took her stand beside her, to follow the music while it was being played and sung. The visitor declined the use of the manuscript, and, without any preliminary affectations, at once entered upon her performance. Her mezzo-soprano was perfectly trained, but not very strong, and anxious rather than pleasing. She had, as it were, two voices. The one, which she chiefly used, was a little too sentimentally soft and honeyed, but every now and then the other made its appearance in a single tone, which affected Nicholas's nervous system as though a sweet, metallic string had been twanged; the sound seemed to go in and in to his consciousness without reaching an end.

The words of the song were more unusual in form than in sentiment. There were only two short verses. They represented a dialogue between a Scottish Highland bard and an aged peat-cutter. The former had just descended from a mountain, where he had spent a night and a morning in order to hear the eagles screaming and to witness the red of dawn; now he was disconten-ted and sorrowful. In the second verse the peat cutter described how *he* had seen nothing all morning but the brown turf and his cutting tool. His hands were sore, his arms ached, and his back was stiff; nevertheless, his soul was full of joy, as the result of his useful labour.

Lore's setting of the poem belonged to her later manner. It was just the kind of music which would be received with discreet applause in all the suburban drawing-rooms in the country, and, from an artistic standpoint, was not to be mentioned in the same breath with the wonderful little sketch which Nicholas had heard on the evening of his first arrival. It was pitifully evident that her art had deteriorated. After her voice had ceased, and while the piano part was drawing to a close, he racked his brain for a way of sparing her susceptibilities without altogether violating the truth, for he was certain that she would challenge him for his opinion. At the risk of another outburst, he did not see how he could honestly compliment her.

The ladies prevented him. Mrs. Sturt was warm in her congrat-ulations, Audrey's banal exclamation of pleasure rang out above the other voices, while even Evelyn felt herself constrained to murmur something. Katherine impulsively bent down to kiss the performer on the forehead, but said nothing. Sturt got up, to approach the piano.

Lore, still sitting on the stool, but facing the room, addressed

Nicholas point-blank:

"I hope I haven't bored you too much?"

"You haven't bored me at all. It has been very interesting."

"Interesting!" She appealed to the others: "He calls it interesting! . . . It's a rather useful expression, and I'll make a note of it."

Sturt had come up. "A dear old friend of mine once made a very excellent comparison regarding this sort of collaboration. He likened poems to statues, and music to the celestial fire breathed into them to enable them to live and walk. Accepting the figure, we must regard Miss Jensen as a second Pygmalion, who has vivified, however, not her own Galatea, but the Galatea of a fellow-artist, working in another medium."

Lore smiled at him, but refused to release Nicholas.

"If the music is no good, what do you think of the words?"

"I'm afraid I'm no judge of poetry, but I don't altogether approve of the sentiment. Peat-cutting may be more *necessary* than mountain-climbing, but, after all, it is the mountain-climbers who have built up civilisation. Columbus was a mountain-climber, and so were Newton and Darwin."

"And are you one, too?"

"Why do you bring me into it?"

"Nicholas hasn't sufficient enthusiasm," said Audrey. "He would be too absorbed in tapping the rocks with a little hammer, to see what they were made of, to get half-way up!"

"Let us hear it from his own lips!" said Lore.

Nicholas began to colour. "It isn't a question of me."

"Are you a mountain-climber?"

"Surely a man has the right to keep his own secrets if he wants to!" remarked Evelyn from her chair, throwing an unpleasant glance at Lore from the corner of her eye.

The visitor returned look for look.

"If you put it in that way!" . . . She went on slowly and thoughtfully: "I believe in everyone's keeping their own property." The words were followed by another and a more significant look, and then Evelyn thought that she understood what Lore wanted. She wished to convey that she had something for her own private ear—perhaps something which concerned Maurice—and very likely she had simply come there that evening hoping to procure a personal interview.

A moment or two later, when none of the others was observing her, she contrived to catch Lore's eye once more and nodded very slightly. The visitor slowly and naturally swung her head to rest her glance on Nicholas for an instant, then returned it to Evelyn. The by-play was managed on both sides with such exquisite subtlety that it passed quite unnoticed by the other members of the household.

Lore, rising, took Katherine's arm and went with her across the room to speak to Mrs. Sturt, and this was Evelyn's opportunity to get a word with Nicholas.

"Do you mind escorting Lore home when she goes, Nicholas? I rather fancy she has a message for me, which she can't get delivered. Don't tell anyone what I have said, of course!"

Nicholas agreed to do as she wished.

Not long afterwards, Lore finally got up to go.

"I see you girls have your hats on, and I didn't come to stay. So glad you like the music, Katherine! I must hear you sing it yourself some time. My voice is enough to ruin any song!"

A short interchange of compliments followed.

"Perhaps you are all going the same way?" suggested Mrs. Sturt. "Won't you see Lore home, girls?"

"I have another call to make on my way back," said the visitor a little quietly. "Mr. Cabot may come with me as far as I am going, if he cares to? He amuses me!"

"How do I amuse you?"

"Your conscience is so funny!"

The girls accompanied Lore and Nicholas down the drive and along the road until they came to the first turning, where their respective ways parted.

"I'm *not* calling anywhere," said Lore when they were alone, "but I have made the detour so as to shake them off. Did Evelyn say anything to you for me?"

"She thought you wanted to speak to her, and asked me to take the message if there is one."

"Otherwise, of course, you would have seen me elsewhere, after your experience of last Saturday!"

"I don't think we need refer to that."

"I'm very sure I don't want to! . . . So that's all that Evelyn said? Did she guess that I came this evening to see her specially?"

"She said nothing about it to me."

"Well, I did. I brought that song along for Katherine as an excuse for coming. If I had called in the ordinary way, it would have meant stopping the whole evening, and I'm getting to love my own home best. . . . I expect you have a cigarette on you? Perhaps you object to women smoking in the street?"

"Not here, anyway, for there's no one to see." He offered his case, and struck a match for her. After a few draws, Lore went on:

"I scribbled the music in my bath this morning, on the back of a hang-up calendar! My reason for fixing on that particular poem was that it was the shortest. I fancy it took me about seven minutes in all. What would dear Katherine say if she knew, I wonder! . . . What do you think of Evelyn?"

"In what way?"

"Are you in love with her yet?"

"Why should I be in love with her?"

"You're at the age of boiling passion, aren't you? And there's no disputing that she's a sweet young thing! . . . However, about this message! You're sure you are authorised to take it?—because it's rather confidential."

"I'll carry back a note, if you prefer it."

"How disinterested we are! . . . Well, how am I to start? It has to do with young Maurice Ferreira, as I've no doubt Evelyn has guessed. He has been misbehaving himself again."

"Again!"

"Oh, it isn't the first time. But I think it will be nearly the last. I've had just about enough of his monkeying. It's high time Evelyn put her foot down, if she's going to, and you tell her so from me! I know they're engaged, or next door to it. If she doesn't feel herself competent to control him, let her give up the job to someone who can. But don't let her run away with the idea that I'm offering my services! I'm sick of the bounder!"

"But why drag *her* into it? Just show him the door."

"To have the excitement of seeing him climb back through the window! You might just as well show your own shadow the door! He's a burr. . . . I'm *frightened* of him, I tell you!" she added, more vehemently

"What can he do?"

"Young men seem to be doing all sorts of things in these days that you only read about in books ten years ago. I wouldn't trust a single man of you in a lonely spot—not even an exemplary youth like you! Probably you're ten degrees worse than any of them. . . . And a revolver is not precisely a bouquet of roses when it's poked under your nose!"

"A revolver?"

"That's his latest toy."

"Do you mean he's been threatening you with it?"

"Oh, no! If I was held up against the wall of my own room last night for three full minutes by his watch, it was only for fun! It was so funny that I had to take morphine when I went to bed in order not to keep awake laughing at the recollection!"

"But what on earth did he do it for? Had he been drinking?"

"Just enough! Why *do* men bully women? Because if they can't bend them they mean to break them, I suppose."

"Then he's really infatuated?"

"We'll say so."

"If you're afraid of a repetition, why not apply for police protection?"

"What do you call police protection? Getting him bound over?" She laughed cynically. "It might restrain his enthusiasm for two days!"

Nicholas cogitated for a moment or two.

"Return to town till he's cooled a bit!" he suggested.

"As if he doesn't know all my addresses! I might borrow a disguise and take rooms in Whitechapel, if that's what you mean!”

“Have you thought of informing his people?”

“I’ve too much sympathy for them. His father left off trying to hold him in years ago.”

“But if he makes him an allowance, as I imagine he does, surely he’s able to control him to that extent?”

“I can tell you about that, since you’re so curious. The doctor allows him spending money at the rate of two hundred a year. Now I hear you’re giving him the equivalent of six months’ allowance in one lump sum. That will last him one month away from home, with economy, and at the end of the month, if he isn’t in jail awaiting trial, he’ll simply go back to the old people in the rôle of the Prodigal Son and draw another quarter’s allowance, preliminary to slipping away again. . . . That’s what *you’ve* done for him!”

“It’s simply the price of his work.”

“The least you can do is make it conditional on his good behaviour.”

“How can I? It’s a business transaction.”

“Then when is he to have it?”

“As soon as the work’s finished. In about a week’s time, most likely.”

Lore took a final draw at her cigarette before throwing it away. Her face looked rather ominously flushed.

“Oh, I can see I’m up against a brick wall all right! Of course *you* won’t see it—and why should you? I’m no friend of yours.”

“If I can do anything I will. I’ll tell Evelyn. But I certainly don’t understand your sudden change of attitude towards Ferreira. You must have known what he was last Monday, yet you sent for him!”

“What you evidently want is women made of putty! You leave them *so*, and they stop *so*. Thank heaven, I’m not a putty woman! If I sent for Maurice last Monday I needed him last Monday, but now I *don’t* need him. Is that clear?”

“Oh, perfectly!”

“I presume you’re working round to an insult, in your usual

sly way! I'm beginning to know you. You're trying to make out that I have been deliberately attracting him, and richly deserve all I'm getting. . . . Well, it's a *damned lie!* If you don't believe me on my bare word, ask Maurice himself. He'll tell you fast enough that I'm not that sort. I've always been too much the other way for his taste. . . . But you're all the same—all you men! An unattached girl is fair game to you. You imagine you may say what you like!"

"I never said or thought anything of the kind!" replied Nicholas shortly.

"Oh, I haven't knocked about the world for nothing! I've met specimens of practically every type of your lovely sex, and you're all alike at bottom. If a woman gives you the slightest handle to think ill of her, you go at her like a dog for a bone. You must be waiting for it all the time. Life's a sordid business, and that's a fact!"

Their detour had by now brought them again into the direct road between the Sturts' house and Lore's. It was already dusk, but, from where they were, The Arbour was still plainly visible at the bend, less than a hundred yards away. Lore turned towards home, but Nicholas continued to look back.

"If you don't like my conversation, I give you your release!" proceeded Lore, misunderstanding his action.

"I was looking to make sure if that is Mrs. Hantish."

She faced round quickly. It was really Mrs. Hantish, moving about with short steps just behind the fence, armed with a basket and scissors, and evidently snipping off rose-blooms for the Sunday decoration of her house. Her white overall gave her tall and slender form a charming air of informality. She caught sight of the two, and waved her hand above her head by way of friendly greeting.

Lore, ignoring her companion, immediately started to walk towards her, while Nicholas followed close behind. Celia came forward to meet them at the gate. Her basket, which she swung in her hand, was nearly full of tea-roses, of the newest fashionable shades.

"How are you, Lore, dear? Good evening, Mr. Cabot! . . . Do both come in!"

"It's too late," said Lore. "I have just been to see the Sturts, and Mr. Cabot is convoying me home."

"I didn't see you come past."

"We came round."

"Oh! . . . You can surely find time to look in for a quarter of an hour? I have had some cigarettes sent me direct from Cairo, and I want expert opinion."

"One would think that you are bored with your own society, Celia, except that you are never bored!"

"And you very often—like all intellectuals!"

"I'm very far from being bored at the present moment, unfortunately!"

Celia noted the remark, but postponed comment on it until they were in the house. Inside the porch she discarded her overall, and set down her basket. The room to which she conducted her visitors was a spacious one, with French windows open to the terrace which overlooked the lawn at the back. It was illuminated by the coloured rays of a rosy-shaded oil lamp, and, with its sparse but expensive furniture and decorations, struck a distinctly challenging note of uniqueness. Through the windows came the cool, sweet, pine-scented evening air.

Celia invited Lore to sit beside her on the settee, at the same time indicating a chair to Nicholas. The latter's eyes kept stealing to her graceful semi-evening frock, which struck him as one of the most becoming garments he had ever seen. She appeared not to notice his regard, addressing herself exclusively to Lore, as the more honoured, or more interesting, guest.

"So you're unhappy?" she asked, with a smile.

"Very much so!" Lore gave a savage jerk to a footstool which she wished to bring closer to her.

"Nothing past remedy I hope? Will you take coffee, or what?"

"Give *me* a whisky-and-soda, my dear!"

Nicholas desired nothing. Celia, in her tranquil way, went out of the room, to return a moment later with a tray bearing a spirit-tantalus, a siphon, and a couple of tumblers. She begged Lore to wait on herself, and the latter rose, with a rather cynical expression, to pour herself out half a glassful of the whisky, to which she added a very small proportion of mineral water. She drank off the whole, standing at the table, repeatedly raising and lowering the glass until it was empty, then sat down again. The second tumbler remained unused; it was merely Celia's delicate way of indicating to Lore that she was not to be considered as drinking alone.

"Young Maurice is running amuck!" announced the visitor abruptly, as soon as she had settled herself. "He has begged, borrowed, or stolen a revolver and cartridges from somewhere. He pointed it at my head last night, and, as his hand wasn't oversteady, it might as easily have gone off as not. By the time I succeeded in pacifying him, I was shaking like a jelly!"

Celia showed just sufficient consternation to retain the other in a confidential mood.

"Where was this?"

"In my own house! I'm quite expecting another visit when I get back home, and I'm in a blue funk about it, I can tell you. What's my best course?"

"I haven't altogether grasped the situation yet. What is the idea? Is he trying to intimidate you?"

"He says he wants to marry me! . . . He always talks like that in his cups. When he wakes up he isn't so sure!"

"But since when has he become violent?"

"Oh, it has been working up for a storm all the week. We had a scene last Monday, and that seemed to start it. Last night he turned up with this revolver."

"And all the time, of course, he is fighting for something quite out of the question!"

"Oh, do I *look* mad, Celia?" Lore twisted her body impatiently. "Do you think I'm so hard up for a man that I'm going to play Katharine to his Petruchio? I'm not quite soft yet!"

Celia, after a nervous little laugh, gazed at the carpet pensively.

"It's all so upsetting to one's preconceived ideas! One always took it for granted that there was such an excellent understanding between you two. And now this!"

"Thanks for classing us together! . . . I did encourage him up to a point. He was young, and refreshing, and somebody to talk to, and all the rest of it. But if you think we are soul-mates, we never were, my good woman! I still have a little pride left, though most of it has been knocked out of me. I haven't sunk to the level of an unfledged cub yet, thank heaven! . . . Besides, it's notorious that his real affinity is elsewhere!"

"Who is that?"

"You know as well as I do. Evelyn Sturt!" She rose to help herself to more whisky.

"I don't fancy anything is likely to take place *there*," said the lady of the house, smiling. "There are far too many obstacles in the way."

"So you may think!"

"But there are!"

"Well, and if there are? A girl like that doesn't stand for obstacles. She's as patient and persevering as the devil! I tell you, she's biding her time, and playing him gently. She'll get him in the end, but I wish she'd hurry up!"

"Present company!" hinted Celia, in an undertone.

"Oh, Nicholas is all right. Far too correct to tell tales out of school."

The young widow raised her eyebrows at the name.

"It slipped out, but I don't suppose he minds," said Lore.

"Not in the least!" responded Nicholas. Celia regarded him humorously.

"Is it to be a practice for everyone, or are certain people excluded? One may as well know."

"None of my friends is excluded, as far as I'm concerned." He attempted to make his tone indifferent but his rising colour betrayed him. She would not release him, however, until she had made sure.

"Then henceforward I am to call you Nicholas?"

"Please do!"

"Just to spare me that feeling of being hopelessly out of it!" . . . She turned again to Lore. "So what have you decided to do about it all?"

"I haven't a notion!"

"I could speak to him, if you thought it would be of the slightest use?"

"You never see him."

"I could."

"I know you're very persuasive, Celia, but what on earth do you suppose you could effect in the present case? You don't imagine he's going to weigh arguments?"

"Outsiders, who have no axe to grind, sometimes get listened to—but if you think my interference would appear officious . . ."

"Oh, you can talk to him if you like! If it doesn't do any good, it won't do any harm. You had better give it to him straight and strong if you do. It's the only way to reach Maurice—he has about as much delicacy of feeling as a Turk! . . . And I shouldn't be at all surprised to hear that he *has* Turkish or Bulgarian blood in him, or something similar. The colouring and the tendencies are there, all right! . . . What will you say?"

"I shall improvise, my dear."

"Don't bargain with the brute! . . . . Mind, Celia, I'll have no more to do with him under *any* circumstances! I'm dead sick of him! I'm utterly fed up with his everlasting glittering eyes and dapper moustache. He has fairly got entangled with my nervous system. I want a complete rest."

"Perhaps the cause of all the trouble is that you made that a shade too clear to him!"

Lore moved her body angrily. "You don't need to provide causes for lunatics! My dear woman, he was *foaming* last night! You haven't any idea what it was like. He kept flourishing that awful pistol of his, and shooting his eyes forward, and saying the most idiotic things you ever heard in all your life, and there was I, cowering against the wall, trying to mollify him and make him see sense, with about a tenth of a second to do it in, for all I knew! I was crying and laughing together—it was so idiotically funny! It is a lucky thing there was no one in the house but Madame and the boy. . . . I'm not sure of the boy, either!" she added reflectively. "How long does a story like this take to get about, I wonder?"

"Surely it's easy to keep the tongue of a small boy silent, my dear!"

"I hope so. We shall soon know, anyway! . . . How will you get to see Maurice?"

"Can I be of service?" asked Nicholas. "I see him every day."

"I heard something about it," said Celia. "Isn't he helping you with your experiments?"

"Yes."

"Perhaps you could bring him along here to tea, without mentioning a reason?"

"I ought to be able to. When shall it be?"

"The sooner, the better. To-morrow, if you can."

"That's Sunday. I'm not sure if he means to put in an appearance on Sundays."

"He's pretty certain not to," said Lore. "He has been going over to Shaftesbury on Sundays, on his motor-bicycle. I expect it's a girl. As it is always on that particular day of the week, it looks suspiciously like a cook or a parlourmaid!"

Celia restrained her laughter as well as she could.

"One can see he's out of favour with you! . . . However, to-morrow may prove an exception. Nicholas"—she uttered the name with the remnant of her laugh, but at the same time with a sort of timid appeal, as though to remind him of his given consent to the liberty—"must act as he is able. . . . If Maurice really doesn't turn up, that's no reason why you shouldn't come by yourself. You promised to come and see me some time." The last remarks were addressed directly to him.

Nicholas lowered his eyes, to conceal the shining which he felt to be in them.

"Thanks very much!"

"You had better not come, Lore, in case *he* does. I'll let you know as soon as anything has been done."

Lore yawned, and said nothing. After a moment she got up.

"Well, we must be going! Thanks for listening to my tale of woe!"

Nicholas followed her example, and Celia made no attempt to detain them. All three drifted through the house to the porch, where they remained for a few minutes longer, chatting desultorily about other things.

"What planet is that?" inquired Celia of Nicholas, pointing a white and tapering middle finger, bearing a flashing jewel, towards the western sky.

"Venus."

"Isn't it exquisite! . . . It happens to be my fortunate star, so perhaps good luck is on its way! I suppose you despise these superstitions?"

"Not *in toto*."

"That's cryptic!"

"I mean, I don't believe in them myself, but I regard them as just as essential a part of a lady's equipment as a hat or a gown. An unsuperstitious woman would be too much like a man."

"I expect there's a great deal in that! Anyway, I'm horribly superstitious! At this very moment, for example, I'm absolutely *positive* that something of an unusual character is about to happen to me. But if you were to ask me my grounds for believing so, I should come to grief at once. Is it intuition, Lore?"

Lore yawned again.

"I wouldn't like to say *what* it is. I know it's getting late!"

Celia, smoothing her nightlike hair, laughed pleasantly and turned to go back into the house, waiving the formality of shaking hands.

VIII

A COUNTRY WALK

Just before four o'clock on Sunday afternoon Nicholas slipped away to The Arbour to tea, without having declared his intention to anyone.

A maid showed him into a pretty, sunlit little apartment, which apparently served the mistress of the house as her writing-room, and there he was left. He wandered to the bookshelves, but could see nothing but novels, many of them French. Five or ten minutes passed and he grew impatient, when Celia appeared, dressed for walking and wearing a small hat. She offered him a light hand.

"It's so good of you to come! I hardly expected you."

"Ferreira didn't turn up."

"So I guessed when they told me you were here alone. I can't pretend to be very sorry!" She gave a little laugh.

Nicholas coloured. "Have you been out, or are you just going out, may I ask?"

"I thought it would be a lovely afternoon for a country tramp. But perhaps you aren't a walker?"

"I'm particularly fond of walking."

"So am I, when I can get anybody to go with. But I may as well be honest and confess that it isn't a case of being attracted, but of being repelled. Visitors may come, and I haven't had you to myself yet! . . . Don't you think it would be rather fun to have tea out? I love those quaint, fusty little wayside inns, where they dole out thick slices of bread-and-butter, and raspberry jam, and water-cress and radishes, and exactly one great hunk of home-made plum-cake for each person, regardless of sex or appetite! Does that sort of thing appeal to you at all?"

"It does!" replied Nicholas, laughing. "You mean out of doors, of course? But do these places open on Sundays down here?"

"Why not? . . . Do you like my hat?" She walked over to the

glass, and straightened it with deft fingers.

"It suits you admirably."

"It's rather sweet! Which way shall we go, then? Are you acquainted with this part of the world?"

"Not in the least."

"And a woman finds places about as well as she throws stones, so the prospect isn't very hopeful! We might start towards Shawford. I don't for a minute suppose we shall get there. It's about five miles."

He glanced at her heels and mentally agreed with her.

"I leave it entirely to you, Mrs. Hantish."

"We shall get somewhere, if not there."

She slipped on delicate, long white gloves, reaching nearly to the elbow of her stylish jumper, then announced herself ready to set out. In passing through the hall she took a slender walking-stick from the stand. Nicholas, walking immediately behind her, was unable to keep his eyes away from her tall, girlish figure. With the assuming of her simple, sporting, gay-tinted attire—which, however, was perfectly fashioned and probably very expensive—she had varied the grace of her bodily movements to correspond. Drawing-room restraint was discarded, and she stepped before him with elastic freedom, swinging her arms. He was unable to decide at once whether he liked her better this way or the old. It certainly made her less formidable, more of a companion and an equal, but he was not quite certain whether he would not rather be condescended to.

But, whatever she had dropped, she remained a somewhat fearful joy! As he viewed the long neck, like an ivory column, supporting her shapely aristocratic head, with its crown of black hair, and, above it, that smart, coquettish hat, it was impossible for him to forget for a single instant that he was actually accompanying the dangerous Mrs. Hantish, against whom he had been warned. So the absurdly unlikely had come to pass, and she had settled in her mind that he was sufficiently interesting (to use Evelyn's expression) to take up! If he could only believe that he had genuinely attracted her, he would not care to answer for his response, but her attentions were discounted, and he had not the least intention of being the latest on her list of victims. It therefore came about that his admiration was strongly coloured by hostility and a very complex state of mind resulted for him, which he was the last person in the world to unravel into its elements, even had there been time at such short notice.

He had not yet fixed upon the correct attitude to adopt towards the advances which he felt were to come, when Celia was already waiting for him outside the garden gate opening onto the roadway. As they started side by side in the direction of Mereway, in order to reach the woods, she glanced at him with a smile.

"I hope you don't consider yourself as being dragged at my chariot-wheel?"

"On the contrary, I think you're being very kind to me. I only hope you won't be bored before we get home again."

"But, candidly, you aren't greatly in love with feminine society? You would prefer to go with a man?"

"No."

"Have you taken any walks with the girls?"

"Not yet."

"I wonder you haven't. You appeared rather good friends with Evelyn that day I called." She gave him a significant smile.

"We're friendly enough."

"Maurice must be wildly jealous of your opportunities, and perhaps that's why he is venting his displeasure on poor Lore!"

"He sees practically as much of Evelyn as I do. We're both stuck in my room from morning till night."

"I can't conceive what she finds in him. His good points are just the ones you would think a girl like that would be unable to appreciate. His qualities are those of a first-class brigand, while she would make an excellent school-ma'am!"

"I haven't thought about it," returned Nicholas a little stiffly.

She said no more until they had passed the turning to Mereway and had entered the woods at another place. It was as delightful an afternoon as on the day of his arrival. To temper the hot air, caressing breezes were moving about, while the deep blue sky was made picturesque by the isolated little clouds, like wisps of cotton-wool, floating low over the forest trees. The leaves were only just beginning to assume the darker green of the second half of summer. Everything was wonderfully quiet. After they had walked some distance through the light woodland in file, on account of the narrowness of the track, they at length came abreast again.

"What do you think of Lore?" asked Celia.

"She seems to have a very excitable nature."

"I had to offer to see Maurice, by way of showing a proper degree of sympathy. I don't for a minute expect to effect anything. . . . Women are like that. We require each other to be demonstrative, at the very same moment that we refuse to give each other credit for being genuine! Lore knows that I'm really not a bit sorry for her—and why should I be? These periodical upsets are her salvation, for when she goes for any length of time without having them, she sinks down and down into the most appalling ennui and apathy—simply for want of emotional occupation—and on such occasions it is no exaggeration to call her state of mind positively *suicidal!* So I suppose we must regard Maurice as a blessing, very cleverly disguised as a curse! . . . Do you like her?"

"Not much."

"They think the world of her at Mereway. I dare say you've found that out—and also that *my* reputation isn't anything like as good!"

"How do you mean?"

"Confess that you haven't heard any hymns of praise in my favour!"

"But I don't know that I've heard any hymns of hate, either."

"Did you mention to anyone that you were coming to my house to tea this afternoon?"

"I didn't, as a matter of fact. There was no one about as I came out."

She looked at him, and laughed. "I understand! . . . Still, you were not afraid to *come!*"

"Why should I be?"

"Hadn't you been warned?"

"Against what?"

"Against *me*. . . . However, I can hardly expect you to answer that. Unquestionably you think I'm being awfully indiscreet to enter into this sort of conversation! But I have a motive for it. If I assure you at once that I haven't any designs on your personal independence, will you consent to drop your reserve and be a little bit more friendly?"

"Really, Mrs. Hantish!—how could I possibly entertain such an idea? . . ."

"You see, Nicholas, I happen to have money enough of my own for all legitimate purposes, and in other respects I realise that we belong to quite different spheres. We can scarcely be supposed to be infatuated with each other after two exceedingly brief meetings in company, and if you can discover any other possible motives for my attempting to seduce you, I shall be extremely obliged if you will point them out!"

"Really! . . ."

"You don't mind my candour? I have a pretty considerable experience of the relations between men and women, and I have always found that personal misunderstandings have a way of beginning at the beginning, just like other diseases, and that, if we leave them to their own devices for any length of time, they are extraordinarily difficult to catch up with. So, if we are to be good friends, as I hope and trust we shall be, I suggest that it would be as well to clear our minds of suspicions now, at once, instead of leaving them to swell and ferment into malice, hatred, and all uncharitableness! Now, are we to be friends?"

"We are!" replied Nicholas, colouring.

She stopped short in the path, and faced him with a smile.

"And you give me your solemn promise to think no worse of me than my actual behaviour warrants?"

"I promise!" said Nicholas, also smiling. "But it's rather superfluous, for I never had any intention of thinking badly of you at all."

Celia held out her hand straight before her, at arm's length, and he took it. The explanation which she had forced might easily have been followed by still greater reserve and embarrassment, but to his admiration for her perspicacity he found, from his own feelings, that the opposite effect had been achieved, and that their relations had quietly been raised by it to an intimate and confidential level. He realised, with becoming humility, how easy women were to get on with, and how well they did these things! . . .

Upon proceeding on their way, the exigencies of the rough track soon compelled them to separate again. Celia pioneered, picking her way through the brush with long, delicate strides, like a young girl. She halted for a moment to draw off her gloves and pass them to Nicholas for bestowal in his pocket, then resumed her lead. With neck and arms bare, her face flushed with exercise, a long rent in one silk stocking from the brambles, and her beautiful hair beginning to stray, she looked a different being from the charming, artificial, self-contained hostess of the previous evening, with her correct manners. Suddenly her foot caught in a thorn-trap, and she fell forward at full length, saving herself with her hands. He jumped to her assistance. It was the first time he had held a woman in his arms, and his heart scurried madly.

She withdrew herself, laughing and unhurt, and started to brush the adhesive rubbish from her clothes.

"Are you all right?"

"Quite! . . . It wasn't a real fall; it was more in the nature of an omen. It is written in the stars that you are to be my protector in some great danger that threatens me! Do you fancy the rôle?"

He admired her ready wit, but that did not prevent her words from making a deeper impression upon him. He wondered whether the remark was to be taken as meaning anything.

"If you'll excuse my saying so, I expect it was those high heels of yours!"

"Shall I wear low ones next time?"

"No."

She looked at him from beneath her lowered lashes, smiled,

and turned her face away almost shyly.

"It's all very well to stand here talking, Nicholas," she said a moment later, "but I'm sorry to inform you that our path has come to an end, and I've lost the way!"

"I suppose we can get out somehow."

"*You* try! It will be something if we can only put a respectable road under our feet. But perhaps you're tired?"

"What a question!"

"It was rather modern! Personally, I feel as fresh as when we started."

Nicholas took his bearings, noted where the trees appeared thinnest, and chose the most unobstructed route through the underbrush in that direction. A few hundred yards farther on they encountered a fence, enclosing a field. He helped his companion over, so that again for a single instant he was in contact with her. When both were across they looked at each other and laughed, without apparent cause. Celia lowered her eyes immediately and constrained her features to a modest, but not altogether convincing, seriousness.

They crossed the field in silence. A padlocked gate on its farther side required to be negotiated, and once more he offered his assistance, but this time she elected to ignore the lifted arm. The gate was the entrance to a lane running past it. Neither had the faintest idea where they were, but as the lane sloped they fixed upon the uphill direction in order to reach high ground and obtain a comprehensive view of the country. The continued silence caused Nicholas some apprehension. He feared she was feeling she had gone too far with him, and, to put matters right, attempted to initiate a new conversation.

"You're not on particularly good terms with the Sturts, are you?" The gaucherie of the question was characteristic.

"I hope so."

"I didn't know. . . . But you don't go round there often?"

"I pay my duty calls, like others. I'm not a familiar of the house, I agree. . . . Why? Has the circumstance been remarked on?"

"They certainly gave me the impression that your visits are few and far between. Don't you care for the girls?"

Celia smiled. "I don't dislike them, but they hold no wild excitement for me."

"They talk well."

"But they don't inspire talk. You see, they happen still to be girls!"

"I see that, of course."

"Don't imagine I'm a hater of my own sex, but I suppose it requires a certain unlikeness before we can be interested to the point of gaiety. I might discuss dress or theatres with Evelyn, but I could never, never let myself *go* with her! You appreciate the difference?"

Nicholas paused.

"May I ask you a question?"

"Twenty, if you like!"

"Why are you so much more concerned with Evelyn than with the others? Is it because you think there's more in her?"

"None of them is anything to me, my dear boy, and I don't know what you mean."

"You've mentioned her name two or three times and the others not once."

"Then it has just happened so."

An invisible church clock somewhere in the vicinity was striking five just as they reached the top of the lane and began the steep descent beyond. High hedges on either side completely shut out the landscape for them.

"What is your real, private opinion of this business between Evelyn and Ferreira?" asked Nicholas.

"In what respect?"

"Don't you think he's rather dragging her through the dirt with him?"

Celia grimaced. "She's of legal age and in full possession of her senses."

"But it's a deadly situation for her, all the same. I had the pleasant task of breaking the news to her this morning of that revolver episode! She hadn't much to say, but I could see she was badly stung. I don't mind confessing that I feel a hundred times sorrier for her than I do for Miss Jensen."

"I expect she knows what she is about," replied Celia, feeling for her hair. "All those girls have stage blood in them, and she is certainly the cleverest of the three. I wouldn't be too sorry if I were you."

He stopped in the lane to stare at her.

"You suggest she doesn't really care for him?"

"I don't know! . . . She allows him an astonishing amount of latitude. You will be exceedingly foolish if you go by appearances in the case of a girl, my dear! Girls aren't the least little bit like men. It may be all right, but you had really better not waste your sympathy at present."

"But what possible motive can she have for pretending to like him if she doesn't?"

"Perhaps we are now bordering on the indiscreet!" replied Celia, smiling and turning away.

They proceeded on their way, and during the new interval of silence, which was a long one, Nicholas had time to read various meanings into her last remark. He came to the conclusion that what she wished to suggest was that Evelyn's infatuation for Ferreira was merely a pretence, and that this pretence was being carried on for the purpose of creating a jealous interest in Nicholas himself. The theory was too full of holes to hold water for a minute, and its absurdity reflected upon Celia's mentality. Yet, as she was a woman of wit and common sense, it did not seem as if it could have been dictated by her *intellect*. It must have sprung directly from her feelings. It was merely a feminine expression of her general antipathy to Evelyn. Perhaps she had an intuitive knowledge that the girl scorned her and was better acquainted with her character than others; and this was how she sustained the feud and took one more revenge. . . . The new conception of Celia as a weak and imperfect being, subject to the petty animosities of her sex, at once had the effect of raising her to a higher level in his esteem. He felt, with a thrill, that she was a *woman*, and, as such, was separated from him by a hundred million miles! . . .

Half an hour afterwards, on the outskirts of a large upland common, they passed a tea-house having pretty pleasure gardens tastefully set out with rustic chairs and tables.

"This will do," said Celia, dragging at his arm.

He looked dubious. "Is it good enough?"

"If not, let's be bad enough!"

They strolled through a side entrance on to the lawn and took their places at one of the tables. The garden was deserted, but a woman immediately came out of the house to serve them. No sooner had she spread a cloth, inquired their order, and returned indoors to procure what was necessary, than Celia's manner changed. Like the ladies of the "Arabian Nights," she began to quiz her companion. She made faces at him, imitated the noises of different fowls and animals, annihilated his conversational openings by the most ridiculous and senseless remarks, and indulged in all sorts of marvellous antics and postures. If he looked nervous or embarrassed, she laughed so that tears stood in her eyes; if he laughed too, she commenced new pranks with a serious face. He could not conceive what had happened to her. It was as if she had suddenly gone back fifteen years, to her schooldays.

While the woman was setting the meal there was a lull rather than a cessation, and after she had disappeared into the house once more the electric storm of irresponsibility renewed itself with other tricks supplied by the materials of the tea-table. Celia ate her companion's food, slipped cake into his pocket, added salt instead of sugar to his tea, and made rabbits out of a corner of the tablecloth. He scarcely knew whether he were awake or dreaming, but, since it was her mood, he had to pretend that it was also his. His complaisance made her still wilder. . . . But the most surprising thing about it was that throughout she remained the *belle dame*. Her movements were graceful to watch, and everything she did was done with such a delicately restrained attractiveness that one might have been justified in believing that in the end it was all for the one purpose of exhibiting her beauty in unusual lights. Before the invisible line dividing fun from vulgarity she drew back on each occasion with unerring tact. Nicholas failed to understand this at first, but it impressed itself upon him by degrees, and then he realised that it was just because she was a *lady* that she dared to enter upon these liberties with a stranger. She was sure of being able to recover herself at a moment's notice. . . . And another thing was that her eyes seemed invariably to return to *affectionateness*, as if that were their natural expression. Yet he had not observed that so much at her visit to the Sturts' house, or last night with Lore. Probably she was happy at escaping for a time from her conventional routine. . . .

The meal ended at last. As the woman of the house came out to receive payment, Celia pulled a white lily head and invited Nicholas to smell its faintly heavy odour. Unsuspectingly he did so, when, thrusting the flower into his face, she well dusted his nose with the yellow pollen. With an air of innocence, she took the empty shell from his egg-cup and professed to sniff gingerly at its interior. The woman was already standing over them when she replaced it in the cup.

"You have some on your nose, Nicholas!"

He laughed and produced his handkerchief, but the woman, with rustic practicalness, had no thought for anything outside her interests.

"Them flowers don't want to be picked, miss!"

"I'll pay for it," said Nicholas hastily. "How much?"

"As you please, sir! I'm not charging for a flower, but if everybody goes and picks 'em there won't be not a great many left, will there?"

A sentimental wave passed through him, and he was about to present her with an extravagant sum when he recollected himself in time. Adding sixpence to the amount of the bill, he turned his back, to slip the lily bloom between a couple of pages of his pocket-book. Celia saw the action, and smiled, but said nothing until they were outside in the road again.

"What are you going to do with my flower?" she demanded then, with a sort of imperious humour.

"Keep it, naturally!"

"Have you a herbarium, then?"

"I'm just starting one."

Celia laughed and looked pleased. It was nearing half-past six. By tacit agreement both turned to retrace the way they had come.

"Have you been correctly shocked by my frivolity?" she asked, glancing aside at him. "I'm exceedingly sorry, but I really couldn't help it. I accumulate!"

"But why apologise?"

"I'm afraid you won't come out with me any more. However, next time I promise to try and be more sedate. I'll take a leaf from Evelyn's book and discuss improving topics all the way."

"Evelyn again!"

"It's lucky I'm not a man, or they would think me to be in love with her!"

"Which, as it is, you're very far from being?"

"Why do you say that? I regard her as a rather wonderful child in some respects. By the time she has attained my years of discretion she will be an accomplished woman of the world."

"You talk as if you were middle-aged already!"

"I have to when you are so humble."

"Humble?"

"You decline the equality I offer you, and, as I have no other superiority over you than years, I have to presume you consider me as belonging to another generation!"

"Please explain! What equality have I declined?"

"Equality of nomenclature! You have become Nicholas, but I remain Mrs. Hantish. If that isn't humility on your part, what is it?"

Nicholas's heart throbbed violently. "What do you wish me to call you?"

"Celia, of course!"

"But not in company, surely?"

"I leave that to your prudence, with which you are so richly endowed."

"Between ourselves, then!" he said, turning red.

"Don't forget!"

No more was said until they began to ascend the lane they had come down earlier in the afternoon. Celia, who had been striding along, whistling under her breath, at this point broke the silence.

"It suddenly occurs to me that I'm wasting your time and that you ought to be at work."

"No, I'm not working to-day."

He was somewhat vexed that she had never once inquired as to the nature or progress of his work. Even now she only pursued the subject in its personal aspect.

"There is nothing worse for a new intimacy than to clash, so I only wish you to give me what time you have left over. Whenever you find a gap, you *will* run along and see me?"

Nicholas looked at her uncertainly.

"No, I mean it," said Celia with a smiling nod. "This isn't one of my polite invitations—I really want you to come. I'm nearly always at home from three onwards, but I am most solitary in the evenings. May I expect you to-morrow?"

"I have to bring Ferreira, if you remember."

"What a bore! . . . Never mind! To-morrow with Maurice, but the day after by yourself. May I rely?"

"If I could believe that you do want me and aren't merely saying so!"

"I do want you."

"I'll come, of course."

It was not yet half-past seven when they were in the woods again, near home. The sun was declining, the ground atmosphere held a warm, mellow tinge, while the shadows cast by the trees were long and almost violet. The clouds had all dispersed from the overhead sky. A delightful odour came up from the carpet of fallen pine-cones.

Celia, hot, gay, dusty and dishevelled, started to prepare herself for civilisation. She stepped into a little thicket, nearly like a chamber.

"Be my maid, Nicholas! . . . Something has happened to my hair, and I don't know what."

He walked completely round her.

"May I touch?"

"What a question for a maid!"

Colouring, he guided her fingers with his own to one fallen tress and two or three insecure ones.

"Is my face clean?" she demanded, laughing.

"Beautifully so! You look as if you were setting out instead of returning home."

"Surely! With a two-inch hole in my ankle! . . . My lips are all cracked and sore." She pressed her finger against them. "Look!"

While he was in the act of bending forward to scrutinise the pouted lips, which happened to be perfectly smooth and healthily crimson, they suddenly parted in a mocking smile. He glanced up swiftly to meet her eyes and saw that they held a meaning. He thought that it was an invitation, but it was too impossible to be true, and during the two seconds he hesitated she uttered a little laugh and withdrew herself from his reach.

Nicholas was very taciturn all the rest of the way home, and Celia did not press him to speak. He saw her to her door, but refused to enter.

IX

MAURICE CHOOSES

By the first post on Monday morning arrived for Mrs. Sturt a letter from Lady Wyburn, enclosing tickets for a subscription fête to be held at her house, Colminster Hall, in aid of the funds of a neighbouring cottage hospital, on the following Saturday week. The tickets were unpriced, but acceptance was expected to be accompanied by a cheque. The entire expenses of the entertainment would be borne by Lady Wyburn, so that the total sum contributed would be handed over to the hospital treasurer without deduction. It would be a mixed gathering, but not *too* mixed; only residents of good social standing were to receive invitations. Colminster was seven miles west of Newleigh. The Sturts were known to Lady Wyburn, though she had never exactly taken them up.

A programme of the attractions was also enclosed. The gala was to commence with tea on the lawns at 4.30, to the music of a string orchestra. On a specially-constructed floor a pair of exhibition dancers would show some new steps. Afterwards, an Elizabethan Masque was to be played, followed by an historic series of Old English dances by the adult pupils of a well-known terpsichorean school. For those guests whose tastes were more modern and robust, the services of a professional concert-party had been secured. No formal meal would be set during the evening, but refreshments in both kinds would be obtainable at all times in the grand marquee. A fancy dress dance in the ball-room was fixed for seven o'clock and would proceed till eleven. Dressing-rooms for both sexes would be provided. Cars at 11.30.

Mrs. Sturt passed the envelope and its enclosures down to her husband, at the foot of the breakfast-table, without comment, but with a dark face. Nicholas had already noticed that she was ominously quiet that morning. Sturt alternately raised and lowered his eyebrows as he leisurely perused everything.

"A very pretty, amateur affair," he pronounced at last, returning the papers to the envelope, "—with the usual amateur weaknesses; *mais, que voulez-vous*?[2] The scheme is sound. Everyone will flock, substantial subscriptions will pour in, and the hospital undoubtedly will be the richer for it."

"Let the girls see, then!" said his wife, rather sharply. "I call it organised blackmail! One has to send one's name in, or people will imagine one has been passed over. Very clever!"

Katherine barely glanced at the letter and programme. She seemed as subdued as her mother.

"We can pay without going, mother. I, for one, haven't the tiniest ambition to support Lady Wyburn's social throne."

Audrey was more impressed by the possibilities of the function. "What could I go as, I wonder?" she inquired pensively, of no one in particular. "Heaps of smart dresses will be there, you may be certain. I shall want some money, father! I can't go slashing up my clothes."

"We shall see!"

Evelyn, having run her eye down the papers casually, pushed them along to Nicholas. He also read, then shook his head dubiously, to express that it was not in his line.

"We shan't let *you* shirk, Nicholas!" said Audrey. "You'll simply *have* to run us over in the car. We'll let you off dancing, but if George drives us we shall get announced as the Misses Turniptops, of Little Ploughborough-cum-Cowfold, or something! You *can* manipulate a car?"

"I can, but it doesn't look as if anyone except yourself is very keen on going."

"I'm not, for one!" said Evelyn.

"And I'm *not* going!" added Katherine, following the statement by a little snap of her jaws. Audrey glared at her indignantly.

"Of course if we really want to make ourselves conspicuous! . . . You quite understand, my dear, what all the girls who do turn up will say about us? That we haven't anything fit to

2. "But, what do you want?"

wear? . . . Mother, I do wish you'd make a remark of some sort!"

"You and Evelyn may run over if you wish, as long as you don't stay till the end."

"Oh, we shall be quite safe with Nicholas!" Seeing the lines of refusal form themselves on his face, she hastened to bring forward an argument: "Mrs. Hantish may be there, Nicholas."

"What of it?"

"You will have somebody to amuse you while we are dancing."

"She will be dancing, too."

"Very likely she won't be!" She looked at him so slyly that he had to flush. Evelyn noticed it, and came to his rescue.

"Even if she isn't dancing, she will have the usual crowd of men round her. Nicholas surely needn't drag over to Colminster to see a woman who is on view here as a permanent spectacle!"

Nothing was decided. It was not till after the conclusion of the meal that Nicholas was enlightened concerning the reason for Audrey's marked allusion to Celia, but then it all came out. Evelyn stopped him on the stairs to whisper hastily that he had been seen on the previous afternoon escorting Mrs. Hantish in the direction of the woods.

"That's why mother and Katherine were so cool just now," she added. "Their feeling, right or wrong, is that as long as you remain our guest it is rather a breach to ignore us in favour of outsiders. I think the contention far-fetched, but you might as well be put on your guard."

"What do *you* think about it?"

"My view is that, short of asking her here, you have a perfect right to do what you like."

"Is she supposed not to be respectable?"

"Oh, no, she's well inside the line."

Nicholas appeared to be very much annoyed at the attempted dictation of his hostess by this attitude of silent disapproval, and he looked as if he would have liked to express his contrary feelings on the subject, but, after hesitating a little and breathing hard, he contented himself in the end with thanking Evelyn for her information. She exacted a promise from him that he would say nothing to the others about the matter on his own initiative, after which she permitted him to continue his progress upstairs.

When Ferreira entered the room, looking rather pale and sullen, some half an hour later, Nicholas's first impulse was to take him to task about his revolver exploit, but again he was sensible enough to restrain himself. A single glance was sufficient to show that his assistant was in no temper to suffer a free discussion of his personal affairs. Celia, also, with her feminine suavity and tact, would handle him far more successfully than Nicholas could hope to do. The only point was to get Ferreira round there.

He announced the invitation at once.

"Mrs. Hantish wants us both along to her place to tea this afternoon. We might close down early for once."

"I don't care about it, thanks! She's no friend of mine."

"I half promised for you, and it will look queer."

"I know! Lore's been speaking to her. I'm not having any! We know the celebrated Mrs. Hantish!"

"What do you know of her?"

"She's a twister!"

"What's that?"

"A mischief-maker. Strongly guaranteed to separate the closest pals at the shortest notice! I've plenty trouble on my hands without her assistance. You go alone, old chap!"

Nicholas, though somewhat disconcerted, did not urge the matter, but at the end of the morning, as Ferreira was shutting up to return home to lunch, he reverted to it of his own accord.

"*Is* it about Lore that Mrs. Hantish wants to see me?"

"It is, as a matter of fact."

"Lore has been spreading the happy tidings, then?"

"I don't know about *spreading*. If we're referring to the same thing, she told Mrs. Hantish and she told me, but she didn't say anything about telling anyone else."

"And I suppose she wants Mrs. Hantish to warn me off?"

"You had better come along with me and find out for yourself what she wants."

"On second thoughts, I will! I may as well know what's doing. . . . But what gets over me, old boy, is where *you* come in! What did she want to go and blab to *you* for?"

"Oh, I was merely representing Evelyn. They couldn't get to talk to one another, so I acted as go-between."

"What the devil has it to do with Evelyn?"

Nicholas shrugged his shoulders.

"So you've passed it on to Evelyn?" demanded Ferreira.

"Yes."

"And what did *she* say?"

"Nothing to me."

"I bet she'll make a personal business of it, the jealous little cat! They're all alike, old chap, and don't you have anything to do with them. There's not one of them recognises the bulkhead system as applied to a fellow. You've got to be theirs all the time, and I just guess I'm not built that way!"

He scowled, and put on his coat.

On arriving at The Arbour shortly after half-past four that afternoon, the two young men were shown straight through to the garden, where a tea-table was already set beneath a white-poplar tree on the lawn. Celia was swinging herself lazily on an upright hammock-seat of striped canvas. She was in unrelieved white, with arms bare to the elbows and a bare neck, and in her beautiful open-air setting of shade and sunshine looked more exotic than ever. An older lady with a dry, scholastic face, and wearing gold-rimmed glasses, was sitting nearby on a hard chair, studying a book of birds having coloured illustrations. No doubt, this was the cousin.

The hostess extended her hand without rising, and the guests took it in turn. Ferreira's manner was cold, jaunty and indifferent. He bowed stiffly to the other lady with whom he seemed already to be acquainted. Celia went carelessly through a form of introduction, and Nicholas learned that the cousin's name was Miss Ogilvie. He sat down beside her. Ferreira was invited to share the hammock-seat with its occupant.

Miss Ogilvie having ministered at the tea-table and sat down

again, Nicholas attempted a conversation with her. He glanced at
the book, now lying on the grass at her feet.

"Are you a nature-lover?"

"Ay!" was the dry response.

"You're Scotch?"

"Ay, I'm Scottish." She followed the remark with a sigh, and
gazed around her restlessly, as though she found the interchange
of banalities already unduly protracted. Nicholas ventured one
more effort.

"Have you been down here long?"

"Four years."

He relapsed into silence, wondering how in the world two
such dissimilar women came to be house companions! He concluded that Miss Ogilvie, notwithstanding the relationship, could
be little more than a resident house-keeper to her smart, modish,
roving cousin, and, at once losing all further interest in her, began
to listen to the words passing on the other side of the table.

"I have a bone to pick with you," Celia was saying with a
smile, "so don't take it into your head to make a bolt for freedom
before I have done! Not now—later!"

"About Lore, isn't it?"

"Possibly."

"That's why I came," responded Ferreira dryly.

He pulled out the familiar cigarette-case and, after lifting his
brows for permission, lit up and sat back smoking, without another word. Celia was too accomplished a hostess to attempt to
construct a party of such heterogeneous elements. She preferred
to put the others at their ease by setting an example of well-
simulated overpowering languor, attributable to the heat of the
day and the pleasantness of their surroundings. All continued
silently to contemplate the sights and sounds of the garden.

The tea ran its course. A maid appeared from the house to
remove the table, and glances were exchanged between Celia and
her relation. The latter bowed to the young men, and retired,
bearing the book with her. Ferreira blew out a cloud of smoke,
and raised his brows again.

"All ready?" asked the young widow, smiling.

"All ready! But is Cabot in this, may I ask?"

"He is. I may need his protection, in case you begin flourishing fire-arms! . . . Now, what does it all mean?"

"I fancy the prosecution usually opens the case!"

"Lore tells me you have been threatening her life. Have you?"

Ferreira examined his finger-ends. "What about it?"

"With a loaded revolver."

"I have a revolver."

"And you have been pointing it at her? You might just as well confess!—it won't go any farther."

"Oh, I've been pointing it at her all right! What's the next question?"

"But upon my word!" exclaimed Celia, laughing. "I had no idea you would plead guilty, and I fear it rather goes outside my experience. One seldom hears of such proceedings in polite society. Was it a joke? Had she egged you on, or what?"

"Oh, yes, she egged me on!" replied Ferreira cynically.

"But how? Had you quarrelled? Were you trying to force her to something she didn't want? . . ."

"Suppose you tell me Lore's story first—then we shall know where we are."

"I gathered the impression that you were trying to intimidate her into marrying you! . . . Do you *want* to marry her?"

"Oh, I want *something*, you bet! But I don't care to discuss it with you, Mrs. Hantish."

"Of course, I don't wish to pry into feelings. I'm only trying to reconcile facts. Forgive my presumption, but I'm acting for Lore, and I'm rather at sea! Haven't you engagements elsewhere?"

"I don't know what you mean."

"Perhaps it would be more correct to say, haven't you *an* engagement elsewhere? I mean the word in its generally-applied sense."

Ferreira gave her a cold and hostile stare.

"I expect you're referring to Evelyn Sturt?"

"Yes, I am."

"I guess we'll leave her out, if you don't mind very much!"

"I don't—and at all—but what am I to tell Lore? Are you asserting that she hasn't a right to discuss it with you, either? You really expect a self-respecting woman thankfully to receive just as much as you care to offer her? . . ."

"It hasn't anything to do with it, and you have hold of the wrong end of the stick altogether, Mrs. Hantish!—but, as I said before, I prefer not to talk about it."

"But I *shall* talk about it!" said Celia, sitting up, with a little laugh. "Here is one of my intimate friends going in fear of her life, and a young man of talent making himself and everyone around him utterly miserable, all for want of a word in season— and I am not to speak that word! . . . Now, let's be practical. Marriage is such a very serious matter that I am in favour of allowing a man every opportunity beforehand of finding out where he means to come down. From a common-sense standpoint there's nothing whatever to urge against your system of investigation by simultaneous comparison—though it may be rather rough on the girls themselves. But there comes a time when you *have* to decide. You can't drag half a dozen young women up the aisle with you, to make your final choice at the foot of the altar steps! . . . But have you decided?"

"I have."

"Lore?"

"Yes."

"Very well, then! Do you imagine for one minute that a girl of Lore's spirit will consent to share your affections with someone else, for all the revolvers in the world? Even if she were willing, would it be fair of you to ask it?"

Ferreira toyed with his moustache.

"Is that her line of argument?"

"May I tell her you will give up Evelyn?"

There was a long pause.

"Very well, you may!" he said, in a tone of reluctance.

"You mean it? You won't go back on your word?"

"No, I mean it."

"Then I'll see Lore this very afternoon, and tell her. Of course there will be no more pistols?" She smiled.

Ferreira rose rather gloomily.

"Mind you, I'm not going to break openly with Evelyn Sturt. She has always been a good pal of mine, and it would be a scurvy trick to let her down suddenly. I shall go on meeting her in a friendly way just as before. That's got to be understood."

"Then what are you promising?"

"Not to marry her."

"But perhaps you have gone too far in to back out?" suggested Celia lightly, as she also stood up.

He was not to be drawn, and she obtained nothing else from him. She escorted the young men through the house to the front door, where farewells were uttered; then, as they passed down the garden path to the roadway, she stood watching them from the porch. Nicholas looked back at her twice. On the second occasion, she beckoned to him to return, and since Ferreira was stalking moodily ahead he understood that the summons was a personal one. He went back.

"Don't you think you had better tell Evelyn?" she asked, in a quick undertone. "*He* isn't going to. I think she ought to know."

"But you know as well as I do that Miss Jensen won't have anything more to do with him."

"And if she won't, you approve of Evelyn's receiving him back?"

"Of course not, but . . ."

"He means to carry on the flirtation with Evelyn absolutely without serious intentions. If you think she is that sort of girl, of course . . ."

"I quite agree she ought to know, but I'd rather anyone else told her."

Ferreira, leaning against the garden-gate, looked back at the two somewhat cynically, but made no movement to return to them. Something unpleasant in his face apparently irritated Nicholas, for he added, half to himself, "There's not much doubt he's a rotter!"

"Give her the intelligence as coming from me if you like, since you don't seem anxious to appear in it. But for heaven's sake don't let her come to grief over a man like that! Supposing it were your own sister, my dear!"

"Well, I'll tell her."

"At once?"

"Yes, as soon as I get back, if I can find her."

"Don't be upset by a few tears! She *may* be in love with him. But I somehow fancy you won't have that ordeal to face."

"If you think she's playing a game, why say anything to her about it?"

"Remember, she's only a child, my dear, and it's early days for her to get involved in scandals. Maurice will go from bad to worse!"

She gave Nicholas a gentle push in the way he should go, but, immediately recollecting something, drew him back by the arm. "You will come to-morrow and tell me all about it?"

"May I?"

"Why, weren't you going to? . . . Come early to tea, and I'll try and get my cousin out of the way for the occasion!"

Without waiting for his response, she turned her back and disappeared into the house.

"What was the palaver?" demanded Ferreira as soon as he had rejoined him.

"Oh, only private affairs!" returned Nicholas gruffly. The other gave him a quick, scrutinising glance.

"You are not double-crossing me, both of you, by any chance?"

"No, we're not."

"I fancy you're straight, but she runs about as straight as a shilling clockwork locomotive. I shall soon know if she's up to any of her tricks."

"If you were half as honest as she is, you wouldn't hurt, Ferreira!" said Nicholas with obvious restraint in his voice.

Ferreira regarded him again, sneered to himself, and turned away. At the first branching of the road they separated to go to their respective homes.

Nicholas realised only too well that his talk with Evelyn would be a delicate one, and he spent considerable time before dinner in preparing and discarding speeches. As it tuned out, the interview lasted precisely two minutes and was unmarked by any emotional incidents. She was rather despondently picking off dead geranium blooms in the dusk when he came up to her. She straightened herself and looked round.

"Oh, I just wanted to tell you!" he began. . . . "Miss Jensen wished Mrs. Hantish to see Ferreira on her behalf. . . ."

"That couldn't have been Lore's suggestion," interrupted the girl. "It must have come from the other."

"Anyway, it was so arranged. So I was to take Ferreira round to tea there this afternoon. . . . The upshot was, Mrs. Hantish consented to try and reconcile him to Miss Jensen, on condition that he left off playing about and made up his mind where he wished to come down. She very reasonably emphasised that Miss Jensen would make that a point. So it was up to him to decide whether he wanted this reconciliation badly enough. . . ."

Evelyn remained perfectly cold.

"And . . . ?"

"Well, I'm sorry to say he decided that he did. . . . I don't know that I care to put it any plainer."

"It's quite unnecessary, thanks! I presume I shall receive official notification in due course?"

"I fancy you won't—that's why I'm telling you."

"I wondered why. But you would not have thought of this. Wasn't it Mrs. Hantish's idea?"

"Well, it was."

Evelyn viewed him for a moment with a slight expression of distaste on her mouth. Then suddenly she threw up her chin and laughed.

"I thought it must be! Be sure to give her my very best thanks for her kindly consideration!" And, almost bowing to him, she turned away to move towards the house.

Nicholas fingered his chin as he gazed after her. He was satisfied that he had performed his duty with sufficient tact, but her attitude completely overturned his notions. Instead of dwelling on the fact itself, her principal concern seemed to be with Mrs. Hantish's share in the transaction. It was unaccountable why women, otherwise perfectly generous and broad-minded, should insist on these uncomfortable jealousies and suspicions among themselves, preventing the coming together of beautiful characters which any man would have expected naturally to gravitate towards one another. He felt irritated by Evelyn's unreasonableness, and began to doubt whether, after all, she possessed the fine instincts with which he had hitherto credited her. Possibly there might be something in Celia's view of her hidden nature.

X

A SCUFFLE

Tuesday was an intensely hot day. There was not a single cloud in the sky, and what little breeze there was came from the east, bringing with it a furnace-like dryness. Sturt, casting an eye upwards at the unpleasant whitish-blue vault—they were breakfasting under the veranda again—prophesied a storm before night. The temper of everyone at table appeared to have an edge put to it by the atmospheric oppression—or, rather, some family disturbance seemed already to have occurred, precipitated by this oppression.

Mrs. Sturt presided at the tray in grim dignity, scarcely opening her lips to speak. Her husband fidgeted and was ill at ease. Katherine's eyes were red-rimmed, as though she had been crying recently, and she, too, hardly spoke. Audrey's face was calm and unsmiling as she applied herself to her food; while Evelyn was pale, disdainful and obstinately mute. Nicholas himself appeared to be in a deep abstraction, unconnected with the household disturbance. He eyed his knife and fork and the food he was eating as though they were miles away. Evelyn occasionally stole a glance at him.

As he was on his way to his room after the meal his host detained him.

"Can you spare a moment?"

"Certainly," replied Nicholas, and they passed together in the morning-room.

Sturt, having drawn at his just-lighted cigar, led him by the elbow to a retired window, where they could not be overheard. He sat down on the window-seat, with legs outstretched to the floor, and studied his ash, while Nicholas remained standing before him, hands in trousers pockets, gazing out of doors.

"Unfortunate incidents are happening around us!" began Sturt with a dry drawl. "How far you may be cognisant of the state of affairs I do not know, but possibly you are acquainted with young Ferreira's latest extravaganza—that with the revolver *motif*, I mean?"

"Yes. What about it?"

"Its sequel, in all probability, you have *not* heard. The ladies, it appears, are making the affair their own, and there is the devil to pay! My wife and eldest daughter have cut Miss Jensen dead in the public street! . . . It is true there appears to have been no one abroad at the time; still, the fact remains as I say."

"That's bad."

"Bad? It is *damnable*, my dear chap! The poor child is pierced to the quick. . . . I chanced to be over there last evening, in all innocence, for I had been informed of nothing. She told me the story—not calmly and consecutively, as you may imagine! The scandal has required three days to become public property, for it seems it all happened on Friday last. There has been a leak. A page-boy, whose mouth, it appears, she had insufficiently stopped, must have babbled to other domestics who had on that evening been out; and these maids have passed the news on to their kind. Whatever the process, the neighbourhood is so thoroughly primed that, damme! one might fancy handbills had been at work. My womenkind must have been among the last to hear, for up to dinner last evening they were in ignorance, and it was less than an hour before my visit to Miss Jensen that the affront was given."

"How are her other friends treating her?"

"She has been out but little, she says. From what one can gather, courteously but coldly. She has not been otherwise affronted. But the symptom is too sharp to be ignored, especially coming from the quarter it does. . . . Imagine what a detestable experience for a girl of pride and heart and sensibility, my dear fellow—conscious of rectitude, and with more to lose in the shape of reputation than others! If ever women were intimate, Lore and Katherine were the ones. For ever visiting, kissing, complimenting, exchanging gifts of poetry and music, writing eight-, twelve-, sixteen-page letters when separated, and what not. And suddenly—not a word, not a reproach, not a request for explanation, but . . . a public cut in the roadway! Was ever anything more unjust and ungenerous? I specify Katherine, since I do not care to call my wife's actions into question, and her interests are manifestly more widespread. But . . . And what has this unprotected child done to be deemed deserving of such treatment? Has she violated in any way the canons of her sex? Has she even been indiscreet? Could she have *avoided* this dastardly assault? They do not say. She is convicted without having been accused. . . ."

"Of course, the real trouble is the sort of life she has been leading. That's probably just come out for the first time. But isn't Mrs. Sturt herself the one to discuss all this with?"

"I am buttonholing you for a purpose, dear boy! We shall come to it immediately. . . . As for what you remark concerning her mode of life, one must not judge the creative artist by the measure of common folk. Imagination is not always at command—a means of stimulation must be found, and quickly. A dry life entails dry thoughts, and a workman might with equal reason pawn his tools as an artist turn her back on the free, lighthearted, rich, coloured society so essential to the formation of moods. . . . Yet the world, which eagerly demands the finished product of art, professes indignation at the indispensable atmosphere! *Quelle bêtise!*[3] Because she serves her muse and makes the sacrifices which that muse demands, is she therefore depraved? Is she to be debarred from the equal friendship of persons of her own sex? Or, if this association be allowed, must she leave her own ground in order to step upon theirs? . . . My dear fellow, you find me impatient, and I am impatient! In my profession, charity and magnanimity are the commonest virtues, and perhaps I have not yet accustomed myself to the ways of the general world. But *passons!*[4] . . . Upon quitting Miss Jensen . . ."

"How has *she* reacted to all this?"

"Over that we will draw a veil, I think. She does not take her

3. "What a stupid thing!" or "What nonsense!"
4. "Let's pass that by!" or "Let's say no more about it!"

passions easily, even for a woman! . . . It is enough to remark that she rendered me, before the conclusion of my visit, nearly as agitated as herself. So much was this the case that, upon leaving her, I felt quite sick and dizzy. It chanced that I had occasion to walk down to the village, and there I was obliged to seek a restorative in the railway tavern—which I ask you to believe is not a common practice of mine. Whom should I see there but Ferreira! The lounge was full, there was great hullabaloo, and he, very undoubtedly, was in liquor, but in the end I persuaded him away, and we walked back together. He also had been to Lore's."

"Are they on terms again?"

"She even declined to see him! . . . Never have I known a youngster more cut up! The more one expostulated, the more unmanageable did he grow, until at last it developed into a direct and personal attack, quite alien to the subject under discussion. In some weird way, he pretended that I was responsible for his dismissal! I do not recall his arguments, and I fancy he will not recall them himself this morning. But his concealed animosity towards me came out in most surprising fashion. It seems he entertains some absurd jealousy in his mind, on the strength of the few friendly visits I have paid Miss Jensen from time to time. He imagines a plot to give him his *congé*[5]—and one knows not what else! He even threatens to inform Mrs. Sturt, who, to be sure, would but laugh in his face; but still, these things are not to be said. . . . So that is the favour I have to ask of you, my dear fellow! You will see him directly. I fancy your word has no small weight with him. Try what can be done to bring him to reason, and report to me afterwards. It is understood, of course, that I have nothing to conceal and nothing to dread, but it is natural, I believe, that I should not wish this further annoyance to fall on Mrs. Sturt. He is quite irresponsible."

"I don't mind talking to him in the least if it will give you any satisfaction. You simply want your name kept out of the whole

5. "Leave". Depending on context, "congé" can be used to denote a holiday, taking one's leave of someone, or (most likely in this case), giving notice (for instance, at work).

business, I take it?"

"That is all I want with Ferreira. . . . Should things go well there, later, perhaps, we will discuss whether it be not possible to reconcile the ladies. Katherine, I suspect, already regrets her friend, while Lore has too complicated a mind to harbour elemental feelings of revenge. It may be that a quite trifling explanation will prove sufficient. But the pot must be permitted to cool before we dip our fingers into it, and animosities are still running high. Ferreira is our first business. See what can be effected with that impracticable youth. If only you do not catch fire from his vehemence and do not suffer yourself to be silenced by his fables—of which he has vast store for all occasions—he will doubtless succumb in the end to your superior calmness of character, and this is what you have to remember. Go now, my dear fellow! Au revoir! And good luck!"

In passing through the hall after his conversation with Sturt, Nicholas encountered Evelyn. The meeting was casual, and at first neither was going to stop, but then each looked at the other a second time, and hesitated. Evelyn halted, and he did the same.

"Are you in a hurry, or can you come into the drawing-room for a moment?" asked the girl.

He signified his willingness. The first object which caught his eye as they entered the room was Lore's manuscript song, dedicated to Katherine, lying on the floor by the piano, completely torn in two. Evelyn glanced at it also.

"You have heard the great news, of course?" she said with a smile. "How Lore's iniquities have come to light at last, and how she has been duly struck off the list of visiting acquaintances? . . . However, I didn't bring you here to speak about that. I want to know if I write a note to Maurice, will you give it to him?"

"What about?"

"Surely that is not a question?"

"If it's the sequel of our talk last night, my information was given you in confidence. You're not supposed to know anything about it."

"I quite forgot that. How stupid! Well, that knocks that on the head, then! Perhaps I shall get the news through more legitimate channels, and then it will be time enough to assert myself. . . . Do you want to say something too?"

"It's nothing much. . . . I don't know if you're still interested, but I promised you—"

Evelyn, looking up sharply, did not permit him to finish. "You have another result to show me?"

"If you care to see it." The surly reluctance of his tone appeared to surprise her, but she did not comment on it.

"Of course I wish to. But was this with your new apparatus?"

"No; that isn't ready."

"Then is it the same sort of thing as before?"

"No. Otherwise I shouldn't have troubled you."

"You're not very explicit. . . . And when can I see it?"

"After Ferreira has gone. Say after dinner."

"At half-past eight?"

"Very well."

"Are you annoyed with me about anything?"

"With you? Why should I be annoyed with you?"

"You seem so extremely short in your manner."

"I wasn't aware of it; but if I am it certainly doesn't refer to you."

"I hope not, for we were such good friends all last week. . . . Well, then, I won't detain you from your work. . . ."

As she turned to precede him out of the room, a new thought struck her, or perhaps it was in the nature of a woman's postscript.

"It is just possible Maurice may say something to you about wishing to see me. I shall be in one of the downstair rooms, or in the garden, all the morning. Perhaps you wouldn't mind letting me know, if he does mention it? I won't bring you into it."

"Very well, I will."

But if Ferreira felt any such desire he had no opportunity of expressing it upon his arrival shortly afterwards. The previous discussion of a different topic had the effect of abruptly curtailing his stay in the house. Hardly had he strolled in sombrely and flung down his hat when Nicholas bearded him concerning Sturt.

"I hear there's a row sprung up out of your business!" he began.

"A devil of a row!" agreed Ferreira. "Have they been talking about it here?"

"I had it from Sturt."

"Oh, he's told you too? He seems to be going round. Yes, Lore's crashed all right!"

"With your assistance!"

"With my assistance, if you particularly want to put it in an unpleasant way. Someone's found the news too warm to hold, and I wouldn't be greatly astonished if it was our dear friend Mrs. Hantish."

"That's nonsense!" said Nicholas sternly. "Mrs. Hantish is a lady, with the instincts of one. She wouldn't do such a thing. It was evidently that boy of Miss Jensen's."

"I'd like to have a quiet five minutes with the party, whoever it was!"

"And if Miss Jensen had a brother, no doubt he'd like to have a quiet five minutes with you. . . . However, it's no business of mine, and I suppose it's no use crying over spilt milk."

Ferreira drew his coat off, threw it on a chair, and leant against the edge of the window-table.

"Said all you have to say, old boy? Because, if so, I'll get on with the job."

"Oh, don't imagine I want to interfere! But is it true you're trying to drag Sturt into the mess?"

"Oho!—now we see daylight! I thought you were working up to something. So the old chap's come to you in distress, has he? And I bet he's made a yarn of it! . . . All right!—I'm very glad you asked. There's no question of my dragging in Sturt, because, as it happens, he's in already—up to the neck! His record for attendances at Lore's takes an easy first, and there's a lot more behind, which may or may not come out. Naturally, he's keen on slipping quietly away in the dark, but why should I stand all the racket?"

"You're responsible for this row, and, besides, however much of an ass he's made of himself, getting him a bad name won't help *your* case at all."

"I don't want to get him a bad name. I'm only trying to screw him up a bit. He hasn't the initiative of a slug. He was too busy thinking aloud to listen to me when I walked up with him last night, so you tell him what I'm after. It's no use anyone of us trying to slip out alone, but things have got to be righted all round. Everyone concerned has got to get back into a position of 'as you were!' And it has to be done through Sturt. It was his women that cut poor old Lore dead outside her own house, and it's up to him to make them take it back, and apologise. I'm not dragging him into a mess; I'm trying to get him out of one. You tell him all that."

"But he said something about your threatening to give the game away to his wife?"

"Quite right!"

"Did you mean it?"

"If he hasn't the decency to help Lore out, he's got to stop in himself—that's all I mean. He can't have it both ways."

"Then you *will* tell Mrs. Sturt?"

"I will if he lets things go on drifting, and I give him just twenty-four hours from now to make a move. At the end of twenty-four hours I'm going to advise Lore to shut up shop, and then we'll all see the pots and pans flying about. There'll be the biggest hell of a commotion in this house since it was built!"

"You realise Evelyn will come in for it, too?"

"I'm sorry about Evelyn, but I'm sorrier about Lore. When I back a pal, I don't stand on punctilio. I go for it straight and strong, with my head down and my eyes shut."

Nicholas reddened.

"Doesn't it occur to you that it's a blackguardly thing to do to throw a bomb of this sort in among a set of decent women?"

Ferreira's eye glinted, as he produced and lit a cigarette .

"I guess we'll go easier with the language, old boy! I have the utmost regard and esteem for your money-bags, but the heavy father stunt isn't in the contract. I have a code as well as you, and don't forget it!"

"Funny sort of code, to make trouble between man and wife!"

The other's face went pale, as he regarded Nicholas for a moment without speaking. Suddenly he stood up, free from the table.

"If you don't like it, you can do the other thing! Give me a cheque for what I've done already, and I'll clear. I fancy I've had just about enough of you, my young friend!"

"You can go if you wish to, but I don't pay you a penny till the work's finished."

Ferreira took a threatening step forward. "I'll see you do! I don't make a free gift of my work to anyone!"

"Oh, you're not bullying a woman now, Ferreira! You'd better not come too close, or you may find yourself going through that window!"

Ferreira eyed Nicholas, then glanced at his coat, which was across the room. Nicholas, guessing his thought, sprang backward nimbly towards it, and felt for the side-pocket. Just as his hand had grabbed the revolver which he had rightly reckoned on finding there, Ferreira made a dash for his wrist, and there was a short, sharp, panting tussle between the two, which terminated by Ferreira's being flung violently against the opposite wall. Nicholas, breathing hard, put the captured weapon in a drawer of his bureau, and turned the key, which he slipped in his trousers pocket.

"It was about time somebody relieved you of that, Ferreira!"

The other, whose face had become as white as chalk, again approached his coat, which he now proceeded to put on. After that, he lit a new cigarette, with as great an assumption of ease as his violently trembling hand would permit. He moved towards the door.

"Don't imagine you've done with me, Cabot!"

"Oh, go to blazes!"

"You'll be dam' sorry for this!" He put his hand on the door knob. . . . "Here's something you can chew on, for a start. Lore's an ex-mistress of Sturt's. She lives here to be on the spot to levy blackmail. If you don't believe me, you can ask him yourself. I'll run round to-morrow and see Mrs. Sturt."

"And if I see you on the premises I'll give you the biggest thrashing you ever had in your life!"

"Perhaps you won't, old boy!"

He went out, pale and sneering, and Nicholas angrily banged the door behind him.

XI

CELIA EXPLAINS THE TRUE POSITION

When Nicholas arrived for tea at The Arbour that afternoon, shortly before five o'clock, he was at once directed to the garden, where his hostess was sitting alone by the tea-table. Although the overhanging branches of the tree screened her from the direct violence of the sun, and despite her unsubstantial attire, she appeared in a state of prostration, but quite pleasantly so. Her head was thrown backwards upon the cushion supporting her neck, while her eyes were dreamy. Her lower limbs were outstretched before her, crossed at the ankle. The contrast between her black hair and the creamy pallor of her skin was vivid, and if Evelyn's remark was just—that her beauty varied—there could be little question that this was one of her fortunate days.

Recognising him, she smiled and held out a friendly hand, without rousing herself immediately from her languid posture.

"I had quite given you up!"

"Yet you were not in tears!"

Celia rewarded his progress in education with a more intimate smile, and instructed him to fetch another chair and sit beside her. While he was away in search of one, she rose to pour out tea for both.

"Before I forget, Nicholas—I'm taking my car to Southampton to-morrow, to do some shopping, and I want you to come with me. If you know how to drive, we needn't take the chauffeur."

Nicholas's heart gave a sudden leap; but then he reflected.

"I'd love to, of course! . . ."

"What is it—your hapless work? Can't you leave it for once?"

"I *will* leave it for once. I'll work late instead. In any case, I've lost my assistant."

"Then will you call here at 10.30 in the morning? It will do you good to get some fresh air. You're looking pale, my dear."

"It's the hot weather."

She viewed him over the brim of her cup. "You say you have lost Maurice?"

"Yes; we had a row this morning, and he packed up and cleared off on the spot."

"How funny! What was it about?"

"Oh, it was really about this everlasting business of Lore's. You've heard the latest development, of course?"

"I've been a hermit since yesterday. Do tell me!"

"The Sturts have struck her off their visiting list. Mrs. Sturt and Katherine cut her in the street last evening."

"On account of last Friday's doings?"

"Yes."

"How rich!"

"Now Ferreira's moving heaven and earth to try and get her reinstated. He's attempting to blackmail Sturt into forcing or persuading his wife to apologise, and when I mildly ventured to call him a blackguard for his pains, he cut up rusty. I had to remove his celebrated revolver to a place of safety. Now he's swearing red vengeance, and I don't know *what* his next move will be."

"And care as little, I expect. But how excruciatingly choice! . . . What has Mr. Sturt been up to, since he fancies he can blackmail him?"

"Oh, he has been going round there somewhat too frequently, and all the rest of it. Ferreira told me some cock-and-bull yarn."

"What was that?"

"He pretends that there was formerly some illegitimate connection between them, and that she's only down here to collect money."

"I'll tell you something about that another time. It's true, and it's not true. . . . Now, what about Evelyn? Did you give my message?"

"Yes."

"What did she say?"

"She said nothing about Ferreira, but she asked me to thank

you for your kindness.”

“Do tell me her exact words, if you remember them!”

“I think that nearly was her exact expression. She laughed, so I suppose she was being sarcastic. Evidently she leapt to the conclusion that you had put a spoke in her wheel.”

“I anticipated that, my dear.”

After sipping her tea in silence for a few moments, with down-cast eyes, she resumed: “I went to see Lore after you two had left me. She refuses to have anything more to do with Maurice, on any conditions.”

“Yes, I know. He went round there himself last night, and she wouldn’t see him.”

“Then we’ve done all that’s possible, I think. They must fight their own battles, without our further interference. I wouldn’t worry any more if I were you.”

“The only thing I’m bothering about is this bombshell Ferreira’s preparing to throw in. It’s a rotten thing to do!”

“Perhaps he won’t do it.”

“He’s going round to-morrow to see Mrs. Sturt specially, he says.”

“Poor old gentleman!”

“I’m thinking more of the girls.”

Celia curled her lip. “Oh, they’ll survive! A mild matrimonial dispute won’t poison their young happiness, even if they are initiated. There will be no divorce proceedings.”

“Couldn’t you have a shot at persuading Mrs. Sturt?”

“Persuading her to what?”

“To undo what she’s done, and make it up with Lore again. I know she has tremendous respect for your opinion. If you were to give her a broad hint that she is making herself look ridiculous . . .”

“She would be mortally offended! I really can’t undertake to lay down the social law to an older woman, my dear. You had better speak to her yourself. Everyone knows that you are a prime favourite of hers.”

“She has hardly condescended to address me since Sunday.”

"Why since Sunday?"

"That was the day of my crime. I visited one lady while staying at the house of another!"

Celia's face expressed smiling astonishment. "You are imagin-
ing it!"

"No, I was definitely informed. Not by Mrs. Sturt herself, of
course. It appears that if I wanted company in the woods the girls
were entitled to the first refusal. I wasn't well enough up in
etiquette to know that."

"It isn't etiquette, my dear! It has a very different name, but I
won't say what! . . . So what are you going to do about it?"

"I'm going to assert my complete liberty of action. If they
don't like it, I dare say there are other paying-guest establishments down here. . . . But what about this other matter? I wish
you would make the attempt."

"I really can't."

"As a personal favour to me!"

"No, for it wouldn't be a personal favour. You are studying
other people. . . . If I were to undertake it at all, it would have to
be as a sporting wager. Will you take a bet?"

Nicholas laughed. "All right!"

"If I fail, I do everything you want for a week. If I succeed,
you do everything I require for a week."

"Very well."

"No backing out afterwards!"

"No."

"Then it's a bet. I may have to tell some fibs, but that doesn't
concern you."

Celia was sitting sideways to the house, while Nicholas faced
it. Suddenly, the cup he was balancing precariously on the saucer
in his hand overturned, with its contents, on to the grass. After
swiftly ascertaining that her precious china was intact, his hostess
left the mishap to seek its cause. Glancing round at the terrace
before the house, she perceived the large, handsome, distinctive
person of Mrs. Sturt herself preparing to descend the steps leading on to the lawn! She jumped up in a graceful flurry, while

Nicholas was still recovering the fallen cup.

"This is witchcraft! What a joke! She has come to have it out with me about *you* dear, and here you are to receive her!"

"Shall I go?"

"No, stay and see how the bet goes!"

She moved towards the terrace steps to meet the visitor, and Nicholas meanwhile went in quest of another chair. By the side of Mrs. Sturt, Celia looked no more than a slender girl, though slightly the taller of the two. She took her affectionately by the arm, and led her forward across the interval of torrid lawn to the shady retreat of the tea-table. Nicholas and Mrs. Sturt bowed to each other rather stiffly, then all seated themselves.

"I'm afraid I am too late for a cup!"

"It has not been standing long, but shall I have a fresh infusion made?"

"Please don't! The stronger it is, the better I shall like it, for I have a slight nervous headache—brought on by worry, no doubt. I meant to have come earlier, but just as I had reached the front door I was confronted by Mrs. Beauchamp, of all people!—and I had to give her tea. She drove me nearly to tears with her eternal harping on her beloved Angus and how well he is doing in Tasmania! I strongly doubt if I should know the boy if I saw him." She accepted the cup of blackish beverage from her hostess's hand, but waved back the cake-stand impatiently.

"I'm sorry you have a headache."

"It's always my unhappy fate the day after I have been thoroughly upset." She continued to eye Nicholas with disfavour, for it became increasingly evident to her that he had not the least intention of taking his departure for some time to come. He reclined far back in the recesses of his hammock-chair, smoking easily, and sometimes closing his eyes. At last, with an angry wriggle of her body, she turned away from him and concentrated decisively, as her manner was, upon the topic which she had already twice hinted at.

"It's this terrible business of Lore's! You know all about it, of course?"

"I've heard about it," replied Celia with quiet cautiousness.

"It descended on all our heads like a veritable thunderbolt! I never could have believed it of her. It was actually on the evening *after* the affair that she had the audacity to call on us. You were there, Nicholas."

"Yes, I was there."

"But isn't she rather to be pitied than censured, don't you think?" inquired Celia with a conciliatory smile.

Mrs. Sturt looked up sharply. "Pitied for what?"

"For being intimidated by a young madman. What a horribly unpleasant predicament for a solitary girl to be in!"

"Very unpleasant!—but how came she to be in it? If a solitary girl encourages dissolute young fellows to visit her in her own home, she must take the consequences! But it is her deceit and artfulness I complain of. She must have had her tongue in her cheek for years! Drug-taking, drinking, gambling, men!—her house has been literally a den of vice and Katherine and I have visited there regularly! . . . . I never could have suspected an unmarried girl of decent education and social standing to be capable of such wickedness."

Celia preserved a sympathetic silence for a few moments.

"Do you think Maurice is really right in the head?" she inquired, lifting her brows.

"I never did think so. I have always regarded him as a shifty and unbalanced young man. The Doctor certainly ought to take measures with him. But all that doesn't exonerate Lore."

"Of course you have heard that he is trying to climb out of the affair on other people's shoulders?"

"No, I have heard nothing."

"That's why I think he is rather crazy. I hear he is going about accusing the most unlikely people. I wonder it hasn't come to your ears."

"Accusing them of what?"

"Of being in the same boat with himself. Of being regular visitors of Lore's. As if that would excuse him at all, even supposing it were true, which I don't for a minute suppose that it is."

"I think it's highly probable that she's been receiving others, considering what sort of person she has turned out to be. However crazy he is, there is no smoke without fire. What names has he mentioned?"

"Your husband for one!" said Celia with a humorous smile.

Mrs. Sturt stared at her, blinking her eyes rapidly.

"He hasn't *dared!*"

"Ask Mr. Cabot!"

"It's quite true," said Nicholas, replying to the elder woman's look of mute inquiry. "He told me a pack of lies about Mr. Sturt only this morning."

"In connection with Lore Jensen?"

"Yes."

"What did he say?"

"I'd rather not repeat."

Mrs. Sturt's bosom laboured, but she maintained a fairly good control over her feelings.

"Of course you understand that it will be impossible for me to have Mr. Ferreira under my roof after this!"

"He isn't coming any more."

"Mr. Sturt will consult his solicitor. You are prepared to sustain your evidence in the witness-box, Nicholas?"

"If necessary."

"A child like Lore and my husband! Why, she might be his daughter—granddaughter, I was going to say! He scarcely speaks six words to her in a month. Are you sure you are not both of you making a mistake?"

Celia laughed. "I quite agree that poor Mr. Sturt is about the worst possible selection Maurice could have made. One can only imagine that his motive is a vindictive one."

"What reason has he for being vindictive?"

"Of course, it's public property, Mrs. Sturt, that he would pay his addresses to Evelyn if allowed."

"Oh, the scoundrel!"

"All the same, I don't think you would be well-advised to take the step you propose. I always regard a law case as nothing more

than a huge advertisement. Instead of ten or twenty people knowing about it, it will very likely get into the London newspapers.
You would get damages, of course, but that won't prevent acquaintances from making your own remark—that there is no
smoke without fire."

"There's no other way of stopping his mouth."

"I think I should simply ignore him."

"Ignore him!—while these lies are being circulated! You must
be mad, my dear!"

"Possibly I am looking at things from a wrong angle. I don't
know. But it seems to me that if you personally kept up relations
with Lore that would be the very best reply to all scandalmongers.
As long as you are on terms with her, there can't be anything in it.
Maurice will soon discover the futility of his campaign."

"I cannot continue to visit that abominable house!"

"It need not be very often, nor for very long. Lore is too proud
to take flight, but as soon as affairs have quietened down somewhat she will be only too eager to shake the dust of the place off
her feet. You will really be constructing a bridge for her to retreat
by. Probably she will sell the house, or, at least, not come back for
a very long time. I believe in the superior efficacy of smooth
methods. One secures better results, with less fuss and anxiety."

"It might have been possible yesterday, but to-day it isn't.
Katherine and I declined to recognise her in the street last evening."

"That can be represented as an accidental omission."

"We met her face to face, and we were the only people in the
road. Quite out of the question!"

Celia reflected.

"But if a temporary resumption of relations could be arranged,
would you be prepared?"

"If it were *very* temporary! I certainly don't want people to be
under the impression that I have broken with Lore for the reason
you state. I expect they *would* think so."

"In all probability they would," said Celia with a light and
nervous laugh.

“On the other hand, I will *not* apologise to that woman!”

“I don’t think you need see her, even, at first. One of your daughters could call and put things on a footing.”

“At that scandalous house!”

“Perhaps Mr. Cabot would escort whichever one you send.”

“With pleasure!” said Nicholas.

Mrs. Sturt pondered for a few moments with a displeased look.

“Then it would have to be Evelyn. Audrey is too young, and Katherine would flatly refuse. Very likely Evelyn will refuse, too.”

“Try to persuade her! You try, too, Mr. Cabot! I know Lore has the highest opinion of her. . . . And if she fails to bring about a reconciliation I will go round there myself. But of course the first advances will be expected to come from you.”

The obliging offer had the effect of considerably modifying the asperity of the eye which Mrs. Sturt turned upon her interlocutor. For the first time since the topic of Lore was raised, her manner visibly softened.

“But really it is no affair of yours, my dear, and I can’t trouble you! . . .”

“Oh, I have received too many kindnesses from you in the past, Mrs. Sturt, not to wish to make a partial return!” responded Celia with a mantling colour and an indescribable intonation of voice.

The older woman rose to go.

“Why do we see so little of you?”

“It’s my incurable indolence!” said Celia, smiling. “When it comes to the point, I can never make up my mind to go anywhere. I really will take you at your word and call one day this week.”

“I wish you would,” said Mrs. Sturt. “The girls are always talking about you.”

The young widow accompanied her visitor through the house, then returned to Nicholas, who still sat obstinately smoking.

“Have I won the bet?” she demanded triumphantly.

“You certainly have.”

“Then you forfeit the stake?”

“I do.”

“And you are to obey me for a week from to-day?”

“So it seems.”

“My first command is that you shall come and take tea with me every day.”

“With pleasure.”

“A slave does not express pleasure, but only obedience. . . . My second command is that you are without fail to convey Evelyn to Lore’s no later than this evening.”

“And if she declines to go?”

“In that case you are not to show your face here any more.”

“Then how can I come to tea?”

“It is merely my way of indicating that I shall refuse to admit the plea of inability. If necessary, you must throw her over your shoulder and carry her that way. But go she must!”

“Very well.”

“And my third and last command, for the time being, is that you shall communicate to her the fact that it is I who suggested that she should go. I don’t wish to hide my light under a bushel.”

Nicholas regarded her in perplexity.

“I say, I wish you’d tell me! . . . I’ll do as you say, of course— but is there anything up between you two? Whenever I go from one to the other of you I always have the curious sensation of being in the thick of a sort of silent *feud!* Have you anything against Evelyn Sturt?”

“My dear, I don’t fight with little girls!” laughed Celia rather hurriedly. “It’s a favourite mode of recreation of mine to mystify people, and these intense young things are such perfect subjects! Don’t tell anyone!”

“So it’s a joke?”

“Does it penetrate?”

“I quite see you’re making fun of her, but why has she been chosen for the honour?”

“Because she is absolutely without sense of humour!” returned

Celia.

Nicholas was more perplexed than ever.

XII

THE VISION

A quarter of an hour after the conclusion of dinner Evelyn knocked softly at the door of Nicholas's room and was admitted. He closed the door after her, and invited her to take a chair, but did not sit down himself.

"Mother is to make it up with Lore," she announced immediately. "She wants me to act as ambassador. I am afraid she will have to find someone else!"

Nicholas looked rather embarrassed. "I was at Mrs. Hantish's this afternoon when they were discussing it."

"What on earth has Mrs. Hantish to do with it?"

"Nothing, I suppose; but your mother opened the subject, and she had no option."

"Did you accompany mother, or did you meet her there?"

"I met her there."

"Did she go round about that specially, do you know?"

"I *don't* know."

"I hope she wasn't foolish enough to go round about something else! . . . But is this strange reconciliation Celia's idea?"

"Yes."

"Then she over-persuaded mother?"

"She put things in a new light for her."

"Celia is rather good at putting things in new lights! What were her arguments?"

"She said that the breach would be misrepresented."

"Why?"

"Because Ferreira is spreading malicious reports."

"About whom?"

"I have no right to say," replied Nicholas, nearly roughly. It was evident that the cross-examination was exhausting his stock of patience. "If you want further particulars, you had better ask your mother."

Evelyn looked at him queerly, and was silenced for a moment or two. At the end of the pause she asked:

"Was it also Celia's scheme that I should be selected for the peace mission?"

"She wishes to take the credit for it. *Why*, I don't know."

"But I know!"

He did not press her.

"It was to put one more humiliation on me!" proceeded Evelyn with a savage little glint of the eyes. "Lore has taken Maurice from me, and I am not to be permitted the consolation of hating her for it. I am to reveal my abjectness of spirit by praying for favours! . . . And, of course, Celia's triumph would be incomplete if I were to remain in ignorance whose hand has aimed the blow!"

"Don't you think all this is somewhat far-fetched? You seem to take it quite for granted that she is actuated by ill-feelings towards you. Why should she be?"

"Oh, you are a man! Can't you understand that it's perfectly possible for two women to loathe and detest each other without a reason? She knows I see through and through her, and that is reason enough, in all conscience! . . ."

Her outburst was succeeded by a dead silence on both sides, lasting for a full half-minute.

"Why did Maurice leave you so quickly this morning?" demanded Evelyn at length.

"We came to loggerheads. He's gone for good."

"May I ask the cause of the dispute?"

"It was connected with Lore's business. He resented my free comments on his behaviour."

"My name wasn't introduced?"

"No."

There was another shorter interval. "How will it affect your work?"

"I shall have to find another workman, that's all. It will put back things, but it can't be helped."

"In the meantime, what have you to show me?"

By way of answer Nicholas walked across to the bracket-cupboard, where his smaller materials were stored. He lifted out the circular metal box with which she was already acquainted, and deposited it on the table before the window. Evelyn watched all his movements in cold reserve, yet with a shade of anxiety. As he prepared, still without speaking, to set the clockwork motor governing the revolving lid in motion, she asked:

"Can't you spare an introductory word?"

"It's hardly worth while. It will only last two minutes, as before."

"But since you say it isn't the same, what is the difference?"

"It's a single exposure. I borrowed a hint from Ferreira. It's an actual record of what I was dreaming from three o'clock to two minutes past, this morning."

"Is it very terrifying?"

"It certainly is impressive. You needn't see it if you don't wish to."

"That's absurd!" she responded quietly. "I came to see it."

Nicholas, who had been pausing with his hand on the starting lever, to allow her the opportunity of withdrawing, should she so elect, now at once pulled it back. Then he took the nearest chair.

Without any shock of surprise, Evelyn found herself walking in a wood. The path she was on formed a rude avenue, just wide enough to permit two persons to pass, dividing the forest which closed in on either hand. It was almost like being between walls, the trees were so thick, straight, branchless and tall. The intervening spaces were rendered impenetrable by the close tangle of underbrush, and there was no other way of getting out of the wood than by the path, in either one direction or the other. The ground was inches deep in loose, fine dust, which upon the slightest disturbance by her foot filled the air with its choking particles, having a peculiarly disgusting, acrid smell, like burnt rags. To a considerable distance above her head everything was in shadow, but above the tree-tops showed a pale blue sky, creating a singular impression of heat and discomfort. The whole atmosphere of her situation was one of perpetuity. The path was only visible to its first bend, about twenty yards ahead; behind her she could see still less of it; yet she had an intuitive feeling that it went on and on, and back and back, for miles without change.

Strangely enough, she seemed to herself to be a *man*, though it never occurred to her to investigate the point, by glancing at her clothing, for instance. Another curious circumstance which she failed to recognise was that her memory belonged to her present experience, not to her waking experience as Evelyn Sturt. She was *continuing* to walk through the wood. Her feminine identity only remained as an under-consciousness, vaguely puzzling her, without drawing attention to itself.

Suddenly she became aware that *something* was about to turn the bend of the path which she herself had rounded a few moments earlier. She stopped, horrified, and attempted to crouch in among the brushwood bordering the avenue. Her heart thudded, her limbs shook violently, while a cold sweat stood on her face, as she thrust her body far backwards in intuitive anticipation of the vision. Her eyes were distended, in fastening themselves on the corner where it was to appear. She knew that she was doomed to a supernatural encounter.

Then she saw it.

It was Lore! But not the Lore of everyday life. This Lore, who glided towards her with such awful smoothness and regularity, was not human. She was a *spirit*. And she was coming straight up to her; there was no escape from the fearful contact. . . . But when she was less than a dozen paces distant, the features of the white face grew distinct for the first time through the gloom, and, as they did so, Evelyn saw on them such a shocking, set expression of agonised despair, that her feelings underwent a sudden revulsion and, forgetting all terror, she jumped up and out of her recess to run towards the other. It was such an expression as a woman might wear who is being removed from a torture-chamber, knowing that she is to return there a few hours later, when her strength has been sufficiently restored. The eyes were lustreless, the chin drooped, the mouth stood partly open, and there were lines of pain. She seemed equally to be past weeping, struggling, and hoping. Her soul was a live nerve, and all that she had to look forward to was dreadful suffering without end. . . .

Evelyn cried out, in the voice of a man, and hurried forward. The blood was in her cheeks. She was moved by such grief and horror that it was as if Lore were someone very dear to her. As they came together, the sufferer looked up with sullen, spiritless eyes. She addressed Evelyn quietly and slowly, and every word seemed to be a pain:

"Do help me before it's too late! It will soon be too late!"

Almost before the appeal was concluded, and while the sound of her voice was still in Evelyn's ears, the whole vision was extinguished! Lore, the forest, the acrid odour of the dust, her own queer masculine sensations—all vanished, simultaneously, unexpectedly, and without warning. Once more she was aware of herself as a girl, standing by the open window, in a familiar room, bathed in the rich reflected light of the sun's afterglow, with Nicholas beside her. Both had automatically risen. Every detail of the dream was present in her memory in such impressive vividness that several moments passed before she was able to understand what had happened to her.

"Thank you!" she said at last.

Nicholas, without a word, lifted the metal box to restore it to the cupboard.

"May I sit down again for a minute, till I have discovered where I am?" asked the girl, with a brave attempt at smiling.

"Do, please!"

She seated herself, and was silent for a few seconds.

Then she inquired, with assumed lightness:

"What do you think of it yourself?"

"As a dream, or an experiment, do you mean?"

"As a dream."

"I think I have struck the real thing," replied Nicholas in a low voice.

"What you called a 'deep-sleep dream'?"

"Yes. It isn't a fantasy, like ordinary dreams. It's an oracle. A *message*, if you like."

Evelyn looked at him intently. "You do think that?"

"Don't *you* feel as if you'd had a visitation?"

"Yes. . . . And will you act on this . . . message?"

"I shall do nothing more till my big apparatus is finished. I shall have more to go by then."

"I referred to Lore. If she is in distress, or if there is some danger or unpleasantness hanging over her head, ought we to sit down calmly and wait? Oughtn't we to warn her, or something?"

"Warn her of what?"

"Of something threatening her." She bent her head downwards, and traced the carpet with the tip of her shoe. It was Nicholas's turn to scrutinise her.

"You don't mean Ferreira?"

"Those awful words of hers are still ringing in my head, Nicholas. . . . 'Help me before it is too late! It will soon be too late!' . . . Either they mean something or they mean nothing."

"She is refusing to see him again, as far as I know."

"Oh, it would be too terrible if anything were to happen! He can be perfectly reckless at times. We ought to try to persuade her to go away at once . . . *at once!* . . ." She started up impulsively. "I'm going round there *now*, Nicholas!"

"I don't see how you can get her to go if she doesn't want to. You can't tell her anything she doesn't know already."

"Oh, you are quite right, I know, but I should never, never forgive myself if anything were to take place which I might have prevented! Please don't try to dissuade me. I'm going now."

"Then I'll come with you."

"If you will."

"I'll just put my things away. Be in the hall in five minutes' time."

Within a quarter of an hour they were outside Lore's house. The air was oppressively close. Although the sun had set, it was still quite light. No words had been exchanged during the short walk; Nicholas was silent and preoccupied, while Evelyn grew more agitated at each step they took towards their destination.

As they walked up the tiled pathway leading to the front door, they observed the profile of the French companion at the open window of the drawing-room. The sallow features were as impassive and inscrutable as ever, as she bent over her eternal needlework. She must have heard the gate swing, yet revealed no recognition of their passage to the house entrance. Someone was playing a Bach fugue on the piano in the same room.

"It's Lore!" murmured Evelyn; but Nicholas had already visualised her at the instrument. There could be no doubt about the ownership of that emphatic, masterly touch. After pausing for a moment or two longer to listen, he pressed the electric bell-push.

The page-boy opened the door. Evelyn gave him her card to take to his mistress, and the boy, after showing them into a reception-room, disappeared on the errand. The Bach fugue continued.

They took chairs in different corners of the room. Nicholas's eyes wandered absently, but the girl studied her shoes. When three minutes had passed thus, the page returned, to notify that his mistress was not at home.

Nicholas uttered an exclamation, and was about to follow it by a sarcastic remark, when Evelyn laid a restraining hand on his arm. She thanked the boy with a smile, and at once led the way out of the room and out of the house.

As they made their way down the garden path once more, the strains of Bach swelled to full majesty. Both turned their heads instinctively to look towards the open window, but of course Lore was not to be seen. The Frenchwoman was still sitting there, in the same attitude and with the same sickly bitterness on her waxen features—except that it now seemed to the two that there was the shadow of a smile on her lips which had not been there before. Evelyn quickly withdrew her gaze, and continued down the path with her eyes straight before her.

"What a fiasco!" exclaimed Nicholas, with a curt laugh, as

soon as they were past the house.

"She is quite justified," was the quiet reply.

"Yes, I suppose the temptation to get her own back was rather strong. . . . So you don't get your interview!"

"I must think of some way of seeing her."

"Mrs. Hantish will probably be calling there to-morrow. She might fix something up for you. Shall I ask her?"

"Why is she visiting Lore to-morrow?"

"Because she promised your mother that if you failed she would try herself."

"Oh! . . . Oh, then she hasn't finished *yet!* She's planning something else. . . . Don't let her go, Nicholas. I believe she is trying to get those two together again, in spite of everything. She mustn't see Lore. Do dissuade her!"

"I'll undertake to dissuade her if you will persuade me she's the sort of woman you think she is! . . . I fancy you don't quite realise how you damage yourself by your continual harping on that string. She's just an average decent-minded person, who wants to help, if it isn't too far out of her road. Besides, I can't ask her to go back on her word to your mother. I'll try and get her to promise to keep away from the Ferreira topic, if you like. She's done all that she contracted to do there."

"Very well, do that," said Evelyn listlessly. "And ask her to try to arrange a meeting for me with Lore, to-morrow. It's the very first time I have ever openly acknowledged her influence, so perhaps she may consent for the novelty's sake. . . . I only hope Lore refuses to listen to mother's overtures. If she really cuts herself adrift, I shall regard it as a token of her speedy departure. She can't live down here entirely isolated."

They arrived at the gate of Mereway and passed into the drive.

"I shall be seeing Mrs. Hantish in the morning, after breakfast," said Nicholas.

"The acquaintance seems to develop!"

"I'm sorry I can't adopt your prejudices."

"I haven't asked you to. However, since we are on the subject, and so as not to have to return to it, may I inquire something personal?"

"What?"

"You won't deny that you are beginning to spend a lot of your time with her. Do you honestly believe that her society is doing you any *good?*"

He coloured. "I'm not conscious of being any the worse for it."

"Still, you continue to place your work first?"

"I do."

"And yet you squander this time!"

"Any time lost during the day I have made up, and shall make up, at night. If it comes to the point, I fancy I haven't 'squandered' any more time in her society than I have in yours— if as much!"

They were actually on the doorstep. Evelyn did not choose to respond to the unmannerly retort otherwise than by a cold, understanding, pitying little smile. She said good night, and went into the house, straight up to her own room.

XIII

CELIA'S DAY

At the breakfast-table on Wednesday the hostess's tranquil, self-possessed manner successfully concealed whether she had thought it necessary to bring to her husband's knowledge what Ferreira was saying about him. Since Sturt, however, though rather more heavy-eyed and depressed than usual, manifested no sign of embarrassment in the few remarks which he made, Nicholas presumed that she was very wisely passing the matter over in silence. Whether wifely tact would be strong enough to sustain the new shock which Ferreira was preparing, was another thing altogether. He cogitated whether it would be better to drop the latter a note to the effect that affairs were on their way to being mended all round, if only he kept quiet, or to treat the threat of exposure as a piece of bluff and disregard it.

But the morning was bright, his hostess was courteous, Katherine was talkative again, and Audrey bubbled with high spirits. Such a day unrolled itself before him as a fortnight earlier he could not have conceived in his fondest imaginings. His healthy young male soul was impatient of underground intrigue, and longed to rise to the surface and sunshine. He was only a paying guest there. Life was too short for that sort of thing. Sturt must get himself out of his own messes! . . . He began to respond in kind to Audrey, with regular returns to his plate.

The conversation circled round the preparations for the approaching fête, which the youngest daughter's unaided enthusiasm had succeeded in transferring from the realm of the hypothetical to that of the actual. The services of a professional sewing-maid had been requisitioned for the fancy dresses. Audrey herself was to go as an *odalisque*; Evelyn as a Roman patrician. Their father had sent to a theatrical friend in town for the stage jewellery and ornaments belonging to those characters. Katherine still declined to accompany her sisters, but she had discontinued her sneers at the function and was displaying a normal interest in the manufacture of the costumes. Evelyn appeared far more bored and indifferent than she.

After repeated hammering, Nicholas had consented to run the girls over in the car. He steadily refused to participate in the actual dancing, and Audrey's persistent offers to teach him his steps threatened to introduce discord to the table, when Mrs. Sturt reduced the combatants to silence by an amazing proposition of her own. This was no less than that Mrs. Hantish—who would certainly have received her invitation in due form—should be requested to occupy the vacant place in the Sturt four-seater, thus completing a private group of friends in a more or less public assembly.

The girls were obviously staggered.

"She's a very charming woman," proceeded their mother coolly. "Why you regard her with such suspicion, I can't imagine. She's modern, she knows good people, and she is likely to be very useful to you. Her only crime seems to be that she is a widow. She can't help that."

"Isn't this rather a *volte-face*, mother?" asked Audrey with an assumption of diffidence.

"Not at all. I have always regarded Mrs. Hantish as a desirable acquaintance, only you girls have been too busy persecuting her to notice it. I think that sort of thing might stop now. She's wonderfully good-natured about it, but it reflects on yourselves. Sarcasm doesn't pay in the long run."

"The only complaint I have against her is that she dresses unsuitably to the country," said Katherine. "I have certainly never consciously been rude to her."

"If you haven't, your sisters have. Evelyn especially!"

"I scarcely ever speak to her," replied Evelyn.

"Exactly! You scarcely ever speak to her, and when you do speak it is to say something crushing. Your manner can be terrible. Has she ever upset you in any way?"

"Not at one time more than another. I simply dislike her."

"One can see that!"

"I can't help it. It's a natural antipathy. One person is disagreeably affected by cats, and another by hyacinths in a room, and I am disagreeably affected by Celia Hantish. It's a pity, but the only remedy seems to be to keep us apart."

From the glance of cold displeasure which Mrs. Sturt threw at her second daughter, Nicholas guessed that even after all these years of intimacy the two still remained strangers to one another. The subject was dropped at once, as though the mother knew from past experience that, Evelyn having definitely expressed herself, it would be mere waste of time to attempt to combat her views. To retain the last word, she contented herself with adding:

"At all events, do try to make things a little more pleasant for her when she *is* here. It isn't as if she were in any way dependent on our society."

After they had risen from table, Mrs. Sturt detained Nicholas for a moment while the others were leaving the room. "I'm sorry you both had your trouble for nothing last evening. I wonder if you would have time to run round to Mrs. Hantish before beginning work? I could send a note by one of the maids, but a personal message would be more courteous."

"I'll go round with pleasure! I shall be away all day, as a matter of fact."

"Are you taking a holiday?"

"I'm going to Southampton."

She did not care to inquire more closely into his plans. "I don't need to tell you what to say. Ask her if it would be possible for her to call on Miss Jensen this morning."

"Very well."

"You will let me know her answer at once?"

"Certainly."

"It's awfully good of you! . . . There's another thing. I have been thinking over this business of Maurice Ferreira. Much as I dislike him, I feel I have no right to permit my personal prejudices to interfere with your working plans, so, providing Mrs. Hantish is able to arrange this other matter for me, I am going to withdraw my objection to his continued visits to your room. You must please yourself about it. Of course, this has to be conditional on Miss Jensen's acceptance of my offer to return to the old state of affairs. You understand that!"

"Of course," replied Nicholas.

At ten o'clock, accordingly, he made his way to The Arbour, anticipating his appointment by half an hour on the strength of this new commission. The morning was a beautiful one. The sun was hot, but clouds had sprung up overnight, and the wind had veered round to south-west, cooling and softening the air. The profusion of roses in the gardens, as he passed along, was un-exampled; they seemed to grow wild. A young and prettily-dressed girl, having long plaits down her back, was met carrying a bouquet of newly-gathered garden flowers, the bouquet being nearly as big as herself. No one else was in sight. Everything was quiet and peaceful, while the tree-tops were swaying in the breeze.

The only connecting-link between himself and the great outside world of men and work was the very faint starting whistle from a goods engine at the junction two miles away. The sound—insignificant as it was, and only one of a hundred sense-impressions—made him uneasy. He felt that he, too, ought to be at work instead of sauntering past flower gardens on his way to an appointment with a pretty woman! . . .

For a moment he hesitated whether or not to turn back and not call on her at all. It was a promise, however, and he also had Mrs. Sturt's message to deliver. He could easily make up the lost time on two or three successive nights. The house, moreover, was just at hand, and he had probably already been seen. It would look like a flight, and it really would be a flight. . . . As he passed through the garden gate he cast off his disagreeable doubts, as one puts off shoes at the threshold of an Eastern temple, surrendering himself to the clean, light, gay atmosphere of the home of this most insouciant of all fashionable women!

He had ten minutes to wait in the elegant, sunlit morning-room before being permitted to see her. Then she strolled in, smiling, and regarded him at a distance, from just inside the doorway. He apologised for disturbing her so early.

"My dear boy, you could have asked yourself to breakfast if you had liked!" was the careless reply. "Has anything happened?"

"Mrs. Sturt wished me to see you. Evelyn and I went to Lore's last night, and . . ."

"And failed, of course, and I am wanted to come to the rescue! . . . But tell me what took place."

"She wouldn't see us."

Celia laughed. "I thought she wouldn't! Was Evelyn angry?"

"She didn't show it. I have another message for you, from *her*. If you are going to Lore's, she wishes to know if you could try and fix up an interview for her."

"What persistence!"

"Oh, this hasn't anything to do with her mother's affair. It's a personal matter."

"Then I suppose her feelings are getting too strong for her at last! . . . Well, I'll slip my things on, and we'll go round there at once."

"Am I to go?"

"So that you can carry back the necessary report, or reports."

"You think you'll be able to make peace?"

"I'll take no bet this time."

"Shall you try and get Ferreira included?"

"I shan't try, for that will probably follow of itself."

"I certainly shouldn't advise you to take the responsibility. There's no knowing what may happen if they get together again!"

Celia looked at him quizzically, without replying. She disappeared from the room, to return a few minutes later attired in a cool, featherweight, light-tinted summer frock, with a gay parasol, but without either hat or gloves. She announced herself ready to leave the house.

As they passed out of the garden gate and turned down towards Yetholm, Nicholas casually mentioned Mrs. Sturt's proposal that she should be invited to accompany the Mereway party to the Colminster Fête on the following Saturday week.

"Would you accept?" he demanded.

"Who is going?"

"Evelyn, Audrey, and myself."

"I had tickets sent me, but I have nothing to dance in."

"You needn't dance. I shan't, either."

"This is rather pointed!"

"Oh, I don't mean that. . . . But I wish you would come."

Celia promptly lowered her sunshade, which only a minute before she had put up.

"Whether I go or not, what difference can it possibly make to your enjoyment?"

"There will be all the difference for me between an exciting time and a boring one!"

"Is 'exciting' really the word you mean?"

"Why not?"

She blushed, and laughed.

"It's frightfully good and sweet of you, but unfortunately I know you're not speaking the truth. Evelyn is to be of the party, you said."

"What of it?"

"You can't persuade me that she bores you!"

"She certainly doesn't excite me."

"I'm not sure."

"Evelyn or no Evelyn, I want you to come."

"But I haven't been asked yet."

"You will be asked."

"As chaperon, perhaps."

"Well, while the girls are dancing you can chaperon me."

"Mrs. Sturt won't want that!"

"Never mind Mrs. Sturt! Say 'yes.'"

"You are a horridly persistent man!"

"Then it's a promise?"

"It appears I have no option."

Nicholas turned away, to conceal his agitation, while Celia once more elected to raise her parasol. As Lore's house by this time was barely a dozen paces distant, the action was foolishly superfluous, but neither of the two noticed anything strange in it. There was no time to start another topic before they were at the gate itself.

Lore was alone in the breakfast-room when they were shown in. The room was sunless, but its open windows looked out on to the bright garden, which gave Nicholas the sense of being in a theatre box. The breakfast things were still on the table, mostly untouched, and Lore remained sitting hunched-up in the arm-chair at the head, yet, to judge by the number of cigarette ends on one of the saucers, her meal, such as it was, had been finished some time ago. She continued to smoke, not getting up for her visitors, whom she regarded with heavy, smouldering eyes. Her black silk blouse, short-sleeved and low-necked, gave her a tragic aspect, which was intensified by the stern immobility of her features, and both Celia and Nicholas immediately guessed that she was attitudinising. Celia seated herself, without invitation, near the window.

"Won't you sit, too?" inquired Lore of Nicholas, in a dull voice and scarcely glancing at him. He did so, and a brief pause ensued.

"This is Nicholas's second shot at seeing you," remarked Celia lightly, by way of opening the conversation. "He came last night with Evelyn Sturt. Were you told?"

"I was told 'a young gentleman,' and guessed who it was."

"Why wouldn't you see him?"

"He didn't send his name in. The person I declined to see was the person whose card was brought to me."

"Oh, it was like that!"

There was another pause, during which Lore drew gloomily at her cigarette.

"Now that you have sufficiently asserted yourself, I should think you might make friends again," suggested Celia, half un-furling her parasol to examine its interior.

"Do you mean with the Sturt women?"

"Yes, my dear. . . . We know they're in the wrong, but it's all so stupid, from beginning to end! Couldn't you be apologised to, or something, and let the affair die a natural death?"

"Have you come from Mrs. Sturt?"

"Not altogether. I suppose I'm really acting for myself. It makes it so wretchedly embarrassing for me, being friends of both of you. Can't something be done?"

Lore eyed Nicholas. "And what are *you* doing here?"

"Oh, he has a watching brief for Evelyn!" laughed Celia quickly. "She has her own peculiar interests, apart from her mother."

"I hope that girl doesn't imagine that *her* entreaties are going to turn the scale!"

"She wants you to see her about something else," said Nicholas.

"What?"

"A private matter."

"Do you mean Maurice?"

Nicholas did not answer.

"Poor Maurice!" said Celia, smiling. "Like Ishmael, every man's hand is against him. Nicholas and he came to fisticuffs yesterday. He took his revolver away from him."

"Why does she want to see me about Maurice? She can have him any time she requires, without my interference. I've done with him finally."

"Will you, or won't you, see her?" demanded Nicholas with increasing irritability.

"I won't, and that's flat!"

"But what about the other business?" asked Celia lightly. "You surely have nothing to gain from pursuing a little local feud to the bitter end! It isn't worth the annoyance it gives you."

"I'm very sorry, Celia, but I'm afraid my brains aren't nimble enough to chase Mrs. Sturt's humours up and down. One day she insults me, and the next day she says it doesn't matter! What's wrong with her? Doesn't she know her own mind, or what is it?"

"She acted in haste and is repenting at leisure, my dear. She will give you all the necessary explanations and apologies, if you will only consent to listen to her."

"I may be disreputable, but I'm not soft!"

"You are neither the one nor the other. Do be sensible, Lore! You're not being asked to do anything *infra dig*.[6] She is the one who will have to humiliate herself."

"I will spare her the pain."

"Won't you be sweet, and let one of the girls call?"

"Oh, I've been sweet quite long enough! . . . She and that old-fashioned frump Katherine! To be in their house always affects me like drinking *eau sucrée*[7] and my digestion is not over-strong! How I have stood it so long, I don't know. And now, to bring it to a climax, they have the crazy impertinence to cut me in the street! *They!*—those society leaders! Who do they imagine they are? It would be a joke if it weren't such appalling impudence! *They* to dispose of *me!* . . . Mrs. Sturt had better be exceedingly careful what she's doing—you may tell her that, with my kind regards! I have a sting, too, if I care to use it, and a tiny bit more venomous than hers, perhaps. The matter with me is that I'm far too easy-going."

Direct persuasion having failed, Celia held her peace and gazed out of doors musingly, until such time as her trump-card could be played with greatest effect. Lore continued to brood for a few moments, then rose impetuously from the table, sweeping the crockery away with her hand as she did so. She flung herself into an easy chair in a dark corner.

"What was the fight with Maurice over?" She addressed Nicholas. "Me?"

"It had to do with you indirectly."

"Was he telling tales about me, and did you object? Was that it?"

"Not quite that, but something like it."

"Oh, he's a cad! I know what particular lie he was trying to negotiate."

This was Celia's opening.

"You don't seem to realise Maurice's present state of mind,

6. Shortened form of "infra dignitatem", "beneath one's dignity".
7. Sugar water.

my dear. Your continued refusal to see him has transformed him into a sort of Mad Mullah. He's hardly responsible for his actions—certainly not for his words. He appears to imagine that you're his personal property, even after all this trouble, and that you are not to be allowed to have any communication with other men at all. That attitude would be perfectly intolerable in a husband even."

"What men are you talking about, Celia. I never see any men."

"I know you don't. Disordered imaginations fight with shadows, and it seems he has been counting up the few visits Mr. Sturt has paid you by way of professional compliment. He threatens to pass on to Mrs. Sturt everything he can rake together, and a bit more."

"The skunk! He's not mad. This is at me!"

"I've done all I can. I have prepared her for the blow, when it falls. She wished to consult a solicitor at first, till I persuaded her to do no such idiotic thing. I told her clearly that her only remedy is to keep up appearances with you. . . ."

"Now I grasp her magnanimous repentance!"

"Because, of course, he will tell others as well, and Mr. Sturt's having been an actor will not assist the prevailing of the truth in the minds of certain simple people. . . . I hope you'll reconsider?"

"I'll think it over."

"In the meantime, while you are thinking it over, won't you let Evelyn come round and see you?"

Lore bit her finger-tips nervously.

"No!"

"Then what shall I tell Mrs. Sturt? I have promised to let her know."

After a brief silence, Lore rose and began to walk about. "Oh, I don't care a damn one way or the other! If she wants to keep up the farce, she may! I don't require any hypocritical apology. Either she can come here or I'll go round there. . . . It's a lovely thing to be a woman, isn't it? You're nine parts reputation and one part human being! I'd rather be insulted by a woman all day long than have to give her a false kiss—though I've given a good many in my time; that's true! Oh, well, it can't be helped!"

"Will you be at home this afternoon, if she comes?"

"No, not this afternoon. They have kept me waiting, and now I'll keep them waiting. If I have nothing better to do, I may stroll round to Mereway to-morrow, after dinner. I'll see."

"And what about Maurice?"

"What about him?"

"Hadn't you better see him too, to find out what he's up to?"

Lore turned suddenly to Nicholas. "You still have that revolver?"

"Yes, it's locked away."

"You keep it locked away, or there'll be murder one of these days! I'll find a way of dealing with Maurice, Celia."

Celia got up to go, and Nicholas imitated her. Lore, still moody-browed, accompanied them as far as the door of the room only. There was no hand-shaking, but as they were moving into the passage she stayed Nicholas with another question:

"Is he still working for you?"

"Not at present."

"Of course he wouldn't be, after that sort of treatment. I congratulate you on being stronger than I gave you credit for! And Mrs. Sturt couldn't very well have him in her house, either. I only thought you might carry a message—but it doesn't matter."

"Mrs. Sturt tells me I can have him back, if I want to; but it won't be to-day or to-morrow, if at all."

"Evidently she likes you as a boarder!" sneered Lore. Celia laughed, but Nicholas became rather thoughtful.

Hardly were they beyond the threshold when the door was kicked to behind them.

In the roadway the handsome, hatless Celia, carrying her gay sunshade furled, walked along by the side of her companion in a subdued manner which was new to her.

"Poor Lore!"

"What is the matter with her, really? It can't be simply this twopenny-halfpenny affair."

"She's an unhappy girl, my dear!"

"By disposition, do you mean?"

"Not altogether; nor do I altogether mean the life she leads. She has sold her art soul to the money-devil—that's the true cause of her unhappiness. She has taken to drugs and drink to make herself forget. You can't understand that, perhaps? Lore is worth all the rest of us put together!"

"Intellectually?"

"Yes; and in heart, and generosity, and soul! If I were a man, I would fall in love with Lore. That's why it is really impossible for me to be angry with Maurice. He has perception."

"Then how comes she to be so mercenary?"

"Because she was down to her last five-pound note, and the public hate genius with a deadly hatred. She simply *had* to make money somehow. She accommodated herself, found it profitable, and now, when she could afford to write good music again, she isn't able to—her inspiration is dried up! Can you imagine a more shocking moral tragedy? . . . And smug, complacent little people like the Sturts look the other way when they meet her in the street!"

They proceeded in silence for a moment or two.

"You were going to tell me something about her relations with Sturt," said Nicholas.

"It's really ancient history, my dear. When she was considerably younger than she is now, they were very much thrown together for a time. In fact he was practically running two establishments. That was in town, of course."

"So Ferreira's statement was correct?"

"He's right, up to the point that Lore was Sturt's mistress. But it's all rubbish about her being here to blackmail him. Not only are they on excellent terms together, but ever since he quitted his professional work his wife has taken money matters into her own hands, so that I doubt whether he could divert a treasury-note without her knowledge."

"Isn't it rather a piece of audacity to select the same district to live in?"

"You can call it audacity or you can call it friendship. He's the best friend Lore has ever had, or is ever likely to have, and I presume she couldn't bear the idea of losing sight of him, though she only spends a fraction of her time here, when all is said and done. The affair was more sentimental than unsavoury, even at its zenith. She was, for him, merely an interesting young foreigner on the threshold of her career. She attracted him, he was able to give her introductions, and the rest followed. He furnished rooms for her, in her own name, where she did exactly as she pleased, treating him just like any other acquaintance. She used to play to him on his sporadic visits, which were chiefly in the afternoons. He was a very much occupied man then. And I think that's about as far as the intimacy extended. If you can imagine a Platonic liaison, that would be a good name for it. . . . Of course, after the failure of his managership, the Sturts had to retrench, and the second establishment went the way of all things."

"How long ago was all this?"

"Ten or eleven years. Maurice is an ill-conditioned wretch to bring it all up, with embellishments, after so long! No one was a penny the worse for it while it lasted, for if he hadn't spent the money on her it would have melted just the same.

"Are they still infatuated with each other?"

"I have been trying all along to tell you that they never were!" replied Celia, rather sharply for her.

"If it is public property, how does it happen that his wife knows nothing about it?"

"Are you quite sure she doesn't?"

Nicholas had no answer ready.

"Some wives are very ready to accept assurances," remarked Celia, by way of concluding the subject.

Outside The Arbour they halted to debate their plans for the day. His proposition was to run round to Mereway, to communicate the result of the visit to Mrs. Sturt and Evelyn. Celia, on the other hand, insisted that it would serve the purpose equally well to scribble a couple of notes while she herself was upstairs dressing, which afterwards she could have sent round. It then emerged that she was uncertain about the shopping expedition to

Southampton. It was Wednesday, and Wednesday (she half fancied) was the early closing day for the shops. There should be a fast non-stop train up to town from Southampton West Station at a few minutes before twelve, unless they had taken it off; how would it be if they were to run up for a matinée, followed by a little shopping there, returning home after an early dinner? It was then eleven o'clock. Celia's man could drive them down to the West Station in well under half an hour.

She urged the scheme with such smiling enthusiasm that he could scarcely have denied her even if he had wished, and he did not wish. They entered the house together. After installing her guest at the writing-table, with the freedom of her stationery cabinet, she vanished. Nicholas, after a moment's thought before each, proceeded to pen a couple of Lacedaemonian notes, to which he added a third.

To Mrs. Sturt he wrote:

Everything is all right. Miss Jensen will call on you to-morrow.

Evelyn's missive was still shorter:

Lore refuses to see you.

The third note, which caused him more perplexity and hesitation than either of the others, was to Ferreira:

Things are in train for a settlement all round. Don't do anything, but come round and see me to-morrow (Thursday).

He had hardly laid down his pen when Celia re-entered the room, equipped for the train journey and town. A smart wrap covered, without entirely concealing, a pretty restaurant frock which was as elaborate as travel permitted; and the toilet was completed by a small coloured hat, coming down nearly to her eyes. While putting the necessary-unnecessary finishing touches to her attire, she walked about, glancing in every direction but his. There was a sort of haughty impatience in her movements which produced an instant chill in him. She did not condescend to speak, and he did not venture to. He was wondering all the time if, and how, he could have offended her since ten minutes ago. Finally giving one more angry twist to the filmy scarf round her throat, she deigned to notice the three envelopes lying on the table, and rang the bell for the maid.

With autocratic peremptoriness she issued her instructions:

"Please see that these are delivered immediately by hand. The addresses are on them. There are no answers required."

The maid took the letters and went away. Celia glanced through the window to see if the car were waiting. The chauffeur had received his orders before she had gone upstairs. Glittering with new enamel, stylishly upholstered, with a low, rakish body and eager-looking wheels, which spoke of speed even in rest, it stood drawn up in the road, just outside the gate. Nicholas also glanced at it, and the spectacle of the luxurious, high-powered machine created in him a sense of hostility towards its owner. He felt that he was being dragged by *force majeure* from his own world into hers, with which he had nothing to do. His clothes sat awkwardly on him, and he was painfully aware of his facial insignificance and his lack of presence generally. She—graceful, beautifully dressed, cool, composed, aristocratic from top to toe—was returning to her element, while he was quitting his, to be the joke of all her fashionable acquaintances, who probably, from an intellectual standpoint, were not worth the little finger of his left hand! . . . No doubt the impropriety of this personal contrast, too striking to be overlooked, was the cause of her strange new coldness towards him; she already repented her impulsiveness in having suggested London! . . .

"It isn't too late to change our plans, if you'd like to!" he brought out, rather gruffly.

"Why should we?" asked Celia in a hard, high-pitched voice,

scarcely qualified by the patronising smile which accompanied it. Giving the wrist of her long glove a final adjustment, she turned from the window and moved towards the door. A flicker of her eyelids, as she glanced round in passing, intimated to him that he was to follow.

After the brightness of the room, the passage leading to the hall appeared nearly dark. Half-way along, she stopped abruptly, as though recollecting that she had left something behind. He crushed up against the wall, to allow her to get by again. Instead of attempting to pass him, however, she seemed to pause, and before he knew what had happened, a perfumed glove was resting on his shoulder. Their faces were level, and no more than a few inches apart. Hers was smiling.

"What is it?" murmured Nicholas quickly, his chief thought being the danger of discovery by one of the maids.

"Now!—*now!*" whispered Celia, coming closer still. He kissed her twice, and scarcely even then realised the situation. She tore herself away, with a low little laugh, to hasten towards the front door. Nicholas lingered for a moment, in order to recover his wits. The whole episode was so utterly unexpected—so dreamlike!

By the time he had reached the car, the chauffeur had already assisted his mistress in, and when Nicholas joined her she was once more rearranging her scarf with all the cold aloofness of preoccupied beauty.

It was not until they were in a deep road-cutting, half a mile from the house, that she smiled at him again, behind the chauffeur's back.

"Shocked?" she asked lightly.

Nicholas shook his head, with a return smile, but would not trust himself to speak. A more introspective nature than his might have been hard put to it to analyse with exactitude the curious feelings that passed through his mind during the seven miles drive to Southampton.

They arrived back at Newleigh Station the same evening as it was growing quite dark. Celia was rather tired, and very quiet, though still sweet. A cab was found, and he put her in it, but both thought it advisable that he should not accompany her. She shook hands with him through the window, after making him promise to visit her on the following afternoon.

Nicholas walked back by the road, as the short cut through the fields and spinney would be too dark. There was no moon, and the sky was already alight with liquid stars, which appeared larger and nearer than those seen in a town sky. His eyes were upturned for the greater part of the way home.

The lower rooms of Mereway were illuminated on his arrival, but, after requesting one of the maids to inform her mistress that he was in, he passed straight up to his room. The night was warm. He produced his pipe, dragged an easy chair to the open casement-window, and sat smoking till midnight. The weird and unidentifiable noises which come from out of doors on a summer night startled him occasionally, but by degrees the stillness of the rest of the world, and the prolonged darkness, solemnised his feelings, and, as one day slowly passed into another, everything seemed to close in upon him, until he appeared to himself to be the only living intelligence in the universe.

Women, vanity, love, no longer occupied his mind. He reflected on his work, and wondered whether it were after all worth while! Those awful stars—all blazing suns—suggested by comparison the absolute insignificance and impermanence of the human race, and the consequent lunacy of the human quest for lasting fame, whether in art, science, or any other sphere. The achievements of the greatest benefactor of terrestrial humanity could not by any possibility survive the decay or destruction of the earth itself, after which—in a few hundred thousands of years at the outside—the curtain would drop, and they would be as completely wiped out, forgotten, and without result as the chalk pictures of a pavement artist which might have existed twenty years ago! . . .

But what was a man to do? He must work. And, after all, it was only while he was alive that he would have the opportunity of attempting great feats. . . . And then, who knew what the ultimate destiny of the human race, and its works, might be? Humanity, in place of coming to an end on an effete and dying planet, might, for instance, migrate *en masse* to another of more likelihood. . . . His own discoveries concerning sleep and death might eventually influence the moral laws and scientific forms of a population numbering, not millions, but billions, on the other side of the universe. His name would be lost, but the fruits of his audacity might survive! . . . More wonderful still, his might be the creative idea which would succeed in bridging the twin-worlds of the living and the dead! . . .

At twelve o'clock he started work. He set the furnace going, and commenced to vaporise, combine and separate his liquids and crystals, until he had obtained sufficient new material to refill the small circular metal box. That done, he stood it for several minutes in cold water, until the sensitive substance should have become congealed into the condition of a stiff gelatine. When that at last occurred, it was ready for use.

By this time it was two o'clock in the morning. Foreseeing the improbability of his falling immediately into deep sleep—so excited was his brain by the events of the previous day—he set the clockwork mechanism which revolved the lid of the box to commence at four, by when, he calculated, he ought to be past the stage of light, restless dreams, if he were ever going to be. Then he stood the box on a table by his bedside, and started to undress.

When four o'clock approached he was still not asleep, though he had been dozing fitfully. Notwithstanding the daylight, there-fore, which was already quite bright, he was once more com-pelled to put the clock forward—this time to five.

Shortly afterwards he fell asleep.

XIV

AGAIN!

My dear Nicholas,

As it is quite on the cards that Lore may choose tea-time for her visit to Mereway to-day, I absolve you from coming to me until you have seen her home. Wasn't yesterday a jolly day?

Ever yours,
C. H.

While Nicholas was still admiring the writer's stylish calligraphy, Evelyn had occasion to enter the hall. It was not long after breakfast. She immediately recognised the handwriting of the note, which she could not very well help glancing at.

"I'm sorry!" . . . Then her lip curled. "What is it—another holiday?"

He crumpled the letter into his side-pocket. "You seem interested!"

"Not in the least. I only hope it will do you more good than yesterday's. You look as if you hadn't slept for a week."

"I was working till two, and then didn't get to sleep till four or five."

"I'm afraid I can't be sympathetic. If you will insist on burning the candle at both ends . . ."

"Do you want to speak to me about anything?"

"Oh, no! . . . Lore declines to meet me, you say? Did she give a reason?"

"Apparently she simply doesn't care to discuss Ferreira. I went round there with Mrs. Hantish. I expect your mother has told you she talks of coming here to-day?"

"Yes. Is Maurice to go back to her?"

"I don't know."

"Is she going away?"

"She didn't say."

"Is Maurice to work for you again, now that this quarrel has been more or less patched?"

"It rests with him. For one thing, I still have his revolver, and don't care about giving it up under present circumstances, so that may stand in the way—unless he would sell it as a compromise. I'm expecting him here this morning."

Evelyn stared at him. "How come you to have his revolver?"

"I thought I had told you. That was an incident in the free fight on Tuesday. I have it locked away in my drawer."

"I don't see why you need have put that humiliation on him. Of course, in another sense, it's a very good thing. It isn't very pleasant to think of his going about with a fire-arm in his pocket. I suppose that was in your head. . . . So there's nothing for me to do? Perhaps it's as well. I've been reflecting, and I have come to the conclusion that we have both been unnecessarily alarming ourselves, on the strength of an accidental dream. I should only have made myself ridiculous to Lore."

Nicholas seemed on the point of replying, but nothing came from him, and he turned away.

"Am I wrong?" demanded the girl.

"I'm afraid you are."

"How is that, then?"

"Perhaps you could come up to my room again after dinner?"

Although his previous manner had anticipated the announcement for her, she turned very pale.

"Must we wait till then?"

"I told you I'm expecting Ferreira."

After an instant's hesitation, she broke away from him and left the hall. Nicholas went upstairs.

Ferreira entered the room shortly after eleven, without knocking. His face expressed haughtiness, while his bearing was stiff. Nicholas jumped up quickly from what he was doing.

"Oh, it's you! You got my note, then?"

"Yes, I got your note."

"Sit down."

Ferreira, retaining his hat and stick, took an upright chair, while Nicholas perched himself on the edge of his work-table before the window.

"Miss Jensen is calling on Mrs. Sturt to-day," said the latter. "The visit has been agreed to. Mrs. Hantish worked it."

"Dam' good of her, I'm sure! Am I included in the armistice?"

"That I can't say."

"Is Lore going to see me?"

"Everything doesn't happen in a minute. Give her a little breathing time. I dare say things will turn out all right for you now."

"Well, I'll wait then."

"I would."

Ferreira lit a cigarette.

"Is this all you had me round here for?"

"If you care to resume work, I'm quite willing to apologise for Tuesday's business."

The other smoked in silence for a few seconds.

"An apology's all very well, old chap; but what about my revolver?"

"I have a suggestion to make about that."

"What?"

"Let me hold it for you, Ferreira, for the time being. No, listen! You're anxious to get back to the old relations with Miss Jensen. Well, you haven't an earthly chance as long as she knows the revolver is still in your possession. Leave it with me and I'll acquaint her with the fact. If you refuse, you might just as well give up all idea of seeing her again."

"Oh, you can keep it till I ask for it."

"Are you going to settle down to work again?"

"I don't mind. A hundred quid is a hundred quid—or was it guineas?"

"It was guineas."

"I'll start right away, I guess. The sooner I handle that cash, the sweeter it will taste. If Lore goes away, I shall want the

wherewithal to give chase! They haven't sent that box from town
yet?"

"Not yet."

"There's no pressing hurry, but I'll be ready for it on
Monday—bar further interruptions."

"And you ought to finish—when?"

"By this day next week."

He stripped off his coat and proceeded to bring out his tools
for the purpose of resuming his task where he had laid it down on
the previous Monday afternoon. While he was in the act of doing
so, a knock sounded outside the door. Nicholas went to open it,
and came face to face with one of the maids of the house holding
an envelope in her hand.

"Mrs. Ferreira has sent this round to young Mr. Ferreira, sir,
thinking it might be important. The boy is waiting downstairs."

Nicholas took it from her and handed it to his assistant, who
tore it open on the spot. He gave a short, explosive laugh and
threw the enclosure across to Nicholas for his perusal. The communication had been scrawled hastily on a soiled and carelessly-
detached half-sheet of note-paper, and was without superscrip-
tion.

Dine with me this evening. 8.
    Lore.

"There's no answer, tell the boy," said Ferreira.

The maid retired, closing the door behind her. Ferreira, still
chuckling, came over to Nicholas and dealt him a mighty thwack
on the back.

"Luck never leaves me for long, you bet, Cabot!"

"What does it mean?"

"What does it mean, old boy? It means I know my own business better than some others know it for me! I guess you were all
thinking I had to grovel. That's not my way. I'll give you a useful
tip, old chap, for the trouble you've taken. Women are *spasmodic*.

Always hang on quietly till the spasm's past!"

Nicholas was less certain than Ferreira seemed to be that Lore meant peace by her note, but as he saw no advantage in attempting to undeceive him he suffered him to talk on.

At half-past four that afternoon he descended to the drawing-room, leaving Ferreira working upstairs. Lore was expected, though she had not yet arrived. In the past her customary hour for visiting Mereway had been after dinner, but it was felt that she would have sufficient tact not to try to resume the old informal familiarity, unless very gradually. Only Mrs. Sturt and Evelyn were in the room. The other girls were playing tennis at a neighbour's house, and their father had still to put in an appearance. Mrs. Sturt, and even Evelyn, looked round with some surprise as Nicholas entered.

"This is indeed a novelty!" said his hostess.

"I felt like it. I hope I'm not in the way?"

"I only wish you would honour us every day."

He took his cup, and went to sit apart. Silence reigned in the room. Mrs. Sturt was in solitary state behind the tea-table, with a countenance composed to icy, impenetrable dignity in anticipation of Lore's visit. Evelyn, at her favourite place by the window, gazed absently out of doors. He wondered mildly whether Katherine was away by chance or by intention. He took it that she was a rather childish girl, having no great control over her feelings.

After this had gone on for about ten minutes Lore was announced, and came into the room, coolly smiling. He had just been making it a test that, if her manner were defiant in any degree, it would prove her nature to be intrinsically vulgar; for he had never yet been able to assure himself on that point. He saw at once that she was very far from being defiant. Her spirits were good, and she appeared to be regarding the whole transaction as a joke; which, however, as the other side would probably be incapable of sharing it with her, she transmuted, for social purposes, into cynicism. He realised that the honours of the afternoon would be with her, not with Mrs. Sturt, who barely troubled to veil her malevolence.

Lore was wearing a black afternoon frock of fashionable yet inconspicuous style, which was the only compliment her *couturière* could pay her somewhat ungraceful form. Mrs. Sturt rose, bowed, and sank down again.

"How do you do?"

"I am very well, thanks. And you? . . . Where is Katherine?"

"She is playing tennis with neighbours, I think—Evelyn?"

"I fancy so."

Lore crossed the room to where the girl was standing rather wearily by her chair.

"I'm so sorry I was out on Tuesday evening when you called!"

"Oh, it was of no importance."

After acknowledging Nicholas from a distance good-humouredly, the guest took a seat by the table and accepted a cup of tea from the hand of her hostess.

"What a wonderful spell of delightful weather we are having!" remarked the latter, in the most frigid tone which was consistent with courtesy.

"Rather too wonderful for my taste!" returned Lore. "Blue skies and green trees and red cows are all very charming up to a point and for not too long a time, but there comes a moment when one gets hopelessly bored by it all. I confess I shan't weep tears at seeing a few motor-buses and painted complexions again by way of relief! I'm returning to town almost at once."

"Indeed!" said Mrs. Sturt hypocritically. "I quite understood you were to be here for the summer."

"I've changed my mind. I thought I should be able to work here, but I find I can't. There's too much distraction, and not enough distraction."

"When do you go?"

"On Monday week. I would disappear sooner, but I have this local fête to attend on the preceding Saturday. I've written the music for the masque. They wished me to conduct it, but I have a whim to hear the effect from a long way off—among the trees, out of sight of everyone."

"How interesting!"

"Is anybody going from here?"

"My two youngest daughters; and Mr. Cabot is to accompany them."

"Then perhaps we shall meet." She began to smile, apropos of some thought in her head. . . . "It's rather funny, but I dare not repeat it. It reminds me of a dream in the small hours of the morning I had about Evelyn and Mr. Cabot—I suppose in consequence of their visit to my house in company. I had forgotten it till this moment."

"What was it?" asked Evelyn, coming forward to replace her cup on the table.

"I really can't! It was far too impolite."

"We shan't hold you responsible for that."

"If you really won't be offended! . . . I dreamt I was sitting in my room with Madame, my companion, when a card was brought in, but it was in strange characters and neither of us could read the name. At my request Madame went out to see who it was, and she came back a minute later, with that sly French smile of hers, to announce: *'C'est le bon petit curé, avec sa femme!'* [8] Not knowing who in the world she meant, I went out myself, and lo and behold! it was you two. Only, Mr. Cabot was dressed in clerical clothes, and you, Evelyn, had a dress up to your ears nearly and down to your ankles! I woke up shouting with laughter. . . . Frightfully rude, wasn't it?"

Curiously enough, Mrs. Sturt was the only one of her listeners who seemed not to take the joke amiss. She laughed: in a wintry fashion it was true, but still, she laughed.

"Dreams can be very absurd. Yet sometimes, perhaps, they have their origin in a subconscious connection of the mind."

"Don't let's discuss it!" said Lore. "I hate the things! I have so many of them nowadays that I am beginning not to know what is real and what is unreal in my life. And most of them throw such a humiliating illumination on one's character. One wanders in public places in one's pyjamas, and so forth!"

8. "It's the good little priest, with his wife."

"I have never had that experience, I am afraid."

The door opened and Sturt entered the room. While still retaining the handle, he cast a calmly dignified glance around the party to ascertain who composed it.

Lore got up with unaffected ease. Sturt moved towards her courteously and bowed over her hand, which he held for a moment.

"And how have you been?" He reseated her in her place.

"I have been well, but not sleeping well. It is interfering with my work, so I have decided to return to town the week after next."

"She dreams a lot," explained Mrs. Sturt to her husband. "She has just been describing a ridiculous adventure she had last night or this morning, in which she saw Evelyn and Nicholas as a married couple."

Evelyn's toe was beating a quick tattoo on the carpet.

"I fear that particular dream will not be prophetic!" she remarked.

"Do you know others that will be?" asked Lore.

"Not in connection with marriage."

"What then?"

"I think that when things are working up towards a catastrophe very often a dream will give the clue."

Lore gave her a shrewd, humorous look. "Have you ever had such a dream yourself?"

"Oh, no."

"I was wondering!"

Little more was said before Lore rose to go. The twenty minutes to which her visit had extended satisfied the requirements of ceremony, she had called officially, the restraint and delicacy on both sides had been admirable, and to seek further to improve an impossible situation was out of the question. Evelyn accompanied her to the front door, while Nicholas reached down his hat to escort her home.

"What a comedy!" commented Lore, with a short, unpleasant

laugh, as they turned out of the drive into the road. "We thoroughly despise each other, nobody cares twopence whether we are friends or not, yet we have to sit in the same room for half an hour by the clock, exchanging false smiles and hypocritical speeches! Can you imagine men doing this sort of thing?"

"Is it this business which is driving you away?"

"This, and everything. I'm fed up generally. Thank your lucky stars you're not a woman!"

"I hear you are having Ferreira to dine with you this evening?"

"I am. Have you any objection?"

"May I ask if that means a reconciliation?"

"It means I'm going to have a quiet talk with Master Maurice! I don't relish having lies disseminated about me. If he fancies we are to fall on each other's necks there is a rude awakening in store for him!"

"I quite see your point of view."

"I'm glad of that! I was afraid you might think I had given up my character as hopeless—!"

"I don't see why you should say that."

"Oh, I'm very grateful to you for standing up for me the other day, and still more grateful to you for taking away his pistol. You still have it?"

"He has consented to leave it in my charge."

"What magnanimity! Now we're on the subject, you might as well tell me what he really did say to make you catch fire in such an unusually energetic manner."

"He professed to have *your* interests at heart. He was threatening to put the screw on Sturt to induce him to persuade his wife to take you back into favour. I told him he was a blackguard."

"What do you mean by 'putting the screw on' Mr. Sturt?"

"Threatening to tell his wife."

"To tell her what?"

"What he told me. Some lie."

"I shouldn't be wonderfully surprised if he said I was once upon a time somebody's mistress?"

Nicholas held his tongue.

"There's a time for modesty and there's a time for free speech," said Lore, raising her head ominously. "Here am I trying to hunt a lie down, and the best you can see to do is put your stick between my ankles! I don't know if you call that helpful. Haven't you any sisters of your own?"

"Well, he did say so."

"I knew it. And did you believe it, or not?"

"I did not."

"I'll give you the facts, then if anyone attempts to spring the same libel on you you'll be prepared for them. . . . Mr. Sturt is my oldest and best friend, and has been like a father to me. He has done me all sorts of good turns—professional and otherwise; and years ago he furnished a pretty little flat for me at Swiss Cottage, and paid the rent. Whereupon, in the eyes of the charitable, sympathetic, chaste-minded world, I immediately became his unmarried wife! I didn't spend a great deal of time trying to assure people that he never as much as took off his overcoat inside the place. There are far too many French and Austrian novels and plays in circulation to let a fairy tale like that pass! Still, it happens to be the literal truth. He was my poor mother's friend before being mine."

"I thought there must be a misunderstanding of some sort."

"You call it that, and I call it a lie! It's a mere trifling difference of standpoint. . . . Shall we go in?"

They were already outside the gate of Yetholm, though Nicholas was walking past it with unseeing eyes. He assented, and they went up the pathway to the house. Lore opened the front door, which was latched but not locked, and at once led the way through to the familiar working-room, with its disagreeable odour of stale tobacco smoke. After carelessly removing her hat and slipping off her gloves, flinging them on a chair, she poured out some whisky, diluted it with a little water, and swallowed it at a draught.

"You're a teetotaler, I believe?"

"Yes, thanks!"

"Then see if you can find yourself somewhere to sit."

Nicholas removed a pile of paper-covered music from a stool and sat down, while Lore herself sank on to the settee.

"You're not looking well, you know!" she remarked, taking a cigarette from an open box and lighting it. "What have you been doing to yourself?"

"Nothing. I was up late last night, working."

"Don't do it! I've had some. You feel a giant for three weeks, and a semi-invalid for the next six months. I suppose you were making up for your day's outing? I saw you getting off with Celia in the car."

"Oh, did you?" said Nicholas, colouring with annoyance.

"Don't be alarmed! I shan't give the game away. I know they want you for Evelyn, and that would be a very good reason for me to balk them. I loathe the girl!"

"Why?"

"Oh, you want chapter and verse for everything! . . . Because I do. She's had a soft, sheltered life, with every advantage thrust on her, ever since she was in long clothes, while I've had to fight and push for myself, always! I'm a democrat; I believe in equality of opportunity. And just because she has never had to work she affects to consider herself as being of finer clay than those who do have to!" Lore smoked on rapidly. "I can stand a lot, but I don't lie down to be walked over by a pert, smooth-haired little doll just back from finishing-school! Maurice has told me all about it. I used to be good enough for her mother and sister, but I never was good enough for her royal highness! She *knew* me, if you please! That type of child suffers from a chronic delusion that she has a gift for reading people at sight. It takes twenty-five or thirty years of all sorts of experience to build any kind of character; and she takes it all in in three glances! . . . That's why I took Maurice away from her. Not because I wanted him."

Nicholas regarded her in silence.

"I needn't ask if she attracts you!" proceeded Lore. "I see she doesn't. Besides, you can't get heat out of ice. She wouldn't attract a Trappist monk. . . . Still, that's what they are after. And these are the persons who put themselves on a moral pedestal!

How you come to be in that house at all, I don't know."

"I know Mrs. Sturt's brother."

"Then you know a first class rogue!"

"I was looking for a quiet place to work in, so he suggested Mereway."

"Yes, it was sure to be nice and quiet, with three young unmarried women on the premises! But don't run away with the idea that Mr. Sturt is in any way responsible for all this dirty business. He doesn't like it, and never did. To be quite open and candid about it, he brought you along here the first time so that *I* might have a long look at you, but I can assure you that you were never in any danger there, from the very first moment! Evelyn's hands may be clean, too; I don't know. I won't answer for any girl or woman on earth. We're a wily crew!"

She concluded with an explosive laugh and rose to help herself to more whisky.

"If you dislike the Sturts so much, how did you come to be friendly with them originally?"

"I thought we had thrashed that out," replied Lore. "It certainly wasn't the women who allured me. They have no heart and very little brains, and if there's any honour and glory to be picked up through knowing them I'm ignorant where it is!"

"So all this has only been a cover for your friendship for Mr. Sturt, whom otherwise you would never have been able to see?"

"Yes," said Lore, sighing and throwing her cigarette away, "and it's a great relief to have someone to confess it to at last. You might not think it, but I hate deception! . . . And that's why I hate my life, for a woman can't live without deception."

After a pause Nicholas got up to go.

"I suppose the fact of the matter is, every single woman needs a male protector," proceeded Lore, ignoring his movement. "They can say what they like; the world's too rough for us. We are not allowed to know anything—every errand-boy in the street has the advantage of us there—yet we have to fight on equal terms with men, and if any innocence gets rubbed off in the process they immediately leap to the conclusion that we're—*cosmopolitan*, if you like! . . . So when we do find a friend—once in a thousand years—we must cherish the acquaintance! . . . But it can't go on like this. The end is in sight, and we might as well make our preparations accordingly. It may astonish you, but I could marry any one of half a dozen men to-morrow if I liked. . . . Perhaps I shall take the plunge yet! . . ."

Suddenly Nicholas staggered; his head swam, and he was obliged to hold on to a piece of furniture for support. It was nervous faintness, brought on by the hot weather, his close chemical work, want of sleep, and emotional excitement. He fought against the passing sensation and refused to sit down.

"Hallo! What's this?" asked Lore. "Aren't you well?"

"Quite well, thanks. It was an attack of dizziness. Liver, I suppose."

"It's what I told you—it's the late hours coming out! What time did you go to bed last night, or this morning?"

"I got into bed by two o'clock, but I didn't fall asleep till nearly five."

"And up again at eight or half-past, I expect! Are you repeating it to-night?"

"Yes," replied Nicholas, not without a trace of conceit in his voice.

"Are the scientific big-wigs getting impatient for your results?"

"Probably not!"

"Would you like some stuff to make you sleep?"

"No, thanks."

"I suppose you've been reading about dope-fiends in the papers! This isn't morphine or cocaine. I forget the name; it isn't chloral hydrate, but it's the next thing to it. I used to take quite a lot at one time. I've developed since those happy days." She opened the drawer of a writing-table, and after a little hunting among the collection of miscellaneous articles there, produced a small glass tube containing white crystals. . . . "Here it is! It won't kill you, unless you want to be killed and swallow half the bottle!"

Nicholas took the phial in his hand, examined it casually, and slipped it in his vest pocket.

"Thanks!"

"I expect you'll throw it in the nearest gutter, but it's no use to me. . . . What was Evelyn talking about with her 'prophetic dreams'?"

"She has it in her head that there's to be trouble between you and Ferreira."

"We don't need a dream to tell us how probable that is!"

"Wouldn't it be better all round if you were to clear off at once?"

"Wouldn't it be better if you were to mind your own business?" laughed Lore, rising to approach the spirit-decanter for the third time.

On his way home Nicholas called to see Celia for half so hour, as she had requested. He found her reclining on a couch in a darkened room, suffering from headache. He described for her benefit Lore's reception at the Sturts', and mentioned how she was to entertain Ferreira that evening to dinner.

"Does Evelyn know?" asked Celia in a weak voice.

"Not yet."

"What a snub for her! It dismisses her with a vengeance! . . . I'm awfully amused."

"But have you quite got it? It isn't for her own sake that she is anxious to keep them apart."

"For whose sake is it?"

"Ferreira's, I imagine. She's afraid he may do something to bring himself within the law."

"You think she really is fond of him?"

"Yes, I do."

"Then can you explain how it is she isn't making a single effort to bring him back to herself?"

"She sees that is hopeless at present."

"It's the most extraordinary way of behaving for a young girl in love that I ever heard of!" exclaimed Celia sharply. "I much prefer to believe that all this show of altruism is for someone else's benefit! You're far too simple and confiding, my dear."

"I may be," said Nicholas, colouring.

"Surely a man like you, who has knocked about, isn't going to allow himself to be hoodwinked by a child who only put her hair up yesterday! I'll wager any money that she contrives that you see twice as much of her as either of her sisters. Confess that she has struck up a *camaraderie*."

"Not exactly."

"I know she has. You think because she is young and fresh that she is without guile; but these young girls are the most dangerous of all. Instinct does everything for them perfectly, and side by side with it they are utterly self-centred and see nothing in the world but their own reflection. If you're not very careful, you will let yourself in for something."

"There's no fear of that," returned Nicholas with an attempt at smiling.

"I'm coming over to tea to-morrow afternoon, to find out for myself what is really happening. I don't like her proceedings at all. Every new thing I hear about her seems to strike a false note. Who ever heard of a slighted girl, just out of her teens, who wasn't a little spitfire? There's something improbable about her whole attitude to Maurice."

Exhausted by her own vehemence, she sank her beautiful head back on its voluptuous cushion and smiled feebly up at him.

"Forgive me if I'm personal. I really hardly know what I'm saying, my neuralgia is such a beast!"

"Is there nothing I can do for you? Can I go or telephone to the chemist?"

It seemed, however, that Celia's medicine-chest was well supplied; and understanding at last that she actually desired him to leave her to silence and solitude, and that she was not merely being "interesting" in order to establish a new and different kind of intimacy, he shortly after took his departure.

Half-way home it dawned upon him as a quiet inspiration that she was being *jealous* of Evelyn! . . .

He went straight upstairs to his room after dinner and got everything ready. At half-past eight, as arranged, Evelyn knocked softly at the door and was admitted. She took her customary chair while Nicholas closed the door behind her. When he came back into the room he stood at the table for a minute, pretending to busy himself with his preparations. Her existence, in some strange manner, had begun to irritate him, and he wished not to have to look at her or speak to her. He regretted having taken her into his confidence originally; but, at all events, was quite determined that this should be the last occasion on which he would show her anything. It grew clearer and clearer to him that she was a different sort of girl altogether! . . .

"Well, shall we start?" he asked in a rather surly tone.

"I'm quite ready," came her cold, clear-cut voice.

"Sit where you are."

He pressed back the release-lever, and the slotted lid of the little metal box immediately began its slow circulatory motion. Then he took his own seat.

Evelyn was again in that wood, with that unpleasant, acid smell in her nostrils. The dry, dusty path was the same, while the trees on either side were just as closely-knit and impenetrable, yet she was considerably farther on than before—though the precise moment of her previous experience was not distinguished in her memory from the intervening period. There was a sort of clearing twenty or thirty yards ahead, and in the very centre of it, interrupting the avenue, which divided itself into two parts to go round it and reunite beyond, was what looked like a little pool of dark-coloured water without banks. Between herself and this pool Lore was walking, away from her, so that only her back was visible.

Once again the odd subconsciousness of being a man was in her mind, and again it did not occur to her to explore the origin of the sensation. Everything around her was so darkly vivid, so *real*, that she seemed to be connected with the world by her emotion rather than by her understanding; her brain was quite incapable of scientific detachment. She never guessed that she was dreaming.

She had no recollection of her waking life.

As she continued to gaze after the retreating Lore, her heart shrunk until she felt that she had a stone there. Grief, terror, and the anguish of suspense battled with and prevailed over her underlying supernatural horror. She understood that Lore was being moved unwillingly—by something, someone—towards that pool, which was in her direct path; and that a dreadful calamity would take place as soon as she arrived there. It was not the alarm of one human being at the danger threatening another which affected her, but it was as if Lore were a beloved sister whose existence was inextricably bound up with her own, and who was about to be brutally maltreated by strangers. . . . She wished to run after her and pull her back by main force, but she was unable to put out a limb. She was in the grip of catalepsy; and she realised the sensations of those who, while still alive and sentient, witness the preparations for their own burial.

Lore neither cried out nor looked round, but her shoulders kept straightening themselves backwards, stiffly and convulsively, as though she were all the time throwing her weight against the terrible unseen force which was drawing her forward. So a woman might recoil from the door of a torture-chamber. . . .

Suddenly Evelyn realised that she was seeing Maurice! He was leaning against a tree, smoking, just beyond the pool, and appeared to be waiting for Lore to come up. He was wearing his ordinary clothes, but his face was the face of a *devil!* Dead-white, sneering and smiling, it was at the same time cruel and childish; and the childishness imparted such an aspect of degradation to it that the cruelty seemed almost a redeeming element. . . .

While Lore continued to advance and the other stood waiting, watching and grinning, all passed swiftly away, and, as if she had emerged from a tunnel into the open, sunlit world, Evelyn found herself once more sitting in the chair in Nicholas's room.

He put away his box in silence. Evelyn kept passing her hand across her eyes, and it was several moments before she spoke.

"My sensations were those of a man. That must have been

because the dream was yours?"

"It would be so. I overlooked that."

Another pause ensued, during which the girl shivered. "I suppose it was a nightmare?" she suggested, as though desirous of relieving herself by a familiar name.

"Yes."

"Yet it was a continuation of the same dream. Had it been a *repetition* of the same dream I could have understood it better."

"Yes, it was a continuation."

"Now that Maurice is working here again, you will soon get your other apparatus completed, won't you?"

"To-day week, I hope."

"And in the meantime?"

"In the meantime Ferreira is dining with Lore this evening."

Evelyn turned so white that he thought she was about to faint.

"Then they have made it up?" she asked as soon as she had found her voice.

"So he thinks; but it appears she has no such intention. She is going to talk to him, that's all."

"Then they are actually together now?"

"Yes."

Evelyn rose and, after a moment's hesitation with another question, which finally remained unuttered, left the room.

When he had shut and locked the door after her, Nicholas began to get together the materials for his night-work.

XV

IN THE WILDERNESS

Immediately after breakfast on Friday morning Nicholas went into the garden to get a breath of fresh air before beginning work, when Sturt unexpectedly emerged from the conservatory and crossed the lawn to join him. His head was a little sunk, a freshly-lighted cigar was in his mouth, and he held his hands clasped loosely behind the tails of his grey morning-coat. They greeted each other.

"I have still to thank you for your most effective intervention," said Sturt in a dry, tranquil way. "You have done great things, my dear fellow. The storm has passed, the ladies are reconciled, and once more we all breathe freely. . . . Ferreira is working for you again, I see?"

"Yes."

"Since we are on the subject—incidentally, how far did he disclose his hand to you in the interview you were to have had together? Was he reticent, or the reverse?"

"He said you were formerly intimate with Miss Jensen, in a bad sense."

"And what else?"

"And that she was blackmailing you."

Sturt's hand trembled somewhat as he again drew at his cigar.

"These are devilish lies!"

"I have no doubt of it."

"And yet you re-accept him as your assistant!"

"It's his brains I'm employing, not his morals. Besides, he's quiet now, and it's best to keep him so."

"At least you will allow me to offer my apologia? . . . Appearances may be ambiguous, but my honour is clear. Miss Jensen's mother was a very dear professional friend." He sighed. "Her death some years ago left me in a somewhat awkward relation to the daughter. She was orphaned, quite alone in the world, and a mere child; therefore, morally, I could not evade guardianship, even had I so desired; though this guardianship had no basis in law, be it understood. On the other hand, it was scarcely feasible that I should require my wife to share this responsibility with me. Not having also shared the acquaintance, she would at once have leapt to the most sinister conclusions. . . . So that is my skeleton, my dear fellow! I did what I could for the child; I helped her in this way and that, and—putting vanity away; for, indeed, it is not a case for vanity—I may say that what success she now enjoys has been in large measure indebted to the introductions it was within my ability to give her during the early stages of her career. At present my guardianship is confined to an occasional visit, to an occasional word of counsel; for she is of an age to be her own manager. But, 'pon my soul! little enough as this is, it seems too much for some. . . . I cannot believe that you permitted his vile aspersions to pass unchallenged! A lady's honour is under the protection of everyone calling himself a gentleman."

"I threatened to give him a thrashing if he went any further into the matter."

"I am grateful."

"I might not have gone so far if I had known about the flat then," added Nicholas dryly. "Miss Jensen herself told me about that afterwards."

"So she has spoken, too! . . . This is a hideous innuendo, my dear boy. Yes, I furnished a flat as well; and why should not I? She must live beneath a roof, and it was in my rôle of guardian. Do you assert that I should have stood upon punctilio in the case of a lonely, penniless, defenceless child, unversed in the ways of the world?"

"Oh, no."

"Affection overrode all such considerations. . . . And it is the same affection . . . it is because a breach between her and my womenkind would finally and inevitably separate us that I have taken an otherwise insignificant affair so much to heart. Damme! I was certainly not thinking of my own domestic peace."

"You haven't had an opportunity of speaking to her since, have you?"

"Since when?"

"Since you called on her that night—Monday wasn't it?"

"No, I have not seen her by herself since then. Why do you ask?"

"I thought, as you know her so intimately, you might be able to say what is really the matter with her. Her health seems to be all right, and this business isn't much to worry about; yet her manner seems to announce that she's arrived at the bottom of the wheel. It isn't natural."

"Pardon me! it is not only quite natural, but the reverse would be cursedly *un*natural—a prodigy indeed. She is a woman, her good name is involved, she sees her friends affronting or forsaking her, and against it all she is helpless! I don't know what you would have, my dear fellow. Would you have her dance and sing?"

"No; but she seems to me like a woman with a secret trouble."

"That is her manner. It is an instinctive yearning for life and occupation; and now this business has underlined it. Her professional work does not and cannot satisfy her, for the most gifted lady of them all cannot live by intellect alone. She needs romance, dear boy. I could wish to see a worthy fellow step forward. . . ."

"She always has Ferreira!"

Sturt passed over the sarcasm contemptuously, and proceeded:

"What her nature needs is not contrast, but community— community of taste, culture, sensibility, ideals, and so forth! What is bad is that the mode of living she has, justifiably or mistakenly, adopted serves to repel just those persons with whom she has most in common; at the same time that it attracts—*bounders*, to state it plainly. . . . You yourself see but little in her, I fancy?"

"I believe she sees still less in me."

His host sighed deeply. "Well, she is still attractive, even as girls go, and Fate holds queer surprises in store for all of us! Yet I could wish to see her established. . . . Once more, my thanks for what you have done, dear boy! We shall doubtless meet at lunch."

He crossed the lawn slowly and dejectedly to the house, and Nicholas, after waiting till he had disappeared, followed him there.

He had barely started work when Ferreira entered the room. He held an unopened envelope in his hand which, without removing his hat and scarcely nodding to Nicholas, he proceeded to tear open. After staring at the enclosed note with raised brows, he handed it to the other in silence. Nicholas took it wonderingly and read:

> *Dear Maurice,*
>
> *I don't wish to intrude in your personal affairs, but if you have any decency you will see that you must leave Newleigh at once.*
>
> *Evelyn.*

"What the devil does that mean?" demanded Ferreira.

"I suppose it means she doesn't care to be mixed up in your scandals. Do you mind telling me when you got this?"

"She gave it me herself as I came through the hall just now. She slipped off again before I had time to say 'How d'ye do?' Queer wench!"

"To be quite open about it, Ferreira, she's frightened of things happening between you and Lore Jensen. She wants to get you safely away."

"You seem to know all about everybody, my friend!"

"She thinks you two are about as safe together as fire and gunpowder."

"I guess I know what's troubling her. Six months ago Lore double-crossed me, and I threatened to have her scalp. But there was an adequate motive then; now there isn't. I'm not writing to Evie, but you tell her from me not to be a little ass. Things are all right."

"What was the other occasion, then?"

"Lore was very much mixed up at the time with one Monro Dawson, a pen-pusher of sorts; and I wasn't having any! . . . Evie came to the rescue like a pal, applied soothing cream and so on, and in point of fact it was from that time that Evie and I got together in a special sense—but we won't open that! Dawson faded from the landscape and was no more heard of, while Lore started another spell of domesticity, with me as first visitor."

"But would you have 'had her scalp'?"

"I would."

"What would you have done?"

"I would have seen 'red,' old boy; and when I see 'red' I don't calculate to be responsible for my actions. In a general way I'm a peaceable sort of chap."

"How did you get on last night?"

Ferreira's face relapsed into the sullenness which it had worn on his first entrance.

"We got on very well."

"Are you to visit her again?"

"I am."

Nicholas said no more. He returned to his work, Ferreira got out his materials, and for upwards of an hour the silence remained unbroken.

At the end of that time Nicholas opened the door in response to a smart tapping. He was confronted by a maid, resting the lower end of a large brown-paper package on the floor while she waited. He took it from her and bore it into the room.

"It's the box at last, Ferreira!"

Ferreira jumped up from his chair, at the same time whipping out a penknife to cut away the packing.

Tea was already served in the drawing-room when Celia arrived at half-past four that afternoon. With the exception of Audrey who was again playing tennis away from home, all the members of the household were assembled, including Nicholas. Mrs. Sturt rose with a cordial smile, the girls came forward, and Nicholas himself, colouring, retreated to the background. Sturt, who, on his accustomed sofa, had been sipping his tea dejectedly, alternately munching a mouthful of cake and keeping his cigarette alight, got up to cross the room as only a professional actor knows how.

Celia favoured each, impartially, with a careless touch of the hand and a murmured word. Every part of her attractive person was adorned for a visit of ceremony. The elaborate frock, which was to be studied as a work of art; the eccentric-looking shoes, with their prodigiously high heels; the huge, dark, curving hat crowning her coal-black hair: Nicholas had seen none of this attire before, and it gave him an impressive notion of the apparently inexhaustible resources of her wardrobe. Beside her, the girls looked like pale, anaemic flowers.

The guest sat down opposite her hostess, removed a long glove, and received her cup. Katherine drew near, to join the conversation, but Evelyn resumed her seat by the window, while Sturt returned to his solitude. Various topics of local and feminine interest were discussed during ten or fifteen minutes, and there was nothing to indicate that the call was to be marked by any intelligence of a more exciting character, when suddenly Celia leant forward towards her *vis-à-vis* with a quick smile.

"By the way!—have you heard about Lore?"

Mrs. Sturt stared at her almost in horror.

"No. What is it now?"

"She's to be married!"

A thunderbolt descending into the room could scarcely have created a greater sensation. Sturt, unnoticed in his corner, set down his cup with a trembling hand, and half rose, only to sit down again. His wife's face retained its expression, as though struck rigid. Katherine uttered a single shrill laugh, like that of a malicious child; then blushed crimson as she realised how she had revealed her secret spite to others. Evelyn turned sharply round to look at Celia.

Mrs. Sturt found her voice at last:

"Never!"

"I had it from her own lips. I looked in at Yetholm before

coming on here. It's Monro Dawson."

"That man!"

"The newspaper scribe?" demanded Sturt, who by this time had approached the tea-table, to gaze down at the guest from his height.

"I don't know if he would accept that definition of his activities!" returned Celia lightly. "I fancy he calls himself a music critic. . . . They were rather thrown together some time ago, if you remember? Lore wasn't quite ready for him then, but apparently she has reconsidered. Whether this latest proposition originated with him or with her, she omitted to say. I understand he always thought highly of the possibilities of her genius. He is practically the only one of the confraternity who has consistently approved her. . . . I expect you have seen his portraits? Forty-two, bald, tall and thin, rather distinguished-looking in a foreign way!"

"I know the man," said Sturt. "He enjoys a select reputation, his musicianship undoubtedly is competent, but his vanity is colossal. He is—dictatorial. . . . In other respects the match may be a suitable one."

"Obviously she is merely aiming at a status," offered his wife.

"And is that foolish? Nevertheless, there may be affection as well. He is older than she, which does not matter. It is her strange reticence in the affair which perplexes one."

Celia smiled up at him gaily. "She didn't know herself at breakfast-time. His letter came by the second post. Her reply may still be travelling, for all I can say."

"When is it to be?" inquired Mrs. Sturt.

"Soon."

Sturt lit a fresh cigarette and strolled to the window, turning his back on the company. Evelyn seized the excuse afforded by her father's obstruction of her view to join the tea-table group.

"Maurice will have to disappear!" went on Celia with a whimsical look on her face. Mrs. Sturt instinctively stiffened, as she always did at the mention of that name.

"It was high time a responsible protector came on the scene! From what I have heard of Mr. Dawson I fancy he will change a good many things in Lore's *ménage*."

"If she will let him!"

"Does he know?" asked Evelyn, ostensibly of Celia, but stealing an instantaneous glance at Nicholas.

"No," replied the latter.

Celia toyed with her sunshade. "Let's hope he won't resort to violence to express his feelings, when he does hear!"

"Mr. Dawson will know how to deal with that contingency," replied Mrs. Sturt severely.

"He is miles away unfortunately."

"Is he coming down, or is she going up?"

"He is to come down, but he will restrain his ardour till to-morrow week. He is taking Lore over to the Colminster affair. You know she has written the masque music? Presumably, his idea is to inaugurate the betrothal by writing a laudatory article in his pet organ."

The conversation drifted, as conversations do.

"Are *you* going?" inquired Mrs. Sturt.

"I may be."

"Have you made your plans, or would you care to join Evelyn and Audrey in the car? Mr. Cabot is running them over."

"It's very sweet of you!"

"But would you care to?"

"I think so."

"It promises to be a very mixed gathering, and they are only children." She smiled. "Possibly, even, you might find Audrey a cavalier from among your numerous acquaintances."

"What has poor Evelyn done?"

"I am relying upon Mr. Cabot to escort her."

Evelyn rose and walked out of the room. There was no essential connection between the action and her mother's remark, yet an uncomfortable silence succeeded.

"Some people have the audacity to say that I require chaperoning myself!" remarked Celia, laughing.

"You belong to a gayer generation, my dear. The girls of to-day are so difficult! I don't know whether it is a good or a bad thing, but everything seems to be done for eternity.”

“The contrast makes one feel terribly young!” agreed Celia, again showing her faultlessly beautiful teeth.

A few minutes later she rose to take her departure. Mrs. Sturt and Katherine accompanied her into the hall, and Nicholas, following them there, unobtrusively lifted down his hat. Celia ignored his escort till they were well away from the house. Then she asked with a smile, still looking away from him:

“You haven’t heard why I am to be taken up? It is the first time in history.”

“Gratitude for services rendered, probably!”

“Or apprehension of possible disservices! I don’t think so. Our solitude is to be invaded. Wherever I am, Evelyn shall be. The fiat has gone forth!”

“I hope you’re mistaken, for I couldn’t stand that!”

“I hope I am . . . but *there she is! . . .*” The concluding words were spoken softly and significantly, and were accompanied by a pointing finger.

They were descending the drive. Evelyn had her back towards them, and was resting both arms on the top bar of the carriage gate, languidly looking over to the road beyond. She did not seem so much to be killing time as waiting for something or someone. She was without a hat.

“Does she want *us?*” asked Nicholas in a tone of surprise.

“Me, I expect.”

The girl’s slim, erect figure wheeled round at the sound of their voices, and she took a few steps towards them. When they had met, Celia looked at her with an expectant smile and halted.

“You’re going?” asked Evelyn, rather unnecessarily.

“Yes.”

“I only wanted to say . . . I think it won’t be wise to tell Maurice about this engagement at present. He may resent it.”

Celia raised her brow humorously. “I shan’t tell him, my dear; but of course he will have to know.”

“He will have to know, but it need not be on our consciences. Lore is going away on Monday week, and the news can very well wait till then. You may not have heard, but there was trouble between him and Monro Dawson once before.”

“Lore will most likely tell him herself, my dear. Why shouldn’t she? Isn’t it rather—*interference* to decide for another girl who shall and who shall not hear of her engagement?”

“I am supposing that she has not told him herself. Of course, if she means to, there is no more to be said.”

“Really, I don’t see how it concerns any of us. . . . It is one of the funniest requests I ever heard!”

Evelyn coloured. “If you wish to take the responsibility for violence, I don’t!”

“And if you are afraid of Maurice’s not knowing how to behave decently, surely it would be better to apply to the police?”

“I shall see Ferreira in the morning,” interposed Nicholas hastily, “and then we shall hear the latest.”

Celia half turned away, and began to dislodge the gravel of the drive with the point of her furled parasol.

“To-morrow is Saturday!” she remarked in a reminding tone.

“I know it is.”

“I expected you would not be working.”

“I am working. Why?”

“I thought you wouldn’t be—but it doesn’t matter!”

“Were you proposing something?”

“A run in the car. But we’ll say no more about it.”

There was a pause.

“Do you mean a whole-day run?” asked Nicholas.

“I did mean the whole day; but I see you are reluctant to give up the time, and it is really of no importance.”

“Oh, I’ll come with pleasure; only, it’s the first I’ve heard of it. Am I to turn up immediately after breakfast?”

“I thought after breakfast.”

“All right, then!”

Evelyn, who had been regarding him with increasing scorn, now spoke quietly, but not to him:

“Nicholas is very, very busy, Mrs. Hantish!”

“That is one reason why I propose a day in the fresh air for him. I see he is dreadfully overworked!"

"You see that, but you don't seem able to see that you are the cause!"

"*I?*"

"It isn't that he is working so hard, but he is working at the wrong end of the day. I understand he is generally up till two or three in the morning. If you were considerate enough not to monopolise so much of his time during the day, he would be able to go to bed at civilised hours, and your medical prescriptions would be rendered unnecessary."

"I'm sorry!" She turned to Nicholas. "I had better release you from attendance to-morrow."

"No, I'll come," was the stubborn reply. "I'm not made of paper! The worst part of the job will be over in a week's time, I hope."

"That is all the more reason for you to put your back into it and get it finished, one would think!" said Evelyn sharply. "You know yourself whether you regard it as important or not! If you mean to play about, it is a pity you ever took it up."

"I can work at night as well as I can in the day."

Evelyn made a grimace expressive of contempt, and turned her back, though she did not go away immediately.

"I leave it entirely to you," said Celia lightly. "If my society really exhausts you, please don't hesitate for a minute to stay away! If you do decide to come, I promise to make it as restful for you as I know how."

"I shall certainly come."

"I think you are mad!" said Evelyn, with quiet incisiveness. And, without waiting for a response from either of the others, she took her departure to the house.

Celia and Nicholas passed through the gate into the road. The former gave a careless laugh.

"What an extraordinary child!"

Nicholas's face was dark, and he said nothing.

"Surely it is phenomenal for a young girl to take so keen an interest in chemistry! . . . Or is it the chemist?"

"Oh, let's talk about something else!" was his surly response.

On arriving at The Arbour, Celia persuaded him to come through to the garden for half an hour. She wished to show him her flowers, which he had never yet properly seen. Nicholas caught at the excuse for staying away from Mereway, the thought of which had begun to be distasteful to him.

They walked round the beds, she pausing every few seconds to pull a withered head here or to stoop to smell a flower-cup there. Her elaborate and artificial apparel was so obtrusively out of place amidst the trees and blooms, and her personal perfume was so much more penetrating than that of any flower, that he was conscious of little else. He could not get accustomed to her beauty, but it grew more disquieting to him each minute. Her conversation excited without satisfying him. His imagination became inflamed.

Their course took them past a gap in a tall privet hedge which shut off one end of the flower garden.

"This is the entrance to my Wilderness!" she informed him, turning in through the opening and pausing for him beyond. "I keep it for my men friends. Men always feel cramped in a garden."

The place, in fact, consisted of about an acre of tangled under-brush, scattered with birches and other small trees, and evidently forming a part of the original uncleared wood. One or two tall standing pines redeemed the enclosed waste from insignificance. There was also a mighty fallen trunk lying extended on the ground, half decayed and covered with mosses and creepers. Narrow footpaths had been made, to permit promenading, while here and there were rustic seats. From some spots the house was invisible.

"This is rather jolly!" exclaimed Nicholas, gazing about him.

"It's not bad, I think."

"I didn't know you had anything of the sort."

They began to walk again.

"I don't know why, but this always reminds me of the woods

at Spa, in the Ardennes," remarked Celia, who was in front but kept turning round.

"I haven't been there."

"Aren't you fond of travelling?"

"Very, but I have had few opportunities up to the present."

"I adore it!"

They came to a seat, out of sight of the house, where she suggested sitting down.

"I've been nearly all over Europe, to say nothing of Morocco and the Canaries," she proceeded. "It's great fun when you have a companion, but for a woman travelling alone. . . !" She concluded with a grimace.

"I expect you're a bit handicapped."

"Handicapped isn't the phrase, my dear boy! It can be made positively ghastly for one. More than once I have vowed never to set foot outside England again. Yet—such is feminine inconsistency—I am already planning another trip this winter to the Italian Riviera."

"Indeed?"

"It's gorgeous there! You really ought to make up your mind to come out. I'm sure you would love it."

"I don't know the language."

"How many do? It isn't at all necessary. Stay at my hotel, and we can form a mutual aid society. You can be my *gendarme* and I can be your interpreter. I know French and Italian. Then we could explore the unfashionable places."

"I should be afraid of boring you."

Celia laughed quietly. "What a horrid thing to say! I thought we put that to the test on Wednesday. Were you bored?"

"I said *you*."

"I'm not physically or mentally obnoxious to you in any way, am I?"

Nicholas reddened. "Hardly!"

"Because you're certainly not to me. I fancy we get on as well together as any two persons can. Why are you so unkind?"

"I'm not; but you wilfully misunderstand me."

"Then let me try and understand you, for a change."

"I was looking at it from your standpoint, not mine. . . . Personally, I could sit in a room with you for twenty-four hours without saying a word, and still not be bored! . . . Is that plain enough?" he continued defiantly. "Or would you like it still plainer?"

Celia laughed, coloured in her turn, and looked confused, yet pleased, all at the same time; but she withdrew her eyes and said not a word. Nicholas thrust a hand in his trousers pocket and stretched out his leg.

"All right, we might as well get it over; but don't forget you asked for it. You happen to be the only lady of my acquaintance I have ever thought of in connection with marriage. And if I fancied there was the slightest chance of acceptance I'd ask you—but of course there isn't! I'm not up to your standard of tone. . . . So perhaps we had better say nothing more about trips to the Riviera!"

While he spoke, Celia became first serious and then thoughtful, as she held a green log a little way off with her eye; but as soon as he had finished she turned quickly round to him.

"Is this a proposal?"

"I'm not such a fool! It's merely an avowal of feelings."

"But you say that if you could be sure beforehand of my accepting your hand, you would offer it. That is a proposal!"

"If you choose to regard it as such." His heart was beating wildly.

"It's rather silly of you! How do you expect me to answer a question which you abstain from asking?"

Nicholas gave her a lightning glance. "Before I dared to ask such a question, I should want to know whether you ruled it a permissible one!"

"Why, of course it is! Why shouldn't it be?"

"All right, then—I do ask it!"

"What?" She smiled.

"Whether you will marry me!" His tone was absolutely gruff, but Celia perfectly well understood that manner stands for nothing on such trying occasions.

"Certainly I'll marry you, and it's very sweet of you to ask me!" she responded, with a still more stylish smile.

Without knowing in the least what he was doing, Nicholas pulled out his cigarette-case and selected and lit a cigarette. His hands trembled slightly during the operation. When he spoke, his voice sounded to himself as coming from another world:

"Then it's a fixed thing?"

"Good heavens, yes!"

They sat at some little distance apart on the same long seat, and neither was looking directly at the other. A silence followed her words.

"I'm so glad you are not being conventional!" she remarked at last. "It would be too appallingly like Hampstead Heath, wouldn't it?"

"Which means that I am being a fool, I suppose!" and he started to move along the seat.

"No, no! please don't! . . ." She sprang to her feet.

"Please!"

Celia retired backwards down the path, laughing, which he took to be sufficient invitation. When he advanced upon her she turned and ran, and upon his still giving chase she took to the brambles. Ten yards farther on he caught her, but not before her frock was ruined. She laughed and struggled in his arms. . . .

"You're a terrible man!" she gasped, successfully disengaging herself a moment or two later. Her hair was very much dishevelled, but her face shone with triumphant excitement. "And I was under the impression that you were so staid and virtuous! You realise you've wrecked my dress? You'll have to buy me a new one."

"Ten, if you like!"

They regained the path, where she put herself in order.

"This will be your first lesson in wifely expensiveness!"

"I can afford it," he answered, with the least shade of boastfulness in his voice.

"I have seventeen hundred a year, and this house. How much

have you?"

"Nearly twice that."

Celia sobered as they started to return to the flower garden.

"I expect we shall manage on it. There will be tons of things for us to arrange and settle now. Where do you want to live?"

"Where you do!"

"Silly boy! . . . But how long do you contemplate staying with the Sturts?"

"Till my work's finished."

"Oh, you are going on with that?"

"For the present." He was vaguely disappointed, not only at the question itself, but at the airy indifference with which it was put. It threatened to constitute the first of their spiritual separations. Then, recollecting that such an attitude belonged to her natural gaiety and irresponsibility of character, he forgave her. They were at the gap in the hedge.

"By the by," said Celia, "do you think it would be exceedingly wise to tell people about this at present?"

"I quite agree," he replied, to her thought rather than to her question.

"I don't see why we should gratify their malicious propensities! The public announcement can very well be postponed until we both go away from here. What do you think!"

"I think it's an excellent plan."

"You will come and see me regularly?"

"Every day!"

She gave him an enchanting smile. No more words were spoken, but it was still a minute or two before they repassed through the privet hedge into the garden.

XVI

EVELYN FAINTS

On Wednesday of the following week, at three o'clock in the afternoon, Ferreira completed his work. He announced the fact to Nicholas, and stood by to light a cigarette while the latter left his own labours in order to inspect the finished result. As he had kept in close touch with its progress all through, there were no surprises for him. He merely had to assure himself that all was ready for use, before finally dismissing his assistant.

The aluminium box, in its dull, silvery beauty, was lying horizontally on Ferreira's working-table. It was circular in shape, having a diameter of thirty inches, with a depth of four inches. Although of somewhat unwieldy size, it was of extreme lightness, the metal casing being very thin. There was a covered reservoir all the way round the circumference, extending one inch towards the centre. The rest of the box was not enclosed, but consisted merely of a bottom of metal to rest on the floor, or wherever it was wanted to lie. The reservoir had two purposes to serve. It was to act as a tank, to contain the chemical in its liquid condition when sensitising the film to be wound through it; and, after the film had been sensitised, it was to protect it from exposure. The narrow exposure-aperture was opened or closed at any required hour and minute by previously setting the clock indicator.

The clockwork revolving the film-carriage was fitted to the centre of the aluminium box, but, for the sake of convenience, was made detachable, in order that the latter when not in use might be stood on end. It was constructed to revolve the film at a given rate of speed past the aperture, which was in the outer cover of the reservoir. The principle was practically identical with that of Nicholas's smaller box; but the exposure, instead of being for two minutes, would be for one hour, and the larger scale had necessitated greater accuracy of workmanship. Ferreira, in spite of the fact that he had regarded the whole thing as a freak rather than a serious piece of work, had made a really excellent job of it, and Nicholas continued to eye and handle the finished product lovingly. At last he lodged it behind the hanging curtain for future use.

Ferreira swept his tools into a handbag which he had brought along for the purpose, while Nicholas produced his cheque-book from the table-drawer. He blotted the wet ink, and handed the cheque to the other.

"One hundred and five pounds! I think that's right?"

"Expenses to town—say five pounds!" drawled Ferreira, standing smoking, with a bored expression. Nicholas made the necessary correction, and this time he accepted the cheque, bestowing it carelessly in his breast-pocket.

"That's that!" he remarked, reaching for his hat.

"Thanks for turning it out so well!"

"That's all right. What are you going to do with it now you've got it, if it's not a rude question?"

"Oh, I'm experimenting."

Ferreira shrugged his shoulders lightly and made for the door.

"Well, good-bye, old chap! I don't suppose I shall enter this darned old house again!"

"What are your plans? Are you going away?"

"I'm running up to town for a few days, but I shall be back."

"Sit down a minute, won't you?" Ferreira did not sit down, but he leant against the edge of the table. "How do you stand now with Lore Jensen?" proceeded Nicholas.

The other blew out a cloud of smoke. "Why?"

"Are you still seeing her?"

"Oh, yes."

"On good terms together?"

"Oh, the glass stands fair to sanguinary. Why?"

"She hasn't told you anything, then?"

Ferreira's face became a question-mark.

"No."

"You were talking about a chap called Monro Dawson, if you

remember. . . . They're engaged!"

After gazing keenly at Nicholas for a few moments in silence, Ferreira drew at his cigarette and stared up at the ceiling. Then he returned to Nicholas.

"Sure thing?"

"It's a fact."

"Who told you?"

"Mrs. Hantish; and Lore told her."

"Excellent!"—and with an admirable assumption of jaunty indifference he went on smoking.

"What will you do about it?" asked Nicholas, still watching him warily for the first signals of an outbreak. Ferreira, instead of answering the question, asked another of his own:

"How long has this been in force?"

"I heard last Friday."

"And to-day's Wednesday!" was the dry comment.

"I purposely kept it back till you had finished with me. I didn't want any more interruptions."

"Oh, well, it doesn't matter! I guess I'll run along now and see Lore. Her version of it may be different."

"You'll find it's authentic, I'm afraid."

Ferreira considered. "Or else I'll keep her in suspense for a bit! Is the rotter coming down here before she goes up on Monday?"

"I understand he's running down on Saturday, to take her over to the Colminster garden-party."

"Most idyllic!"

Nicholas, who had been filling his pipe, stopped the tobacco with the ball of his finger meditatively.

"You'll accept the situation, of course?"

"Not exactly, old boy! If I was Dawson I wouldn't order a new silk hat for that wedding yet! He forgot to make inquiries."

"You're not going to make a fuss?"

"Oh, there won't be a fuss. That bald-headed scarecrow doesn't stand up to fight. An angry sheep would make his heart go pit-a-pat. All he knows how to do is turn over music for half-dressed women at the grand piano, and tell the world all about it afterwards in violet ink on rose-coloured paper! If you shake him by the hand he shudders. I know Monro Dawson."

"Still, I don't see what grounds you can interfere on."

"Don't you worry about grounds, old chap! We'll take action first, and then find the grounds. I'm running over to that swank-gathering on Saturday afternoon. You can tell Lore that, if you like. I'll get up to town this evening, and come down specially on the day. Perhaps I'll run up against Dawson on the platform."

"What do you think you can do at Colminster?"

"Do? I guess I can describe his own character up and down to him, for a start! You bet, the audience will be one of the biggest and most enthusiastic *he's* ever seen clustered! . . . Incidentally, I'll trouble you for my revolver now."

"No, I won't take the responsibility."

"I'll thank you for that revolver!"

"You don't get it."

"Righto! I'll get downstairs, and see if Mrs. Sturt approves of her house being made a receiving-office for stolen property."

"It has nothing to do with Mrs. Sturt."

"Then I'll find something that *has* to do with her."

Nicholas, glancing at the other's pale face, thin, sneering lips, and narrowed eyes, had no doubt as to the nature of his threat, and he credited him with sufficient hardihood and unscrupulousness to carry it into effect. He went over to the bureau, unlocked it, and took out the revolver.

"Here you are! . . . You know the fête is an invitation one, of course?"

Ferreira did not trouble to answer, but, slipping the weapon in his coat-pocket, stood up to go.

"Miss Jensen won't put up with personal indignity," suggested Nicholas. "You'll only be doing yourself more harm than good."

"Did she ask you to break the happy news to me?"

"She did not."

"Then where the devil do you come in?"

"I may not come in anywhere," replied Nicholas, nettled. "I

can tell you one thing. I shall be at the fête myself on Saturday, and I shall keep a good look-out for you. If you insult Dawson while in Miss Jensen's company and I'm on the spot, you'll have me to deal with as well. She's had quite enough persecution from you. So you had better go slow."

"And if you come inside a yard of me when I'm on the warpath, you'll get stopped by a bullet for sure! I'm taking this little friend with me"—tapping his pocket —"so don't tell the hospital staff I didn't warn you!"

Clapping his hat on at an insolent angle, and picking up his bag, he left the room. Nicholas wandered to the window, wondering how he might best give the alarm to Lore, in order to keep her away from the entertainment. He resolved to seek counsel from Celia, whose *flair* in such matters amounted to genius. It was already her hour, and he retired to his inner room to make himself presentable.

Beyond the barest civilities, Evelyn and Nicholas had exchanged no words since the previous Friday, when she had so indignantly left him with Celia. He was all the more astonished when, upon his returning from The Arbour shortly after six o'clock, he found her sitting back in the easy chair in his workroom, with her eyes closed. She opened them at once, but did not offer to get up. Nicholas shut the door and came over to her.

"You want me?"

"Presumably, since this is your room! Have you just come back from Celia's?"

This question he did not answer.

The girl moved her body impatiently, and went on: "I saw Maurice come and go with a bag to-day. Does that mean he has finished here?"

"Yes," said Nicholas, marvelling at her astuteness and observation.

"I won't tell you how relieved I am! It's like the ending of a nightmare for me—being in the same house with him, at such a time and on such conditions! . . . I gave him a note last week. Did he make any remark about it to you? That's what I came to ask."

"He thought you were foolishly and unnecessarily alarming yourself."

"And he declines to go away?"

"He's going up to town this evening, but only for a couple of days; he's returning on Saturday to attend the Colminster garden-party. After that, I don't know his movements."

"He *is* going to the garden-party?" Her voice trembled a little.

"So he threatens."

"Threatens?"

"Yes; he's going to try and work up a scene with Dawson."

Evelyn spoke more quietly each time she opened her mouth, until her voice was now little more than a whisper:

"Then he knows of the engagement?"

"Yes, I told him to-day."

"Oh, you told him!"

"I did."

There was a pause.

"You still have his revolver, of course?" she inquired, with a sickly, apologetic smile.

"No, I gave it to him back this afternoon."

"What!"

"It was his property."

Evelyn clenched her hand until the knuckles were white, but he saw nothing but a chagrined girl who was persistently endeavouring to put him in the wrong. Celia at last had succeeded in opening his eyes.

"You will warn Lore? Or does she know?"

"No, I shan't warn her. Dawson's no friend of mine."

"But she is."

"Oh, well, if Ferreira is to be violent, it will be better in public than in private. There will be attendants and so forth to come to the rescue."

She looked up at him. "That argument isn't *yours*, Nicholas!"

"Whose do you think it is?"

"No man would abandon a girl in such a cowardly fashion as

that! Celia has been persuading you."

"And why should she 'persuade' me, as you call it?"

"She wants Maurice to disgrace himself publicly, because she knows I shall be the chief sufferer. . . . Oh, you needn't expostulate! She hates me more and more every day, that woman!"

Nicholas turned pale.

"I can't say that she doesn't, of course; but I've seen no sign of it, and if she does it must be because she hates hypocrites."

Evelyn straightened herself in her chair. "Am I a hypocrite?"

"At least you are playing a farce."

"What farce?"

"You know as well as I do! If you really cared for the chap as much as you make out, you would make some sort of effort to get in touch with him again. Instead of which, his presence in the same house is a nightmare! If all this is for my benefit, I may as well tell you I'm not the least little bit impressed by it."

"I don't quite understand. For *your* benefit?"

"That's what I said."

"I'm afraid I'm very dense."

"No, you're not dense, and you understand perfectly well. If it isn't a farce to pretend devotion to a man, *behind his back only,* what is it?"

Evelyn uttered a sharp, incredulous laugh. "But really! one must have some sort of motive. . . ."

"The motive is quite transparent, thanks! I don't wish to be unnecessarily brutal, but you are certainly wasting your time."

After regarding him for a moment or two, she got up suddenly, and as she did so the blood surged into her face.

"I *do* understand you now! . . . It was my stupidity. I thought you were a gentleman, but I see you are a *cad!*" And she started for the door.

It was the one epithet of all others calculated to penetrate Nicholas's complacency, and he weakly hastened to justify himself before it should be too late.

"You must admit . . ."

"The only thing I admit is that you are not responsible for your own words. She has hypnotised you. That does not excuse your insults, but it explains them." She paused with one hand on the door-knob.

"If I am mistaken I am quite willing to be convinced."

"That is a matter of indifference to me. You must think what you please."

"If I could think you really cared for Ferreira I should admire you tremendously for trying to prevent his running into mischief, but I can't see any personal signs of it. You always seem anxious to keep out of his way. You must admit that's unusual?"

"Then would you *force* your company where it isn't wanted?"

"Very likely not."

"Haven't you any generosity of nature at all? Must you always credit people with sordid motives? How can you go on living like that?"

"Well, I apologise. . . . I'm sorry."

"You know it has always been against my wish that you are in this house. I must have had a presentiment that some such thing as this would happen. The situation was false to begin with."

"Well, I'll get out as quickly as possible; and in the meantime we'll say no more about it. I certainly hadn't any intention of insulting you."

Evelyn turned her back on him for a few moments while still holding the door-handle. Then she slowly released it and came back into the room.

"As Maurice has finished his work, you must be ready for . . ."

"Not yet," said Nicholas, strangely flushing. "I haven't manu-factured enough sensitive stuff to coat the entire film yet. I hope to be ready on Friday or Saturday. I'll let you know."

"You have made no further experiments with your *little* box?"

"I made one early this morning."

"Oh! . . ."

"I said nothing about it because I didn't want to add to your worries, but you may see it if you like."

She gave him a mild, penetrating look. "You said nothing about it because you thought we were no longer friends. As long as there is someone to stir up trouble between us, we shall hardly be; but I want you, under any circumstances, to remember your promise. You have promised to let me witness the first reproduction of a dream secured on your large machine."

"All right! That will be on Saturday or Sunday."

"Then why are you—" She did not finish.

"Why am I wasting time on this minor experimenting? Oh, I wanted to see the end of that dream!"

"And have you?" asked Evelyn in a whisper.

"You must judge for yourself."

He moved to the cupboard to lift down the metal box, while the girl dropped slowly into her chair again. As he was about to release the spring of the revolving mechanism, she interposed an inquiry:

"Without wishing to raise further unpleasantness, may I just ask you one more question?" And, on his silently assenting, she proceeded, "Does Celia Hantish know anything of all this?"

"Nothing whatever!"

"Thank you!" said Evelyn.

Nicholas drew back the little lever, and sat down.

Again she was in the wood, within sight of the pool in the clearing. But she felt faint and ill, and had only just risen to her feet. She had swooned, although she could not remember the exact circumstances. After seeing Lore approach Maurice, everything was a blank until a minute ago. The wood was now silent, no one was visible, and she was alone with those sinister trees, under that ominous sky, with the harsh, penetrating smell, as of burnt rags, in her nostrils. It was terribly real.

Just before the vision had commenced she had caught a solitary glimpse of a man's back disappearing round the bend of the avenue in the direction from which she herself had arrived. He had now vanished, and she was only *remembering* him; moreover, she had hardly seen him; yet she knew it had been Maurice! . . .

Her heart threatened to stop beating, and she was obliged to cling to a tree for support. The quiet forest-way had an atmosphere as if an awful crime had been committed there. The acrid air felt polluted, so that it physically sickened her to breathe it. She wished to get away—quickly—into the open! A leaden paralysis chained her to the spot. She did not know what was to happen . . . but there was nothing to happen. *Maurice had killed Lore!* . . .

She thought neither of Maurice nor of Lore, but only of the crime itself. It took shape in her consciousness as an immense fact which filled the whole universe, and which would render all joy and innocence impossible thereafter, for *everyone*. By no possibility could things be the same in the future as they had been in the past. The ideal world was ended, and reality had burst in to take possession. Her anguish was inexpressible. The sky grew white and bleak.

Somehow, she was both a man and a woman. She was identified with the dreamer of the dream; yet, underneath everything, she remained herself. She was perfectly aware that she was on the point of swooning again. The silence around her became intensified, and the only sound she heard was the dull, heavy, laboured thumping of her own heart. . . .

As the dream gave place abruptly to normal consciousness, she really fainted. When she came to her senses, Nicholas was in the act of moistening her neck and forehead with a cold sponge. He desisted as soon as her eyes opened.

Neither referred to the experience they had passed through. He asked her if she felt able to walk to her own room, which was in the same passage, only a few doors away. She begged a minute longer, and then accepted the assistance of his arm.

No one was about, so he remained outside her door for a few moments after she had shut and locked it from within, to reassure himself that everything was all right with her. A bed creaked, profound silence succeeded, and, guessing that she was lying down to recover herself before dinner, he returned thoughtfully to his room.

XVII

THE FÊTE

Evelyn and Audrey, who had been dressing upstairs, at last made their appearance on the veranda, where Nicholas was waiting for them, smoking a pipe. It was half-past three on Saturday afternoon. July was in, and the girls' flimsy, light-coloured frocks were very appropriate to the day, which was sultry and cloudless. Audrey was bubbling with excited spirits, but Evelyn did not look herself; her brow was wrinkled and she was paler than usual. She took the opportunity of her sister's returning into the house to fetch her father to snatch a word with Nicholas:

"Is your new apparatus ready now?"

"Yes, I sensitised the film this morning."

"Then you will try to-night?"

"Probably."

Audrey came back, leading her father by the arm; and almost immediately afterwards Mrs. Sturt and Katherine emerged through the French windows, attired for visiting.

"Hasn't Celia come yet, then?" demanded Mrs. Sturt, addressing no one in particular.

"Not yet," said Evelyn.

"What is she to appear as, by the way?" asked Audrey. "Are you in the grand secret, Nicholas?"

"She isn't dancing."

"Why not?"

"Of course, she knows it is only a boy-and-girl affair," explained her mother, with quiet decisiveness.

"But she isn't a grandmother herself!"

"She certainly isn't a junior, my dear."

"I know juniors who would willingly take some of Celia's years off her hands if they could dance half as beautifully. If she's standing out, there must be another reason, and I wonder what it is!" She glanced slyly at Nicholas.

"You had better ask her," said the latter, feeling pleased and vexed at once. "Here she is."

Celia, in fact, was already advancing upon the veranda group through the interior room, escorted by a maid, who turned back as soon as contact was effected.

She greeted everybody pleasantly, without shaking hands; meanwhile taking in with a rapid scrutiny the outdoor garments of Katherine and her mother, and endeavouring to deduce therefrom their destination. Her own wrap permitted glimpses to be caught of the charming garden frock within, while sitting closely to her head was a small, gay hat, to match the equally gay sunshade, of Indian colours, in her hand. Katherine tried once more to penetrate the secret of her fashionable dress. It was not her clothes, or her shape, or her way of holding herself; it was some sort of elusive mannerism, which always just evaded her, but one of these times she would suddenly realise of what it consisted, and then she could proceed to put it into personal practice. Evelyn, in the single glance she bestowed on Celia, had an impression, little more than an intuition, that she was growing coarse.

"I'm not unpardonably late, I hope?" asked the arrival.

Nicholas pulled out his watch. "Just on time! A quarter to four."

"George has the car waiting outside, I fancy," said Mrs. Sturt. "Nicholas, you are driving?"

"Yes."

"It does twelve easily on the level," said Audrey.

"However, what matters time in the society of the fair?"

"It's quite a decent car," returned her mother. "This senseless craze for speed is only another symptom of the modern unrest."

"The modern practicality, mother! In the olden days travellers used to need to pull up every fifty yards or so to admire a tree or a cow, and note the circumstance in their diaries. Nowadays we are grown up, and learn the last word about trees and cows at school, so as to have done with it. Nicholas, our dressing-bags are in the hall."

"I've heard about your dresses," said Celia smilingly. "I hope they are as beautiful as the description!"

"That must be Nicholas! Nicholas, you're a fraud!"

He coloured, without attempting to defend himself. Katherine took pity on his confusion.

"You aren't dancing yourself?" she inquired of Celia.

"No; my foot hurts me."

"Oh!" exclaimed Audrey so ingenuously that everyone was forced to laugh.

Mrs. Sturt led Celia into the house, maintaining a confidential pressure on her arm until they were in the hall, while the others followed behind.

The girls slipped on their wraps, Nicholas lifted the cases containing their dance costumes, and all moved to the porch, where farewells were exchanged. After this the little party started down the drive to join the car, over which George was mounting guard in the roadway outside the gate. Celia, to whom, as the guest, the choice of places was offered, appeared to prefer to sit behind, whereupon Evelyn took her own seat by Nicholas. Audrey sat next to Celia.

Colminster Hall was seven miles almost due west from Newleigh, towards the New Forest. The country road along which they rattled was scarcely more than a lane, running through pretty enough woodland scenery, but having a surface which left much to be desired until the last mile was reached, when they picked up a more important and better metalled thoroughfare. Here they found that they had become captured by a procession of other cars, evidently all bound for the same destination. Their occupants were smartly dressed, but the Mereway members of the party, at least, saw no one they knew. Celia's smile was fixed and enigmatical, and it was impossible to say whether she had made any recognitions. Audrey reflected rather ruefully that in a mixed assembly of this sort there would not be much fun to be had unless some introductions could be obtained.

Inside the lodge gate, twenty or thirty cars were already parked in line along the right-hand side of the carriage-drive leading to the house, and others were continually arriving. Commissionaires dealt with each car as it came up, assigning to it its place, and handing each driver a numbered check, which on the conclusion of the entertainment would enable him to locate and claim his property without confusion. Other attendants took charge of the hand-baggage. By a simple system of numbers and counterfoils, those who proposed to participate in the fancy dance were relieved of all care concerning the cases containing their costumes, which would be delivered straight to the dressing-rooms, for retrieval when required. While Nicholas was obtaining his checks, the feminine members of the party discarded their wraps, in order to leave them in the car. Self-conscious beneath the eyes of other women, they followed with their escort the thin stream of new-coming guests moving to augment the already large concourse assembled on the great park-like tea lawn before the house.

The Hall itself proved to be a rambling Charles II erection of considerable size, but small pretensions to beauty. The forecourt was formed by the main building and the two low-lying wings which jutted out from either end of it. Judging from the dimensions of the windows, the rooms inside were probably lofty and spacious, and the decorations and art treasures of the house were celebrated. Beneath her aged haughtiness Lady Wyburn was secretly proud and delighted that this should be the case, and whoever else might seek her acquaintance in vain, she was always at home to the press photographer. She had outlived most of her affections, so that each remaining year of her life saw her more rooted in her rank, local standing, and estate. Her neighbours of the free modern school regarded her as an interesting survival, which did not prevent their leaving her very much to herself; and though she was ruled by a resident nephew, her next-of-kin, it was generally whispered that his scheme of alteration and retrenchments in connection with the estate was already prepared and locked away in his desk, in view of a certain contingency.

Celia, who already had the honour of her personal acquaintance, unhesitatingly led the way at once towards the little group of notabilities who surrounded the lady of the house as a court of honour, a little to the left of the grand marquee which had been set up on the lawn. Short, alert and vigorous, despite her seventy-seven years, with a face like yellow, wrinkled parchment, containing a pair of small, black, darting, malevolent eyes, Lady Wyburn extended a horny, fleshless hand, and expressed her gratification at seeing dear Mrs. Hantish there that afternoon; helpers were so scarce, she had had so many disappointments from her friends! Audrey's fresh and youthful face attracted a moment's attention, but Evelyn was quickly dismissed, and Nicholas not even glanced at, in her anxiety to greet a more important knot of women guests who were just then approaching.

"Go and get some tea, all of you," she called out, after they had already turned away. "You'll easily find a table."

The lawn extension behind the marquee, indeed, was thick with small tables, scattered irregularly, in the manner of the tea-grounds of a public exhibition. Tail-coated waiters were bustling about, receiving and executing the orders of the guests, who already began to fill up the vacant places. The refreshment tent from which the needs of these guests were supplied was not the marquee itself, but another less imposing canvas structure, discreetly hidden from view behind a shrubbery. The train of black-coated waiters moved to and fro between the tables and this tent like so many ants. Audrey began to find it amusing, especially when an unseen orchestra, whose existence they had not suspected, struck up a fashionable hesitation valse. The orchestra was concealed, perhaps, to emphasise the strictly private character of the gathering.

In the very centre of the lawn, where the tables were thickest, was an empty space, and in this space was a raised platform. It was for the exhibition dancers, who even now were to be observed threading their way in gaily-coloured attire through the interested sitters, who invariably turned to stare after them. The effeminate-looking male dancer was in traditional Spanish bull-fighter's dress, while his partner was charmingly apparelled as

Carmen. They smirked as they passed along, with a strange mixture of confusion and self-confident vanity. The girl was pretty.

While Audrey and Celia were gazing after them, Nicholas espied a vacant table which promised to give a decent view of the proceedings. He persuaded Evelyn to sit down, whereupon the others were induced to follow suit. A waiter approached to take their order. Audrey would hear of nothing but eclairs, meringues and ice-creams, but Celia expressed a desire for tea. Before they were supplied the valse came to an end, and the dancers appeared on the platform. An Argentine dance suddenly burst from the orchestra. Simultaneously the pair advanced towards each other with graceful, rhythmical steps, from opposite ends of the platform.

The gay, swaying music, the dancing, the brilliant sunshine, tempered by the softest of breezes, the broad expanse of velvet lawn, interrupted here and there by a mighty, overbranching tree, the multitude of pretty women, in their interesting frocks, the well-groomed, brown-faced men, many of them so jolly-looking, the funny waiters, the dainty, cautious nibbling of a pastry promising to be all cream inside—all this combination of delightful circumstances exhilarated Audrey to such a degree that she presently became audacious.

"It's awfully topping here, but oh! for a man," she exclaimed, half laughing, in the interval between two dances. "Don't say that we four are to stick together all the time!"

Celia smiled. A minute later, as if the secrets of white magic were at her command, she leant backwards across her chair and pulled at the coat of one of two young men who happened to be passing by in quest of a table, accompanied by a stylish, painted woman, no longer quite young. Nicholas thought that he recognised her face as that of a well-known actress, but of course it might be a case of deliberate imitation. The young man, with his superb chest, bronzed, haughty-looking face, and dark moustache, covering teeth like snow, was as smart in appearance as his feminine companion, and far handsomer. He turned rather impatiently to discover who had arrested him, but no sooner did he recognise Celia than his face lit up and became quite pleasant.

"Fancy meeting *you* here!" he said, in the affected, high-pitched voice of his kind.

"Which of you two boys is free?" asked Celia smilingly, still retaining his coat, as she leaned one arm over her chair-back.

The young man laughed. "By Jove! that rather depends, doesn't it?"

"Don't be alarmed! It isn't myself. Who has Sybil—Harry?"

"She rather has the two of us in tow, but I suppose it's Harry."

"Then why don't you give the man a fair chance? Let me introduce you to a very charming new acquaintance! Mr. Hedder-wick—Miss Audrey Sturt! . . . I won't make you known to any more of us, or you'll get confused. Run along, Audrey! Miss Sturt has a great thirst for knowledge, Philip, and wants to see everything. You may return her to her sister in the dressing-rooms at six-thirty. You're dancing, of course?"

"This is somewhat informal, I'm afraid, Miss Sturt!" remarked Hedderwick, showing his magnificent teeth in a smile. Audrey had promptly sat down again after the introduction.

"Oh, Celia is only joking."

"Yes, but it happens to be a joke which just manages to reach my limited intelligence. May I have the honour?"

"No, thanks!"

Celia raised her brows, but said nothing for the present. Hedderwick smiled more than ever. "If you refuse, I shall go down on both knees before you—and remain there!"

"I can see you doing it!"

He dropped on to his knees on the grass. Celia, with great presence of mind, hurriedly and deftly dropped the handkerchief she was holding before him, as though he were down there for the purpose of picking it up.

"Say *yes!*" she commanded Audrey in an intense whisper.

The young girl was in a complex state of wrath, fear, pleasure, mirth, and bewilderment.

"Get up! get up! and don't be such a madman!" she said with

low vehemence, glancing nervously about her to see if others were looking. "I'll come!"

Hedderwick captured Celia's handkerchief, and rose to his feet with an energetic bound. He handed the article to its owner with a bow, which she got up, with mock gravity, to return. The people seated at the neighbouring tables, to whom the spectacle of an elegantly-garbed young man on his two knees before a lady had come as a rather unpleasant shock, exchanged among themselves smiles of tolerance and understanding as soon as they realised that the incident was no more than an audacious joke. Audrey laughed, blushed, and she also got up.

"I don't know you from Adam," she remarked, looking him straight in the face with not unkindly eyes, "but it's clear you are a desperate character, so I suppose I must uphold my sex's good name for submissiveness! Where are you taking me?"

"We'll go and feed the ducks!"

"What, is there a lake or something?"

"No—a river. It's right at the other end of the grounds, so probably the mob haven't hit it yet."

"Are you going to fill your pockets with crumbs?"

"No; we'll give them worms. I'll sing to them, and you can dig them out with the spike of your parasol as fast as they emerge!"

They walked away together, continuing to chatter nonsense.

"Who is that chap?" inquired Nicholas.

"The youngest son of Lord Benfleet," replied Celia.

Evelyn looked up. "I expect she'll be all right with him?"

"In daylight, yes. Under the light of a full moon, I won't guarantee!"

They gazed awhile at the dancing. The man's vigorous methods had begun to make him distressed, but the girl was posturing and smiling with greater effect than ever. The seated onlookers grew bored. Suddenly Celia gave a little start.

"Here come Lore and Dawson!" she announced in a low voice.

The others turned their heads quickly. The pair were about six tables away and he had fallen to the rear to allow Lore room to pass between the chairs. Her rather heavy figure was tastefully dressed in the dark colours which were the only ones she could wear. Her face seemed fuller and softer than usual, and her expressive lips bore an almost amiable smile as she recognised her friends, but the eyes remained strong and cynical. Dawson's long, thin, ill-shaped body had a slight bend forward, while his neatly-shod feet perceptibly turned outwards. The face, which was pale, oval and somewhat pampered and stupid-looking, bearing as its ornament a small black moustache, expressed imperturbable dignity and the consciousness of superior culture; but Evelyn, who had not seen him before, thought it contemptibly vulgar. She failed to understand Lore.

When they had come up, the latter proceeded to effect the necessary introductions. Dawson at once turned his back on Nicholas, and began to talk in an affected voice to the two ladies. They did not sit down again, but the whole group, still talking, moved away towards the open lawn. Lore fell behind with Nicholas.

"May I congratulate you?" he asked, with an embarrassed smile.

"Thanks!"

He could think of nothing else to say appropriate to the occasion.

"We are just off to the sunk garden at the back of the house," explained Lore. "That's where they are giving my masque. I say *my* masque because the music is mine."

"Have you succeeded with it?"

"I haven't the remotest idea."

Though her words were curt, her manner was soft; yet somehow this new softness did not strike him as proceeding from happiness, but seemed rather the consequence of depressed spirits, as though she no longer had energy enough to antagonise people. He felt profoundly sorry for her, and wondered how he could get her away before Ferreira appeared on the scene. Notwithstanding Celia's over-persuasion, he was privately convinced that a public contretemps would be disastrous to Lore's reputation, which was already very shaky, even if no actual violence occurred. But perhaps she knew that Ferreira was coming, and was prepared to accept the risk with her eyes open, in which case his interference was uncalled-for.

"You know Ferreira is going to turn up here this afternoon?" he demanded point-blank.

"Evelyn wrote to tell me."

Nicholas had not contemplated this possibility.

"Begging you to stay away?"

"That's it! But *why*, she and Heaven alone know!"

"Because he has heard of your engagement, and intends to make a row."

"So Evelyn said. But that doesn't explain why I should stay at home. I'm not responsible for Maurice."

"Still, when you have heard your music I suppose you won't have anything else to stop on for?"

"Oh, you're another! For your information, I'm stopping on to the bitter end."

It was evident that some vein of defiance had been opened in Lore's nature, and that the more earnestly he attempted to combat her decision the more obstinate she would become. And at that very moment Dawson turned round to reunite the two sub-divisions of the little party.

"We mustn't be late for the start, Lore!" he said rather pompously, trying, even while he spoke, to stare Nicholas's eyes down. The latter instantly gave up the contention and looked away.

"Are you coming to the masque, Celia?" inquired Lore. "It's just going to begin."

"Where is it to be?"

"At the back of the house. Shall we all go together?"

"I'm rather looking for some people I know, my dear. You two go on ahead. Besides, Mr. Dawson won't want chattering women with him if he is to listen professionally!"

Dawson eyed her in such a fashion that one could see he was

perfectly prepared to combine business and recreation on this occasion. As, however, it was his dignified rule never to press people, and as in addition all the conventions of the situation were against the expression of sociable instincts, he kept silence, affecting entire indifference. Lore watched him for a moment with a queer, cynical drooping of the eyelids, as though reading with distinctness the thoughts passing through his head. Celia took Evelyn's arm and turned away, and Nicholas, raising his hat to Lore, followed them.

"It's a dummy engagement!" remarked Celia negligently, when they were out of earshot. "She can't marry that man. I give them twenty-four hours for hopeless boredom, and half a week for a first-class quarrel!"

"Oh, it's an escape!" said Evelyn quietly.

Celia looked interested. "An escape from what, or whom?"

"An escape from herself. . . . and if this fails her . . ."

"Well?"

But Evelyn had no more to say, and the older woman, after smiling at her strangely, prepared to take her departure.

"I dare say you two won't be sorry to be left to your own devices for a short time! I am really going in search of some people. You had better run along to the masque." She proceeded to address Nicholas alone: "After Evelyn has gone upstairs to dress, if you feel particularly lonely and friendless, you may reclaim me. I shall probably be found wandering in the vicinity of the marquee. . . . Au revoir!"

She departed across the lawn with her inimitable step, the envy of all other women, and Nicholas watched her out of sight before returning to his companion. She herself was too absent to observe his preoccupation. They automatically joined the procession of guests skirting the house across the lawns, to arrive at the sunk garden in the rear. As they drew nearer to the open-air theatre, faint music was wafted to them round the side of the house, and all footsteps instinctively quickened.

"Perhaps he won't come," suggested Evelyn, still occupied with her thoughts.

"Of course he may have found town too attractive."

"I would give a great deal for to-day to be safely over!" said the girl, with a shivering little sigh.

"Then there would still be to-morrow and the next day."

"No, it's to-day—it's to-day! I am as certain as if an archangel came down from heaven to announce it that this is to be an ill-omened day for all of us!"

"Is it that dream?"

"You cannot have dreamt it three times for nothing."

They came within sight of the dug-out lawn, in the centre of which the masque was in progress. The long-fronted terrace behind the house, with its beautiful Italian balcony, was thronged with guests, who had also overflowed on to the tops of the sloping grass banks of the hollowed-out arena. The lawn itself was clear for the players, whose stage scenery consisted of the large ornamental fountain of white stone in the middle, with its surrounding basin, a stone garden-seat to accommodate four persons, a few skins of wild carnivora for use as rugs to sit on, and nothing more. The organisers of the spectacle did not wish to compete with the theatre, but preferred to preserve the authentic atmosphere of the ideal pastoral era. Shepherds and shepherdesses—not beribboned, but in flowing Grecian attire—fauns, satyrs and nymphs crossed and re-crossed the grass, to strike aesthetic postures, dance their emotions with carefully-modulated grace, and make love in recitative. On the printed programme they were named Perigot, Daphnis, Chloe, Amoret and Iphis, but it was impossible to tell who was who, and it did not matter. The feminine half of the audience agreed that the effect was charming, while the men could always find something to laugh at. Lore's music was rather chained by the pedantic requirements of the art-form; it was laboured, dull, and did not go well; but among the predominating oboes and flutes of her orchestra was a solitary kettledrum for the comic relief, and this kettledrum, whenever it sounded, produced the happiest success. The men roared with laughter, and the ladies thought it most quaint.

Evelyn and Nicholas took their stand with the rest, and remained looking on for quite a long time. Towards the end she touched his arm, as he leant gloomily over the stone balustrade, watching the performance with lack-lustre eyes.

"I think I'll go now to dress. Are you staying to see the Old English dancing?"

"No; I'll come with you, if I may."

They had been informed that the dressing-rooms were in the house itself, and accordingly made their way to the main entrance. A good many young people were already ascending the great staircase. Nicholas offered to stay with her in the upstairs corridor, out of which the doors of the numerous dressing-rooms led, until she had met Audrey, as he had somewhat stupidly retained the checks for their cases in his possession, so that the latter would not have the remotest idea where to go.

It was ten minutes before Audrey appeared, and then Hedderwick was with her. Both looked very pleased with themselves.

"You've dropped Celia, then?" asked the younger sister.

"She dropped us."

"We've seen every square inch of the grounds and every frock, and Mr. Hedderwick is an angel without wings!"

Hedderwick uttered a mighty laugh, and was manufacturing a response, when someone caught Nicholas's elbow from behind.

"I say old chap, have you seen Lore anywhere?"

He turned quickly, to confront Ferreira. At the same instant Evelyn came forward quietly.

"What are you doing here, Maurice? and why do you want Lore?"

"I want a chat with her."

Evelyn half turned away faintly; then again faced him.

"The masque is over, and she may have gone home."

"But you don't know that she's gone home?"

"No; but I think it is most likely."

Ferreira laughed. "You bet, if she is to be found, I'll find her!"

"I want you to go home yourself, Maurice. I ask it as a favour."

"When I've had my palaver with Lore, and not before! Has

Dawson turned up?"

Evelyn did not reply.

"Yes; Dawson's here," said Nicholas.

Audrey, growing weary of the debate, exerted gentle force to drag her sister to their room, and she offered no resistance.

"Nicholas, you will go with Maurice?"

"Very well."

The five young people separated: the two girls and Hedderwick to retire to their respective rooms, Ferreira and Nicholas to redescend the main staircase.

Once in the open air, Ferreira lit a cigarette and blew a cloud of smoke into his companion's eyes.

"Do *you* know where Lore is, or may be?" he demanded, with an insolent smile.

"If I did, I shouldn't pass the information on to you."

"Then you can fade, as fast as you like!"

"Where do you intend to start looking for her?"

"That doesn't signify," said Ferreira. "You may see a crowd running together soon, and that's where we shall be!"

Nicholas watched him out of sight before going to rejoin Celia.

XVIII

A TRAGIC INTERRUPTION

It was nearing seven o'clock. There was a rather large circle of well-dressed men and women talking and laughing together in the very centre of the lawn before the house, and Celia was among them. Intimidated by their appearance, Nicholas hesitated for some minutes to draw nearer. One of the young men observed him loitering and casting uneasy glances, and apparently resented it, for he left the conversation in order to stare at him, and it was these stares which led Celia at last to look round curiously. The moment she saw their object she excused herself in a laughing way to the others, and started to back out of the group. The desertion was accompanied by a chorus of expostulation on the part of her friends, to which, however, she only responded by waving her gloved hand teasingly. Without the least attempt at concealment, she came straight over to where Nicholas was standing and lightly caught his arm.

They began to stroll across the lawn, away from the house, in the opposite direction to that of the entrance lodge.

"I hope you haven't left your friends out of compassion for my lonely state?" asked Nicholas, smiling.

"I've been expecting you for ever so long! Evelyn found her room all right?"

"Yes; and Ferreira has turned up, and is looking all over the place for Lore!"

"How desperately funny! Somehow, I didn't think he would."

"You don't seem to take it very seriously."

"Maurice is such an utter boy! Why can't he possess his soul in patience a little while longer? The engagement will break itself off; anyone can see that."

"I wish you'd convince him of that fact."

"I will if I see him."

"Evelyn is very much concerned. So much so that she begged me to shadow him."

"And are you shadowing him?" asked Celia humorously.

"Oh, I had to meet you. Besides, he wouldn't have me with him, and I couldn't very well go dodging him behind trees!"

"Otherwise I might have waited in vain!"

"You seemed to be passing the period pleasantly enough."

"Surely you don't intend to be absurd?"

"Not at all; only I'm not sufficiently conceited to imagine that my failure to keep the appointment would have caused you any particular pang. A lady isn't in universal request for nothing!"

"Do you mean those men? How foolish you are, my dear! Creatures of that sort are turned out by the thousand. I hardly know one from another."

"Yet you seem to relish their society!"

"Because I was with them by compulsion of circumstances? Didn't I leave them directly I saw you?"

"You did."

Celia was an artist who put her paints on with the palette knife, as well as the brush, on occasion.

"You know I'd a hundred times rather be with you than any-one, my dear!"

"But would you?"

She threw him a look and a smile. "One's own property is always the best."

"It's very good of you to say so," muttered Nicholas, who began to respond with difficulty.

"The whole fact of the matter is, you are far too modest, and don't realise your own worth. Do you think I am a woman to take up anybody?"

"No, I don't."

"Very well, then! let it stop at that. I rather flatter myself I'm a connoisseur!" and she erected her lovely neck with a proud backward swing.

By now they had passed outside the territory of the grand marquee. Tables, waiters, guests were left behind, and they found themselves walking silently over a great, solitary expanse of grass, which was a continuation of the lawn before the house, but each moment approximated more closely to a park. The beeches, birches and oaks occurred with greater frequency as they strolled on, while the turf underfoot gradually grew coarser and lumpier, indicating a transition to a region of brush. The country was quite level, and in the background was a wood. It was unexplored land, appealing to their romantic instincts. The trees became denser, yet they were still inside the estate, and there were no signs at present of their approach to a boundary wall. The declining sun hung like a great ball of ruddy, molten gold straight before them, not very high in the sky. The shadows of the trees were long and poetic. An occasional faint burst of music from the dance-room reached their ears; otherwise, the only sounds to hear were from the birds and the quietly-rustling leaves.

"The river must be this way," suggested Nicholas, after a somewhat long silence.

"Perhaps."

"Shall we go and look for it, or do you want to see the dancing?"

"Let's be unique!"

The grounds certainly were mysteriously deserted. They were almost out of sight of people, and even the few they saw were far away, towards the house. Celia slipped her arm through his.

"My reputation is empty-headedness and frivolity," she proceeded confidentially, "but at least I can appreciate the other thing. The sedate miss everything. They can be neither frivolous nor ideal, but just like to feel themselves in a herd! I haven't a word to say against dancing—but not on a July evening! Isn't this divine?"

"*Divine* is the word!"

"I fancy you are worrying about that encounter? You can't do anything, my dear. If they meet in the crowd there will be plenty of men to interfere. This journey of discovery promises excitement!"

Nicholas threw off his doubts and entered into her enthusiasm.

"What sort of excitement?"

"Perhaps we shall find a little gate."

"A little gate?"

She glanced behind her hurriedly. They were now quite alone and no one was in sight. The wood was all around them.

"Yes; a little gate." She laughed. "A little gate, with two little red doors, which open—so!" and she parted her lips charmingly in a long bow.

"Oh! . . ." he exclaimed with surprised comprehension, as her meaning dawned upon him.

A moment later he was kissing her. She stood swaying, with her two arms hanging limply down by her sides, and her eyes closed.

Presently they came to the river.

Through a narrow open gateway in the moss-grown wall which marked the boundary of the woods, they entered quite unexpectedly on a broad, grassy walk, following the course of the curving stream. All the way along the inner side of the walk was a ten-foot wall, completely overgrown with flowering shrubs and creepers. Across the stream, which was little wider than the walk itself, were trees, thick rather than high, whose overhanging branches drooped to the water surface, quite concealing what lay beyond. At the bend of the river, about fifty yards ahead, a part of a white-walled cottage was visible through the intervening green vegetation. It was evidently an outhouse belonging to the estate, perhaps a dairy-building.

"Oh, how sweetly entrancing!" cried Celia, clasping her hands in rapture, as they emerged on to the walk.

Nicholas responded with the tolerant smile of a man for feminine enthusiasm, and they continued gazing about them where they were, trying to comprehend all the beauties of the spot at once. Although the sun was already behind the trees, the air remained sultry. The sky was cloudless. A multitude of tiny midges swarmed above the surface of the stream, while wild bees, butterflies, dragon-flies and beetles still pursued their business in the shrubberies and on the banks. An unseen bird was trilling delightfully close at hand. The air was nearly faint with the evening odours of the flowers.

Nicholas had just remarked on the great apparent depth of the still water, which he calculated at six feet in the section of the river by which they were standing, when his companion quietly held up a cautionary hand.

"What is it?" he asked, after an obedient pause.

"I was sure I heard voices."

They walked on for a few yards. Then Celia turned her head, to see two persons—a man and a woman—coming through the gateway by which they themselves had entered. It was Lore, followed by Dawson.

Courtesies were exchanged, and everyone expressed gratification at the strange reunion in so remote a corner of the grounds. When Celia come to regard her friend more attentively, however, she detected that her cheeks were hectic, and that her manner, now that the first effusions were over, relapsed into abruptness and taciturnity. Her bosom, also, was slightly labouring. She was visibly trying to control her breathing. From that basis, Celia proceeded to observe that Lore and Dawson did not once address each other. His face bore a sulky expression, and he kept turning away irritably, curling his small moustache. A recent quarrel was diagnosed. It caused Celia no disquietude, but she was curious concerning the details.

She began by congratulating Lore on her wonderful music.

"Oh, it was rotten!" was the scornful reply. "My day's done! I have this afternoon to thank for being able to realise it at last."

"What nonsense, my dear! But you artists are all the same. Ideals prove unapproachable, so you will sell your tools at once! That kettledrum was positively inspired!"

"So I've already been told fifty-seven times! I try to write music, and I achieve fame as a buffoon. But it doesn't matter."

"I'm sure Mr. Dawson calls it a triumph."

"Oh, yes—yes," said Dawson, obviously vexed at being appealed to, and at once retiring again into his shell.

Lore smiled bitterly. "You needn't play the consoling angel for my benefit, Celia. I'm past all that. There was a time when I should have been sickened at making such a public idiot of myself, but now I don't care a damn! I'm not even thinking about it."

Discerning that she spoke the truth, Celia allowed the topic to drop.

"Maurice is here," she announced casually and watched with flickering eyes the effect of her words. Lore looked contemptuous, but said nothing.

"He's looking for you," continued Celia. "I don't wish to appear officious, my dear, but hadn't you better go home?"

"Why should I?"

"He may have been drinking, or something. I don't say he has. In any case, a meeting with him won't make for your enjoyment."

"My enjoyment!" Lore laughed. "Oh, yes, my enjoyment! . . . Yes, I'm enjoying myself tremendously!"

"Then why stay on, my dear?"

Lore snapped her fingers in the air. "Just to show Maurice he can go to the devil!"

"But is it quite fair to Mr. Dawson?"

"Who is this person?" asked Dawson.

"Maurice Ferreira. A young man who has been persecuting Lore with his unrequested attentions for some time past. Do persuade her to leave!"

"If he is to create unpleasantness, I certainly think we should leave. . . . Have you any definite purpose in staying?" he added, addressing Lore.

"Yes, I have."

"May I inquire?"

"To put off going home till the last possible moment! I loathe that house I live in!"

"I think you ought to go," persisted Celia.

"Monro may go if he wants to. I'm sure I haven't the faintest desire to detain him against his will."

Dawson coloured faintly.

"Be sensible, my dear!" said Celia. "How can he go without you?"

"Oh, he can have the car. I shall manage somehow."

"You know that isn't it!"

"Oh, I know what you mean, but I can assure you there's nothing of that kind between us. We are far too reasonable, both of us! . . . Perhaps you had better go," she continued, with a sarcastic smile, half facing Dawson. "Maurice is younger than you, and has shockingly primitive methods!"

His colour deepened as he bowed. "I accept my dismissal."

Lore stretched out her hand. . . . "Good-bye!"

But Dawson declined to see it. Removing his hat and retaining it in his hand, he made her a second and more profound bow from his waist. Then, turning to Celia, he gave her a friendlier and less ceremonious salute. Nicholas, who had been watching the proceedings in gloomy silence, he nodded to casually, and immediately clapped on his hat. As he was in the act of departing, he bethought himself.

"I shall *not* take the car, so I had better hand you the check." And he started fumbling for his pocket-case.

"You won't secure another conveyance, and it's two miles to a station," returned Lore. "Anyone will give me a lift."

He replaced the pocket case, and silently bowed acceptance, as though not trusting himself to dispute the point. Disguising his anger under a mask of exaggerated nonchalance, he turned on his heel and started with short, affected steps for the wall gateway. In the gap he paused for a moment, with his back to the watchers, to produce and light a cigarette. Celia thought it the most characteristic so far of all his actions. It was a piece of studied rudeness and insolence which at one stroke destroyed all his pretensions to superior culture, and displayed the intrinsic caddishness of his nature. After he had disappeared, the two women exchanged indirect and uneasy glances.

"It's all over between you, then!" ventured Celia.

"It is."

The other placed a light hand on her arm. "You're not greatly upset, are you, my dear?”

“I, upset!” Lore uttered a nasal laugh. “O Jupiter!—can’t you see it’s a deliverance?”

“I suppose you fell out before we met you?”

“There’s no need to make a mystery of it. He tried to force his scheme of the universe down my throat, and I rebelled. I told him he was to marry *me*, and not my habits. . . . I seem to be floundering from one bog to another these days! What sensible thing shall I do next, I wonder!”

“At all events, my dear, you can be thankful you weren’t very far in.”

“I’m thankful for nothing—*nothing!* I feel as if Fate were kicking me out of sheer spite!”

“Won’t you walk back to the house with us?”

“No, thanks! I’ll stop here a little while. I don’t feel like a crowd. You go.”

“If you meet Maurice, you will tell him the news before anything else?”

“Perhaps.”

“Be as nice to him as you can.”

“Oh, I’m all bitter—I’m all bitter! I couldn’t be nice to a seraph at the present moment. If you see him, tell him what you like, but get him to run away home like a good boy and leave me alone! That’s all I ask of anybody—to be left alone! I feel as if the least spark would explode me!”

“There is still no hope for him, of course?”

“For Maurice? No; I’m through with marriage. Let him turn his attention to Evelyn, or anyone. I’ve given up the idea of being happy in this world. Happiness isn’t worth the bother of getting it. I suppose nothing is worth anything, if you look at it in the right way.”

“You’re in an evil mood, my dear! You’ll see things differently by and by. . . . You really won’t come with us?”

“No, thanks,” said Lore again.

They left her, to retrace their steps to the house. When they looked back at the gateway, she had a lighted cigarette in her mouth and was wandering slowly and despondently along the river-walk, in the direction of the white cottage. Celia sighed, which was an unusual phenomenon for her. As they re-entered the wood she said:

"I rather pride myself on my prophetic powers, but I can't place Lore at all. I simply can't imagine what the continuation of her life is to be."

Two minutes later she sighed again. . . . "Oh, well, I suppose we must hope for the best!"

Nicholas said nothing.

They continued walking through the wood. When they were still in the very thickest part, his unprepared eyes received a momentary impression of a man's back disappearing behind some trees. It was at a considerable distance away to the left, and the man had seemed to be going in the direction of the river.

"Did you see that?" he inquired of Celia.

"No."

"There's a fellow making for where we've just come from."

"Don't say it was Maurice!" said Celia quickly.

"I think it *was*."

He indicated the spot, and both stood still to stare at it for some moments, but there was no reappearance.

"Anyhow, there's no ground for a scene now," remarked Celia.

It was the signal to go on again. Neither spoke for a long time, and it appeared as if Celia were sharing her companion's uneasiness regarding Lore, but her resilient temperament was the first to recover. Music, glitter and gaiety were secretly calling to her; she wished to see the dance dresses and to pass the time of day with her friends; yet it would be unfair to Nicholas to drag him about with her wherever she went. As they approached the marquee, her restlessness was increased by the strains of dance music issuing from the farther wing of the house, and she began to ponder ways and means.

People were streaming in and out of the entrance of the marquee and, reminded of the desirability of refreshment, they too entered. They ate sandwiches, standing at the buffet. Celia accompanied them with a glass of sherry, but Nicholas observed his rule. It was half-past eight, but still daylight. On coming outside again she smiled, hesitated, and bit her gloved finger-tips.

"I ought really to pay my respects to Lady Wyburn. She's a horribly touchy personage, and I don't want to fall out with her superfluously. How can you amuse yourself?"

"How long will you be gone?"

"That depends on how soon I can find her. Wouldn't you care to see the dancing? The girls will be disappointed if you don't report the success of their costumes."

Something in her tone caused him to give her a peculiar look, but he raised no opposition to the proposal.

"Then where shall we meet again?"

"Oh, we shall be sure to see each other; but if not, meet me here at ten o'clock. We'll make it a rendezvous."

Nicholas's brow darkened, but still he made no comment.

"Very well."

"And this interlude will afford you a capital opportunity of discovering which you really prefer: your own society or that of a certain irresponsible and exacting lady!"

He pretended not to hear her very well; whereupon, deciding to waste no more coaxing on him in his present humour, she accomplished her escape. Nicholas set out sullenly towards the ball-room.

A few steps farther on, the impulse entered his head to ascertain which direction she was taking, and he looked back. Another of her innumerable friends had already arrested her—a smartly-apparelled youth—and they were chatting together almost within hearing distance of himself. Celia was standing with both hands resting on the handle of her parasol, which propped her from behind, while her head was thrown backwards in the act of a hearty laugh. Although the youth maintained a solemn face, it was sufficiently obvious that he was amusing her—in fact that he was a jester after her own heart. . . . Nicholas resumed his way, crimson in face and with a heavy scowl disfiguring his features. More than one person stared after him indignantly as he jostled against them—really unconsciously, but apparently with deliberate rudeness—in passing.

There was no difficulty in locating the dance-room, for its entrance door was the nucleus of the throng. It was an isolated hall lying beyond the farther of the two wings of the house, with which it communicated by a covered passage-way. The public entrance was the wide double door opening directly on to the lawn. The hall, which was large and lofty, had been decorated profusely for the occasion with coloured stuffs, tinsel and streamers. Although it was daylight outside, electricity was blazing from a dozen overhead chandeliers. A small string orchestra played in the centre of the upstairs gallery. The two long sides of the same gallery were crowded with guests in ordinary attire, staring down at the gay spectacle on the floor, while other throngs had congregated about the door downstairs, peering in as well as they were able. The dance-floor was reserved to those in fancy dress. As many as thirty couples were in motion, and others were seated on the long, curved seats round the walls. One of the new American dances was progressing.

Nicholas could see nothing from the door. The double crowd—one on either side—was too dense, and in the middle he kept being elbowed aside by the masqueraders who, singly or in knots, were continually passing to and from the lawn. He made a detour to the gallery entrance, which was round the side of the building, and having ascended the staircase, eventually squeezed his way into a gap left by a guest who had had enough. Standing with both elbows on the balcony ledge, he leant over with the rest.

There were many pretty women on the floor and, as they outnumbered the men, some of them were dancing together, but Evelyn was nowhere to be seen. Audrey he detected after a time. Her fresh, generous young beauty was admirably served by her harem dress. The ever-moving white silken tunic and trousers and the swaying ropes of imitation pearls formed almost the most conspicuous object in the room, while, to judge by her laughing, blushing face, she had every appearance of thoroughly enjoying herself. Her dancing partner was no other than Hedderwick, cleverly disguised as a Kurdish bandit, or something of the sort, with wide, coloured breeches, and a dangerous-looking dagger stuck beneath his sash. In his audacious way, he looked even handsomer than she. He kept his eyes constantly fixed on her face, and the very movements of his lips indicated the daring, humorous character of the monologue he was addressing to her.

Presently Evelyn entered, from outside. She was unescorted, and stood just inside the doorway for a moment or two, as if in doubt. Nicholas wondered whether she had been looking for Maurice, or Lore, or both. As he continued trying to attract her attention, it occurred to him that hers was the only masquerade in the hall which appeared not to be a masquerade at all but a personal dress. It was not that her Roman draperies approximated to modern fashions—though perhaps they did so more closely than some of the fanciful costumes there—but that she seemed totally unconscious of her apparel, remaining as cold, grave and thoughtful as if she were wearing an everyday frock in her own home. Only her gorgeous bracelets and necklaces were rather out of place on her, but of these, too, she appeared to be unaware. There were handsomer women present, but none so aesthetically striking. A young cavalier minced up to her and swept off his plumed hat, but upon a few unsmiling words from Evelyn he took his departure, this time walking more naturally. She remained standing in the doorway, without espying Nicholas.

The dance ceased, a new one started, and Audrey went up to her sister for a moment, leading Hedderwick by the hand. Evelyn just condescended to smile at what they said to her, then gave Audrey's shoulder a gentle push, to send them back into the dance. Nicholas thought he would go down and speak to her.

He was actually looking over his shoulder to calculate his retreat, when suddenly, rapidly finishing the phrase on which they were embarked, the orchestra ceased playing!

The dancers halted and uncoupled in astonishment, every face staring up towards the gallery, to discover what was amiss. The guests in the side galleries were no less dumbfounded. The whole hall was filled with the low babel arising from the murmur of individual interrogation, each inquiring of his or her neighbour what had happened, as though others were likely to be better informed than themselves. A master of ceremonies, in evening dress, was perceived talking very earnestly to the band conductor, who bent down from his stand in order to hear better. Finally the latter gave an acquiescent little nod of his head, straightened himself, spoke an incisive word of instruction to his subordinates and, with a smart rap on the desk before him, raised and brought down his baton. The orchestra raced through the opening bars of the National Anthem, and immediately got up with their instruments. Descending from his stand, the conductor followed the last of his men through the exit door.

The dance obviously was at an end. It was barely nine o'clock, however, and it had been announced to last till eleven. A confusion of surprised and indignant voices filled the room. No one went away but group encountered group, demanding an explanation which no one could supply. A few audacious youths started booing. The master of ceremonies had vanished hastily. Just as the tumult was threatening to become a riot and many of the ladies had begun nervously to thread their way towards the door, a short, rotund, red-faced gentleman in evening dress, having the appearance of a barrister, whom several present recognised as Lady Wyburn's nephew, made his appearance in the centre of the gallery and, mounting the conductor's stand, faced the assembled company, with an upheld hand for silence. The uproar subsided rapidly, and in less than twenty seconds he obtained the full hush for which he waited.

"Ladies and gentlemen," he began, in a rich, measured voice, which seemed far too large for his body. "I exceedingly regret to inform you that an unfortunate accident to one of our guests renders it desirable that our entertainment should be brought to a prompt conclusion. As it is realised that many of you here present may be temporarily separated from your friends, we have thought it best to reassure you at once by giving the name of the lady to whom the accident has occurred. It is Miss Lore Jensen, of

Newleigh. Any of her personal friends who may desire more particular information will find me in the main entrance hall of the house during the next half-hour or so. We courteously request everyone else present personally to assist us in bringing the proceedings to a close as rapidly as possible."

He descended from the stand and went away. Whispering succeeded the first silence which his announcement had produced, and then the babel recommenced. All talked together, debating the possible nature of the accident, whether it were really essential to close down the entertainment, whether it were *she* who had composed the music for the masque, when she had last been seen, etc. While they talked they moved towards the doors, and the dance-room rapidly emptied itself. There was no more rowdiness, but everyone seemed awed by a tragedy which was all the more impressive to the imagination because its details had been withheld. Those in fancy dress were anxious to discard it.

Nicholas had hardly reached the head of the stairs when the electric lights were switched off. Out of doors, however, it was a bright twilight. He wished to find the girls, but as everyone was leaving the ball-room he guessed that they would most likely be making their way with the rest to the hall of the house in order to learn the particulars of the accident. It was five minutes before he was able to work his way through the crush up to the great double front doors leading into the house. Lady Wyburn's nephew was standing in an alcove of the hall, besieged by a queue of curious guests, and he was responding to each in turn with a brevity and an unflurried courtesy which spoke volumes for his trained mental alertness. Nicholas did not care to approach him until the throng should have thinned somewhat. Meanwhile, he looked round for the girls, but failed to see them.

It was not till a few minutes later that they came in. Evelyn was deathly pale and faintly smiling, while her sister appeared to be supporting her. He went forward to them.

"Evie has fainted," explained Audrey briefly. "You had better help me with her upstairs."

Evelyn caught at Nicholas impulsively. "Oh, what has happened?"

"I don't know. I'm waiting to speak to that fellow."

A woman guest, who was hastening past them to the door, overheard question and answer.

"She was found drowned in the river!" she whispered swiftly and, bestowing a single glance on the little group, resumed her passage.

Evelyn threw such an expressive smile at Nicholas that he was dismayed. He was about to obey Audrey's injunction to assist her to her dressing-room upstairs, when the massive door of a room which communicated with the hall opened about a foot, and a woman's hatted head appeared through the gap, exploring the crowd. It was Celia. Everybody turned to stare at her, but it was not until she had caught sight of Nicholas and the girls that she fully emerged, softly closing the door behind her. She stepped across to where they stood. Her face was serious, rather than agitated.

"What a horrible thing, my dears!" Her voice was very low. "Lady Wyburn is in that room, and I want you all to come in and see her."

She led the way, and the two girls followed immediately behind. Nicholas, who brought up the rear, closed the door again after him as soon as he was inside. Those in the hall who had witnessed the episode began to whisper among themselves.

Lady Wyburn was alone in the room, sitting very erect in the exact middle of a sumptuous sofa. She appeared to be in a vile temper. Her face was copper-coloured, her hundred wrinkles were as if graved, and her voice, when she spoke, was hard and staccato. Celia reintroduced her friends. They were invited to sit down.

Nicholas was addressed:

"I understand that you can throw a certain amount of light on this terrible business?"

He abstained from glancing at Celia, but he at once saw that she had been speaking, and his reply, when it came, was dull, cold and heavily deliberate:

"On the contrary, I am still waiting to hear the particulars."

"But you are a friend of the deceased lady?"

"I am an acquaintance."

"The details are very simple. Less than an hour ago my dairy-man, living at the other end of the estate, discovered Miss Jensen's body lying in eight feet of water in the stream which runs past his cottage. Life was extinct. The doctor who was summoned finds no trace of violence on her person, but there are footprints on the path by the side of the stream which may require investigation by the police. It is hardly conceivable that she could have overbalanced herself accidentally and been unable to regain the bank. A cigarette-case was also picked up on the bank, close to her handbag, which was there as well, and out of which it may, or may not, have fallen. The police have been notified, and should be here shortly."

Evelyn uttered a little gasping sigh, upon which Audrey, who sat beside her, pressed her hand reassuringly.

Nicholas preserved a gloomy silence.

"Perhaps the cigarette-case and handbag should have been left *in situ* for the police," proceeded Lady Wyburn grimly. "However, they were brought to me. Here is the case. Do you recognise it?"

It was of silver and was engraved with the monogram "M.F." He had seen it produced from Ferreira's pocket often.

"I know nothing about it," he replied half sulkily.

Celia shot him a queer little glance.

"Do you know anyone with those initials?"

"I know a Maurice Ferreira."

"Is it his?"

"I haven't any idea."

"Was he in the neighbourhood of the river this evening, do you know?"

"I don't know."

Lady Wyburn looked up sharply in surprise, while Celia bit her lip and changed colour. Evelyn began to realise that a conflict was in progress; she kept her eyes feverishly on Nicholas.

"That is all the more strange," said Lady Wyburn, "because Mrs. Hantish tells me you encountered him close by the river, and on his way towards it."

Evelyn gave a little cry, and started up; but her sister drew her back. Celia's foot was drumming the floor.

"That is not so," replied Nicholas coldly.

"Then how came you to make that statement?" She turned to Celia.

"I simply repeated Mr. Cabot's own words. I did not see him myself."

"Do you accept that?" Lady Wyburn returned to Nicholas.

"No. . . . I saw a man's back for the tenth part of a second in the woods, and mentioned the fact. Mrs. Hantish asked me if I thought it had been Maurice Ferreira, and I said it was possible. I presume it *was* possible. That is the whole story, as far as I am concerned."

"Then you cannot account for her being in the river?"

"I certainly can't."

Evelyn's bosom, beneath her Roman dress, continued to rise and fall, but her eyes, as they rested on Nicholas's face, had a new light in them.

"Yet you were the last to see her there, Mrs. Hantish tells me?"

"It may be so."

"Who was with her?"

"No one. She came there accompanied by a Mr. Dawson, but he left while we were still with her."

"May I have your card?"

He produced one in silence, and Lady Wyburn rose to place it on her writing-table, beneath a paper weight. Instead of sitting down again, she turned briskly and extended her withered hand to Celia.

"Come again when all this miserable trouble is over and forgotten."

Celia responded coldly. The hostess made a small, stiff, general bow to the others, and the interview was at an end. The party made for the door, glad to be away from the gloomy splendour of the apartment and its atmosphere of death.

Outside, everybody paused or turned to stare at them, while a few of the ladies looked as if they were mustering courage to come forward and speak. Audrey glared back indignantly and, hastily requesting Nicholas to wait where he was for them, slipped her arm through Evelyn's and hurried her upstairs. To escape unwelcome attention, he and Celia paced slowly towards the outer door.

"Well, you have succeeded in putting your affront on me, and I hope you are satisfied!" murmured Celia, with a spiteful little smile.

"I'm afraid you are too egotistical!" returned Nicholas stonily. "I wasn't thinking of you in the matter at all, but I certainly wasn't going to give evidence against Ferreira at the present stage of the proceedings."

She still smiled. "Oh! no, my dear; it was your abominable jealousy! However, you have done it this time! I have too much proper pride to endure that sort of treatment. . . . I am going home with other friends; and you need not call on me again."

"As you please," said Nicholas, turning pale.

"In any case, I do not care to number an accessory after the fact among my acquaintance. Perhaps you may still have cause to repent the line you have chosen."

"It's suicide, and you know it."

She gave him a singular glance. "You think so?"

"I am sure of it."

"Then ask Evelyn *her* opinion."

He sombrely watched her descend the steps to the drive, without remembering even to remove his hat. A minute later she had disappeared.

Shortly afterwards the girls came down in their own clothes.

"Where's Celia?" demanded Audrey.

"Oh, she isn't coming home with us."

"Why not?"

"Have you had words?" asked Evelyn.

"We have."

"Because you refused to back up her statement to Lady Wyburn, I suppose," said Audrey. "I shouldn't worry about that, if I were you, Nicholas. It was one of the finest things you ever did. Of course, you did see Maurice?"

He returned no answer.

"Why did Mr. Dawson leave her there?" asked Evelyn, after a pause.

"It was the tail end of a quarrel they had had. The engagement was broken off."

An eager look appeared in her eyes, only to fade again at once.

"But that could have had nothing to do with it," she said in a low voice.

"It may have been the last straw."

"Do you think it was suicide, then?" asked Audrey, as quietly as her sister.

"Probably. She was in a very depressed state when we left her."

"Of course there will be an inquest, and you will be called upon to give evidence?"

"I expect so."

He picked up their dressing-cases and they left the house together. The crowd had considerably thinned by now. When they were in the dusky drive Audrey gave him a keen side glance.

"And shall you repeat the statement you made to Lady Wyburn?"

"As far as I'm asked, I shall."

"But if any new facts come out—about Maurice—in the meantime?"

"They must act on them. I can't help that."

"So in any case . . ."

"In any case I decline to be forced into giving damning evidence which I'm not at all sure about in my own mind. Of course it's a hundred to one that nothing of all this will arise."

Audrey glanced uneasily at her sister's white, thin, careworn face, which seemed to have put on years within the space of half an hour. As she did so, she had an instantaneous sensation, impossible to describe to herself or to recall, but which was as if a huge, formless, black shadow had advanced on Evelyn from behind, enveloped her, and passed away again in front. At first she was merely startled, but a few minutes later she made up her mind that it was a presage of some evil fortune about to overwhelm her sister. She said nothing about it to the others, but was very quiet all the way home.

They found their car. The majority of the other cars had already departed, so that the road was practically empty as soon as they were well past the lodge gate. They arrived at Mereway about half-past ten.

Katherine had gone to bed, but her father and mother were still sitting in the drawing-room. The lamp was lighted, but the window remained open and the blinds were undrawn. Mrs. Sturt was writing to a friend abroad, while her husband was on the sofa, smoking a cigar, over a volume of theatrical reminiscences. Both looked up in astonishment as the girls and Nicholas came into the room.

"What's the meaning of this? Why are you home so early?" asked Mrs. Sturt, mechanically laying down her pen.

"Evelyn fainted," began Audrey.

"Oh, dear! . . . Sit down, Evelyn! Are you better now?"

"But that's not the reason, and it isn't the worst, by a long way," continued Audrey. "The affair was closed down suddenly. There was an accident."

"An accident?"

"A tragedy. One of the guests was accidentally drowned in the river."

"Good gracious me, child! How was that? It wasn't anyone we know?"

"Yes; and very well, too! Someone who lives at Newleigh."

"You had really better sit down, Evelyn!" The girl did so. Even the mellow light of the lamp failed to flatter the frailty of her appearance and the delicacy of her colouring. When she removed her hat there were new lines on her forehead. Mrs. Sturt rose, to continue the conversation standing. Sturt, who retained his place on the sofa, gently laid down his cigar and held his right hand over his heart as though trying to quieten it.

"Who was it?" demanded Mrs. Sturt of Audrey.

"I'm doing my best to break it gently, mother, because I think it will be rather a shock to you. It's a woman you know almost better than anyone down here."

"Not Lore!"

"Yes."

There was a painful silence, during which Mrs. Sturt slowly resumed her seat.

"Lore *drowned!*"

"Yes, mother."

Another pause.

"How was that, then?"

"It happened about eight o'clock—wasn't it, Nicholas? The river is quite a long way from the house, at the other end of the grounds, away from everything. I was there with a man earlier in the afternoon. Nicholas and Celia were actually with Lore right up to the time of the accident, nearly. She had just quarrelled with Mr. Dawson, and he had gone away. Nobody knows how she came to be in the water."

"Mr. Sturt isn't very well, I think!" said Nicholas suddenly.

Audrey glanced swiftly towards the sofa, and sprang to it almost in the same instant. Her mother also hurried over, and Evelyn, turning still paler, made an effort to follow them, but was compelled to sit down again. Sturt, who had been sitting in an upright attitude, had fallen over on to the raised end of the sofa. He was unconscious, and it was only by a lucky chance that he had not dropped to the floor. He was breathing stertorously. His face had taken on an alarming purplish tinge.

His wife tore off his collar, and sent Audrey post-haste out of the room for water, while she herself flew to the cupboard for brandy.

"Go round to Dr. Ferreira at once, Nicholas!" she commanded

breathlessly. "Take no refusal, but bring him back with you, even if he's in bed, as fast as you can both run. You know the house?"

"Yes, I know it."

Without pausing to put on a hat, he tore out of the house, down the drive and along the road. The doctor's house was quite close. By a fortunate accident the owner himself was neither out nor retired for the night. He was a thin, nervous-looking man of fifty-five or sixty, rather handsome in a clever way, with a clean-shaved face, and plentiful hair which was not yet completely grey. He set down the scientific treatise he was perusing and listened to what Nicholas had to say. After putting a few questions, he hastily collected some appliances in a bag, snatched up his hat, and motioned to his caller to precede him out of the house.

As they strode along side by side hurriedly, Dr. Ferreira stole a glance at Nicholas.

"I believe I have heard of you in connection with my son?"

"Yes, we've done some work together."

"So he said. May I ask if you know anything of his private affairs?"

"Very little."

"He came home from an entertainment in the neighbourhood little more than an hour ago, and without a word either to his mother or myself, and without changing his clothes, left the house five minutes later with a kit-bag in his hand. We are wondering what his intentions are. I don't know if you can throw any light?"

"I can't. Perhaps he's running up to town?"

"There is a train, as a matter of fact. But surely he would not make such a journey at this time of night without one word to anybody!"

Nicholas had no hypothesis to offer, and a minute later they arrived at Mereway

Sturt had been taken upstairs to his room. The doctor followed him there. He was not a great while examining his patient, and when he came down again he passed straight out of the house without seeing Nicholas. Audrey informed the latter that her father had regained consciousness, and that he was in no immediate danger, but that the doctor had warned her mother that for some time to come he would need to take the strictest precautions with regard to his health.

Evelyn had retired to her own room, and Mrs. Sturt was busied upstairs with her husband. Audrey, after requesting Nicholas to extinguish the lamp when he had done with it, also disappeared for the night. He put out the lamp at once, and made his way softly into the garden to smoke.

XIX

EVELYN'S VIGIL

Sunday opened with a bright and solemn stillness. The sun was hot, the sky was of a leaden blue, the air was without a breeze, yet the house was like a house of the dead. An oppressive mournfulness hung over everything. The different members of the household went about their respective duties without reference to the others and scarcely exchanging a word. Breakfast was set in the morning-room, but there was no family party. Sturt remained in his room, Evelyn did not come to table, while Mrs. Sturt had snatched a hasty mouthful before anyone else had appeared downstairs. She grudged every minute spent away from her husband's bedside. When she had come down he had been dozing peacefully in the half-darkened, half-sunny room, but he might need something when he awoke. She intended to arrange with her daughters a nursing scheme for the day which would ensure that someone would be always in attendance. Audrey also had breakfasted. She had taken it upon herself to superintend the household during her mother's preoccupation.

Katherine and Nicholas sat down together. Her eyes were red-rimmed, she ate hardly anything, and neither of them spoke. After breakfast he seized an opportunity of asking his hostess whether he could be helpful in any way, and upon receiving a negative reply took his hat and effected his escape from the house into the pine woods. He lighted his pipe and strolled in the direction of the lake.

The idea occurred to him that during his absence the half-anticipated visit from the police might take place, but, since he intended to tell them nothing, he saw no reason why he should stay in on their account. They would have to take their chance. On arriving back at nearly one o'clock, however, he was informed that no one had called.

The midday meal on Sundays at Mereway took the form of dinner. Mrs. Sturt had a tray sent upstairs to herself, while Nicholas sat down with the three girls. Evelyn had recovered from her alarming indisposition of the previous evening, but it had left its mark on her. She sat like a marble statue, keeping her eyes fixed on her plate, and not once opening her lips to speak. Before the meal was concluded Katherine broke down suddenly. Hastily fumbling for her square of lace handkerchief, she rose from the table and quitted the room. It was her first trouble, and she had no resources of character with which to meet it. Audrey's mouth twitched in sympathy, but, catching Nicholas's eye, she bravely summoned an unconvincing smile.

"I'm afraid it isn't a very jolly house for you!"

He made some sort of response, but the thought which passed through his mind was that the inner nature of this young, un-formed, irresponsible girl was revealing itself, in a time of trouble, as stronger and more unselfish, more mature, than that of either of her elder sisters. Three weeks earlier such an observation might have germinated into something very different, but now it spent itself in respect and admiration.

The hours crept. In the middle of the afternoon, while he was endeavouring to concentrate his mind on a book, sitting alone in a screened-off part of the garden, Evelyn came to him. She had been looking for him, she said. He offered to rise from his deck-chair, but she would not permit it, seating herself on the grass beside him instead. Her eyes were sunken, as if with the effort of fruitless thinking.

"Can't *something* be done?" she asked, abruptly and quietly, staring away into the distance.

He shook his head slowly.

"We must wait."

"I went to see Mrs. Hantish after breakfast this morning. . . . Maurice left home last night, directly he got back."

"I know."

"He must have gone up to London. Oh, it's horrible! . . . She wants you to see her this afternoon."

Nicholas's heart beat rapidly.

"No, I couldn't go."

"I understand. However, I think you ought to. It isn't for yourself. There may be something . . ."

"Oh, I'm not afraid of meeting her, if you wish me to go. Shall I get round there at once?"

"No; don't be in a hurry. I want to talk to you. You haven't changed your mind since last evening?"

"Oh, if Ferreira comes to grief it won't be through me—you can make your mind easy about that. I've been thinking it over, though; and it's *suicide*. I'm convinced of it."

"Then why has he run away?"

"He may have had to get back to town last night."

"And that cigarette-case! It was his. I recognised it."

"He may have given it to her, or left it at her house."

"And your seeing him by the river—for I know Celia told the truth about that!"

"I won't swear it was he."

"Oh, it's a fearful business! It's very noble of you to shield him so—if you are doing it for him—but if he—if he is in any way responsible for poor Lore's death, what does it matter what we say or do about it! The fact will remain. . . . Then all those terrible dreams of yours! . . ."

"We mustn't lose our heads. There's a right and a wrong way out of every trouble. All we can do for the time being is to wait. If the police had anything to go on, I should probably have had an official visit before this. Either it was pure accident or it was suicide. I say it was suicide, knowing what state she was in. . . . Besides, Ferreira hadn't any motive. She was a free woman again."

"We don't know! We don't know anything! I would willingly give all I possess to see and speak to him for five minutes only. If I knew where to find him I would go up to London. It's the uncertainty that is so killing. You seem to think that if it is brought in suicide, that will end the matter, but you miss the point. There will be an inquest, and everybody will talk a great deal, and they will find some verdict or other. Do you imagine that, whatever they find, I shall be satisfied? If they find that she fainted and overbalanced herself into the water, do you think that will make any difference to me? As long as a shadow of a suspicion of doubt lingers in my mind, how can I regard him with normal eyes? It will be like a slow corroding acid, eating away my—my *affection*." She whispered the last word.

"Then, unless you are going to accept Ferreira's own assurance, I don't see quite how you propose to satisfy yourself as to what happened."

Evelyn was silent for some moments. Then:

"Of course, you did not experiment with your new apparatus last night? You would scarcely have the heart to."

"I'm thinking of doing it to-night."

"Hasn't the strangeness of the coincidence occurred to you?—if we are to be afraid to call it anything else. You dream three times that Lore is going to her death, and after the third dream she is drowned! . . . Aren't we the real murderers, Nicholas? We took no steps to warn her, although we were given three chances. Was it callousness, or obtuseness, or what?"

"I agree it is a remarkable coincidence," said Nicholas shortly.

"You will set the machine just before going to bed, I suppose?"

"Yes."

"May I come to your room and see you do it?"

"If you wish to. It will be about half-past nine."

Evelyn got to her feet, and stood looking away from him listlessly. Then she gave a quick, nervous turn, to glance down at him where he was sitting.

"Couldn't we run over to Colminster this afternoon in the car—just you and I?"

"To find out what is happening, you mean? No, I don't care to. It will be a bit too marked."

"But we must do something! To sit here hour after hour, waiting for news which never arrives—I shall go out of my mind! . . . Oh! . . ." The exclamation was brought out as if a new light had suddenly broken in upon her.

"What's the matter?"

"Why haven't we thought before of going to her house? Madame Brion, if anyone, will be able to tell us what is taking place."

"Is that the companion?"

"Yes. Come, let's go at once!"

"Very well."

He got up from his chair, and they proceeded indoors together. While Evelyn went upstairs to put on her things, Nicholas stood waiting in the hall with his hat on, gazing out through the open front door. It was like a deserted house, everything was so still. The dullness of a brilliantly hot Sunday afternoon without occupation was intensified by the domestic gloom almost to the point of despair. The visit to the French-woman prompted no excitement, and the thought of that to Celia afterwards oppressed his heart like a leaden weight. Although she had sent for him, and although they might come together again, something had disappeared for ever from their relation. . . .

When Evelyn came down again, it was without speaking that they walked down the drive together and into the road. Yetholm was not seven minutes distant. The page-boy who opened the door to them bore a scared expression on his face, and the disorganised state of the household was disclosed in his invitation to them to follow him to Madame's room without the formality of a preliminary announcement.

The room was the principal one in the house, though no one had ever heard Lore's name for it, and she had scarcely ever used it. The companion doubtless was taking advantage of the interregnum between the death of her mistress and the arrival of the trustees to indulge luxurious tastes which hitherto she had been compelled to repress. It was a large, airy, sunny apartment, beautifully furnished and possessing a remarkable outlook on the garden in the rear of the house, with its backwoods. Madame was sitting by one of the windows, the blind of which was half-drawn, busily plying a pair of black knitting-pins. Her fine, sallow face was impassive, unsmiling and inscrutable, as she rose barely six inches above her chair-seat, with a slight inclination. She silently motioned to her callers to sit down, and immediately resumed her task.

Evelyn gave her a penetrating look.

"I've called to inquire if you have any fresh news."

Keeping her eyes obstinately down, but slightly elevating her brows, Madame raised one hand from her work to make a gesture. It signified that she had no news to impart, that the affair was very sad, but that in dealing with such a complex personality as that of her late mistress it was always necessary to be philosophical. Her callousness was so openly displayed that Evelyn felt herself growing hot.

"She has not been brought home yet?"

"Not yet." The words were spoken with the sharp, unaccented precision of a foreigner who has learnt the English language late in life.

"But surely they have communicated with you from Colminster!"

"Well! . . . A policeman has called this morning—*eu gentilhomme*.[9] He has asked me this and that." She lifted her chin for an instant in an extraordinary silent laugh, which to her callers was like a descent into a clever, wicked brain. Then the mask fell again. . . . "His face did not please me. I have told him what I would."

"What sort of things did he ask?" inquired Nicholas, gazing at her with distrust.

"About Mlle. Jensen. When have I seen her the last time? What has she said before going out? What affairs has she? Who visits here? What is her family? What is this cigarette-case which they have picked up? . . . I do not know what!"

"Did he seem to regard it as an accident pure and simple?"

"I did not ask. He said nothing. I told him that I do not love that M'sieur Dawson. He brings back Madame's auto alone, and too early. Then he departs to London."

9. "A gentleman", or "as a gentleman".

"There's nothing in that. She sent him back with the car. I was there when he left her."

"I did not know that, but I do not love him. I think it was an accident."

"Was she subject to sudden fits of dizziness, or anything of the sort?"

"The policeman, too, has asked that. I have told him 'yes.' Her head"—she hesitated for a word—"*swims* . . . the world goes round, and she tumbles! It is a common thing. Yes, she has fallen in the water! . . ."

"Have you seen Mr. Ferreira?" demanded Evelyn suddenly.

Madame bent more closely over her knitting, while her face acquired an anaemic tinge, as of pale green wax. "M'sieur Ferreira has called for one minute last evening, immediately after M'sieur Dawson. He desired that I should tell Mlle. Jensen that he too had departed to London."

The joyful relief which for a solitary instant flashed through Evelyn's brain was quickly succeeded by suspicion as she continued to regard the Frenchwoman's disingenuous features. Without appearing to notice the girl's scrutiny, Madame's snake-like eyes gave a single sidelong flicker at her from underneath their heavy lids as she proceeded with her work.

"Do you wish to assert that he was ignorant of what had happened?"

"It is quite certain. He would not leave a message for the dead."

"Not if it was *bona fide!*" said Nicholas.

Evelyn broke in upon him:

"Then you are convinced in your mind, Madame, that he has had no hand in this awful affair?"

"I am very sure," was the quietly-spoken reply as the companion bent still further down to her work. Suddenly, as if her pent feelings were forcing an outlet for themselves, her bosom rose. Getting up quickly, she turned, her back on the visitors, and began to draw up the blind, regardless of the fact that the sunshine was still as intolerable as ever.

During the pause which succeeded, Evelyn kept her eyes fixed steadily on her.

"Has the theory of suicide been considered, do you know?" asked Nicholas with assumed carelessness.

"That is also possible," said Madame, settling herself in her seat once more and preparing to resume her knitting.

"What I mean is, what is the official view?"

The companion shrugged her shoulders. "*Qu'importe?*[10] I think that the police are great fools!"

"What do you believe yourself?"

"I think perhaps she have thrown herself in the water, M'sieur. . . . She was malcontent with life. Many times has she spoken to me of poisons, of gas, of the railway-line. I think that this water has *tempted* her. She has not sought it, but it has come in her way."

"Very likely," agreed Nicholas thoughtfully.

"Then how do you account for the presence of the cigarette-case?" demanded Evelyn.

"Ferreira may have left it here by accident, and she may have been using it," suggested Nicholas.

"I do not know. I think so." The pins worked on rapidly.

"You are telling lies!" broke out Evelyn vehemently and unexpectedly. "You have an understanding with Mr. Ferreira, and you are trying to shield him by false statements and impossible hypotheses! Tell me the truth!"

Madame's features remained immobile and waxen, and the outburst did not even cause her to look up.

"You talk fiddle-faddle, Ma'm'selle!" she said, almost gently. But the very restraint of her voice showed how thin was the crust which imprisoned the fires of her woman's nature.

"He has paid you money!" proceeded the girl, completely relinquishing herself to the new thought which had been rapidly swelling within her during the last few minutes. "Confess that you are in his pay!"

The Frenchwoman's knitting dropped from her as she clutched

10. "What does it matter?"

the two arms of the chair she sat in and closed her eyes.

"Rest well assured, Ma'm'selle, I do not sell myself for money!"

"Then something else!" She uttered an abrupt, hysterical laugh. "Oh, heavens! don't say you are in love with him too!"

Madame reopened her eyes and fastened them sombrely on Evelyn's face.

"I think M'sieur Ferreira has not done this crime, Ma'm'selle. Thursday, Friday, perhaps, but yesterday, no! The other had already departed, there was no more need, and he is not imbecile. I think he has not done it any more than M'sieur!" and she indicated Nicholas by an inclination of the head.

"Have you his address in London?" asked the girl.

"No," replied Madame quickly. She got up, as though to indicate that the interview was terminated, and the others rose after her.

"One more question," said Nicholas. "Are the police inquiring for him?"

She folded her hands together against her waist. "The policeman has not said, M'sieur. . . . The police are very great clowns!" she added as an afterthought.

Without wishing her good day, Evelyn made for the door, and Nicholas, after a stiff bow, followed. They were permitted to find their own way out. The girl could scarcely contain herself till they reached the roadway.

"She's screening him, Nicholas!"

"Or defending him—which isn't quite the same thing."

"You see how terrified she is! She must know something that we don't."

"I doubt whether you were justified in accusing her to her face like that. She may be simply muddle-headed."

"No, it's a clear case of collusion! Why should he have called here to leave a message for Lore? It was a deliberate attempt to mislead. This is by far the most unpleasant development we've had as yet. Everything goes from bad to worse. Oh, I can't see how it is all to end! . . ."

"Of course, we have to recognise that a scared man might do silly things in a panic. If he realised that he was the last one who had been with her . . ."

"Oh, no! that we can't think," said Evelyn, cutting him short. She suddenly ceased discussing the subject, and they walked on in silence.

When they were passing The Arbour, Nicholas dragged his pace and turned to her inquiringly:

"Do you wish me to go in now?"

"I think perhaps you'd better. I think we ought to know what she wants with you. You won't stop long?"

"Only just to hear what she has to say. Perhaps you would like to come in with me?"

"No; I fancy she wants to see you by yourself. . . . Of course—I expect I have no right to speak of it, but it is just possible she wishes to make it up with you. If so—if you do make it up together, it won't be at the expense . . . I mean it won't affect your decision about the evidence?" She jerked out the question nervously, with her eyes fastened on the pavement and with an unwonted colour in her cheeks.

"In the first place, we shan't make it up," replied Nicholas, rather grimly, "and in the second place, if we do, I'm not in the habit of allowing other people to force my judgment. I thought I had made you understand that already."

"Yes, but . . . Then you will come straight back?"

"In a few minutes."

Evelyn remaining silent, he raised his hat to her, and entered the gate.

He was shown into the same room where he and Lore had been on his first visit to the house. As he walked in, Celia was standing before the mirror in outdoor attire, adjusting a hat and veil of unrelieved black. She was in light mourning for Lore, though it affected only the colour of her garments, and not their modishness. Still, it was a tribute of respect which the Sturt girls had omitted—for it did not occur to his young man's imagination that they might possess no black frocks—and it already made him regard her more favourably. She was alone in the room. Tea was set on a table, but apparently she had finished and was on the point of going out.

She turned her head carelessly to glance at him, without smiling.

"I'm glad you have come. Won't you sit down?"

He obeyed stiffly and a moment later she left the glass and took a chair herself.

"I'm just running over to Colminster. Lady Wyburn wants me about something. It's fortunate you came now, for in another five minutes you would have missed me."

"You wished to see me?"

"Yes. You understand, of course, that there is to be an inquest, and that both you and I will be required as witnesses, as the last—or nearly the last—to see poor Lore alive. What I wanted to talk over is what our evidence is to be. If our two statements in the witness-box disagree, we shall be made to look idiots, if nothing worse! Am I right?"

"I suppose so."

"I propose to tell the truth. Have you come to any decision?"

Nicholas coloured.

"I propose to say as much as I think justifiable. . . . I'm very sorry, but the case is far too serious to treat theoretically. If I were convinced that Ferreira had a hand in it, I wouldn't keep back my quota of evidence, such as it is, but . . ."

"Aren't you rather usurping the prerogative of the coroner?" interrupted Celia impatiently. "Surely that is just what his trained legal mind is for—to weigh one piece of evidence against another, in order to arrive at a balance of truth? Supposing everyone withheld their evidence for the same reason!"

"I don't care to argue it. I may be right or I may be wrong, but that's the line I have fixed on."

"In other words, you mean that your sympathies are with Maurice rather than with poor Lore?"

"I certainly don't care to fasten a stain on a man's character for life—to say the least of it—without knowing more about the business."

"That is all right. But, on the other hand, aren't you fastening a stain on poor Lore's character? Suicide is still a moral and legal crime, though people are apt to forget it."

"It may have been an accident."

Celia regarded him severely.

"I can tell you at once that in the absence of new evidence it will be brought in 'temporary insanity.' Maurice's strange flight to London proves nothing by itself, and Madame Brion—her companion—is prepared to swear that the cigarette-case which was picked up was in her possession when she left the house. So everything hangs on your having seen him on his way to join her by the river, and if there is to be a miscarriage of justice the responsibility will rest with you."

Nicholas stirred uneasily on his chair, but said nothing.

"The fact that she had just broken off relations with Mr. Dawson will provide all the motive that is required," she proceeded, "and then, of course, her drug-taking propensities and general depression! All suicides nowadays are drug-takers, so that the two terms have come to be practically synonymous. . . . But may I ask what makes you so sure of his innocence?"

"And may I inquire why you are so sure of his guilt? That seems to me very much more to the point."

"Now you are fencing!" She rose. "Well, it is no use discussing it, but I sincerely hope you will think it over quietly without prejudice. You will probably receive your summons to-morrow. . . . One thing I feel I must warn you about. If you are adopting this unusual and illegal attitude on Evelyn's account, in order to spare her feelings, you are purely punishing yourself for nothing at all. The girl is play-acting, according to her breed. Her pose of Maurice's heroine is nothing but a disgusting hoax, intended to win your esteem. Oh, you needn't trouble to defend her! I am only telling you what I know."

She moved towards the door, so that Nicholas had no option but to get up also. A pale gleam of hope shot through him as he fancied he recognised feminine jealousy underlying her words.

For if she still regarded Evelyn with unreasoning hostility, it seemed to prove that he himself could not be the object of indifference to her which her grand manner pretended. Perhaps she was already prepared to relent, if he would make some necessary little concession to her womanly dignity. He wondered how they could compromise matters.

Celia drew herself up like a beautiful statue by the side of the door, waiting for him to pass out.

"Aren't you going to give me another chance?" he asked, smiling, but in a very low voice.

"Do you deserve one, do you think?" was her equally quiet response. She looked away from him with a disturbed face.

"My fault was unintentional, and I hope you will forgive it. I never had any manner worth speaking of. You should take pity on me and educate me!"

"No, it was an affront; and the affront still remains. I am now going to see Lady Wyburn, and it is probably just about *you* that I am to be cross-examined. All this is highly disagreeable to me, as you may imagine. Yet you expect me to smile and to return to four-and-twenty hours ago, as though nothing were different!"

Nicholas's heart sank.

"Then what do you want me to do?"

"I *ask* you to do nothing, but I certainly cannot be on terms of friendship with a man who is willing to see me placed in such an ignominious position." She offered to leave the room, but he detained her by an eager gesture.

"May I have a little time longer to consider?"

"To consider what?"

"If I even suspected Ferreira, I would agree . . ."

"No, that isn't it at all. You seem to think I want to bring trouble to his door, innocent or guilty, but why should I? Maurice is nothing to me. I merely wish to leave all the responsibility to the law. The only thing I am personally anxious about is that Lady Wyburn and her circle should not regard me as a prevaricator. Hitherto I have preserved my name for honesty."

"Yes. I see that."

"You see it, but you are not disposed to prevent it! . . . However, it is for you to decide. I must go now."

"I wish you could help me a little. I'm only anxious to do what's right, but the question is what *is* right—for me, I mean. I grasp your standpoint absolutely, but you don't seem able or willing to grasp mine."

"Then what is yours?"

"I think Ferreira is an innocent man who has most likely got himself into an awful mess, only partly through his own fault; and of course his back relations with Lore won't stand investigation. We know the ins and outs of it, but the lawyers and police aren't going to take a sympathetic view of his case, and that's why I don't want to offer them a handle. The only thing that would induce me to do it would be if I suspected him myself."

Celia glanced at her wrist-watch.

"Well, I'm afraid I can't stay here and argue it. We certainly seem to have come to an impasse, so I suppose the best thing for us to do will be to agree to separate. . . . I must really be off!"

"Will you allow me till to-morrow morning only?"

"To do what?"

"To reconsider the whole matter carefully between now and then. May I wait on you early to-morrow?"

"Oh, yes," said Celia, with cold indifference, gently rubbing her chin with her gloved finger as she viewed him.

She accompanied him to the front door, and watched him as far as the gate before proceeding to join her car, which had just been driven round. As she settled herself in the back corner seat, her mouth formed itself into a bitter, cynical smile, such as very few even among her intimates had seen there. Fifty yards farther along the road the car, running silently and smoothly, over-took Nicholas, who was walking back to Mereway. He lifted his hat, but though she eyed him with a sort of mournful tranquility she made no acknowledgment or sign of recognition.

He had forgotten Evelyn, and the vision of her standing by the gate, awaiting his return, came as an unpleasant reminder of her existence. He dismissed Celia's allegations as the fantasy of a jealous woman, and he could not doubt for a minute that the girl's solicitude concerning Maurice was genuine, yet somehow her standing there waiting for him struck him as a piece of hypocrisy. Could not she just as well have spoken to him in the house? And surely her pale face could not have been drawn into wrinkles like that all the time she had been by the gate! They must have been just put on for his benefit. She was certainly posing, but whether consciously or instinctively it was difficult to say. Perhaps her idea was to keep him up to the mark.

As he drew closer she swung the gate open for him, and when he was through they continued up the drive together towards the house.

"Well?" she asked quietly but rapidly. "What did she want?"

Nicholas found himself wondering whether the question were not feigned. He could hardly believe that she had failed to have it all out with Celia on her visit to her that morning. If she had not known that there was no prospect of a reconciliation, she would not have sent him there, and she could not have known that unless Celia had expressly stated the nature of her business with him. . . . However, two people could play a game! He determined to lead her on, as though completely unsuspicious of her deceit. It was with surprise that he discovered that he could not keep anger out of his voice:

"She merely wished that we should come to an agreement about our evidence. It seems that we are both likely to be summoned as witnesses at the inquest."

"And have you come to an agreement?"

Why did she ask that? . . . It suddenly occurred to him that, had she been really anxious that he should not inform against Ferreira, she would not have run the risk of Celia's over-persuading him. Her conduct was growing clearer and clearer to him.

"Not yet," he replied, with a curt rudeness which would have been intentional had not his voice been independent of his deliberating faculty. Evelyn glanced at him strangely.

"What do you mean by 'not yet'?"

"I mean what I say. I shall think over my evidence between now and to-morrow morning, and let her know then."

"Oh! . . ." She stopped short in the drive with a start, as if shot. "But you told me your mind was made up!"

The abrupt halt and the frightened tone appeared to Nicholas as no more than a piece of clever acting, so that he made less effort to conceal his growing anger.

"Well, now it isn't made up! I shall go to sleep on it."

"She wants you to contradict your statement to Lady Wyburn and substitute hers?"

"It isn't a question of what she wants. The question is, how far is Ferreira entitled to the protection of my silence? In plain English, is he an innocent man or a criminal? That's what I am going to sleep on."

"And when you say 'sleep' you mean 'dream'?" inquired Evelyn quietly. "You intend your decision to be governed by the result of your new dream record?"

"If you like! We don't know that it will have any bearing on the case. I'm going to try, anyway. If it endorses those other records, I shan't feel justified in holding back my evidence."

Evelyn made no reply, for at that moment they entered the house.

"I think there is tea in the drawing-room," she remarked with attempted lightness. "Have you had yours?"

He growled a negative response, and they went through together. The room was deserted, but, as she had anticipated, the tea-tray was still standing there, with cups both clean and used. Nicholas sat down, but Evelyn remained standing by the window, looking out, a distracted, absent expression in her eyes, and her lips occasionally forming silent words.

Five minutes passed without speech, and then an incident happened, insignificant in itself, but which impressed itself upon him as strange at the time and which disturbed him more and more for the rest of the evening. Katherine, entering the room, came over to where he sat and proffered him something which she held in her hand. It was a small bronze sphinx, not more than two inches in length. He took it and regarded it curiously.

"You probably won't be with us very much longer," she re-marked, still standing over him with a serious face. "I thought you might like to have this as a memento of Lore. She gave it me when I expressed my admiration of her 'Sphinx.' I can't say it has brought me any particular good fortune, but perhaps it will be otherwise with you. I don't feel that I can keep it myself."

"Thank you," said Nicholas simply. After contemplating the object for a few moments longer, he slipped it into his pocket.

Katherine left the room again.

Evelyn came across to him. "What did she mean by your not being with us very much longer? Have you announced to anyone your intention of leaving us?"

"No."

"*Are* you leaving us?"

He misinterpreted the expression on her face, and his suspicions in that moment completed themselves. Instead of replying to her question, he reverted to the little gift.

"It's rather extraordinary she should have given me that now. It's nearly ominous. The Sphinx has asked us her three riddles, in the shape of those dreams; we have failed to understand them, and she has claimed a death! No doubt you remember our conversation?"

"Why do you say that so cynically?"

"Because I don't think you regard all this business quite so seriously as you pretend. I am simply falling into your vein."

"I don't understand you," said the girl.

"But I am beginning to understand you!" Avoiding her bewildered stare, he left the room and, going to the hall, reached his hat down from the rack. He went out through the kitchen garden into the woods, intending, if possible, to exorcise the black devil which had settled on his spirits by continued hard walking in solitary places.

The exercise fatigued his body without composing his mind, and by the time he had returned home he had developed a feverish headache, with disagreeable shiverings and an irregular pulse.

He went to lie down in his room. It was eight o'clock.

In order to afford their mother the night's rest of which she stood so obviously in need, the three girls had arranged among themselves that they should take it in turn to remain on duty in their father's room throughout the night. There were to be three watches of three hours each, commencing at nine o'clock. Evelyn requested that as she had not yet completely recovered from her indisposition she might take the first watch, as the easiest. Her sisters made no opposition. At nine precisely, accordingly, she relieved her mother in the sick-room, armed with a shaded candle and her knitting.

Her father was slumbering peacefully. It was still daylight outside. The window was partly open, and the air of the chamber was cool, fresh and sweet. There was no need to light the candle at present, but at the foot of the bed she noiselessly set up the large folding screen behind which she proposed to sit and work. She was to call Audrey at midnight. Her father was unlikely to awake during her watch, but, if he did, such requirements as might be wanted were at hand on the little bedside table. She sat down behind the screen, gazing out of doors at the quietening garden, and at the same time trying to hear her mother and sisters retire to their rooms. She was uncertain whether they had all closed their doors, and the suspense kept her nervously irritated for a long time.

At half-past nine she rose silently, went round to her father, and bent over to assure herself that he was still asleep. The light, regular sound of his breathing satisfied her that she might safely desert her post for a few minutes. Cautiously manipulating the door-handle, she let herself out and closed the door again behind her, after which she stole along the passage in her moccasins as far as Nicholas's room. Upon her scratching gently on the panel, he opened the door from within. Had the light been better, she might have noticed that his face was flushed and his hair ruffled from lying down.

"I mustn't stay above a minute," she said rather breathlessly.

"It's my turn to be with father. He's asleep now, but he may wake. . . . Where is the box?"

He pointed silently to the table by the window, upon the surface of which the great aluminium box rested horizontally. Evelyn moved towards it quickly, and tested its weight by lifting one side an inch or two. She was astonished at the lightness.

"Is it ready for use?"

"Yes."

"Then how do you start it?"

He explained the mechanism to her.

"I see you have set it for eleven," said the girl.

"Yes; if I get to sleep by then."

"Then it will run for one hour from eleven till twelve?"

"Yes.

"And to reproduce afterwards?"

"The spool comes round to the starting point, where it is stopped by a pin. You raise the pin—so!—and continue winding with this handle a few times. That gets you past the pin, when all you have to do is wind the whole machine for another revolution."

"You don't require to treat the sensitised surface of the film chemically before reproducing?"

"No; the original exposure itself fixes it."

"Are you having the box in this room, or in your bedroom?"

Nicholas would have wondered more at the question had he not felt so unwell.

"I shall place it on a table by my bed."

Evelyn threw bird-like little glances about the room while considering quickly if there were more questions to be put before leaving him. Her eyes rested accidentally on a poison-blue phial on the mantelshelf. She looked from it to him.

"What is that bottle?"

"It's some stuff Lore gave me for sleeplessness, but I've never taken any."

"Do you suffer from that regularly?"

"Every night lately."

"Then it may interfere with your experiment?"

"It's more than likely. To-night especially. My head's in a sort of fever."

"In that case, hadn't you better take some of it? What is it?"

"She couldn't give me the name. I don't know that I care about risking it." He went over to the bottle and took it in his hand. . . . "On the other hand, what the dickens does it matter? I don't suppose it will kill me, and I certainly shan't get any result otherwise. One takes it in water, I believe. I'll get some water from the other room."

He passed through the communicating door, leaving it ajar behind him. No sooner was his back turned than Evelyn snatched up and uncorked the phial with lightning speed, and poured a quantity of the crystals into the palm of her hand. She recorked and replaced the bottle on the table just as he came back, carrying a tumbler half full of water.

After reading the instructions on the label to ascertain the dose to be taken, he turned to face the light from out of doors, which was fast fading, and cautiously poured into the glass the approximate quantity stated. The crystals refused to dissolve immediately.

"Now we want a spoon."

Evelyn caught swiftly at the chance.

"Run down and get one out of the kitchen. But go very softly, in case you wake father; and please be as quick as you can. I ought to be with him."

"There's no necessity for you to wait."

"No, but I want to."

Nicholas kicked off his slippers and left the room in his socks. The moment he was outside the door Evelyn dropped the crystals which she still held in her hand into the tumbler, to double the dose it contained. She scarcely knew what she was doing. It had entered her mind three minutes ago that if he were to sleep *longer* she would have more time to . . . to think what was best to be done . . . yes, to test the result alone, before he woke up! It was not a conscious plan, but it was a sort of instinctive motive, as what had to be done under the circumstances. And, as with other instinctive actions, every detail fell into place mechanically. If the record proved too hideously impossible she was to suppress it, without allowing him to see it. Afterwards she could pretend that she had been frightened at the possibility of a disclosure and had on that account destroyed the film beforehand. His anger would be tremendous, but it would be days before he could try again, and in the meantime the inquest would have been held. Yet perhaps a lie would not be necessary. . . .

She gazed at the unmelted crystals standing at the bottom of the glass, and wondered dully whether he would notice the addition. . . . then it occurred to her that he would be sure to lock his door before retiring for the night. She quickly opened that communicating with the passage to ascertain whether he were yet returning, but she could hear nothing. Taking a risk, she darted into his bedroom and, having first satisfied herself that the door was unlocked, quickly removed the key and dropped it into the side-pocket of her woollen house-coat. . . .

She was staring out of the window of the outer room when he re-entered it a minute later with the spoon in his hand. He at once took up the tumbler and began stirring and crushing the crystals vigorously. Evelyn faced round to watch his operations.

"Lore little anticipated on what occasion you would be making use of her drug," she remarked.

Nicholas did not reply, but set the glass to his lips and, throwing back his head, drained the contents.

"Now I'll go," said Evelyn.

"Yes, you had better."

"At what hour may I look in in the morning?"

She continued to carry on her instinctive campaign of deception.

"We had better make it after breakfast."

"Then good night!"

"Good night!" said Nicholas.

He closed the door softly behind her, then bore the aluminium box into the other room and placed it beside his bed on a table which had been cleared in readiness. That done, he went to the passage door and, without thinking about it, reached out his hand to turn the key in the lock. Its absence caused him a mild shock of surprise and irritation, but he had no suspicion of the truth, and concluded that a maid, in cleaning the room, had accidentally dislodged it. He did not trouble to barricade himself in, but he closed and locked the communicating door.

Meanwhile Evelyn returned to her father's darkening chamber. She shut the door quietly and went on tip-toe to his bedside. The breathing was as light and regular as before, while there was the suspicion of a smile on his sensitive, well-shaped lips. Never had she seen such a look of *innocence* on a grown man's face. It was as though he were dreaming of purer worlds, where he had become as a child again! . . .

She took her seat behind the screen and picked up her knitting, but it fell out of her hands as she continued gazing through the window-gap with wide-open eyes.

What a contrast between her father's sleep and that morbid, artificial one of Nicholas's, and if only the tables could be turned! . . . At first it was no more than a mental phrase of regret, but the comparison refused to leave her, and a minute later her brain was stabbed by a sudden inspiration. Why should not the record be of her father's dreaming instead of Nicholas's? . . .

She had only to transport the box from that room to this at eleven o'clock, and take it away again at midnight. In all probability Nicholas would never realise the deceit she had put on him. He would be pleasantly relieved that, in place of the tragic nightmare which both of them dreaded, a simple, happy, childlike dream had been recorded. However that might be, it would assuredly determine the nature of his evidence at the inquest! . . .

It was already a decision in her mind, though she was unaware of it; but there was no hurry. It was barely ten o'clock, and there was still nearly an hour before she could do anything. The clockwork was set for eleven, and she was afraid to tamper with the time for starting, in case she should put something wrong. . . . She hoped her father would sleep on. . . . Afterwards, before restoring the box to Nicholas's room, she could take it to her own to test the result. Her watch expired at midnight, so that she would be at liberty then. . . . She wondered how long it would be before that drug took effect! He had not said a word to her about its nature or strength, but if it was to act at all, surely a full hour would be an ample measure of time! . . .

So the minutes passed.

At a quarter to eleven she stole along the passage once more to Nicholas's room. The house was in a deathly silence, and it was nearly quite dark. She first of all cautiously attempted the door of his work-room, but that was locked, so she returned to the bed-room door. After listening outside very intently for a moment or two, and hearing nothing, she turned the handle softly with a rapidly-beating heart. When the door was opened sufficiently to admit her she again stopped to listen, but everything was perfectly still, and she concluded that he was sleeping soundly.

The silvery grey of the aluminium box was still quite conspicuous. The whole apparatus did not weigh above a few pounds. Its dimensions, however, rendered it rather unwieldy to carry from place to place, so before venturing to touch it she first made up her mind how it was to be handled. She decided that it would be a little more awkward, perhaps, but safer, to bear it horizontally, since that was its present position and she wished to disturb nothing.

The plan was at once put into effect, and the box successfully conveyed to her father's room without untoward incident. Her modesty had prevented her from observing Nicholas at close quarters to ascertain if he were really asleep, but as he must otherwise have seen her, and he had made no movement, she had no doubt that this was the case. It was not a very pleasant adventure, but she had not to consider her own feelings.

After setting the box temporarily on the floor, she cleared a table, put it behind the screen, and then lifted the box again on to it. . . . Suddenly she realised that if she were to stay in the room during the hour of exposure, that would spoil everything. Her waking thoughts would clash with her father's dreaming, and the result would be a negative one. She would have to go away during that hour, running the risk of his waking up. She could retire to her own room, which was only just across the passage, and leave both doors ajar, so that she could hear him if he needed anything. It was not very likely that anyone else would be wandering about the house. Her mother was tired out with her day-nursing, and Audrey would wait for her watch. Katherine she dismissed. . . .

It was on the point of eleven. She hastily gathered up her candle and knitting, and peered down at her father's face for the last time. It appeared even more tranquil than before. The almost preternatural peacefulness worried her. She hoped it did not foretoken a change for the worse; she hated leaving him, even if only for an hour. . . .

A faint whirring came from behind the screen. The clockwork was moving, and she must go. . . . Oh, it was so ghastly, so almost monstrous, that this inanimate machine should be capturing the impressions thrown off from her sleeping father's brain, one by one, as he lay in total unconsciousness! She was, after all, intensely thankful that she had not to stay there, for had she been compelled to go on listening to that mechanical grinding, knowing all the time that his private soul was being picked, she must surely have become hysterical! . . .

She stole to her room, and continued till just before midnight sitting on the side of her bed in the dark, doing nothing.

XX

AT MIDNIGHT

Evelyn lit her candle, adjusted the shade, so that her father should not be disturbed by its direct rays, and at twelve o'clock precisely stepped softly to his room. Without stopping to do anything else, she passed behind the screen, to lift the box, which she bore silently away to her own room. Having laid it on the bed, she shut the door behind her and hurried back to her father.

He still slept, but the smile had gone and, from his puckered brow and the convulsive little movements which he kept making, she guessed that he was about to awake. Profoundly thankful that he had not done so earlier, she immediately went away to summon Audrey. At the thought of what yet remained to do, a sort of sick fear paralysed her heart. That long look into the *other world* which she had now to take—the first among all mankind— seemed to her little less terrible than death! But she did not permit herself to catch at the alternative of evading or postponing the ordeal.

Roused from sleep by her sister's gentle shake, Audrey, who was not fully undressed, threw off the eiderdown which alone covered her, and sat up yawning. As soon as her stupefied brain realised the situation, a look of anxiety came into her face.

"Is it time? Is everything all right?"

"It's just after twelve. Father is still asleep, but he looks like waking."

Audrey struggled off the bed and slipped on her dressing-gown with awkward haste.

"May I have your candle?" Then, as she perceived that the pointed end was still intact: "You haven't been sitting in the dark?"

"Oh, it was light till eleven nearly."

The younger sister having taken the candle and picked up a

book with which she proposed to while away the time, they left the room together, but Evelyn did not design again to visit her father.

"I feel thoroughly done up," she whispered in the passage. "If you want anyone, do call Katherine. I'm dying for sleep!"

"You look a wreck," agreed Audrey candidly. "All right, have your sleep."

Evelyn paused just inside her own door until she heard the sound of that of her father's room being latched from within. Then, turning the key in the lock, she switched on the electric light and pulled down the blind. For a moment or two she remained standing beside the bed, gazing apprehensively at the box. Her own involuntary sigh aroused her, and with an impulsive movement of determination she bent over the apparatus, to follow Nicholas's instructions with regard to setting the film in readiness for another revolution. She raised the pin, and wound the band past it into position to start anew. After that, she wound the motor spring. Finally she pointed the hands of the indicator to twenty minutes past twelve. It was then between ten minutes and a quarter past, but, of course, she needed a few minutes in which to get ready.

She brought a small table to the further side of the bed, and placed the box on it. Then she switched off the electric light before lying down on the bed, dressed as she was and without covering herself.

The interval of waiting was awful! She was perfectly ignorant what form the shock would take when it came. It might come at this very moment, or in one, two or three minutes. She bit her lip and clenched her hands. It seemed to her as if at least ten minutes must already have passed. . . . Perhaps the experiment was a failure? Had she omitted any process? The blackness of the room was so intense that she could see absolutely nothing, while the only sound which broke the eerie stillness of the house was the sullen, evil pumping of the blood through her arteries. . . .

Very quietly and smoothly, and without realising the transition, she was launched into the heart of her father's dreaming! It neither appeared to her a dream, nor did she know that anything had changed. Her memory belonged to the dream, so that what she was experiencing was merely a continuation of what had already taken place.

She was also her own father, yet it did not strike her as a metamorphosis. It had always been so. Deep down in her brain, she knew at the same time that she was herself—Evelyn—but neither did that trouble her. She reconciled the two identities as though it were a quite normal condition. But the dreamer was Leslie Sturt; Evelyn was like a very small inward voice, a thousand miles away.

Her spirits were strangely excited, as when one wishes to laugh and cry at once, which was all the more singular as there was no apparent cause for it. Perhaps the beauty of her surroundings was stirring her feelings, or perhaps it was her feelings that caused these surroundings to seem so beautiful. Then there was a grave music playing in the air. Yet somehow this also seemed to result from her emotion, as an overflow. But her mood was not introspective. She made no attempt to analyse this life into its elements. She had no standard of comparison, for the common life had passed from her; otherwise she would have marvelled how far more real, how far more important and significant was her present experience! . . . She did marvel. Everything around her was so real that she could no longer understand, she could only be overpowered. It was a world without details; not because they were not there, but because her excitement prevented her from dwelling upon them.

It was early morning on a lonely sea-shore. The immense vault of the sky was all rosy, milky, opalescent, like the interior of a sea-shell, but a solemn half-light reigned on land and sea, for the sun had not yet risen. The shore was flat and wide, continuing into the gloom both before and behind her, without change, and in whichever direction she looked, wildness and solitude met her eye. Nothing of human labour or suggestive of men was visible.

On the shore itself were only the delicately-coloured,

fantastic-shaped rocks, the pools of sea-water left by the ebb, and the gleaming, wet sands, reflecting the tints of the sky and disappearing at each end into obscurity; while the visibility of the landward side was bounded by low-lying marshes, the bright green hue of which appeared in the twilight as metallic and luminous, as though their slime were exhaling gases. The sea was a vast, swelling, blue-green surface, and enormous white-crested waves continually came tumbling in, breaking with periodic thunder, like the regular breathing of some mighty monster. A strong, rough salt breeze was blowing off the sea, and each impregnated gust seemed to bring her another message from the dawn.

She had never known anything so mysterious and sacred. She did not understand where she was, or how she had got there, but perhaps she had become translated to a new planet which was still in its pre-historic period. The dusky, wildly-beautiful landscape seemed the habitat of spirits and gods. . . . She was seeing all things through her heart. It was the music. It was a peculiar music, for it did not come from without, it did not sing to her ears, but it existed as an *atmosphere*, which she breathed with her lungs. It had a stern, noble rhythm, in the time of a slow waltz. The mental vision repeatedly recurred to her of great white pillars supporting a Doric temple, which at the same time rotated on their axes and revolved about the sides of the hall, in a gigantic, mystic dance.

The contrast between this uninvited fancy and the lonely, savage, melancholy reality encompassing her—or perhaps it was their combination—so uplifted her sensations that she kept pulling at the chains of her body. Strange beauty, inward and outward, flowed together in a higher, still stranger beauty, exciting her to a degree of rapture which was fearful to her physical frame, and which she was obliged to suppress.

She had other feelings.

She was alone and bereaved there. A brutal sorrow was pressing her heart down like a heavy slab to prevent it from rising. She had lost someone, who was not to return. Wild joy and electric beauty might come to her, but she must know them alone; she could not share them with that *other*. . . . And that was why her exaltation was made subtle with tears, and why, her brain giving up the contest, she surrendered herself to the blind will to laugh and weep together. . . . Yet, though her life was ended, she seemed to herself still to be waiting for something. . . .

After she had stood for a long time on the shore, understanding everything with her heart, yet failing to understand her heart itself, a new sound gradually entered her consciousness, coming from a definite quarter, and resolving itself some moments later into an unmistakable, but extremely faint, thudding of hoofs of some galloping animal. By the rapid increase of sound the beast was evidently approaching her, but at first she could distinguish no more than a glimmer of white emerging from the dusk, half a mile away, along the sands.

Then it swiftly acquired the shape of a riderless horse, racing the beach towards her, on a course parallel to the sea. It was without bridle and saddle, and was running free. Its magnificent head alternately lowered and raised itself as it came on, and now she could see it much better. It was a thing of savage beauty, a snow-white stallion, slender and noble in all its lines, but still retaining the deep chest and wild vigour of its original stock. Mane and tail were caught by the wind. She would not have been amazed to see it ascend into mid-air, such light, facile grace of motion it possessed! As it swept past her, not two yards away, like a snowy missile, she longed to mount and fly with it into the unknown, could she have brought herself to attempt such a violation of its noble freedom.

Its bulk sensibly diminished, and in an incredibly short space of time it had replunged into the opposite gloom. The dull thud of the departing hoofs grew less and less, until the sound could no longer be caught.

There was a small, circular pool in the naked sand, a little way higher up towards the marshes, which for some while had attracted her eye by its perfect geometrical shape and the circumstance that it was not there as the result of obstructing rocks retaining the receding tide. Presently she stepped across to it to see what it might be—not out of intellectual curiosity, but because she felt that something might happen there.

She was looking over into a natural well of water, the surface of which reflected the colours of the sky. It could not be sea-water, otherwise it would long since have drained away into the porous sand. She fell on her knees, to peer down over the edge at close quarters. The pool was only a few feet across.

What she saw seemed to her perfectly natural, yet she would have had the utmost difficulty in describing it to another person.

A rocky tunnel passed completely underneath the water, from end to end of the little pool, in such a way that while both its floor and walls were composed of the rock, the roof consisted of the surface of the pool; yet the inside of the tunnel was free from water—quite dry. The rosy glow of the overhead sky was shining through the water on to the floor of the tunnel, beautifying it. She could not understand whether the rough, rocky walls were high or low. She also could not understand how long the tunnel was, but it seemed to wind and twist its way along for mile after mile, and yet it was included in the pool! It was like a kind of dungeon under the water.

Then Lore appeared, walking and stumbling through the length of the tunnel. She was very small, like a person seen from the top of a high cliff as walking on the beach below, yet her features were as distinct as if she had been only a few feet away. Her face and neck were illuminated by the glow from the sky, but the under-part of her body was in darkness, so that the fashion of her clothes could scarcely be distinguished.

She was midway through the tunnel, and seemed in deep distress at her inability to find a passage out. Each time she approached another bend the same look of strained anxiety came into her face, only to fall back once more to an expression of hopeless endurance as she seemed to realise that there was still to be no escape for her. Her pace varied according to the nature and intensity of her moods. Sometimes she stopped to lean against the wall, with her face bent and covered, and sometimes she flew forward wildly for several yards, as though overtaken by panic. The greatest anguish, however, appeared on her features as often as she turned them upwards to the sky, as seen through the water-surface. The realisation of a light, fresh, free, beautiful world, lying immediately overhead, which she was unable to reach, seemed to be more than she could bear; and Evelyn, dreaming her father's dream, perceived that after each occasion of looking up through the water she staggered a little and pressed her hand quickly against her heart, as though a pang were shooting through it.

But what was inexplicable was that it never occurred to her to escape through the pool itself! It needed but one spring into the air, and she would penetrate the water-surface and be up in the world, standing beside herself. The thing was so easy and so obvious that she must surely be blind! She tried to call to her, but though her mouth articulated the words, no sound came forth. . . .

Suddenly, and for the first time, she observed that both Lore and the tunnel through which she walked were throwing *shadows*. But they were not ordinary shadows. Although cast by the physical forms above, they possessed an independent existence of their own; and, in place of being black and unsubstantial, they were coloured and solid. They were shadows in the sense that they owed their presence there to a certain obscuring of the upper light, so that the general direction of the shadow thrown by the tunnel, as well as Lore's progress along it, were determined; but they were independent existences in the sense that they allowed her new and different things. She could not quite understand how she had failed to see them before.

Underneath the rock tunnel, still lower down in the depths of the pool, ran the shadow-passage. She vaguely remembered it. In fact, she was familiar with it, but it had been in other dreams, of another dreamer. It was Nicholas's forest avenue! She knew nothing of that. Then, moreover, it had been her whole environment, while now it was diminished to a distant spectacle, though it was true that its details, although minute, were extraordinarily clear and distinct.

In the same way she simultaneously saw the two Lores, one immediately beneath the other in the water, each walking along her enclosed passage, which was as a prison to her, each vainly struggling towards the open world which never came, each despairing and agonised, but neither apparently aware of the other's existence, and the shadow-Lore, in truth, just because she was a shadow, not comprehending her own desires. The real Lore of the tunnel wished to escape into the free world which she could see above her, whereas the shadow-Lore of the forest avenue longed only to escape from her confinement—she was aware of no other place. And that, perhaps, was what constituted her shadowhood. But she continued to behave as if her motives were produced by her own environment.

And now, as Evelyn's eyes grew more accustomed to the pool, she discerned a *second* shadow-plane underneath the water, as far below the forest avenue as that was below the rock tunnel. Away down in the depths was a third Lore, the shadow of a shadow, yet still substantial—seemingly no bigger than an ant, but as clear-cut and distinguishable as if Evelyn had held that ant on the palm of her hand to examine it. She was standing on the winding path which ran by the side of a beautiful little stream; and this path, imprisoned, as it were, between the stream and a high wall bounding its other side, was the shadow of the forest avenue, just as the latter was the shadow of the tunnel. All three ran forward in the same direction, one beneath another, without an opening. The little river was in shadow, but the tops of the taller trees shading its banks were bathed in mellow, golden sunshine. It was a summer evening.

The third Lore was talking to Ferreira. Oddly enough, the Lore of the forest avenue was now also confronting him, beside a little pool in a clearing she had come to. But when Evelyn looked upwards to discover the original of these shadow-Ferreiras, she saw nothing answering to them, unless it was a black, shaft-like orifice caused by a sudden descent of the tunnel floor. At the place where Lore was standing, the ground had climbed high up towards the surface of the water, so that the top of her head was nearly touching it; but immediately beyond it dropped sharply again, while the rock walls shot up on either side. It was the mouth of this dreadful descent which seemed to correspond in situation to the two shadow-Ferreiras. What confirmed it was that in the forest Ferreira's image kept coming and going. At one time he was a man; at another time a *fear*. Evelyn understood it while she was seeing it, but it mystified her afterwards.

Lore and he had halted and faced one another on the path by the river, and he appeared to be persuading her anxiously to something. She listened patiently and with perfect composure, but it was plain that he was making no impression. Evelyn was unable to hear the sound of their voices. When Ferreira realised that his words were failing to shake her resolution, he grew still more vehement and agitated. She waited till he had finished, then, smiling with a strange mingling of tranquillity and bitterness, spoke a few sentences in response. Suddenly he whipped out a pistol from the side-pocket and presented it at her head. So violent and abrupt was the action that a silver cigarette-case flew out of the same pocket and fell on the path, unnoticed by either.

The end of the barrel was not more than twelve inches from her forehead, but she did not even start back. Her smile remained, and a few seconds later she deliberately crossed her hands behind her back, staying so. She spoke again, with a slight sneer.

Ferreira glanced at his revolver, then back at her, and finally allowed the weapon slowly to sink, until its muzzle was pointing at the ground beside him. With a careless side-jerk he sent it into the river, where it disappeared with a splash. After flourishing a bunch of bony fingers almost under her very nose, and ending the gesture by snapping his thumb and finger high in the air, he turned his back on her, and started walking away, with long, violent strides. Lore gazed after him, threw back her head in a silent laugh, then at once became thoughtful again. Her eyes, after roving contemplatively around her for some moments without settling, at last remained stationary on the stream. . . .

Meanwhile the Lore of the tunnel was standing gazing upwards at the thin sheet of water which alone separated her from the upper air. She appeared to be mentally measuring the distance which she would require to leap. Evelyn, by reaching down her hand through the water, could have touched her, but she feared to do so, lest the vision might be shattered.

Quickly and unexpectedly Lore stepped, rather than jumped, up through the surface of the pool, into the free, pure atmosphere of the open world! The action was performed with such unobtrusiveness that Evelyn, who was still regarding the lower of the two shadow scenes, only vaguely comprehended what had happened. As Lore passed through the water—somehow, without disparting its mirror-like surface—to join her in the upper air, she saw her shadow-shape deliberately cast itself into the stream. Her final disappearance beneath the liquid hole produced by her plunge exactly synchronised with the uppermost Lore's final emergence from the pool on the seashore.

At the very same instant of time the Lore of the forest, standing at the edge of the pool in the clearing, no longer facing Ferreira, who had once more vanished, but staring in terror at the place where he had been beyond the pool, threw up her arms with a *silent shriek*, and jumped in, so that the water closed above her head.

And had not she already been sure of it, the coincidence in time of these three actions would have certified to Evelyn the unreal, shadow-like character of the two lower Lores. Their leaps into the water were not willed, but necessitated. . . .

They embraced in tears: Lore and Evelyn, in the personality of her father.

"Father!"

"My dear, dear daughter!"

Evelyn experienced surprise neither at Lore's presence in that lonely and unheard-of world nor at the manner of her entrance into it. It seemed quite natural that the world from which she had escaped should lie, as it were, at the bottom of a *hole*. She was as little stirred by the new relationship expressed on both sides, for it had been a basic thought throughout with her that Lore was her—

that is, her father's—daughter. She did not remember that Lore was dead; or, if she did, the fact did not disturb her in any way. Two emotions were battling within her for supremacy, while the sea continued to thunder in and the atmospheric pillar-music to sound.

That individual of all others dearest to her heart was here alone with her at last. The obstructions of the world had ceased, and they had each other. The realisation of this was like a *final* joy, the ending and completion of all desires, almost amounting to apathy. Even Lore's noble, lovely mother had not been dearer in the ancient days. *Her*, perhaps, they two together were presently to meet! . . . But Lore was to depart again immediately, for they were in the mid-world and must travel in opposite ways. And this knowledge was like death! . . .

They walked slowly away together along the shore, not speaking at first, but suffering the music to speak for them. The sea-horizon became splashed with red colours. The salt gusts of wind brought laughter to their hearts between whiles, and all the world grew still more beautiful. A glorious day was breaking. A dark coast appeared, miles distant, across the sea.

Lore pointed to it with her finger.

"That is where I have to go, father!"

The remark struck upon Evelyn's heart like nails being hammered into a coffin-lid.

"Without me?"

"You are not here, dear! I am here, because I am dead; but you are in your body, dreaming everything."

"But later? . . ."

"In a few years. It will soon pass."

"I am the elder, and should have been the first."

"I precipitated matters, but I could not help it."

"Yes; I saw you and your shadows."

"You saw it very brokenly, father. Between reality and experience there is an unbroken line of shadows, but your eye was not quick enough."

"How came Maurice to be there?"

Lore smiled. "I thought I was running from him, but I was running *towards* something all the time. I wish I could see him, to tell him how little angry I am."

"Will he suffer?"

"Yes; but it will change him, so we need not mind. He is to throw off the old life, and go abroad. You ought to be kindest to poor Evelyn, dear, for he will cause her far more pain than ever he did me!"

They sauntered on, while the music became sterner and more pathetic, and the colours of the sky still more extraordinary.

"Why cannot the dreaming go across the sea?" asked he who dreamt.

"The cord cannot be farther strained without breaking," replied Lore.

"Then let me break it!"

"It will not rest with you, dear!"

Shortly afterwards Evelyn again caught the sound of the galloping hoofs, but this time the noise was confused, as though there were more than one beast.

"Courage, father!" said Lore, smiling. "Here they come for me! Remember, it is only for a very, very short time!"

"I refuse to see them! They cannot take you against your will!"

"It is my will. It must be so."

"But you cannot ride the sea on horseback!"

"Yes, indeed!"

A minute later the two horses—for there were two of them—dashed up and came to a violent halt just past them, with their quivering bodies nearly erect and their forelegs pawing the air. One was riderless—the same snow-white stallion that she had seen before—but on the bare back of the other, a huge silver-grey beast, was a man. He was lightly clad in antique-looking garments, and was detaining the free animal by the mane, in readiness for Lore to mount.

Evelyn, through her father's eyes, looked at him a second time. It was Nicholas! . . .

Far from being amazed, she felt greatly relieved that Lore was to travel in company with an old friend.

"You are making the journey too, then?"

Nicholas said nothing, but smiled pleasantly as he soothed his horse by fondling its neck.

Lore embraced the dreamer passionately. It seemed to Evelyn that her soul was losing itself in tears. No words were spoken. . . .

Lore disengaged herself, laughing, lightly shook out her graceful draperies, as though finally casting off her grief, then vaulted easily on to the stallion's back. She sat astride, like an Amazon, and gently resting one hand on the animal's neck for support, saluted the dreamer encouragingly with the other. Her movements were so marvellously beautiful that she appeared already transfigured.

At the same moment the ruddy-golden disk of the sun peeped above the low line of land beyond the sea. A hundred exquisite colours shot across the world. The waves crashed in. The rhythm of the music became so pronounced that it seemed like the throb of a mighty engine, yet the theme was sad and majestic beyond description. The two horses bounded forward, unurged, into the surf. Nicholas looked straight ahead, but Lore turned back, to wave once more. . . .

The dreamer, standing alone on the beach, on the very verge of the water, perceived without astonishment that the beasts had already quitted the rude sea, to take flight in the upper air. They were speeding forward with great, with miraculous rapidity. Before she had taken six sighing breaths they were of the size of small birds. Immediately afterwards she could no longer distinguish them. . . .

She flung herself down on the sands, and wept without restraint.

Upon the abrupt termination of the dream record, Evelyn lay quietly on her bed for at least ten minutes, trying not to think of what she had just experienced, and concentrating her forces instead on the restoration of her physical equilibrium. Her heart was beating dangerously, while she feared that she might suffocate. When presently the sensations modified, she rose in a subdued manner to switch on the light. Upon glancing at her watch, it was twenty minutes to two.

Sitting on the side of her bed, she pondered for a short time longer what she should do. . . . She *knew* what she should do, but she refused to entertain the terrible thought. . . .

She forced herself to ask whether Nicholas ought to be shown the record, and even went into reasons for and against. He would understand at last that poor Lore had destroyed herself and that Maurice was innocent. But at the same time he, a stranger, would be introduced to her father's dreadful secret! She had no right! . . . Of course, he was not to know that the dream was her father's, but did not it speak for itself?

Therefore (she endeavoured to convince herself) it might not be wise to demolish the record at present, in case its testimony were hereafter required, but she ought at least to take it out of the box and hide it somewhere. . . . Nicholas (she thought on, glibly and desperately) would make angry inquiries as to what had become of it, and either at once or afterwards she would be obliged to confess to the theft. Oh, how gladly and thankfully she would do so! . . . How could he continue to be angry when she assured him that it concerned her father's honour? . . .

And all the time she knew that Nicholas was *dead!* . . .

Suddenly she burst into suppressed weeping, burying her face in the pillow. . . .

A few minutes later she stiffened herself, and once again resolved not to believe the worst. Opening the cover of the container, she lifted out the exposed reel of film, rolled it carelessly together in her hands, and thrust it away at the back of one of the drawers in her chest. Then she replaced the cover and bore the box from the room.

It was fearful to enter Nicholas's bedroom, but it was dangerous to linger outside. She turned the handle noiselessly and went in. The room was in total darkness, so that she had to feel her way by instinct and recollection, but at last she found the table. After depositing the box, she listened for a moment without breathing. There was not a sound. . . . Her heart turned cold with fear. She could not think what she ought to do. Oh, she *dared* not! . . .

Half-way along the passage, while she was dragging her feet in the direction of her own room again, Audrey looked out from her father's door, a lighted candle in her hand. She went forward to meet Evelyn.

"What in the world are you doing up and dressed?"

"Oh, nothing. How is father?"

"He woke up soon after you left, but now he's sleeping again. He was worrying about a wonderful dream he had had, which he couldn't remember. But whatever have you been doing along the passage?"

"Oh, Audrey! . . ." She stopped; then went on again: "I thought I heard a sound in Nicholas's room."

"But you haven't been to bed!"

"I was too tired and worried. I lay down just as I was. . . . Won't you come with me, to see what is the matter?"

"But what kind of sound was it?"

"Oh, I don't know! I can't describe it! It might have been a groan. Please come!"

"But is his door unlocked?"

"Yes, it is. I peeped in, but I could hear nothing—not even the sound of his breathing."

"It's your imagination, my child!" said Audrey. "However, to satisfy you . . ."

Evelyn took the candle from her, and they went along together to Nicholas's bedroom. The door was still ajar. They listened intently outside.

Audrey straightened herself again. "He's fast asleep, that's what it is!"

"No; we must go in."

"It isn't a very nice thing to do, you know!"

Evelyn did not reply but pushed the door open, and so holding the candle that its direct light should be away from the bed, stole across the room to where he was lying. Audrey kept close behind her.

Nicholas was in the exact middle of the bed, with his face upturned to the ceiling above. The clothes were not disarranged, and for a moment they thought he was sleeping. Then both girls simultaneously noticed that there was something not quite right about the look of his face, which almost resembled that of a waxwork, although the eyes were closed.

Evelyn clutched her sister's arm convulsively.

"Don't say it! Oh, don't say it, Audrey!"

Audrey borrowed the candle and held it so that its light should fall on Nicholas's face, though she did not bend down for the purpose. She bestowed a long and troubled look on the inanimate man, and when she glanced round again at Evelyn her own countenance was white.

"I think he is dead!" she whispered. "We must go at once and fetch mother."

"I must know now. I must! We dare not waste time; he may be simply in a faint. . . . I am going to feel his heart, Audrey, but I daren't do it alone. Hold my other hand!"

Audrey, now frightened, did as she requested, while Evelyn, repressing a sob, fearfully drew the bedclothes from the upper part of Nicholas's body. Averting her eyes, and with a face like chalk, she laid her free hand first lightly, then more firmly, over the place where she judged his heart to be.

Not the faintest tremor responded.

"He is dead, Audrey!"

Then she ventured to finger his face lightly. It was cold and awful. . . . She replaced the clothes reverently, and both girls came away from the bedside. They left the room. Evelyn was the last to pass out, and as she was doing so, through the open window came the strange, melancholy note of a night bird. It was succeeded by a quiet rustling of the trees by a breeze, resembling the sighing of the sea.

With a haggard face, which was almost that of a middle-aged woman, she closed the door behind her. Audrey had gone forward to call their mother.

About David Lindsay

David Lindsay (1876–1945) is best known for his first novel, *A Voyage to Arcturus*. Published in 1920, it has been called "the greatest imaginative work of the twentieth century" (Colin Wilson), "a stupendous ontological fable" (E H Visiak), "a masterpiece... an extraordinary work" (Clive Barker), "that shattering, intolerable, and irresistible work" (C S Lewis), and "less a novel than it is private kabbalah" (Alan Moore). John Grant, in *The Encyclopedia of Fantasy*, called it "a masterpiece of allegorical fantasy".

Lindsay himself said that as long as publishing existed he would have readers, however few, and has been proved right. *A Voyage to Arcturus*, and his subsequent novels *The Haunted Woman* (1922), *Sphinx* (1923), *The Adventures of Monsieur de Mailly* (1926) and *Devil's Tor* (1932), have found a growing audience of devotees, enabling his unpublished novels (*The Violet Apple* and the unfinished *The Witch*) to be brought out in the 1970s. He has been translated into French, German, Spanish, Dutch, Bulgarian, Russian, Japanese, Catalan, Romanian, Turkish, Icelandic, Finnish and Greek.

www.ingramcontent.com/pod-product-compliance
Lightning Source LLC
Chambersburg PA
CBHW071219210726
48293CB00002B/499